ILLUSION OF FEAR

PARIS KAUFMAN

Second Edition: February 2026

Cover Art Copyright: GetCovers

Edited by: Michaela Bush

Formatted by: Paris Kaufman

Library of Congress Control Number: 2026900197

ISBN: 979-8-9916725-4-2

*To the guard rail on
Misty Lane where this cast
first introduced itself.
Thank you.*

Also by Author

The Mageye Trilogy
The Mageye
Illusion of Fear
Beldestine

Unbound: A Mageye Novel

The Return of the Mageye Trilogy
The Kidnapped Queen

Theater of Memories
Paris Kaufman & McKenna Rowell

Middle Grade
The Empty Manger

PRONUNCIATION GUIDE

Ackley Elephants: Ack-lee Elephants

Alveraada: Al-ver-ah-duh

Mageye: Magi

Otologicoal: Otuh-logi-coal

Volcaniacs: Vol-can-ee-acks

Wolvien Guard: Wool-vin Guard

Author's Note

I started the first ever draft of *Illusion of Fear* in early July of 2020. Back then, I was still fully a "pantser." (As in, I knew Point A and Point B, but everything else was up to the draft itself.) And truthfully, pantsing works! Though, I am now a plotter, and create an outline first (who would have guessed that an outline makes the drafting process smoother)? Now, working on this current version in 2025, I can really see how much I have grown as a writer.

As you will soon see, our main cast has grown from two main characters in *The Mageye* to five in *Illusion of Fear*. And 2020 pantsing Paris found this to be a *challenge*. Poor Mercy got forgotten more than a few times. But now, I have books with as many as ten or even fourteen main characters. These five sweet characters aren't a struggle to juggle anymore. This time around, they are my home.

And now I turn them over to you. The five characters who have lived every day for the past five-plus years in my head. Creating a second edition of their story has been an experience I am tremendously grateful for. If I were forced to claim a book from the first editions with the "roughest" start, it would be *Illusion of Fear*, but that has turned out to be a blessing, because it meant I got to add more of *everything*—and that includes the unexpected.

~Paris

Chapter 1

The doors to the Elite Guard's private training quarters creaked as I entered, and Myles's voice rang out across the large room. "I told you Rose was coming to cheer you on, didn't I, Raymond?"

Raymond muttered something in response that I didn't quite catch and I stared at him. When he announced his first trial towards becoming a member of the Elite Guard was to train for forty-eight hours straight, I had imagined he would be practicing fighting techniques and survival skills. What I had never considered was that he would be dangling a foot off the ground from a metal rung. Sure, he needed to do something to keep him awake, but this seemed a little excessive.

Myles stood under him, and my twin brothers, Ren and Ryder, sat sprawled on the mats.

"What are you doing?" I asked, my footsteps echoing off the stone floor until I stepped onto the mats.

"Myles told him to see how long he can carry himself as deadweight," Ren said, tilting his head back to look at me. His blue eyes seemed to be alight with mischief. "I suggested putting nails under him to motivate him to hang longer."

"You can lay under me," Raymond huffed, red-faced and arms trembling. "Break my fall."

"A foot is hardly a fall," Ryder said. He sat up, pinching his fingers to estimate the drop. "Not to an *Elite Guardsman*, anyway."

"You're almost three quarters of the way done," I encouraged Raymond, taking a seat between Ren and Ryder. "How do you feel?"

Raymond adjusted his grip, the trembling slowly strengthening. "More exhausted than I've ever been."

Myles patted Raymond's side. "I survived this trial when I was eight, there's no reason why you can't do it, too."

"Never said I was going to fail it." Raymond attempted to kick his foot at Myles, but ended up losing his grip. He landed on his feet and staggered, nearly falling backwards.

I hurried to my feet. "Are you okay?"

He put a hand to his temples, but nodded. "What's next?"

I assumed he was addressing Myles, but I intervened, grabbing Raymond's hand, but hesitating to heal him with my powers. "Can I heal your sore muscles, or is that cheating?"

His eyes widened and he slipped his hand from mine. "You can help me with that when I'm done."

"The more he survives, the prouder he'll be when he finishes," Myles said. "That's why he keeps refusing to take rests."

"I thought the whole point of this was training forty-eight hours nonstop?" Ren asked.

"It is, and no sleeping." Myles shrugged. "But the goal is to prove your endurance and commitment to the guard, not to die trying. A few minutes to catch your breath can be allowed."

"But guests cannot," a new voice said. I jumped, turning to face General Cornstone. He wagged a finger at Myles. "You know better, General Duncan."

His tone held teasing in it, and Ren and Ryder exchanged amused looks. Myles smiled sheepishly. "There's technically no rule that it needs to be one-on-one the entire time."

"You and your loopholes." General Cornstone rolled his eyes at Myles. At a glance, he was an intimidating man. Standing above six feet, eyes the color of dust, and the king's right hand, he was above even Myles in line for the throne. But I had fast learned not to be intimidated by him, and he often teased when a break in his duties allowed it.

"If it helps," Raymond said, "I'm pretty sure the guests made focusing twice as hard."

"Are you calling us distractions?" Ren quipped.

"Yes," Raymond answered. "Very much so."

I giggled. "That's another part of the trial you've overcome, then."

He smiled and General Cornstone chuckled. "I've come to take over the next section of your training, Raymond, and you will be relieved to know these four *distractions* are excused. But," he paused as he picked up a wooden staff, "I won't go easy on you in their absence."

At the sight of the staff, everyone—excluding General Cornstone—froze. He paused before putting it down and passing Raymond a short wooden sword instead. "I'm sorry," he said. "We won't touch that again."

My gaze lingered on the staff, and I noticed Ren doing the same. It looked near-identical to the staffs we had used to fight against the Volcaniacs hardly two months ago. A battle we had all almost died in.

Raymond tested the sword and huffed. "Wish me luck," he said to us. "I don't think General Cornstone would exaggerate about not going easy on me."

His quick recovery from the reminder of the Volcaniacs only seemed to solidify how fitting he would be amongst King Duncan's Elite Guard, and my posture relaxed.

Ryder helped Ren to his feet, and Myles laughed. "He doesn't go easy on anyone."

General Cornstone scoffed and shooed us out. "I don't go easy on *you*, Myles. But you enjoyed your first trial, didn't you?"

"Did you train him during it?" I asked.

General Cornstone smiled. "The final part, as I am going to do with your brother."

"The hardest part," Myles whispered ominously, holding the door for the rest of us to file out.

After Ren and Ryder left the palace, Myles took me on a walk through the market. King Duncan had asked him to pick up a new tablecloth he had ordered.

"Why didn't your dad send a servant to pick this up?" I asked.

Myles shrugged. "I've been restless and nagged him to give me something to do. He promptly gave me a list of chores."

I laughed, and Myles poked my arm. "Not funny."

"How do you manage to be restless when you are constantly working or training? I mean, you practically wrote a novel from your signature alone on all those documents last week, and you have been helping Raymond train non-stop."

He shrugged, nudging me around a puddle in the center of the market. People—non-Mageye and Mageye alike—bustled by. The sandstone streets all eventually led towards the center of the city and the palace. When I glanced back, I could see the East Tower over the rooftops.

Before Myles could reply, someone called our names. "Hello, Ms. Kaser," he greeted as a woman approached.

Ms. Kaser had introduced herself to my mom soon after we settled into Mageye City. She smiled as she joined us now, revealing her fangs. Her brown hair was tied in an elegant updo and her yellow cat eyes seemed to flash. "What are you both up to?" she asked.

"Shopping," I said, waving my hand around the market. "Well, kind of shopping. We're picking up an order for King Duncan."

"Running errands for a loved one," she practically purred,

showing us the basket she carried on her hip. "I'm doing the same."

"I like to think they appreciate it," Myles said. "But sometimes I feel used."

Ms. Kaser shook her head, winking at him. "We appreciate it more than you realize, *General*."

"I think I'd appreciate it if Myles ran errands for me," I mused.

Myles groaned. "I have enough chores as is."

"I imagine teleporting makes things easy," Ms. Kaser observed. "Well, I suppose I better get going. Tell your mom I say hello, Rose."

"I will," I said, holding out a hand to get her to wait. "Mom wanted me to tell you, there is a stray cat that keeps showing up around our house. She seems healthy enough, but I know you like to keep numbers on any strays."

The sunlight glinted off her fangs as she smiled. Her affinity to cats stemmed from her power—the ability to shift into the form of a small housecat. "I will most certainly keep an eye out for the pretty kitten. Have a good night's rest, you two."

When she left, Myles stared, then looked at the sun, which shone from high above us. "I'm not going to bed for at least eight hours. You?"

I laughed, putting a hand over my mouth in case Ms. Kaser looked back. "Well, she could have left without any well-wishes."

"Or, she could have left with bad wishes," he added.

"Bad wishes?"

"I once told General Cornstone to have an extra bad night, and the look he gave me might have scarred my very aura."

"Why did you tell him to have a bad night?"

He shrugged. "I could be honest and tell you I was being a brat, or I could lie and say he was being annoying."

I hummed, straying to a booth to buy some treats for my family's horses. My favorite horse, Lucy, was expecting, and I had taken it upon myself to be as accommodating as possible. "I feel like even if he was being annoying, you were being bratty."

He gasped in offense and I giggled, counting out treats for each of the horses. Since settling into Mageye City, not a day went by where Myles and I didn't see each other. He often teleported to my house, or would appear right beside me, striking up a conversation like no time passed since our last one.

Myles had fast become my closest friend besides my brothers, though as we left the booth to finish our errands, he fell silent.

"Are you all right?" I asked, unnerved by his silence.

He hummed. "Just thinking. I've been meaning to ask you something."

"Ask me what?"

A young boy suddenly ran between us, and we stepped apart around him, but that hardly slowed our conversation as Myles slipped into my mind. *I think I'm ready to start going on missions again.*

My eyes widened. After we had returned from The End, Myles had asked King Duncan for leave from missions outside of the city. During his leave, Myles had continued with work around the palace, but he hadn't referenced when his missions would begin again.

By now, I had heard dozens of stories about the trips he had gone on in the past, and he never failed to get an electric gleam in his eye whilst sharing them. And now, the air between us almost felt electrified, as if his aura were full of pins and needles. I smiled. *Have you talked to King Duncan? That is exciting news.*

Lightning sparked in Myles's purple iris. *You're all right with me doing that?*

I frowned. *Why wouldn't I be?*

Well... I don't know. I figured you would want me to stay in the city.

Since we can talk telepathically, I don't need to worry about distance. I can annoy you anytime, day or night.

"Not if I block you," he said cheekily as he ducked through the doorway of the shop King Duncan had ordered the cloth from. "And no, I haven't asked my dad yet."

"You wouldn't dare block me," I scolded.

He smirked before turning to the shopkeeper, an elderly Mageye with jasmine-colored eyes. "We are picking up an order for King Duncan."

"Paid for in full already," the Mageye declared, pulling a bundle of cloth from a shelf. "Here you are."

"Thank you." Myles accepted the cloth. "Have a good day."

"And the same to you."

I waved and followed Myles from the shop. He paused on the steps and turned to face me, a serious expression on his face. "You're really okay with me leaving the city again to find and help more Mageye?"

"It's your job," I said. "You never quit—only took a break to help my family settle. I'll miss you, but you won't be gone forever."

"I will talk to King Duncan soon and see what missions he comes up with." Myles smiled, his voice dropping. "Maybe he'll even let me take Raymond on one for his training. He should be cleared for some apprenticing within the guard after he passes his trial."

I grinned, looking over the rooftops at the East Tower. "I used to be nervous about him joining the Sunset Guard, but I don't feel that way anymore. Not now that we live in Mageye City, at least." I glanced at him. "And not since we saved them from The End."

Myles nodded. "With the Volcaniacs and Wolvien Guard gone, the biggest threat to me is getting scolded."

I laughed, patting the bundle of cloth he carried. "We should hurry this back to the palace, then. Your first mission back on duty."

"I'm glad you're the one accompanying me for it. Lead on,

Miss Crawford!"

Chapter 2

Heat radiated from the lava surrounding the Volcaniac leader's throne. My breath shallowed and I looked around the amphitheater. The nine entrances from last time were gone, leaving only one exit behind me, and a staircase between the rows of seats that led to the lava. The throne was empty and I took a cautious step back, my breaths shaky.

Lava lapped against the lower floor and bubbled over, frothing towards me. I spun on my heel and ran down the corridor, entering it as the entire amphitheater filled with lava and flooded after me.

The corridor twisted and turned, nearly tripping me until I ran out onto an obsidian floor. Cracks split the obsidian and lava rose up around me, creating another corridor, and the lava continued flowing from the amphitheater.

Splashes of it burned my arms and face, and I screamed as my hair caught on fire, now running through a corridor of glowing fire.

A lone figure stood to greet me at the end of the corridor, laughing as our gazes met.

"Did you really think I died?" the leader of the Volcaniacs asked. "You see, unlike you, I can't burn."

I woke with a scream and flailed my arms as I fell off my bed. The sheets seemed to ensnare me and I fumbled with them, jumping as my door burst open and Mom ran in.

"Rose, are you all right?"

My heart raced and I trembled, but nodded. "Nightmare," I whispered. "I'm okay."

"Are you sure?" She hugged me. "You aren't hurt from falling?"

"No."

She cupped my face in her hands, studying my expression closely. "King Duncan told me Myles has been getting nightmares. Have you been getting them, too?"

Myles was getting nightmares? I took a shaky breath and shook my head. "Just this one. I'm okay, Mom. Really."

"Are you sure?" She took my hand and squeezed it gently. "I worry about you."

I squeezed her hand back, forcing a smile. "I'm sure."

"All right." She stood slowly and put my sheets back onto the bed.

When she left, I pulled my hair over my shoulder and examined it closely. My nose scrunched and I breathed in the smell of my hair deeply. For an instant, it had smelt smokey, but as quickly as the dream had ended, the smell faded, too.

I stood slowly, pausing when a pressure in my head signaled Myles's presence. He didn't say anything and anxiety gripped my heart until his presence faded.

That wasn't like him, and I frowned as I dressed. Since when was he getting nightmares?

A door shut across the hall and I combed my fingers through my hair, shaking my head as I left my room.

Ryder sat at the kitchen table while Mom cooked breakfast, and he looked up as I walked in. "Did you drop something? I heard a crash."

"I had a nightmare and fell out of bed."

"So that's what that was," Ren said as he walked into the room. "Could have sworn it was an earthquake."

I rolled my eyes. "Well, Ben Chireton is showing signs of earth-related powers. It could have been him."

"You mean the Ben Chireton who lives next door?" Ren's voice pitched awkwardly, and he shot a look at Ryder.

"Ben's not even one," Ryder assured him before turning back to me. "Come here. Let me fix your hair."

I smiled and sat on his knee like I used to do with all my brothers when I was younger. He gently braided my hair while Ren distracted himself with a book.

"What's that?" I asked.

He turned the book to show me the page he was reading. "I found this in Raymond's room. It's all about magic fighting."

"You know you aren't supposed to snoop in Raymond's room, Ren," Mom scolded, looking up from the bacon she was frying.

"I wasn't snooping. He asked me to bring him an extra dagger to his general trial thing. And I took this too and asked him if I could borrow it when I saw him."

"He said Ren can borrow it for however long he wants," Ryder told Mom, and she shook her head.

"Let's keep it that way," she said, turning back to breakfast.

I slid off of Ryder's lap and took my own seat, fiddling with my freshly-done braid and reflecting on the dream again. Even my family had never overheard the Volcaniac leader's name whilst being imprisoned, so why had that dream seemed so *real?* A nameless, dead man...

"Rose," Ren said, leaning close. "Snap out of it."

"What?" I blinked, turning to face him.

He grinned. "Were you talking to Myles?"

"No..." I shook my head and turned to Mom. "But can I visit him after breakfast? Raymond should be nearly finished with his trial, and I can walk him home to ensure he doesn't pass out halfway."

Mom laughed. "That might be a good idea. We are going to

have a nice dinner tonight to celebrate him making it through. But for today... I expect he will be sleeping."

After breakfast, I hurried out the front door. A cloud of butterflies fluttered through the sky, and I stopped outside the Chiretons' house, admiring them.

Mrs. Chireton sat on her front porch, bouncing Ben on her knee. "Why are there so many butterflies?" I asked.

She laughed. "My guess is some young Mageye either pulled a prank, or let things get a little out of control."

Ben reached his hands towards the butterflies, and Mrs. Chireton smiled. "He likes them."

"I like them, too." I waved as I walked off through the butterfly-filled city. "Have a good morning."

"You too, Rose."

At the palace, General Agar opened the towering front door for me. His eyes resembled clocks, ticking by the seconds of the day. The day I met him, I tripped and dropped a mug I had bought for my mom. Before I could fret about it shattering, the mug was back in my hand as if nothing had happened at all. General Agar's gift of rewinding the last thirty seconds of time, or even erasing thirty seconds from memory, certainly had its upsides.

"Good morning, Rose. Are you here for Myles or Raymond?"

"Both. But Myles first. I think Raymond still has another thirty minutes or so."

He chuckled and stepped aside to let me in. "Myles hasn't left his room yet, but I suspect he is up in his office. General Curran said he could hear him pacing before the sun had fully risen."

I laughed. General Curran could hear whispers from behind locked doors. He and General Agar were very close and often the first to be informed of secrets within the palace, thanks to their powers.

12

"Thank you." I walked through the front foyer and up the large staircase. Myles's room was on the west side of the palace. After making my way down several more corridors, I arrived at his room.

Before I could knock, he opened the door. "Good morning," he said, though he didn't sound as upbeat as he had yesterday.

"Did you sense my aura?" I asked with a smile, hoping to cheer him up.

"I've been waiting for you." He stepped back to let me into his bedroom, although it was really more of a private tavern room. There was a washroom, a large closet that served as a small room of its own, and his favorite part of his room, the office in the back.

The bed wasn't made, which was unusual. I couldn't remember ever seeing it unmade before. "Are you okay?"

He followed my gaze to his unmade bed and blinked a couple times, as if only just noticing it. "Yeah... I'm fine. Are you?"

"You seem distracted and not... yourself."

"I've just..." He sighed. "I've been having weird dreams, and the one last night..."

He didn't finish his sentence, and I studied him in concern. Mom had said he was having nightmares and his aura had been filled with anxiety this morning.

Before I could question him, he went to his office, waving for me to follow. I gasped when I walked in; it looked like a thunder storm had swept through the room.

Myles was normally a neat freak, especially when it came to his work. But now, books and papers were scattered everywhere. He bent over a messy pile of papers on his circular desk, silently mouthing words to himself as he read.

I peeked over his shoulder. The pages he was looking at were torn from a book that lay open at the edge of the table. I picked the book up, flipping it over to read the title. "*Prophetic Horrors*... What is this for?"

"Dreams," he answered, hardly glancing up from the papers.

I flipped through a few pages of the book. "You think the weird dreams you have been having are prophetic?"

He hesitated, slowly putting the torn pages down. "I didn't want to tell you and scare you, but I have been dreaming about the Volcaniac leader. At first, I thought it was just reliving nightmares from my fight with him, but now..." He trailed off. "They've been getting worse."

Unlike you... I can't burn... My heart raced at the memory of my own nightmare and I shuddered. "Worse, how so?"

Myles continued to hesitate, and I shut the book. "I can't exactly help if you don't tell me what you need help with."

He shook his head, riffling through more torn pieces of paper. "I don't really know how you could help. I've gotten nightmares from traumatic stuff before, but these are different. They, well," he grimaced, "when I fought the leader, I jumped into the volcano and teleported at the last second, but in the dreams I'm not fast enough. Twisted version of what really happened; it's happened before with other things, but this time..."

"How did you stop it before?"

"Time. But these dreams have only gotten worse with time, not better. Last night, I saw the Volcaniac leader in the dream. He *spoke* to me, and if the dreams are prophetic like I suspect..." He pointed at the book in my hand. "Then, well, I don't know."

"What do you mean, he spoke to you?" I asked nervously, reflecting on my own dream. Surely, this was a coincidence. A lava-filled coincidence.

"He asked if I really thought he died, because unlike me—"

"He can't burn," I finished in a whisper.

Myles stared. "Did you read my mind?"

I shook my head, putting the book down as if it had burned me. "I had the same dream. But it was only a nightmare, right? Maybe our telepathic connection can link to dreams as well?"

The papers he held fluttered to the floor. "What do you mean?" His voice was cold and I hesitated, looking down at the papers he had dropped.

"Well, I haven't had many nightmares about The End before, but last night, I did. I was running through a tunnel of lava, and..."

I stopped when Myles made a sound similar to a gag and snatched a book from his desk. "Nothing," he whispered, tossing it aside and grabbing another book from one of his bookshelves.

"Myles?" I questioned, stepping after him but hesitating. "My mom told me you've been having nightmares, and I felt your aura when I got up this morning. So we probably just connected, right?"

He shook his head. "No... No, if you shared the dream, then that has to mean—" He stopped again, ripping out a page from the book and comparing it to the ones he had been looking at.

"Myles, what's wrong?" I asked.

Lightning flickered in his purple iris and he went pale, his voice hoarse. "We need to talk to King Duncan."

Before I could respond, he scooped the papers into his arms, not caring to organize them.

"What do you mean? Why do we need to talk to King Duncan?"

"He'll know what to do," Myles answered. "Dad always knows."

"Know what to do about what?" I caught his arm before he could leave. "Myles, what's wrong?"

"I don't think we shared a dream last night. I think we witnessed a prophecy."

"A prophecy? Like a prediction of the future?"

Did you really think I died?

"You don't think the Volcaniac leader survived the eruption, do you?"

His green and purple gaze met mine. "That's exactly what I think."

Chapter 3

Myles led the way out of his room. "We need to tell King Duncan. He will better know how to handle this."

"Handle what, exactly?" I asked, shutting his door behind us. "Myles, I know the signs point to him being alive, but... how?"

"That's why I want to talk to my dad."

When we reached King Duncan's office, I knocked. King Duncan's smile at the sight of us quickly faded when he saw the looks on our faces. "What's wrong?"

Myles pushed past him. "We need to speak with you. I believe Mageye City is in danger." He strode to a large circular table in the center of the room, and dumped the papers onto it. Several fluttered to the floor.

I walked more politely into the room and picked up the scattered papers, attempting to hide my shaking hands.

King Duncan's silver eyes swirled like pools of mercury. "What do you mean? What has happened?"

Myles took a deep breath. "Remember how I told you I was getting nightmares again, and that they... felt different? This past week, they have gotten worse, still feeling like more than a nightmare."

"What?" King Duncan interrupted. "You didn't tell me that."

Myles accepted the papers back from me and dropped them on top of the pile. "I wanted to research them. I thought maybe they were memories reflecting back, or some kind of prophetic dream. Then, last night... I had the worst dream yet, and Rose shared it."

King Duncan glanced between us. "What happened in the dream?"

"The leader of the Volcaniacs was there." Myles's voice lowered. "He asked me if I really thought that he had died and said that he couldn't burn. He said the same thing to Rose in her dream. I think he's alive and looking for revenge."

I turned to Myles. "How are you so sure he is back? Maybe it *was* only a nightmare. We can talk telepathically, so who's to say we didn't accidentally merge dreams last night?"

"Sometimes Mageye have prophetic dreams that predict part of their future. I think that is what this was." Myles turned to King Duncan. "I remember you telling me about that a few years ago."

King Duncan picked up a few of Myles's papers, bearing an unreadable expression. "That would be correct."

A chill went through my body. Was I going to run through a corridor of lava again?

Unlike most kings, King Duncan didn't often wear his crown. And though he didn't wear it now, he held himself with a regal authority that only amplified the concern I felt at his unreadable expression.

"Then do you think that is what we had last night?" Myles asked, raising his brows. "A prophetic message?"

"A prophecy would imply something that is destined to happen in your future, not a warning that he is alive," King Duncan said slowly, putting the papers aside. "If you had seen each other in the dream, that would align with some kind of prophecy, but it sounds as if you both witnessed the same dream alone."

"Maybe the prophecy part was running through the lava corridor," I whispered.

King Duncan's expression softened as he faced to me. "I stand by what I said about seeing each other. Or if the message given was a more direct threat..." He trailed off and his expression darkened.

He shut his eyes and shook his head. Myles's brow furrowed as he waited for King Duncan to speak.

When King Duncan looked up, he took a steadying breath. "I believe these dreams are something worse."

"Worse?" I asked. "What is worse than a prophecy foreshadowing... fiery... death..." I trailed off, fidgeting with one of the papers.

"I don't think the dream you shared last night was a dream or a prophecy; I believe it was a vision."

I recoiled from the papers I touched. "Isn't a vision another way to say prophecy?"

"A *controlled* vision," he clarified. "I believe someone sent that dream to you. It wasn't predicting the future, but conveying a message."

Myles picked up another paper. "So, someone wants to tell us something," he stated. "Do you think that someone is the Volcaniac leader himself?"

King Duncan rested his hand on Myles's shoulder, shaking his head enough to send some sort of personal signal. Myles forced his shoulders to relax and put the paper down.

"Do you have reason to believe he is alive?" he asked instead.

"I have feared it," King Duncan admitted with a sigh. "But have not confirmed it, and I was hoping I wouldn't need to tell you. I wanted to give you more time."

Myles leaned forward, lightning sparking in his purple iris. "What do you mean? What do you know?"

King Duncan looked at me and then back at Myles. "We need General Cornstone for this. He should be finishing up with Raymond soon. Myles, can Raymond rest in your room while the four of us have a discussion? I will likely call a meeting for the Elite

Guard this morning and want him there."

"Of course," Myles said, studying his dad closely. I had a feeling he was attempting to read his mind, but King Duncan must be blocking him. After a moment, he glanced back at the papers. "I want to know more about controlled visions."

"I will tell you. But first, there is someone else we need to speak with."

"Who?" I asked.

King Duncan looked grim. "We found a Volcaniac."

"Did you find him when you went to patrol The End?" Myles's voice echoed off the walls as we descended a spiral staircase into the lower levels of the palace.

General Cornstone nodded. "Yes, and he was injured very severely in the eruption. We have been allowing him time to heal before we interrogate him further."

"Why didn't you say anything when you first brought him here?" Myles asked.

"You know I hate holding prisoners in the dungeon," King Duncan said, but General Cornstone corrected.

"He has been trying to convince me to move him to the city prisons and out of the palace."

"Isn't the palace more secure?" I asked.

"My point," General Cornstone said, winking at me.

We reached the bottom of the staircase, and General Cornstone unlocked a door, allowing us to pass him. The dungeon was warmer than I would have expected. In stories, they were always described as cold and damp.

"Is he a Mageye?" I asked.

General Cornstone shook his head. "He is not."

We walked down a torchlit hall, our footsteps echoing off the stone floor and creating an eerie atmosphere. General Cornstone stopped by another door and turned to King Duncan. "Would you rather we bring him to a private room or discuss in the cellblock?"

King Duncan shook his head. "He is the only one in the cellblock; I see no reason to drag him out when he is still healing."

I stepped closer to Myles. Interrogating an injured prisoner in the dungeons was not at all what I would have expected to do today.

"Rose, if you get uncomfortable, you may leave," King Duncan told me. "He hasn't been violent."

My heart raced but I managed to thank him as General Cornstone opened the door. It led to another empty hall; we hadn't passed a single guard since coming down here.

Only members of the Elite Guard can open the door we just walked through, Myles said. *And a few trusted guards to check the cells.*

So, no one is down here because the dungeons are escape-proof?

Yes. Magical seals.

I looked back at the door curiously, before following General Cornstone and King Duncan down the cellblock. Each of the cells looked to be square with stone backs and sides, and bars in the front. Benches along the back wall served as cots and all were empty, except for one.

The Volcaniac appeared to be in his twenties, though it was hard to judge his age with all of his scars. He sat on his bench with his feet up, reading from a book.

"Good morning, Marlon," King Duncan said, holding his chin up.

Marlon lifted his head, not looking at all surprised to see us. "Your Majesty," he greeted, his voice hoarse. He stood to bow, grimacing in pain. His dark skin was heavily scarred and the burns on the left side of his face were only recently healed. "For what do I owe this visit?"

His hazel eyes bounced between us, not showing an ounce of

nerves.

"We are here as we are in need of information on the Volcaniacs. Will you be willing to answer our questions?" King Duncan asked briskly.

Marlon's face was expressionless. "I do not suppose I have a choice."

Myles's voice suddenly filled my head. *I remember him. He was one of the men who saw us soon after we broke in. The one who thought we were new recruits. Remember, he commented that the Volcaniacs were recruiting younger and younger?*

I studied Marlon closer, and recognized him from when we first snuck into the volcano. He and the man he had been with, had been the reason we realized we could try to blend in... Until the map we had stolen from Gray's hut exploded.

"Thank you," King Duncan said. He straightened his stance, his expression appearing much less stressed than I knew him to be. "Your leader, what do you know about him?"

Marlon laughed hoarsely, then winced from the pain of it. "I know those two children stole a map and the entire volcano erupted mere hours after."

I took a step back, bumping into Myles and feeling exposed as Marlon watched me flinch. Myles steadied me as I nervously held Marlon's gaze; it seemed he recognized us too.

"We have our doubts on whether he truly died in the eruption," General Cornstone said.

Marlon's gaze snapped to him. "I have no way of confirming nor denying that."

"We aren't asking you to confirm the rumors. We are asking you to provide us with the information needed to confirm it for ourselves," King Duncan said.

Marlon squinted. "What is there to tell? He was and perhaps still is a very powerful Mageye—persuasive too. I have seen him touch lava before, you know, walk through it without so much as a wince. But if he was injured prior to the eruption, I would assume he was injured after it, if he survived."

I looked at Myles, and he shook his head. "He wasn't hurt."

That seemed to pique Marlon's interest, and he stepped closer. "You fought with him? Are you the one to blame for the eruption? It was not coincidence?"

"Yes," Myles said, lifting his chin. "You may address me as General Duncan."

"Perhaps King Brenton was not the one recruiting young, but King Duncan. And you are his son?"

At the mention of the name, we all startled. "Your leader went by the name of King Brenton?" King Duncan clarified.

Marlon's hazel gaze flicked back to King Duncan. "Yes, Your Majesty."

General Cornstone and King Duncan shared a look before King Duncan turned to Marlon once more. "Does King Brenton have a way to create controlled visions?"

A flash of unease swept across Marlon's face, though he quickly suppressed it. "Why do you ask?"

"We do not owe you a reason."

He set his jaw. "And I do not owe you an answer."

I wrung my hands together, recalling the ashy smell of my hair after the controlled vision. If there was any chance these controlled visions were as awful as King Duncan seemed to imply, they must be stopped. "Would you help us in return for something?" I asked.

Myles caught my arm. "Rose," he scolded, but King Duncan motioned him with his hand.

"What do you wish to trade, Rose?"

My cheeks burned as everyone's eyes turned on me. I met Marlon's eyes again and for a fraction of a second, his expression seemed to soften with the same look Raymond gave me when I was terrified, as a part of me was now. "He's in pain," I answered

King Duncan. "I can heal him."

"He's a Volcaniac," Myles replied. "And he is already receiving medical treatment, more than your family ever did. Raymond didn't receive any treatment when his leg broke, and now you are offering help to Marlon?"

"We are citizens of Mageye City, not Volcaniacs," I argued. "Why would we withhold help from someone in need?"

"Rose," General Cornstone scolded gently. "You cannot make propositions like that in front of King Duncan. It is disrespectful."

Embarrassment licked my skin and I stared at my feet. "I am sorry, Your Majesty."

King Duncan rested a hand on my shoulder. "You may heal him."

I looked from him to Myles, who nodded. King Duncan turned to Marlon. "Rose has healing powers. If you answer our questions, she will heal you."

"Proof?" Marlon demanded, the softness gone.

I winced, and Myles's hand slipped into my grip, helping ease my nerves.

"Tell us about the controlled visions first," King Duncan said coolly.

Marlon started to shake his head, then his eyes flashed, and his aura filled with the presence of magic. His eyes no longer appeared hazel, but as if they were reflections of glass. Glass that led to... memories? I blinked rapidly, but couldn't seem to tear my gaze away as voices echoed from within Marlon's irises.

King Brenton stood in Marlon's eyes, another version of Marlon standing before him. More images flashed—nightmares. The Marlon in the memory sank to his knees with a groan, and King Brenton laughed. "Perhaps controlled visions are no longer a lost form of magic. Thank you, Marlon. You are free to go."

Marlon blinked, and his eyes returned to their hazel color, the magical hold that kept me staring at his eyes fading with the memory. Myles stepped forward, lightning arcing between his fingers.

"You're a Mageye," he stated.

"Yes," Marlon rasped.

"What did we just witness?"

Marlon turned away. "You activated one of my memories."

"What does that mean?" King Duncan demanded. "Why didn't you tell us you could do that before?"

"You never asked." Marlon turned back, a shadowed look crossing his hazel eyes. "So why would I offer that information?"

"Show us what you know that could help us stop King Brenton," General Cornstone ordered coolly, ignoring Marlon's frustration.

"That is not how it works," Marlon's voice lowered. "I can hide the fact I am a Mageye so well because my aura is weak. My memories activate of their own accord. I cannot force them to play."

"Can you play others' memories?" General Cornstone asked.

"Only my own. My power allows others to see what I have seen, witnessed, and lived. I do not know how he did it, but King Brenton found a way to force memories out of me."

"Force them?" General Cornstone asked.

Marlon frowned. "When he wished to view a memory, his aura forced it from me."

"Did you not work for him by choice, then?" King Duncan asked.

Marlon raised a brow. "I came to him. Our deal was he would take my power from me when he had finished his mission. The controlled visions were a part of that." He sighed, shaking his head. "I presume your questions stem from him sending controlled visions?"

"Possibly," General Cornstone said. "Our interpretation of what we know will depend on the information you provide."

Marlon curled his lip. "He is the only Mageye I know of who can send them. If you are asking these questions because someone has been receiving controlled visions, then all I can say is they will continue until King Brenton is dead."

"So, you suspect he is alive?" King Duncan confirmed.

"Given what you have alluded to, that is my guess."

"Do you know where he could be hiding, or if there is a chance that other surviving Volcaniacs are with him?" General Cornstone asked.

Marlon shifted, his gaze flicking between the four of us. "I know where he might be," he admitted.

"Where?" Myles asked.

Marlon shook his head. "You must understand that if the Volcaniacs ever learn that I have betrayed their king..." He stopped, and looked down the hall the way we had come. "They would take away the only reason I have left to live, and they do not need to enter this dungeon to do it."

I followed his look down the hall. The cruelty of the Volcaniacs seemed to extend even amongst themselves.

King Duncan sighed. "You being our source will remain classified. Besides my Elite Guard, no one else will ever know."

Marlon licked his lips, considering the offer. "And Miss Rose will heal me if I answer?" he asked, inclining his head toward me.

"Yes," King Duncan said.

"If you imprison any other Volcaniacs, I ask that you do not inform them that I am here," he decided. "It would be preferred that they are simply brought to their cells and notice my presence. I will maintain the impression of my loyalty and keep hidden the fact that I have aided you."

"Impression of loyalty?" General Cornstone questioned. "You told us before you were not there by force, but that you approached King Brenton."

"You would have to torture this information out of me if I

recognized King Brenton as my king," Marlon responded coolly. "I am offering it in a trade."

"What made you change your alliance?" I asked.

He glanced at me, and his hazel eyes flashed, though no memory played. "King Brenton broke a promise." With that, he turned back to King Duncan. "Will you accept my offer?"

King Duncan nodded. "Yes. Now, where do you suspect King Brenton has gone?"

"There were rumors that he intended to build a palace. The End was his fortress, but this palace was where he intended to hold his most powerful weapons. If everything was truly lost in The End, he would be there."

My eyes widened; King Brenton had a *palace?*

"Rumors or fact?" General Cornstone clarified.

Marlon smirked. "It depends on how much you trust my word. I have never been to the palace, but it is to the east." He waved his hand. "And I presume more impressive than the volcano."

King Duncan was silent as he contemplated Marlon's words. "And what of King Brenton's ultimate goal? He must have a motivation, a reason to be targeting..." He stopped, correcting himself. "If our suspicions are correct that he intends harm to the citizens of Mageye City, why is that?"

"Is it not obvious?" Marlon motioned to where King Duncan's crown would sit were he to wear it daily. "He desires to be king."

A shudder passed through me and Myles tightened his grip on my hand. "He wants to overthrow Mageye City, you mean? Why?"

A solemn expression crossed Marlon's face and he stared past us, his whisper contemplative, "I have heard it said that powers can become poison. Too much..."

"Taints you," Myles finished and Marlon's gaze snapped back, nodding.

"His motivation is his addiction to power and hunger for revenge against anyone whose knee does not hit the ground before him."

General Cornstone flexed his jaw. "The Volcaniacs have built themselves up for decades, haven't they?"

"Since well before I was born," Marlon answered, his hazel eyes again flashing without a memory.

"As I suspected," General Cornstone hissed, swallowing hard before turning back to King Duncan. "Do we need to know more?"

"Yes." King Duncan looked more stressed now, but his tone was calm as he asked Marlon, "The number of survivors?"

"You are the ones who told me I was the only survivor. I have not a clue about anyone else."

King Duncan narrowed his gaze. "For a man who has learned it is possible every friend he had in the world is dead, you are rather stoic and willing to turn your back on their graves."

"If I begged you on my knees, would the circumstances change?" Marlon challenged.

King Duncan grimaced. "No, they would not."

"Then why would I allow you to see my grief?" Marlon raised his brows. "Besides, I was not always a Volcaniac. I had a different life once." He again looked down the hall. "My choices led me here, not my loyalties."

"All right. Thank you for your honesty." King Duncan motioned me forward. "You may heal him."

I held my breath as I stepped up to the bars and reached my hand through. He didn't attempt to grab me and I took a steadying breath. "Give me your hand, and I will heal your wounds."

He grasped my hand, and I sent my powers to him. As the pain of burns lit up my left side, taking away the pain he felt, his irises flashed and another memory played.

King Brenton sat on his throne in the volcano's amphitheater, a purring mountain lion rubbing against his knee. It turned its yellow eyes towards Marlon, and he blinked, the memory fading from his hazel eyes.

"Thank you," he rasped, holding my hand for another moment. "You should know that I am one of very few Volcaniacs who do not hurt children. You say Mageye City is not as cruel as them..." He released my hand, his hoarse voice dropping even lower. "It was very dangerous to enter The End all alone. King Brenton will not take kindly to it, nor will he forget your faces."

"We were and still are aware of the risks," Myles said, putting a hand on my shoulder. "But thank you."

Chapter 4

"I want you both to stay together," King Duncan said once we exited the dungeons. "Be in the throne room in one hour with Raymond."

General Cornstone shut the door that led into the dungeons and I stepped away from it nervously. "Why do we need to stay together?"

He sighed. "Keep each other distracted." He gave Myles a pointed look. "General Cornstone and I will discuss everything, and you will be informed about what was discussed during the meeting alongside everyone else."

Myles tapped his fingers against his thigh but nodded, stepping past him. "We will be in my room."

"Thank you," King Duncan said as I went after Myles.

I looked back before rounding the first corner, and the two men appeared to be in deep discussion, both seeming stressed. General Cornstone glanced up and when he saw me watching, he put his hand on King Duncan's shoulder, steering him away.

One hour, Myles said, and I looked at him as he continued, *practically a life sentence.*

His smile faded quickly though and he held out his hand with a sigh. "Let's go to my room."

I took his outstretched hand and a purple orb formed around us. When it snapped, we stood in Myles's bedroom.

Raymond slept on top of the blankets of the unmade bed, and a soft thrill of pride crept through my nerves. "He did it," I whispered.

"First step to becoming a general," Myles agreed, walking over and straightening Raymond's boots, one of which had fallen on its side.

I stood by Myles's dresser, my gaze lingering on the leg Raymond had broken whilst being held in The End. "What do you think King Duncan is going to do about King Brenton?" I asked.

"Defeat him," Myles answered, his tone sounding as if he too had been defeated.

"How?"

He shrugged. The flickering lightning in his irises seemed to amplify whatever negative emotions he felt. "I don't know. King Duncan was blocking me the whole time we were in the dungeons."

I shifted my feet, pausing when Raymond stirred. He lifted his head, mumbling, "That was not an hour..."

"Actually," Myles corrected, the lightning fading from his irises, "you technically have another hour if you want to take it. Dad said to be in his throne room then."

"Wait..." Raymond rubbed his eyes. "I was told my presence might be needed for that."

"It will be needed," I whispered.

He pulled his hands from his face, propping himself up and looking at me with a frown. Dark bags circled his eyes, but his exhaustion seemed to have evaporated at the fear leaking into my voice. "What's wrong?"

I stepped up to the foot of the bed, forcing a steady tone. "King Duncan and General Cornstone took us to the dungeons to meet with a Volcaniac. We think their leader—King Brenton—survived."

He shot upright the rest of the way. "What?"

"He survived the eruption," Myles said, sitting on the edge of the bed. "Now he wants revenge. I endangered Mageye City."

"Well, don't go blaming yourself without the full story," Raymond replied. Though he rubbed his leg that had been broken, blinking a few times. "Rose said you think, but you're saying you know. Which is it?"

"We are fairly certain," I whispered. "And... Mageye always say to expect the unexpected to be unexpected for a reason."

His frown deepened. "Even magic has some predictable limits. And I would assume surviving the eruption is one of them."

Myles shook his head. "King Duncan has been blocking me from his mind. I think he knows more than what he told us."

Raymond looked to the window, sudden concern filling his tone. "This is suspicion based off of what the Volcaniac told you, right? Not because of some attack on the city? Should I go home and check on Mom and the twins?"

My heart raced at the thought and I hurried around the bed, crawling up and plopping down beside Raymond, shoes and all. "It isn't immediate danger," I whispered. "At least, I don't think."

Myles lay back, his head resting on Raymond's legs. "But it is a danger that exists," he finished, shutting his eyes. "I'm sorry."

X

As the seconds ticked closer to the meeting, Myles explained to us how they tended to go, before teleporting us directly to the throne room. A long table stood in the middle of the room, where the Elite Guard convened for meetings such as this one.

The Elite Guard created King Duncan's top advisors and there were currently twelve generals enrolled in the guard, including Myles. A few were here now, and I glanced between them. While I had no qualms with any of them, seeing them standing around the table at such a formal setting was intimidating.

General Agar smiled at us though, and General Laplin—one of

the longest standing members—nodded a welcome, her green eyes shifting with the shadows of leaves.

As we crossed the room, a small, brown cat suddenly brushed past me, scurrying under the table by General Curran's feet. Its yellow eyes followed me as I crossed the room.

A few more generals filed in, including General Cornstone and the second youngest general besides Myles, General Avery Ansley. Her father, General Silas Ansley, was also a member of the guard.

The full guard was now assembled, and the next time the doors opened, King Duncan was the one to enter. He held his head high as he strode to the head of the table, his tone taking on a practiced authority.

"Thank you all for coming," he addressed us. "I have called you together in response to our city being in grave danger. This morning, Myles and Rose came to me about dreams they have been having. Shared dreams, or more specifically, controlled visions."

"What is a controlled vision?" General Curran asked. His eyes were a pale color and his dress shirt was perfectly starched, not a wrinkle in sight.

King Duncan sighed. "A controlled vision is a vision sent to an individual in their sleep to convey a message. They are a *very* advanced form of magic; one I have not seen in decades. My first exposure to learning about them was after a woman attempted to create one and lost her life due to cool-down related to the vision."

My breath caught and I inched closer to Raymond. His fingers brushed mine under the table, also appearing uneasy.

Instead of looking appalled, General Curran looked intrigued. He rested his hands on the table and his gaze scanned the faces around him in a slow swoop.

"Who could have sent the controlled vision?" General Laplin asked. "Surely no one in the city would play around with something so dangerous."

King Duncan squared his shoulders. "You're right. It was not sent from within the walls of the city. I believe it was sent by the leader of the Volcaniacs, King Brenton."

"Forgive me, King Duncan," General Silas Ansley said. "But I thought we were operating on the assumption no one besides Marlon survived the eruption."

No one seemed surprised by the mention of Marlon, and Myles tapped his fingers against his leg, clearly miffed.

"Based on the contents of the dream Rose and Myles shared, as well as information given to us by Marlon this morning, we now believe our assumption was incorrect," General Cornstone said from his stance at King Duncan's right hand.

Myles stopped tapping his fingers, his brows drawing together. "I know the proof we have points to his being alive. But *how?* Dad—King Duncan, surely he acquired magical burns when I broke his hold. He *shouldn't* have survived."

King Duncan stared at the table, his tone quiet, but not defeated. "I don't know."

Myles faltered his defense, staring at his dad. After speaking with Marlon and while waiting with Raymond for the meeting to start, Myles had accepted the truth that King Brenton was likely alive. But now, lightning flickered between his fingers and it was clear he had expected King Duncan to have more to say. "Do you have any doubts about the truth of all of this?"

"Not one." King Duncan looked up, holding Myles's gaze. "It is something I have feared prior to when you and Rose met with me this morning, though I had no proof to offer. And yes, he should have died during the eruption, but if Marlon could survive it, why couldn't he?"

The fire king himself... King Brenton stood much better odds of surviving unscathed than a weaker Mageye like Marlon.

"My first nightmare was the day we returned, and even then it felt different. More so as time went on," Myles said. "King Brenton shouldn't be strong enough."

"But he is," King Duncan stated. "He *is* strong enough. We saw him using controlled visions in Marlon's memory."

A deadly silence settled over the table and Myles swallowed hard. "All right. How do we fix it, then?"

The silence continued and a pained look crossed King Duncan's face. "That is a question you need to ask yourself, Myles. You and Rose."

I froze. "What do you mean? You want us to..." I stopped, glancing around the many faces in the room. If Myles and I were meant to ask ourselves about the solution, was King Duncan wanting us to plan an attack?

King Duncan shut his eyes, his somber expression solidifying the concerns I dared not speak aloud. "Controlled visions are similar to searchlights. When he calls upon your auras to send them, he gets a sense as to where you are. The reason Myles has reported them worsening with time is because King Brenton is getting stronger. As he continues to grow stronger, the visions will continue to worsen and eventually, they could become partial reality." He looked between me and Myles. "He will also get a better sense to your location every night if you remain in the same location... but if you were to travel, things would be different."

"Travel?" I echoed in a whisper, exchanging a look with Myles. "You mean... you want us to leave the city?"

He gave a single nod. "For your safety as well as the safety of the city. I would like to create a team of Mageye to overthrow the Volcaniacs and King Brenton for good. A team they won't deem an immediate threat, but will have the combined strength needed to defeat them."

My mouth felt suddenly too dry to speak, but Myles nodded slowly, leaning forward. "I can fix it, then," he whispered, before raising his voice for everyone to hear. "You want us to go to the palace Marlon referenced?"

"Yes," King Duncan confirmed.

"But we almost died last time," I said, blindly reaching for Raymond's hand. "And if he is angry and looking for revenge..."

"You won't be working alone. I have a few more Mageye in mind to join your team," King Duncan assured.

"How many other Mageye?" Raymond asked, squeezing my hand.

"Three," King Duncan said slowly.

"Are you wanting volunteers from the Elite Guard?" General Curran asked, raising a brow.

King Duncan shook his head. "No, none of who I have in mind will be from the Elite Guard. I am catering powers."

Several generals looked suddenly uneasy, and Myles paused. "I don't want a team of miscellaneous guards. Rose and I faced King Brenton before and with our connection, we are practically in sync. We can handle this alone."

King Duncan ran a hand down his face. "I want you to permanently defeat King Brenton and any Volcaniacs he has close to him. That is a job that requires more than two."

I steadied myself on the table and Raymond shifted his stance. "King Duncan, Rose is only fifteen. Even if she were traveling with the entirety of the Elite Guard, I would have to insist she is too young."

"Mageye often choose strength over age," General Cornstone said. "Rose and Myles have two of the most powerful auras in the city. This is not the same as sending two non-Mageye teenagers."

"And remember, the visions will worsen the longer they remain here," King Duncan said. "Not only will the worsening visions put them in danger, but all of Mageye City. King Brenton may eventually be able to intertwine his aura with the city."

My grip on the table tightened. "So, it's not just me and Myles in danger?"

"No," King Duncan said softly. "It is not."

Myles didn't hesitate. "Then we'll leave. Before tonight. It's one thing to endanger ourselves, but a completely different thing to endanger others."

Raymond put a hand on my shoulder. "Surely there is *time*," he pressed. "If last night was the first time Myles and Rose shared a dream..."

"I believe that connection means our time has already expired," King Duncan said.

I placed my hand over Raymond's, my heart racing. The dream had happened in my *house*. Mom had run into the room right away, Ren and Ryder had been in their room across the hall when it happened, and on most nights, Raymond would be there as well.

Myles had sworn to protect Mageye City above his own life when he joined the Elite Guard, and that was a promise Raymond would also be making very soon.

While I had no obligation to that promise for the city, there were thousands of innocent citizens who were now in danger because of my presence. And even worse, four of those innocent people owned my entire heart.

It was my love for my family that had led me to Myles in the first place. I couldn't risk putting them in danger again. Almost losing them to The End was bad enough, much more if I were to stay here and allow it to happen again. "When do we meet the rest of our team?"

King Duncan relaxed. "After this meeting. I will send for them to come to the palace so we can meet in my office and discuss your combined powers."

Raymond tugged his hand from my shoulder as a murmured assent swept around the table. "Your Majesty, I'm sorry, but no." He took a shaky breath. "I... I can't allow Rose to go. And our mom would never allow it either, even against your orders."

I turned to Raymond, shocked by his defiance. "Raymond, I

want to go."

"No, you don't," he argued. "You don't *want* to go. You feel obligated; there's a difference. And while I am willing to follow whatever path is best for Mageye City, I... I can't do that at your expense." He swallowed hard, looking at General Cornstone in shame. "Even if that means being declared unfit for the Elite Guard. I will vow everything above my own life, but not Rose's."

"I have to," I interjected. "It is safer for everybody if I go."

"Not you. How is this safe for you?" he challenged, tearing his gaze from General Cornstone.

"The visions won't get worse if I go," I whispered.

His blue eyes filled with a battling agony and he glanced around the table. "I would like to go with them if they insist on going."

General Cornstone cleared his throat. "That would be much too risky, Raymond. You are a powerful soldier, but not a Mageye. Your presence would cause more harm than good. Even something as simple as going through a portal with you would slow them down."

"You're asking me to let my little sister risk her life!" His voice began to rise, but he caught himself. "I'm sorry, but I... I can't let this happen."

King Duncan shook his head. "It breaks my heart to send Myles. But sometimes we are forced to make sacrifices our very soul screams in protest against."

Raymond's chest heaved. "She's fifteen," he whispered.

"I broke into The End," I said. "I have experience."

"A rescue mission is different from an assassination," Raymond replied.

"Last time was a battle too," Myles said, looking over my head at Raymond. "I'll keep Rose safe."

Raymond opened his mouth to protest again, but was interrupted by General Avery Ansley. Her eyes were the color of pink peonies, and like her twin sister, Sadie, she could stimulate positive emotions. "King Duncan has elected Rose for this mission to help protect her," she said. "He doesn't want her visions to get worse and endanger her as well as the rest of the city."

"Maybe that makes me selfish," Raymond said. "But we haven't even considered another way."

"That's because this is the *best* way," she said.

Raymond's stance seemed to falter, but then he blinked and shook his head. "Avery, no. You're using your power on me, aren't you?"

"Rose ran away in the middle of the night to save you last time, wouldn't you rather let her go of her own accord than have her run away again?" Avery asked without missing a beat. "And when Rose returns, she will be a hero. Won't that make you proud?"

"I..." Raymond touched my braid with trembling fingers, and tears welled in my eyes at his next words. "I'm already proud of her."

"But you'll be even more proud," Avery whispered.

"You're right," Raymond admitted. "And the Elite Guard is meant to put the city above themselves..." He blinked a few times, pulling back. "But this is different." He swung his gaze back to Avery. "I would be proud, yes, but—"

"Myles has never failed a mission," Avery said, her irises seeming to bloom with a deeper pink. "Neither has Rose."

Raymond stilled, whispering, "I trust them."

Hot tears burned my eyes as I watched his fearful expression slowly melt away with the help of Avery's words. Myles quietly ushered me from the room, and a few of the other generals nodded or waved as we left, but I never looked away from Raymond.

"Stay safe," I whispered as we ducked out of the room. "I love you."

Myles released my wrist. "He will forgive us," he whispered.

"I... I'm sorry, Rose."

I hugged my arms around myself, sniffing as King Duncan followed us out. He looked grim, but nodded. "Thank you for agreeing to this. Let's head to my office. I want you to meet the rest of your team."

Myles straightened as if shocked by his own power. "I don't want a bigger team," he decided. "Dad, this has happened because of my screw-up. Why are we putting others on the line for it?"

King Duncan shook his head. "It is not your fault, and General Cornstone and I have already picked out the rest of your team. If all five of you work together, you will stand a much better chance of succeeding."

Lightning flickered in Myles's purple iris. "Rose, what do you think? We can do this ourselves, *right?*"

I wiped my eyes, my hands shaking. "I don't know."

He stepped closer. "We traveled to The End ourselves," he implored me. "We can do the same here."

Both men watched me and I looked between them in vain. Myles and I had done the impossible once, something told me that facing the impossible a second time was pushing our luck. "I'm sorry, Myles..." I began, straightening my stance. "But I agree with King Duncan. Even five people seems like hardly enough."

Lightning flickered in his purple iris but he stepped back. "Fine. We'll see who these other Mageye are first."

Chapter 5

King Duncan led us back to his office. The pile of papers Myles had dumped on his table had been straightened and placed neatly on the desk in the back of the room. We took seats around the table and waited.

King Duncan stood behind Myles, hand on his shoulder. Myles leaned his head back on the chair to look up at his dad. "I'm ready," he said. "Rose and I were talking yesterday. I was going to ask you to start assigning missions again."

"I had a feeling you were going to ask me soon," he answered, pulling his hand away. "With your restlessness."

"Yeah." Myles stared at the table. "And now I have given myself a mission. King Brenton is alive."

"How could you have known?" I asked. "When the volcano erupted, you shattered his hold. All of The End came back to life. Even though he survived, you injured him."

"But not enough," Myles answered.

King Duncan clucked his tongue and took a seat beside Myles. "Rose is right. Clearly the Volcaniacs hold more power than we have ever known."

I chewed my lip and stared out a window. "If he is so much stronger than us, how will we ever beat him?"

"No one is invincible," King Duncan said softly. "I would not have chosen the group I have if I did not have complete faith you all will succeed. King Brenton has power and cruelty and lava. You five have power and loyalty and all of Mageye City in your hearts. That is where your advantage lies." He smiled sadly. "And most importantly, you have faith and you have God Himself."

"And my family," I murmured, looking back. "Can you make sure they're okay, King Duncan? While I'm gone."

He smiled. "Of course. I will keep an eye on them, even Raymond." His smile widened. "I respect him for standing up for you. I prefer my Elite Guard to be unafraid to challenge me."

"I'm unafraid to challenge you," Myles said, leaning back in his chair.

My lip twitched and King Duncan sighed heavily. "You're too unafraid to challenge me."

Myles's gaze drifted around the room now, as if memorizing every detail, and King Duncan stood to look over the papers on his desk.

Someone knocked lightly on the door and King Duncan strode to it, letting a young girl inside with a warm welcome.

Myles snapped to attention. "Soph, what are you doing here?"

Thirteen-year-old Sophie Hughes was like an adopted little sister to Myles. He had saved her life on one of his first missions to find Mageye, and ever since, the two had a bond like no other. She had been one of the first Mageye Myles introduced me to, her white quartz eyes, long, blonde hair, and shy demeanor representing her ability to turn invisible beautifully.

"King Duncan asked me to come," Sophie explained. "A messenger came and said he wants me to meet with you and Rose."

Myles froze and slowly turned to King Duncan. "Is Soph one of the three you have in mind for the mission?"

When King Duncan nodded, Myles shook his head. "I'm not taking Soph. This is way too dangerous."

Sophie flickered, her body disappearing and reappearing in the same spot. "What's too dangerous?" She stepped back, and parts of her body began to grow translucent, revealing the wall behind her through her skin.

"Nothing is dangerous in this office," King Duncan soothed. "I want to ask you if you would be willing to help with something, alongside Myles and Rose."

Sophie flickered and Myles opened his mouth to argue, but King Duncan shot him a look. "I am asking, not forcing," he warned, motioning Myles to sit.

Sophie sat beside Myles and I smiled at her. "Good morning, Sophie."

"Good morning," she echoed softly.

Myles crossed his arms and glared at the table. *She's too young,* he said to me telepathically.

I glanced at Sophie and nodded. *King Duncan seems to be doing this because he has no other choice.*

I know. Myles shut his eyes. *Doesn't mean I have to like it.*

I didn't have a response to that and turned to the door when there was another knock. This time, two young Mageye entered.

Both appeared to be a little older than me and bowed and curtsied to King Duncan, appearing nervous yet excited.

The girl had medium length brown hair and her eyes resembled the night sky, creating a beautiful galaxy of their own. Rather than wearing a dress, she wore a lavender-gray tunic and pants.

The boy stood a few inches taller than her, and his eyes looked like sunlight reflecting off water. He had an energy about him that seemed to fill the whole room, and when he nodded at Sophie, Myles, and me, his hair seemed to ripple in waves around his face.

King Duncan motioned to the table. "Mercy, Will, thank you both for coming. Please take a seat."

When they were seated, King Duncan cleared his throat. "I have called you five here to discuss an important mission I would like you to be a part of."

Mercy and Will exchanged looks and Sophie flickered again, though she relaxed when Myles reached over and took her hand.

"I want to begin by telling you that you don't need to commit to this," King Duncan continued. "It is very dangerous, and if you do not wish to go, I will not force nor shame you." He acknowledged Myles, adding, "All five of you have the ability to decide for yourselves."

Myles drew a deep breath and nodded reluctantly. "Yes, sir."

"Thank you." King Duncan turned back to address the table. "I don't believe you have all met, so let me introduce you." He motioned to Myles. "I am sure you recognize my son, Myles, though you may also know him as General Duncan. And perhaps you know Rose, as well."

Myles nodded, but continued to frown, and I smiled at everyone as King Duncan waved to Sophie. "Sophie." His hand swept across the table. "Mercy and Will."

The three of them all offered smiles, though Sophie's was very faint.

"I want you five to be a team." King Duncan began to explain everything we had learned that morning, forging on even when Sophie began to grow translucent. When he finished, we sat in stunned silence.

Will broke it. "You want *us* to blow up a palace and kill a rampaging psychopath?"

King Duncan nodded. "Yes, that is exactly what I want. With your combined powers, I believe you can do it."

"With our combined powers?" Mercy repeated, glancing around the table. "What can everyone do?"

King Duncan nodded. "That is a good question. Your powers are why I think you five, out of all the Mageye, are our answer." Despite the confidence of his tone, his irises swirled with silver mist that suggested he was uneasy. He turned to Myles. "Myles can teleport, as well as create other similar forms of electricity.

Including force fields and lightning bolts." None of that seemed to surprise anyone, until King Duncan finished, "He can also read minds."

Will raised his brows, and waves began crashing in his irises. "No wonder your aura is so powerful. Mercy and I have always wondered what else you can do."

Myles nodded stiffly. "Not many Mageye outside of the palace are aware of it."

"Yes," King Duncan agreed. "And Myles has been a general in my Elite Guard for six years now. This is far from his first mission. You will be safe with him."

King Duncan motioned to me next. "Rose can heal herself and others. With her help, you won't be set back when injured. She and Myles can also speak telepathically at any distance. This will allow you to temporarily split up if needed."

Mercy nodded, the stars in her irises appearing to burst and glow. The connection Myles and I had was unheard of, and we were lucky the price we had paid for crossing the magical boundaries of life was more of a blessing than a curse.

King Duncan continued his introductions. "Sophie can turn herself invisible, which makes her the perfect spy. If she masks her aura, she won't be detectable. Mercy can communicate with the stars, and they can guide her through the quickest and safest path. This will help you to sneak around in unexpected ways only she can follow."

When King Duncan turned to Will, his expression grew serious. "And Will. You can breathe underwater as well as control it. Water can douse fire; you may be the one best-fit to put out King Brenton's flames."

Waves crashed in Will's irises, no longer playful, but stormy. He nodded anyway. "Yes, sir."

Myles studied Will now, and when he looked to Mercy and Sophie, his tense posture seemed to falter. "I can see why you picked them," he admitted.

"Me too," I agreed. From the auras flooding the room and the powers surrounding the table, it was obvious why we had been matched together. I clenched my fists, digging my fingers into my palms before uncurling them and watching the wounds fade.

Mageye City needed us... and if Mageye City needed us, then so did my family.

King Duncan met and held each of our gazes individually before asking, "With that understanding, are you willing to travel to King Brenton's palace and defeat him and his Volcaniacs for good?"

The five of us glanced between each other and while Mercy, Will, and Sophie looked nervous, and Myles looked frustrated, everyone was nodding.

Myles was the one to speak for all of us, echoing the same conclusion I had come to. "Mageye City needs us; we will do it."

King Duncan smiled, though I could sense worry behind it. "God protect you all. And thank you. We will meet at the entrance to the city in an hour."

Chapter 6

Myles took me back to his room so we could pack together. The realization that I was going to be leaving without a single goodbye had hit me hard, but Myles had assured me this was to keep my family safe. Even so, I had decided to write them a letter to apologize and promise them I would be careful and that I *wanted* to do this.

And I did. To protect them.

I sat at Myles's desk now, while he packed bags for both of us. Mercy, Will, and Sophie had returned home, and I could only hope they wouldn't need to run away like I was doing. Regardless, they were now a part of our team. A team that would be fighting the Volcaniacs together soon enough.

I shuddered, signing my name and adding a heart for my mom and each of my brothers. Once the letter was sealed, I turned to Myles. He frowned at the coins he was counting. "Why are you so against working as a team?" I asked.

He looked up. "I prefer working solo. That is why most of my duties are one-person jobs."

"Well, you worked well with me. What's the difference between what we did as a team before and working as a bigger team now?"

"That was different," he said, dropping the coins back into the bag. "When we first met, you were going to save your family with or without me. We came together by choice."

I furrowed my brow. "But your job is to bring Mageye home, so you are with other people a lot."

"Yes, but I'm supposed to guide them. Take Soph. She was being hunted after her powers were discovered. I helped her, and we're still friends, but going on a mission like this..."

"It's dangerous," I said. "But you have told me before you swore to protect Mageye City no matter the cost, even if it takes your life."

"No one in the group my dad picked has made that promise," he said, voice low.

I took a shaky breath and nodded, turning back to my letter. "Maybe not technically, but we did all agree to go of our own accord."

Myles pulled out a chair and sat across from me. "It's my fault we need to do this, Rose. No one else should risk their lives for a mistake *I* made. I don't like relying on others when I'm to blame."

"I don't blame you," I said. "No one we have talked to today does."

"I should have dragged him down with me," Myles whispered.

"But then you would have died," I said. "I'd blame you for that... but not this."

He looked down for a moment, then met my eyes. "You're right. I messed up, but I'll fix it... *We'll* fix it."

I reached across the desk and took his hand. "There's a reason King Duncan picked us five that goes beyond our powers. He trusts us to be a *team*."

The entirety of Mageye City was surrounded by an impressive wall. A true envy of architectural design, sandstone pillars were connected with gold. Sunlight reflected off of the golden gates now, seeming to shine outside of the city. Broad stairs led to a frequently-used path into the midst of Alveraada.

A group stood to the right of the gates, and I recognized Will and Mercy. They stood with who I could only assume were their parents. Their dads looked very alike, both had the same brown hair that Mercy and Will had. As Myles and I grew closer, I got a glimpse of their eyes—Mageye—and the biggest difference between their identical faces. I smiled softly, wondering if they were twins, which likely made Will and Mercy cousins.

Mercy's mom held both her hands, speaking softly, while Will's mom sorted through his satchel, ensuring he had packed everything he needed.

Before we left the palace, Myles had gone to speak with King Duncan privately, and had taken me to the gates when they finished.

King Duncan approached the gates now, alongside General Cornstone, and Sophie arrived with her parents soon after.

My gaze flit behind them to the empty streets. I was the only one without family to see me off, but I had made my choice. And I could apologize for it when the Volcaniacs were defeated for good. When my family was *safe*.

King Duncan looked between the five of us. "Remember, I wouldn't have chosen you if I didn't believe you were capable. I have created many groups to defend our city as king, and the five of your auras combined together outweighs many of them." He turned to me and Myles. "Chances are the visions will continue, but as long as you don't stay in the same place for more than one night, King Brenton won't be able to tell that you are on the move. My hope is that the visions might get better, because he will unwillingly be searching for you to send the visions."

Myles nodded. "We understand, Dad."

Mercy picked up her pack. "We won't let you down, King Duncan."

Her mom smiled proudly, but tears threatened to spill from

her eyes. "You all be careful. Come back and tell us the stories after."

"We will, Aunt Cindy," Will said, waving her off jokingly, as if she were being overprotective. "No need to worry."

His mom pulled him into a hug. "We raised you, Will. We know we need to worry."

He laughed, protesting her before hugging back. "I'll be okay, Mom. So will Mercy and everyone else."

Sophie's dad picked her up in a hug, and her mom kissed her cheek before they bowed their heads together.

As everyone said their goodbyes, Myles turned to King Duncan. "Three months?" he asked. "If we aren't back by then..."

General Cornstone stepped forward and put a hand on Myles's shoulder. "I will leave the second past midnight on that day if I must. But you better not make me do that."

Myles's lip twitched. "Thanks, General Cornstone."

He hugged Myles before stepping back, and King Duncan took his place. General Cornstone smiled at me and offered a hug, whispering, "I will visit your family often."

"Thank you." I breathed, relief rushing through me. "And can you tell them I'm sorry?"

He stepped back and nodded. "You are brave for doing this."

I only smiled this time, and when our goodbyes were finished, Myles stepped up to the gates. "I want to get as far from the city as we can before nightfall. So let's pray a portal calls us quickly."

The city gates were held open, their golden magnificence shining in the sun and welcoming us back into Alveraada.

"Rose!" someone shouted. "Wait!"

I turned to see Ryder and I shook my head. "Ryder, I have to go, you won't be able to stop me. I'm sorry."

He weaved through the crowd seeing us off, panting. "That's not why I'm here." He glanced over his shoulder, scanning the empty streets behind him. "I have to be quick. I don't know how much longer Ren can hold Mom and Raymond back."

My lips parted in my surprise. "You mean you're okay with me going?"

His expression grew serious. "No, of course not. But I know I won't be able to stop you, so instead I wanted to give you this." He handed me a small box. "Ren and I got these for you. The bird let us take them, so they should work if you need a boost with your powers."

I lifted the lid of the small box and my breath caught. Three golden feathers lay inside. "Thank you," I breathed, snapping the box shut.

My eyes found Myles's, and he nodded his head, stepping aside to give me and Ryder space. But my gaze lingered on his chest and how it rose with every breath he took. Hardly two months ago, that chest had been still.

During our first escape from the Volcaniacs, Myles's powers had been pushed past their limits and he gave his entire life to get me and my family out. If it weren't for a Golden Dove offering me a feather that enhanced my power... Myles wouldn't be here.

These feathers had the potential of being life or death to our mission... and to us.

I turned back to Ryder, and he gave me a grim smile, holding out something else. "Ren wanted you to have this, too. He said it is a tradition to give it to you before a dangerous journey."

The familiar jackknife fit in my palm perfectly, and I traced the intricate *R* burned into the handle. After taking the jackknife with me to save my family from The End, I had returned it to its rightful owner. And yet, here it was again, Ren's most prized possession. "Thanks, Ryder, and tell Ren thanks for me, too."

Ryder pulled me into his arms. "I'll do that if you promise to stay safe," he whispered. When we separated, he gave a shaky laugh. "Now I need to get home before Raymond murders me. But good luck, and don't die." He looked over Myles, Will, Mercy, and Sophie. "That's the same for the rest of you."

I nodded, blinking back my tears as I put the box and jackknife in my apron pocket. "I promise," I whispered back. "And you stay safe, too... so you all can scold me when I get back."

His fingers traced my braid. "I look forward to it."

Chapter 7

"Marlon told us that King Brenton's palace is to the east," Myles said once the golden gates of Mageye City had officially blended into the trees. "But he has never been there, so he had nothing else to offer about the location."

Will glanced at the sun, then at Mercy, then Myles. "Uh... if it's to the east, why aren't we walking east?"

Myles waved at the path ahead of us. "This path splits a few miles ahead and will let us get some extra distance between us and the city."

"I was wondering if you were directionally challenged." Will snickered. "I stand corrected."

Mercy laughed and Will grinned, waves crashing in his irises. Myles shrugged but didn't otherwise respond, and Sophie and I shared a look, both fighting our smiles.

I quickened my pace to walk alongside Myles. "Sounds like a good idea to me."

His shoulders relaxed a little and he nodded. *I am hoping it makes the controlled visions better.*

I put my fingers to my temples, grimacing at the reminder. *I have only had the one, and I am already dreading another.*

Regardless of whether they are as scary or not, at least he won't be able to sense us.

My gaze flit to the east and I sighed, walking in silence

alongside him until the path forked. A light breeze rustled the leaves on the trees, and a bird sang merrily somewhere in the upper branches. Myles turned to the path leading east, but Mercy paused between the two.

"It will be quicker if we take the other one," she said.

Myles looked down the other side of the fork. "That path is going west. We need to go east."

"I know, but the sun is telling me to take the western path anyway."

His brow furrowed, though he looked faintly curious and stepped back. "King Duncan said the stars guide you? How does that work?"

"It is like a whisper in my ear." Mercy shrugged. "The stars tell me their secrets and give me direction. One thing is for sure, we won't ever be lost with the stars guiding me."

"I'm happy King Duncan chose you to come with us," Sophie said quietly, stepping beside me.

Myles tilted his head. "So, we will be following a map made of ink only you can see?"

"Exactly like that." Mercy traced her finger through the air in front of her. "Though, I can't physically see it either, the stars direct me."

"Interesting..." Myles looked down both paths, before turning to the one Mercy had suggested. "We will follow the stars."

"It's what I always do," Mercy agreed.

"Do the stars have voices?" I asked.

"It isn't so much a literal voice as a metaphorical one."

"Didn't realize stars have metaphorical voices," Will mused, rubbing his chin contemplatively. "Not sure what that means, to be honest."

"Wouldn't you like to know," she quipped, waving him away, and he snickered.

"Nah, you can keep the stars and I'll keep the water."

"And Myles has lightning," I said. "Kind of a connector between the sky and water, right? Storm clouds and rain..."

Myles sighed. "King Duncan did say our powers go well together," he admitted. "And... I can see why."

"He didn't choose us for nothing," I agreed, catching his eye. "Any of us."

He raised his brow but nodded, turning to Sophie, who kept a shy distance. "Come here, Soph. We don't bite."

She flickered a little but smiled, stepping between me and Myles. She was the youngest in our group, but her power was one Myles had wished we had when breaking into The End. And while she was shy, this wasn't her first risky journey with Myles.

Mercy and Will whispered together, and we continued farther and farther to the west.

"We should leave the path now," Mercy announced, turning from her conversation with Will. "We've gone as far as we can before losing distance."

Myles scanned the trees. "Straight in?"

She pointed past him to a tall oak tree. "Past that."

"There's a stream along our non-path, path then," Will said.

I looked at him in surprise. Besides the chatter of birds and rustling leaves, the woods were silent—no sign of water. "How do you know there's a stream over there? Can you hear it?"

He shook his head. "Sensing water is what I do."

Myles nodded. "That makes sense. Everything has its own aura. Water must have a stronger aura to you."

"A stronger aura, but not a voice," Will said, poking Mercy's arm.

Before we passed the oak tree, I took one final look at the trail behind us, back towards Mageye City. *Stay safe... Please, stay safe...*

Myles put a hand on my shoulder. *We'll see them again. It isn't goodbye forever.*

Mageye City is safer already with us outside of it, isn't it? At least, as long as these controlled visions continue.

He grimaced but nodded. *I think so.*

I took a deep breath and tore my gaze from Mageye City. *Goodbye for now, then.*

Goodbye for now, he echoed, stepping into the woods.

It wasn't long until we heard the gentle bubbling of a stream and Will strayed to our left, hopping into it. "See? I could sense it, and here it is."

Sophie frowned. "You'll get your boots wet."

"No, I won't." He lifted his right foot to reveal it was perfectly dry. "I'm waterproof if I want to be."

"If you want to be? Do you mean you can choose when you get wet?" I asked, peering at his feet.

He nodded. "Yeah."

"So, if it rains, you won't get wet?"

Mercy answered for him. "Yes. He loves to invite me places when he knows it is about to rain so I'll get soaked. Then he'll be dry and warm, and I'll be miserable."

Will laughed. "You fall for it every time, Mercy. Do you really think I'm going to pass something like that up?"

I looked between them. Besides their hair, they bore other resemblances, such as similar face shapes, and they had a closeness that suggested more than friends.

"Are you cousins?" I asked. "Your dads looked like they could be twins."

"They are," Mercy said. "Will's dad is the older twin, but *I'm* the older cousin."

"By a *month*," Will grumbled.

"Best month of my life." She sighed wistfully.

Will motioned towards Mercy with his hand and an arc of water rose from the stream and splashed her.

She jumped. "Will!"

He laughed. "You deserved that."

Sophie giggled. "Are you going to dry her, or is she stuck being wet?"

"He better dry me," Mercy complained, holding her wet shirt away from her skin.

"I'll half-dry you," Will decided.

Myles glanced at the bickering cousins. "You live by the fields on the northwest side of the city, right?"

Will looked up. "How'd you know that?"

"I've seen you around."

"Well, that's not creepy at all," Will joked. "Though we've seen you around too, *General Duncan*."

Myles nodded. "I'm sure you have," he agreed.

"Everyone probably has," I said. "At least, people always seem to recognize you."

"Yeah..." He turned his gaze ahead of us, his expression solemn. "And apparently people outside of Mageye City recognize me, too."

Like King Brenton. I shuddered; after all, hadn't Marlon warned us King Brenton would remember our faces?

✕

As the sun set, Mercy paused and turned to face the west. "There is a portal that way. Off our current path, but we will gain any lost ground back."

"Really?" Myles asked, narrowing his gaze in the direction she pointed. "I don't feel it at all."

"Me either," Mercy said. "The stars are telling me."

"How far is it?" Will asked, kicking a small stone so it bounced into the bushes.

"Too far for tonight," she said. "Unless we want to travel in the dark."

Sophie flickered. "I'd rather not do that."

Myles crossed his arms over his chest. "It's usually better to travel during the day to keep a routine. I think we should find a camp near here, and first thing tomorrow, we will teleport to get a boost towards the portal."

Will's eyes went wide. "What's teleporting like?"

"You won't feel a thing," Myles said. "I'll create an orb around us and when it snaps, we will reappear somewhere else."

"If you shut your eyes, you'd miss it," I added.

"I won't be shutting my eyes," Will said. "I want to see it happen."

"It's fun," Sophie said quietly. "Or, it can be, depending on where you're going."

Myles nodded. "Let's make a camp and prep for an early morning."

"Works for me," I said, glancing around us for a good spot.

With all five of us searching, it didn't take long to find a suitable camp. A large group of bushes tightly interwove with each other, but appeared to have an almost hollow center that we could all fit inside, and even stand in.

Once settled, Will pulled out a bag with what looked like five round loaves of bread the size of a large orange, each with a beautiful flower design on top. "My mom made these," he explained. "There's jam inside. Pretty sure she said it's apple."

"Thank you," I said as I accepted mine.

Sophie traced her finger along the flower design. "It's almost too pretty to eat."

"There's plenty more where it came from," Will said, splitting his in half. "Our fields, as Myles not-creepily knows, are a shared farm. Our parents grow most of what we eat."

"And lots of hay," Mercy said. "We have cows, too."

"Do you help in the fields?" Myles asked, tearing his bun in half.

"From shoveling stalls to helping birth cows," Will said. "We'll be inheriting the farm one day, you know... in a long, *long* time."

Myles nodded slowly, swallowing a bite before speaking again. "How much experience do you all have with something like we are doing? Fighting or defense, endurance, knowledge of strategy?"

Sophie flickered, staring at her lap. "I know everything you've taught me."

Myles reached over and flicked hair over her shoulder. "Yes, you are a good fighter, Soph. And I know you're small, but your power will help keep you safe."

I rested half my bun on my knee, wiping my hands together to hide the shaking. "I have experience from... you know."

"And you've practiced fighting techniques before, too." Myles nodded, turning to Mercy and Will. "What about you?"

"I once won a fight against a rooster," Will offered.

Mercy giggled, drawing her knees to her chest. "Not what he meant."

Myles was frowning, but Will sighed. "I know. Our dads both served in the guard when they were in their twenties. They've taught us a lot from that, and I like to think we're pretty strong, given all the manual labor we do."

"And we are both proficient with daggers and a few other weapons," Mercy said, drawing a dagger from her waistband. "We can fight."

I pulled out my own blade, Ren's jackknife, and ran my finger over the R in the handle. "Marlon said the Volcaniacs have been growing for decades."

"That's..." Will stopped, staring at his half-finished bun. "Well, that just means a lot of them probably have rickety bones."

"It means we need to train," Myles said, annoyed. "We can't rely on powers alone, and Mercy and Rose don't have powers that will necessarily help in a fight. And Soph's power is best for defense. That leaves Will and I with powers we can wield like weapons, so we need to make up for that."

"And how we will do that?" I asked, a pit forming in my

stomach.

"We practice," Myles answered. "I can teach you all some fighting techniques in our camp, at night. We can learn each other's weapons and weaknesses so we can best protect each other. And we can stage attacks on each other—Rose can heal us if anyone gets cut."

A heavy silence fell over the bushes, and even Will didn't have a remark.

Finally, Mercy stretched out her legs. "All the travel to get there will be good endurance training."

"My dad picked us for a reason," Myles said, though he was frowning. "Tonight, we can focus on getting to know each other. In some ways, that is better than any amount of practice we can do."

"I agree," I said, forcing a smile. "Favorite colors?"

Will laughed, and Sophie's shoulders relaxed, the solemn atmosphere slowly easing as we questioned each other.

Myles kept silent though, his gaze continually bouncing between the three of them.

Are you okay? I asked as we finished our dinner.

He turned from Sophie. *I'm still not happy with this being a group of five.*

I'm sure it won't be as bad as you think.

Maybe.

He didn't sound very convinced and I looked between Mercy, Will, and Sophie. *What are your thoughts on everyone? It sounds like they all have some experience with... well... fighting.*

Mercy is a good help. She can save us time with her directional skills. I can see Soph's power being useful too, but she is so young...

She is older than you were when you went on your first mission, I reminded him.

True, but she's different. I don't want her getting hurt.

That was fair. *What about Will?* I prompted.

He turned his gaze to the stars. *He is as committed to the mission as the rest of us, but I don't like how he is treating our traveling like a camping trip.*

A camping trip? I studied his expression. *He was at the meeting with the rest of us. He knows the stakes.*

Playing in the water. The constant jokes... He's immature.

He's older than me. When Myles frowned, I added, *Mercy said they're sixteen.*

Age doesn't always define capability.

Powers and auras do. Isn't that exactly why King Duncan picked us despite all of us being young?

He looked back at me. *He did, but he was also blocking my mind from some things.*

My eyes widened. *Even after the meeting in his office?*

Yes. All morning and even at the gates.

I looked in the direction I assumed Mageye City to now be in. *He wouldn't have kept something from you if it put our lives in danger.*

He sighed aloud but nodded. *You're right,* he admitted.

Mercy stretched her legs out, her eyes locked on the stars. "Beautiful," she breathed.

When she looked back down, I tilted my head. "Your eyes look different," I observed, leaning forward to study her face. The same constellations from above us now shown in her irises.

She smiled. "They show the whole galaxy from afar during the day, and at night they zoom in to show what is above me."

Sophie smiled shyly. "They are very pretty."

"Thank you."

As we settled down to sleep, I nervously scanned the bushes. King Duncan had said that Myles and I would most likely continue to be sent controlled visions, but since we were travelling, they wouldn't get worse. I just hoped that he was right.

Chapter 8

I knelt at the rim of the volcano and peered at the bubbling lava far below. A lone figure stood in the center of the sea of orange and began to rise alongside it. King Brenton's one-eyed gaze met mine, and his lips curled into a cruel smile as lava arced from around him, aimed directly at me.

I woke with a gasp, now surrounded by green leaves and a sky hardly touched by the rising sun. Myles was up beside me, and from the looks of it, had been for a bit.

"Another vision?" he asked.

I nodded and shut my eyes. *Just a vision... Not real...* "Yeah. Another vision," I agreed.

Myles looked back at the fading stars. "Were you at the top of the volcano?"

"Yeah."

He sighed. "Me too. I think we're still sharing the same vision, but at different times. I've been up for about an hour."

An hour difference, and two nights in a row... "General Agar told me you had been up for a couple hours when I got to the palace. We didn't have it at the same time last night, either."

"True..." Myles sighed.

"Do you think the timing is a bad thing?" I asked.

"I don't know. It is only the second time we've shared them." He quietly began packing our bags, adding, "Maybe we had them at different times because he isn't strong enough to do them simultaneously."

"I hope so."

He offered a tight-lipped smile. "I can feel the portal this morning. I think it might be stronger than we realized last night."

I passed him a bandage that had rolled from one of the satchels, and he stuffed it inside his bag.

When Mercy awoke, she smiled at us. "Morning."

"Good morning," I replied.

She shut her eyes as she sat up, and when she re-opened them, they had changed to resemble a distant galaxy. The official start to the new day.

Myles shook Sophie and Will awake. "It's time to get up. The portal wants us to follow the pull."

Will rolled onto his stomach and hid his face with a groan. "The sun isn't even fully up yet."

"We want to get to the portal early, remember?" Myles said shortly, frowning at Will as he reluctantly lifted his head.

Sophie had fallen back asleep, and Myles knelt by her. "Soph, it's time to get up. You won't feel as tired once you're on your feet."

She yawned and sat up, her shoulders slumped with exhaustion, but she didn't complain. "I'm up."

Mercy had wandered out of the bushes to watch the rest of the sunrise, and I sorted through my bag for something to eat. Sophie's head hung towards her chest and her long hair hid her face.

"Myles," I said, guilt washing over me. "Maybe we should wait a little longer, at least give Will and Sophie time to get more awake."

Myles looked towards the portal and sighed. "How about we take a break after we leave the portal?"

I glanced at Will, who was dragging himself to his feet, and Sophie, who was still barely awake.

Will ran a hand down his face with another groan. "Fine. After the portal, I'm going to hold you to that."

Sophie grabbed an apple from her pack. "After the portal," she agreed.

"Deal," Myles said. "And now we're all up. We can grab Mercy and find the portal before anything else takes it."

Sophie lowered the apple from her mouth. "Wait, *right now, right now*? Myles, can't I finish my breakfast first?"

He looked to the portal. "Can you eat while we walk?"

"Ugh." Will dramatically crumbled to the ground. "Early risers!"

Mercy rejoined us now that the sun had fully risen, nudging Will with a foot. "The sun is awake, so why shouldn't we be?"

"Because," Will answered, draping an arm over his eyes.

Sophie stood, holding her apple in one hand and grabbing her satchel with the other. "I can eat while we walk," she answered Myles.

"Thank you," Myles said, relaxing his stance. "Will, get up. The portal has been nagging at me for over an hour."

Will held up the hand not covering his face. "Five minutes," he decided. "Let me mourn my dreams and Sophie eat her apple. If the portal wants us to take it, it's not going anywhere."

Lightning flickered in Myles's right iris. "We agreed to go early, and I said we're leaving, so let's leave."

Will moved his arm and glared at Myles. "Who says you get to call the shots?"

"My experience, age, and title," Myles retorted. "I said we can take a break after the portal, didn't I?"

I glanced at Mercy, who also looked uncomfortable. "Five minutes won't hurt, Myles," I said.

"That's not the point," he said. "Get up, Will."

"Nope," Will stated. "Early doesn't mean before sunrise."

"This isn't a camping trip," Myles snapped.

"I never said it was," Will snapped back, sitting up. "Last I checked, this is a mission to overthrow a group of Mageye who have been threatening Mageye City for decades. And your dad wants my powers to douse their fire, and I agreed. We *all* agreed. Don't single me out because I don't have your etiquette."

Sophie's outline began to fade. "Please don't fight."

Myles shut his eyes and took a steadying breath. "If Will gets up, no one needs to fight, Soph."

"You started it," Will said as he finally stood.

"You kind of started it, Will," Mercy said, stepping closer to him.

He glowered, but caught himself before snapping anything else. "You're right that you're more experienced, Myles, and I know we agreed to leave early, but you practically dragged me and Sophie out of camp in your rush. That's not fair."

Myles paused and studied Will closely, before nodding. "All right. Take your five minutes, and I'll be better at my communication when it comes to making decisions."

Waves crashed in Will's irises, but his stance relaxed. "Thank you."

✕

When everyone was fully awake, we gathered to teleport for the first time. The tension seemed to have faded, and Will now stepped up next to Myles. "How do we teleport?"

Myles's lip twitched and he held a hand out to Will. "A purple orb of lightning is going to form around us, and when I snap it, we will reappear somewhere else."

Mercy smiled. "Will we feel it?"

"Nope," Myles said, offering his other hand to me. "Since we are standing, it will feel like nothing at all. If we were running, there would be more exhilaration."

"I think it's fun however we do it," Sophie said, taking my

other hand.

"I agree," I said, waiting as Will linked hands with Myles and Mercy, and she grabbed Sophie's free hand.

A purple orb formed around us and Will and Mercy exchanged looks as it snapped. The orb faded away altogether and we now stood in an entirely new spot of forest.

"That was crafty," Will declared, crouching and touching the grass. "We should do a running one sometime, too!"

"I think that can be arranged," I said with a giggle. "Though right now, we need to find the portal."

Mercy stepped around us, taking Will's hand and tugging him after her. "Follow the stars and the portal's pull," she declared. "It isn't too far."

"We'll let them lead," Myles said with a soft sigh.

No more arguments flared up between us, and when we found the portal hovering above a cluster of wildflowers, we gathered around it.

Myles turned to Mercy. "Where should we go? You know how to get the most mileage out of it, right?"

She studied the sun before kneeling and cupping the portal gently with both hands. "Follow what the sun says."

The portal blinked in response, and grew until it reached about Will's height.

"I forgot how beautiful portals are," Sophie awed once inside. The quartz in her irises sparkled as she admired the crystalline walls and swirling rainbows of images surrounding us.

Will reached a hand through the wall over an image of a lake. "There is magic in that lake."

I peered over his shoulder. "How can you tell?"

He shrugged. "It's like explaining how to raise an eyebrow. You can just do it."

Mercy frowned. "How *do* you raise an eyebrow?"

Will raised his left eyebrow with a mischievous grin. "Like

this." She rolled her eyes, and Will waved her away. "You're jealous."

"Sure," she drawled, trailing a hand through an image of a sunshiny field.

Myles watched them and unlike yesterday, he looked amused by their antics.

"The end is up ahead," Sophie called.

"Let's take a short break when we get out so I can figure out the best route from here," Mercy suggested.

"Well, Myles promised us a break anyway," Will said. "I'm not tired anymore, but I'm taking the break."

"I told you that you won't be as tired once you're on your feet," Myles said.

"To be fair, Myles, you are wide awake the second you open your eyes. Most of us aren't like that," I pointed out.

"True," he mused. "But it sure is frustrating waiting on everyone every morning of your life."

I giggled. "I've waited on you more than a few times."

His expression lightened a little and he jokingly waved me off. "Hush!"

Will and Mercy stepped out of the portal, and Sophie followed. A peaceful feeling washed over me as Myles and I followed, and I glanced around. We now stood in a small clearing at the foot of a tall tree.

"Mercy, can the sun guide you to another portal?" Myles asked.

"Sometimes. It depends on whether the portal wants us to find it naturally or not."

"So... are there any portals nearby that are okay with us using your power as a cheat sheet?" Will asked.

Mercy tilted her head as if listening to the sun. "Not at the moment, but—"

A loud scream cut her off, and we all jumped, turning too late to witness Sophie disappear.

Chapter 9

In Sophie's place were two armed men. They stepped out of the bushes, rifles pointed at us, and Mercy gasped, stepping closer to me. Will raised his hands in the air and Myles stepped forward, his posture tense but his tone calm. "There's no need for the weapons. We aren't going to hurt you."

Huh? Why would these men think we were going to hurt *them?* I clutched Ren's jackknife in my pocket and took a small step back, my gaze darting around for Sophie. She had gone silent after her initial scream.

"What black magic are you using?" one of the hunters demanded.

Will stiffened as the second man adjusted his grip on his rifle, and he shoved Mercy closer to me, adjusting his stance to shield us. "We're not using black magic," he said.

Myles raised his hands in the air as he took another step closer. "Listen, you both need to leave now."

"Witches!" the first man said, pointing his gun at Myles's chest.

"No!" I shouted as he prepped to pull the trigger, but Myles had already reacted. Purple lightning crackled and both men dropped to the ground, unconscious.

Will stared at the men. "Were they actually going to kill us?"

"Yes," Myles rasped, looking away from the unconscious men.

"Is everyone okay?"

Mercy shook her head. "Where's Sophie?" She ran to where the scream had come from. "Sophie?"

I ran after her, pushing through the bushes the hunters had come from. Surely, we would have heard a shot or more screaming if they had harmed her, but where had she vanished to?

"Soph is right here," Myles said. "She isn't hurt."

"What?" I turned back, but Sophie was nowhere to be seen.

Myles hadn't moved, but his posture was more relaxed than it had been. "She is invisible," he explained. "You can calm down, we are all safe."

Will ran a hand through his hair. "Are you sure? What if she is invisible and hurt, or...?"

"She's okay," Myles insisted, turning and talking to seemingly no one. "Soph, you can come out. It's safe now."

Sophie's outline slowly crept out from behind the tree, and I sighed in relief. As she stepped closer to Myles, she became more and more visible until she was solid again.

"Are they dead?" she whispered, staring at the men.

Myles caught her arm and tugged her close. "Unconscious," he soothed. "They'll be fine, like us."

She flickered as she hugged him. "I thought they were..."

"I know," Myles whispered. "It reminded me of them too, but... but it wasn't."

"Wasn't who?" Mercy asked, eyeing the men. "We should probably leave before they wake up, especially if you both... recognize them?"

"They're not connected," Myles said, staring at the men in disgust. "Let's teleport."

"Good idea," Will said. "Maybe not directly east, just in case."

Myles nodded and a purple orb formed around us before snapping. When we reappeared, Sophie still clutched Myles and she flickered again. "How far did you take us?"

"Ten miles," Mercy answered for him. "Even if they are waking up right now, we will have disappeared without a trace."

Sophie nodded and her quartzlike gaze flooded with tears. "Can we take a break?"

"I think that's a good idea," I agreed. "Is anyone... hurt?"

Myles sat with Sophie, and Will flopped down across from them with Mercy. I completed our circle and sighed in relief when no one voiced being injured.

Mercy leaned towards Sophie and Myles. "You both have seen hunters like that before?"

Myles grimaced and Sophie stared at her lap, nodding. "I'm not from Mageye City. I'm from a town in Alveraada called Silverton, and... when I was eight..."

She trailed off and I hugged my knees to my chest. While I knew the gist of the story from Myles, Sophie had never voiced her version of it.

Myles took her hand. "It's your story to tell, Soph. No pressure either way."

Mercy leaned back and nodded. "You don't need to tell us."

"No, it's okay." Sophie wiped her eyes with her free hand and took a shaky breath. "My host family found out about my powers."

Will sucked in his breath, waves crashing in his irises. "They weren't Mageye themselves?"

She shook her head. "They were so nice to me, but not after they discovered my power. They said I was witch and... and my host dad kicked me out of the house with nothing. I tried finding help, but then I met this man who tried to kidnap me, and I ran away. He was shouting all of these horrible things and hunters came after me." She looked between us, eyes flashing. "That's how I met Myles. He saved me."

Myles grimaced. "I got lost before I met you and I'm glad I did, or we never would have met."

Sophie flickered but smiled a little. "I'm happy you got lost, too."

"Me too," Mercy whispered. "I'm sorry that happened."

Will stretched his legs out, asking cautiously, "Can I ask how you both got away? Teleporting?"

Sophie stared straight ahead. "When those men came at us with their rifles, it reminded me of them. But... the three men who chased me out of Silverton are gone."

"Gone, or...?" Will fidgeted.

"Dead," Myles said simply. "They're all... dead."

Will's eyes widened. "Sounds like that is for the better."

Purple lightning flickered in Myles's irises. "I know."

I pulled out Ren's jackknife to roll in my palm. "You're brave for telling us, Sophie."

"Thanks," she whispered. "Should we... keep going now? I want to get farther away from them."

Myles pulled himself up. "I think that's a good idea." He stopped, looking over us before smiling. "That was our first time defending ourselves as a group. I think we did a pretty good job."

I dropped Ren's jackknife back into my pocket. "You're right," I agreed. "It was like we were a real team."

"We are a real team," Sophie whispered. "At least, I want to be."

Myles played with her hair, smiling softly. "You're stuck being in our team, Soph."

That got a giggle, and Mercy stood, her gaze turned towards the sun. "There is another portal willing to help us."

"Really?" I asked, standing and offering Will a hand up. "I love your power."

She laughed. "It is too far away to sense yet, but the sun knows it's there."

Will accepted my hand. "You can speak to the sun, but you can't raise an eyebrow?"

Mercy groaned. "Are we still talking about that?"

Sophie giggled again, and visible relief crossed Myles's expression as she relaxed. "If it makes you feel any better, Mercy, I can't raise an eyebrow either," she said.

Myles waved his hand ahead of himself. "Most people can only do one or the other. I can do both."

Will turned to him. "Really?"

"Yeah, like this." Myles raised his left eyebrow, then relaxed his expression and raised his right eyebrow next.

Will raised both his brows at the same time. "That *is* impressive."

Mercy shook her head and walked closer to me, whispering, "I can practically hear Will's thoughts as he considers ways to create competition with Myles."

I laughed. "I know I can read Myles's mind, but even if I couldn't, I would be able to hear those thoughts, too. I have three older brothers; I see this kind of thing all the time."

"*Three?*" Mercy questioned.

"Three what?" Sophie asked.

"Rose has three older brothers," Mercy said. "Does that make you the only girl?"

I nodded. "It also makes me the most mature."

Myles glanced over. "That is such a *blatant* lie."

I smiled innocently. "No, it isn't... not completely, anyway."

Sophie giggled. "I don't think it's a lie. One time, when I was over at your house, I walked into the kitchen to find Ryder on the floor, pretending to be poisoned. He said Ren put sugar in his eggs instead of salt."

Will laughed. "That's a good idea. Sugar instead of salt."

"I can never trust Will with making eggs again," Mercy said in dismay.

"You could also do salt instead of sugar on other things," I mused. "Maybe I should suggest Ryder does that to Ren when we get back?"

"Sweet revenge," Will said, then paused. "No, salty revenge."

"Do it," Myles said, smirking at me. "Ren's been trying to prank me for weeks. Said he is going to one-up a mind reader eventually."

I laughed. "Remind me when we get home."

"Deal."

Chapter 10

Every night that passed without a controlled vision was like a breath of fresh air, and yet it brought more anxiety as we made a camp each evening. The only shield our constant travel offered against the controlled visions was blocking King Brenton from seeing us, there were no other promises. And the vision Myles and I had shared the first night of our mission prevented any hope that maybe they were fully thwarted by our travel.

This morning marked the fourth day in a row without one, and it was only a matter of time for another to happen.

We had gone along with Myles's idea of practicing our training, and we had all successfully disarmed him at least once during it. With him being the most experienced, that had been declared a good marker that our training was already paying off.

Sophie pulled a small comb from her bag and I sat by her, offering to help. She smiled. "Thanks, Rose."

I combed her hair carefully. "Do you want me to braid it?"

"No, thanks." She twirled some strands between her fingers. "I don't want it getting crimped. It is kind of hard to coordinate baths out here."

Will leaned over. "I can help with that. Dry you off in seconds after."

I looked down at myself and nodded. "I'd appreciate that."

"Me too," Sophie agreed, smoothing her skirts. "I would still like it down today, but maybe tomorrow we can braid it."

Myles and Mercy were discussing the best path to take, and seemed to have agreed that continuing with our current straight-shot east was best.

"I will talk to the stars about any shortcuts," Mercy declared. "Will and I once got to a campsite a day's journey away in half that time."

Will laughed. "Dad and Uncle Jace were shocked when we already had the camp looking lived in."

"You traveled there alone?" I asked.

Waves crashed in his irises. "Can't get lost with Mercy around."

"I guess that's true," I said. "My mom only let my brothers and I camp overnight if all four of us went together."

Myles suddenly stood, turning south-east.

"Is something wrong?" Mercy asked.

He took a few steps forward, tilting his head as he examined the expanse of woods before himself. "A portal started calling me," he murmured. "Its aura is faint, so we must be outside that inner radius."

I put the comb away as I finished Sophie's hair. "If it's calling from so far away, that must mean it is a strong one."

"And if it is calling us, then it wants to help us. Can the stars tell you anything about it, Mercy?" Myles asked.

She turned her gaze to the sun and shook her head. "No, but that's okay. Not every portal reveals itself to the stars."

Will tugged his boots on, glancing at Myles. "What do you mean by it started calling you? Did you... move over in camp and trigger it?"

Myles shrugged. "I don't think so. I didn't feel it one second and then felt it the next. It's possible it was just born."

"Born?" Sophie echoed.

"Baby portal," Myles said with a smile. "That's what I used to call them.”

“Aww.” I stood and offered Sophie a hand up. “Let’s find the baby portal.”

X

“I see it,” Myles declared, waving at the small orb we had spent the past couple of hours looking for. “Baby portal.”

“It doesn’t look very babyish,” I observed.

Myles held a low-hanging branch out of our way and we stopped at the edge of a thicket of thorns. The portal hovered in the middle, glowing cheerfully. If anything, this portal appeared brighter than usual, which often suggested a stronger portal.

Will crossed his arms. “We’ll be torn to shreds by the time we get to it.”

“I can heal us all when we get inside,” I reminded him.

“True, but it still isn’t preferable. What about our clothes?”

“It’ll be fine,” Myles said. “A few pricks won’t hurt us, or our clothes.”

“Don’t complain about it, Will,” Mercy scolded. “It’s only a few hours old.”

Will waved his hand over the thorns. “And it was born in an annoying location. I wouldn’t be offended if people complained about me being born in a thorn patch.”

Sophie giggled, nudging a thorny bush with her boot. “I would feel bad for your mom if you were born in a thorn patch.”

“Do portals have moms?” Will asked, raising his brows. “How exactly did it birth itself?”

“A mommy magic portal and a daddy magic portal decided to have a baby and poof, a baby portal appeared,” Myles said, stepping into the patch.

We laughed, but the giggles quickly stopped when the portal flickered, then died. Myles paused. “What happened?” When no one answered, he added, “We would have seen if someone else used it."

"We didn't actually offend it, did we?" Will finally asked, seeming genuinely shocked. "It's magic. It doesn't have feelings."

Myles shook his head, brow furrowed. "That would be like a tree disappearing because you said you thought it was an odd shade of brown. This portal just... decided not to let us take it."

"Why?" Mercy asked, crossing the thorns and standing where the portal had been. "It was *calling* us. When a portal calls you, it is because it is waiting for you to take it."

I stepped into the thorn patch after her. "Maybe it will come back?"

"Maybe," Myles murmured, going suddenly rigid.

The hairs on my arm rose as the suffocating presence of danger laced its way through the air. I reached for Ren's jackknife, clutching it tight as I turned, scanning the trees behind us.

Sophie had started to fade, and I could see Mercy through her, who was also searching for an answer to the aura.

"Let's teleport," Myles whispered, taking my hand and bringing me back out of the thorn patch. "Mercy, come here."

She hardly took a step when a trumpet call echoed through the woods. Myles recoiled from me, pure terror lighting his eyes.

"Myles?" I asked, peering towards the sound. "What was that? It sounded like—"

The trees before us parted and snapped back into place as a huge elephant emerged. Its large ears flapped and it huffed as it dug at the ground with its front foot.

A strangled sound escaped me and I fumbled with the jackknife in my pocket, tugging it out only to stare at the elephant. What could a small blade possibly do against an...

I stopped, turning to Myles, who opened and closed his mouth, looking like he wanted badly to scream. Lightning sparked wildly off of him and his cheeks were tinted with a shade of green.

"What do we do?" Will hissed, talking out of the side of his mouth. "It looks angry... Myles, you need to shock it before it charges."

"Or stomps its foot," I croaked, fear constricting upon my heart as I recalled the story Myles had told me about his parents' death. A magical Ackley Elephant had killed his parents in front of him by stomping its foot and turning them to stone. No wonder he was so petrified. "We'll die if it stomps its foot."

"I-I..." Myles stammered. "Yeah... stop it..." He didn't make any action to stop it though, but stood frozen, as if he had already been turned to stone.

Mercy took my arm, her hands trembling violently as she stepped off the thorns. "Sudden movements?" she whispered. "It's just standing..."

Sophie tugged on Myles's sleeve. "Myles?" her voice quavered. "Please... no one else has your power."

Another trumpet call bellowed from the elephant and I bit nearly through my lip, flicking open my jackknife and holding it towards the elephant. It dug at the ground angrily, its beady eyes locked on Myles.

Will stepped forward. "I can try to distract it, but blasting it with water might only make it angrier."

"No, that's too risky. It might stomp its foot," Mercy said, holding her arm out to him. "If we run, it might get stopped by the trees."

"But it already got through those trees," Will whispered, motioning at the woods behind it.

"Myles," I pleaded.

Sweat dripped from his brow, and his lower lip trembled. His aura, too, was electrified with terror and I could only take a step closer to him before it became suffocating.

We have a window, Myles! I shouted in his mind. *If anyone else does anything, it will get angrier.*

His gaze slowly made its way to me and he stilled his trembling lip. "Get behind me," he rasped.

Relief flooded me in a rush and I staggered backwards, still keeping my jackknife pointed to the elephant. Will tugged me closer to himself, and Mercy pulled Sophie farther from the thorns.

Myles raised his hand towards the Ackley Elephant, screwing his eyes tightly shut when it let out another trumpet call.

But no sooner had the call ended than a purple bolt of lightning hit it square in the chest. It raised its trunk and its final bellow echoed through the trees before it disappeared, like the portal.

Myles collapsed, sharp gasps escaping him as he clutched his throat. My own throat felt constricted too and I stumbled to him wordlessly.

Lightning flickered in his purple iris and I looked to where the elephant had been before turning back to him. "Are... are you okay?"

He shook his head, slowly lowering his hand from his throat. "I have never experienced fear like that before. It... it was like my veins were pushing fear into my heart instead of blood."

My fingers trembled as I took his hand, but no injuries reflected onto my power, and Myles hardly reacted to my touch. Instead, he stared at the spot where the elephant had stood, the green tinge to his skin being replaced with a pale color. "Why are there no marks?" he whispered.

"Marks?" Mercy asked as she tiptoed closer. "What do you mean?"

"Where it was digging." His finger trembled as he pointed. "There should be scratches on the ground, but there's nothing."

Will took a few cautious steps forward, stopping when Mercy grabbed onto him. "I don't think that elephant was real," he whispered.

I nearly dropped Myles as I helped him to his feet. "What do you mean?"

He shook his head, staring at the untouched ground. "It vanished like a cloud of smoke, and even the trees bent without so much as a twig cracking."

"Felt real," Myles whispered, wiping his face with his sleeve.

"Very real," I agreed, easing Ren's jackknife into my pocket. "Too real... we need to leave."

"Myles!" Sophie screamed, running towards us with her arms outstretched and pure terror written across her face.

Three armed men stepped out of the trees behind her and I yelped, plunging my hand back into my pocket for my jackknife.

Myles spun on his heel, the fear evaporating from his expression and instead being replaced with... recognition? He grabbed Sophie, practically sweeping her off her feet in his rush to hide her behind himself.

"Witch!" one of the men shouted, pointing his rifle at Sophie.

"No!" Sophie squeaked, cowering behind Myles.

His lips had drawn into a firm line and I inched closer to him, doing my best to stand tall and block Sophie from sight.

A wave of water suddenly appeared from the woods. Will stood to the side of the clearing and made a throwing motion, causing the wave to rush at the men, but it went right through them.

When the wave splashed the trees behind them, all three men still stood, perfectly dry.

Will's jaw dropped. "How?"

The leader stepped forward, sneering at Sophie. "Hand over the girl," he ordered.

Lightning arced between Myles's fingers, and he stepped forward, his left hand reaching behind himself for Sophie. "She isn't an object to be passed between us," Myles hissed. "Leave. Or I will end your lives *again*."

Mercy paled, half-lowering her dagger in her surprise. "Again?"

Stars flickered in her irises, and she raised her voice. "You've been chasing a child for *five* years? Leave us alone."

The men didn't even glance her way and my heart sank. "They should be dead," I whispered.

A bolt of purple lightning hit the heart of the lead man, but it simply flew through him and blackened the bark of a tree.

I jumped backwards, my flinch not eliciting even the slightest reaction from any of the men. "The witch dies," one of the men called and the others voiced their agreement.

Half a dozen more bolts followed the first, and another gush of water swept over the men, but not even a hair on their heads fluttered.

I glanced behind myself, where the elephant had been. No marks. Vanishing... dead men. My chest heaved and I looked back at the men. "You're not real," I whispered. But the realization only seemed to spark more fear—what else could these men possibly be?

"Why can't you stop them, Myles?" Sophie sobbed. "Will?" She flickered wildly, cheeks flushed red with her tears. "Please!"

Mercy's head whipped between Sophie and the three men, before horrified understanding settled over her expression. "Because *they* can't." She stepped closer. "Sophie, it has to be you."

The men again demanded Sophie, and Will scowled, starting to uncork a waterskin, but I caught his hand, addressing Sophie. "Mercy's right," I said. "You need to stop them, Sophie. Just like how Myles made the elephant disappear, you need to make these men disappear."

She shook her head, hiding her face in Myles's back. "I can't."

"You can." Myles stepped back and put a hand on her, keeping his gaze locked on the men. "You have to. The fear will go away as soon as you get rid of them." He pulled the dagger he wore at his waist out with trembling fingers. "Throw it."

"No..." Sophie soft plea seemed to die in her throat and she took the dagger instead. Her hand shook, but she faced the men anyway, hurling the dagger. "Leave me alone!" The dagger sailed through the lead man's head, and like the elephant, they disappeared.

Sophie threw herself into Myles's arms, burying her face into his chest. "I don't want that to ever happen again."

Myles hugged her close, a tear sliding down his cheek as he stared at the spot the men had been standing moments prior. "You faced your fear, Soph. Now we... we need to get out of here." He turned to me, Will, and Mercy. "I don't know if this is some kind of magical trap, or something else, but we need to leave."

"Gladly," Will said, glaring at the spot the men had stood. "You can teleport here, right? It's not going to get tainted?"

"I don't sense the bad aura anymore," I whispered, cautiously picking up a small stone and tossing it where the men had stood. It rolled into the trees, leaving faint marks in the dust that the men had not.

Myles grimaced, exchanging a look with me. "It doesn't matter," he answered Will. "I would rather be tainted than have us stay... here."

"Rose!" Raymond stumbled out of the woods, clutching his side. He appeared to be covered in burns, and blood poured from between his fingers.

"Raymond?" No sooner had his name flown from my mouth, than I froze as the worst fear I had ever felt in my life filled me. A paralyzing fear. An uncontrollable fear that took over my entire being, aura and all.

"Raymond!" I screeched again as he collapsed to his knees. Coughing, he spat out blood. Our eyes met, and a tear slipped down his cheek as he slumped to the ground, unmoving.

"No!" I broke into a run towards him, but a warm hand grabbed my forearm, causing me to skid to a halt.

It was Ren. "Help me." He sobbed.

I grabbed him, but he seemed to slip from my fingers,

collapsing to the ground.

"Rose," Myles shouted. "It's a vision. They... they aren't really here. It's not real."

But I couldn't focus on him because Mom and Ryder had appeared from the woods, succumbing to their wounds before I could scream.

They had been meant to stay safe in Mageye City, but now here they were. Dead.

Chapter 11

The paralyzing terror released its hold, only to be replaced with the worst physical pain I had ever experienced. *Grief.*

"*Mom.*" My voice didn't seem to be my own, and tears blurred my vision. "No..."

"Rose!" Myles threw himself down beside me. "They're not dead. They're not dead, Rose. None of this is real." He took my shoulders. "Look at me. I need you to look at me."

"This was to keep them safe," I whispered, doubling over as I hugged my gut. "They were supposed to be *safe!*"

"They are," he insisted. "They are safe. You are seeing your worst fear like me and Soph. You need to stop it."

I shook my head, my chest heaving with each breath I took. "But... but..."

Look at me.

I met Myles's gaze, clutching his arm as if my life depended on it.

They're not dead. It is an illusion; tell the world it isn't real. My fingers dug into his skin, but he hardly flinched, repeating, *It isn't real.*

I shook my head again, trembling until a soft touch on my shoulder told me Sophie was here, invisible. I blinked, my panicked breaths steadying as Will and Mercy knelt on either side of me, blocking the blood and bodies from sight.

"It's not real," I whispered, screwing my eyes tightly shut and raising my voice. "I don't need to be scared of losing you because you are safe in Mageye City. The Volcaniacs can't touch you again. You're *safe*."

As I spoke the final word, the fear and grief and pain evaporated from my veins, leaving me gasping for air. When I opened my eyes, my family and all of the blood was gone.

Myles gripped at his heart as if it were causing him pain. "It's over," he whispered. "You faced it."

Fresh tears flooded my eyes and I collapsed into him. He trembled and his voice filled my head. *That is one of my worst fears, too.* He slowly pulled back. *The words you spoke to make them go away were the truth.*

I wiped my eyes, staring at the spots where my family had lain. "Mercy and Will haven't faced an illusion yet." I sniffed. "We should leave before they do."

Sophie reappeared, taking my hand and squeezing tightly. Mercy and Will also appeared shaken, but agreed instantly that it was time to leave.

Myles created a wavy purple orb, but when it snapped, we were left crouching in the same spot. He attempted another orb, snapping it with the same result. Lightning flickered in his irises and he jumped to his feet, whirling around with his arms thrown to the sides. "What trap is this?"

When there was no answer nor stir of auras, he swallowed hard. "We need to leave on foot. There is something over this thorn patch that is stopping me from teleporting, even though the auras are gone."

"What do you mean?" Mercy asked, clutching the dagger at her waist.

Myles shook his head. Lightning sparked between his trembling fingers. "I don't know."

Will stood, stepping back to examine the spot where the portal had originally been, but he was abruptly thrown forward, crashing into Myles and knocking them both to the ground. Walls shot up from the ground, cutting off our view of the sky and cloaking us in darkness.

"Ugh." Myles groaned, and Sophie clutched me tightly.

"The stars!" Mercy's voice pitched and she choked on her words in her panic. "N-no... no! The stars!"

Will scrambled over me in his rush to grab her. "Mercy, it's only a fear," he insisted. "They're not gone."

Before she could reply, the ground shifted and threw me into the air and out of the box. I crashed to the ground in the middle of the thorns, pricking my arms and face.

"What happened?" Will wheezed from across the shrubs. He staggered to his feet, dazed from the crash. "Where's Mercy?"

Myles and Sophie pulled themselves from the thorns, but Mercy wasn't anywhere to be seen. Instead, there was what looked like a black box, and as it shrank, Mercy sobbed from inside.

Will hurried to it, shouting her name. He ran straight into its side and fell backwards with a grunt as the breath was knocked from him. "Mercy," he croaked, pressing his hands to the box. "It's not real! I know it feels solid, but it's not real."

Her voice was a hysterical screech as she responded incoherently, and Will pulled himself to his feet, leaning against the box. "I know it's small, but the sun is shining right outside. The stars aren't going anywhere, Mercy, but you need to face your fear to see them again."

"I need the stars to know where to go." Mercy sobbed.

"No, you don't," Will insisted. "The stars don't make your decisions, and small spaces have nothing on you. You need to believe that."

Mercy made no reply, but as Myles, Sophie, and I gathered around the box, also pleading with her to face the fear, her sobs began to slow.

"I am going to stand up," she announced. "And face the sun… because I know that no matter what blocks me from them, the stars are *above* me."

The box flickered and Will stumbled forward, crashing into Mercy and sending them both toppling to the ground.

She grabbed onto him. "That was horrible!"

He rolled onto his back and hugged her close. "I know, but you did it. You were brave."

Myles stepped closer, his posture tense. "Will, what's your fear? That one was different. It was real, or partially real, at least… What will we face next?"

Will sat up slowly, shaking his head. "I think it's over. I'm not scared of anything to that degree."

I frowned. "It amplifies fears."

Myles grimaced. "Everyone is scared of something, and with the amount of fear these illusions are creating, even if it is something small, it could become much worse."

"No, I'm serious. I'm not scared of anything. The dark, natural disasters, being attacked, animals, I'm practically fear-free."

He helped Mercy to her feet, and she sniffed while wiping her eyes. "This isn't the time to be embarrassed, Will. If… if my fear can become real, yours can, too."

"I'm over it. Dad and I slept over in the loft for a week last summer, remember?"

My gaze flit around us nervously. "Could there be another fear?" I asked. "Besides… the loft?"

"Maybe something with dried water?" Sophie suggested.

He shook his head. "I swear—" An invisible force cut him off, sending us all flying again, with Will being pushed away from us.

As we scrambled back to our feet, Myles glared at Will. "If you don't have a fear, then what was that?"

"Not my fear," he insisted. "I don't know what that was."

Sophie took a few steps toward Will when the ground

disappeared from under her feet. She screamed and flailed her arms, catching a thin ledge with one hand and gripping it with all her strength.

"Soph!" Myles shouted. He ran forward, ready to jump over the canyon that had appeared and teleport her to safety, but I grabbed his arm and yanked him back.

"If you can't teleport, you'll fall," I gasped, my voice trembling as I stared at Sophie.

"I have to help her!" he insisted.

I tightened my grip, tears filling my eyes.

Will stood at the edge of the canyon, staring at Sophie with fear-filled, blue eyes.

"You're scared of heights, Will," Myles accused, tugging his arm from me.

"Help!" Sophie shouted desperately, scrambling for a better hold.

Myles's voice shook. "Will, you have to help her. You have to face your fear to save her and it will be over."

Will's face had turned a shade of green and he shook his head. "Sophie..."

"You have to, Will." Mercy waved her arms. "Face your fear!"

He trembled, slowly lowering to his knees and holding a hand out. "T-take my hand."

Sophie struggled to reach for him, but swiftly grabbed the ledge again. "I can't reach." She sobbed. "You need to reach down."

Will shut his eyes tight as he lay on his stomach and braced himself, reaching for Sophie. She caught his hand and he strained to lift her until the illusion disappeared. Both of them now lay on their stomachs, outstretched hands gripping each other tightly.

Will released Sophie and gripped the grass with both hands, wheezing as we ran to them.

"Are you okay?" I demanded. "Are either of you hurt?"

Both shook their heads, and Myles turned on Will angrily, but before he could speak, Sophie sat on her knees. "Will," she began. "The next time we have to face our fears, do you think that you could tell us that you're scared of heights *before the ground actually gives out from under us?*" Her voice raised to a yell at the last part.

Will winced, pushing himself to his knees. "I'm sorry, Sophie. I really thought I was over it. And I didn't... I didn't think that could become an illusion. Not like that, at least."

"Oh, don't worry," a man drawled. "I can create an illusion out of anything... but fears are what I do best."

A Mageye leaned casually against the trees the elephant had stood by, smirking. His eyes resembled prisms—somehow carrying all but no color.

"The rumors were right; King Duncan matched your powers fairly well... it's simply too bad he didn't consider what fears accompanied them." He straightened from the tree and bowed. "Nice meeting you. I will be sure to tell King Brenton we need to prepare for guests." With that, he vanished.

Chapter 12

The crackling of lightning filled the air as Myles shot a bolt at the spot where the Mageye had stood.

Instead of shocking him, the lightning blackened the bark of the tree he had leaned against. More purple bolts followed, but they did nothing but hit more trees, and Myles soon stepped back, panting.

I clutched Ren's jackknife. "I don't sense his aura."

"Masking," Myles said urgently, turning to us. "We need to leave. King Duncan expects us to finish off every Volcaniac, but whatever he just did…" His voice dropped and Mercy stepped closer.

"We're not prepared," she whispered.

"But that's not his business," Will added, pointing an accusing finger at the blackened tree. "We'll be back," he promised as a purple orb formed around us.

Myles seemed to be gripping the air in his left hand and Sophie's faint outline reappeared as the orb snapped. This time, it flashed so brightly, I shut my eyes, and suddenly found myself tumbling down the side of a grassy hill. The others crashed after me and I came to a stop in a divot on the side of the hill, the world spinning.

"Ouch." Will grunted as he landed beside me, groaning as he squinted at the clear sky above us.

I coughed, blinking as the world regained focus. The aches from falling were fading quickly and I dragged myself to my feet, looking around in concern. Will and I had been lucky to land on grass, as much of the hill was rocky.

Mercy sat up nearby, rubbing her ankle and grimacing. "I think I sprained it."

"I'll help," I promised, looking around. Sophie tugged her dress out from a scraggly bush it had gotten snagged in, and Myles lay on his back farther down the hill.

"Myles!" I called, hurrying to him. Like the rest of us, he was covered in dust, but he had stopped rolling when he hit a boulder, and hugged his chest tenderly.

His gaze was unfocused when I touched his face and a pounding headache made me grimace, whimpering as the pain from his ribs bloomed within me.

"Is he okay?" Sophie whispered, flickering wildly as she knelt beside me.

"Yeah, Soph," Myles croaked, attempting to sit up.

I pushed him down. "You're not healed yet."

Will helped Mercy limp to us and he sat down heavily, grimacing. "At least we're away from that Mageye."

Myles put an arm over his face, shielding his eyes. "That took a lot out of me."

The aching from his wounds faded as I released him, and I turned to Mercy, pausing when I saw her expression. Stars shot across her irises and she looked at Myles, then back at the sun. "Myles..." she whispered. "Isn't your max about fifty miles?"

"Yeah," Myles huffed. "Feels like that's what I did now."

"No." Mercy shook her head. "Myles, you took us hundreds of miles."

"What?" Will asked, looking around. "That's not possible. Wouldn't that kill him?"

Sophie grabbed Myles's hand, peering at him worriedly. He

pulled his arm from his face to look at us. "Hundreds?" he questioned.

"Hundreds," Mercy confirmed. She stood slowly, swaying a little. I grabbed her ankle, healing it as she stared at the sun. "Myles, you took us... far. Really far."

Lightning briefly flickered in his purple iris before fading, the physical effects of cool-down fast becoming clear. The last time Myles had pushed himself past his limit, his heart had stopped. I scrambled through my pockets, looking for the Golden Dove feathers, but he caught my wrist, his grip loose. "I'm okay," he croaked. "I... I don't know how I took us so far, but consider it... a blessing."

"Blessing is right," Will murmured. He put the back of his hand to Myles's head, and Myles wrinkled his nose.

"What are you doing?"

"Trying to see how half-dead you are," Will quipped. He grabbed a waterskin and held it to Myles's lips. "Now drink."

Myles took a few sips before resting his head on the ground. "Mercy, do you know where we are?"

"Not yet," she said, stars still darting across her irises as she sat. "Myles, are you sure you're all right?"

Despite his clammy skin and shaking hands, he nodded. "Don't worry about me yet. We need to worry about that Mageye."

I looked back up the hill where we had reappeared. "Well... if you took us hundreds of miles, then... then he won't be able to track our auras, right?"

"Largest radius I've ever heard of is seven miles," Myles said. "But that Mageye lured us in from much farther than that."

"What do you mean?" Will asked.

"The portal," Myles rasped. "We were following its aura all morning, and when we arrived, it disappeared, like... the elephant... and," his voice cracked, but there was no need to finish his sentence.

"Illusions," I whispered, reaching for Will to heal any bruises he might have. "How did he do that?"

Sophie loosened her grip on Myles's hand. "I want to know how he found us. You need to know who you are hunting to set a trap, and he... he seemed to know us."

"I don't know," Myles croaked. "He admitted he created the... illusions, so that must be his power. And the bad aura, all that fear, it must have been him."

I grimaced. "And when it would stop between illusions, he must have been masking."

Myles only nodded and I frowned. Masking was draining to your aura, and the ability to do it so well was a sign of a powerful Mageye.

Sophie held a hand out to me. "Can you heal me?"

I took her hand and aches slowly crept up my arms and legs. "None of us got very injured," I said with relief as Sophie's pain swiftly faded. "Except for Myles, and he is all right, just in cooldown."

Myles grunted, shielding his eyes again. "I'll survive."

Will rubbed the nape of his neck. "It wasn't only illusions and masking, but also creating other auras and fear. Does him being around mean we can't trust portals anymore?"

"Portals?" I echoed. "Why can't we trust them?"

"Because he lured us in with one." Waves crashed in his irises. "How will we know which is real and which is a trap?"

"The stars." Mercy pointed at the sun. "They never told me about that portal, remember?"

Sophie flickered. "The stars wouldn't lead you into a trap, right, Mercy? If they say it is a portal, then we know it is a portal?"

"Yes." Mercy shut her eyes, and when she opened them, the shooting stars had stopped. "You can't trick the stars."

"Then we rely on the stars from now on," Myles mumbled. He pulled his hand back. "Can I have more water?"

Will passed it to him and I looked around. The grasses swayed lightly in the breeze, and the boulders created hiding spots. "If we need to fully rely on the stars, then we can't trust our own auras anymore."

Myles lowered the waterskin. "I know. And... he said he will be telling King Brenton about us. That means the Volcaniacs will know we are coming."

Sophie grew suddenly translucent. "Myles, if he can create fake auras, mask, and make us see illusions, what if he didn't really disappear? What if he only made it seem like he did and let us go?"

Myles's already pale skin grew even paler. "You're right... but why would he *let* us go?"

"I think that stems back to how he found us in the first place," I whispered. "He mentioned rumors and he knew King Duncan matched our powers."

Mercy looked between me and Myles. "Have the controlled visions gotten worse?"

"No, we haven't had one in a few days," I said.

"Is it possible that King Brenton was able to see more of your surroundings than we originally thought?" Mercy asked.

"I don't think so," Myles said. "King Duncan said that as long as we never spend more than one night in the same place, he won't be able to locate us."

"Then how did he find us?" Will's expression darkened. "How did he know we are looking for the Volcaniacs in the first place?"

None of us had an answer for that.

After a few beats of silence, Myles struggled to sit up. "I want to get away from here. If my jump was really as big as we think, he shouldn't have a way to know where we went. But I don't want to risk that."

I put my hand on his shoulder to stop him. "I think we should let you rest, at least for a little bit."

He grimaced, resting his head in his palm. "Fifteen minutes."

"Do you have a headache?" I asked, concerned.

"Cool-down," he mumbled. "That's it."

Will stood. "I am going to find the bags we dropped. Looks like a few of us lost stuff."

"I'll help," Mercy said.

Sophie and I waited with Myles, and when they returned, he lifted his head. "If you're going to force me to rest, we might as well talk about this mission. It has gotten much more dangerous, and I think we need to consider a new plan."

"New plan?" Sophie asked.

"Rose and I can't go home, not only because of our acceptance of the mission, but because our presence puts the city in danger as long as we continue getting the controlled visions. That same rule doesn't apply to the rest of you."

Will frowned. "We all accepted the mission and I, for one, am not backing out because of one scary day."

"There is a lot more than a scary day ahead of us," Myles answered. "And if we are now risking the Volcaniacs trying to make our fears a reality..."

"He made us face our worst fears," Mercy said. "And we did it. We faced them once, we can face them again."

"I think our experience today is more of a reason for us to stay together," I said.

Myles tapped his fingers to his thigh. "We still need to consider a new plan. Right now, we are heading straight there with the intention of an ambush, but now that they know, that is risky."

"Anything we do is risky," Will said. "I don't think we should change a thing. Don't you think King Brenton and that illusion Mageye will *expect* us to change our plan? Our Plan B can be Plan A with added danger."

"Added danger?" Mercy asked skeptically.

Will shrugged. "Yeah. They know about us now, so it is more dangerous, but we are still going to stick with the original plan."

Myles furrowed his brow. "Your backup plan is no backup plan?"

Will bobbed his head, giving his wavy hair the effect of looking like liquid. "Pretty much."

I pulled out Ren's jackknife, running my thumb over the engraved *R* on the handle. To change our plan and no longer make a direct shot, or to try another risky maneuver to throw them off when the Volcaniacs know we are coming regardless... Will's idea was risky, but no riskier than those ideas. In fact, it might be less risky, because it was unexpected—like magic.

You're on board? Myles asked.

I think so.

He nodded slowly. "Rose and I are on board. What do you think, Mercy? And you, Soph?"

Mercy sighed. "I don't like it, but I don't think there is a better plan. And maybe Will's right. They won't expect us to stick with a direct attack."

Sophie fidgeted, but when she stilled, her quartz eyes seemed to harden into chiseled stone. "Let's make Plan B, Plan A."

Will grinned. "It's official. We stick with our original plan."

Myles nodded. "Yes, but I do want to make one change. I think we need to start having someone sitting guard at night. We have a lot of questions about that Mageye: how he knew about us, how he located us, how he attracted us... We need to be ready for an ambush at any time."

Will raised his brows. "Fair. I can take first watch."

Myles blinked, clearly taken aback. "All right... Plan B is Plan A with the exception of a guard at night." He nodded in satisfaction. "I think King Duncan was right that a team is a better idea for this."

I nudged him. "Told you."

He groaned. "I said, I *think*. Now... should we leave? We should find somewhere safe to make a camp for the rest of the day."

Sophie stood, dusting off her dress. "We are out in the open," she mused. "I don't like it."

Will offered Myles a hand up. Once on his feet, Myles swayed and put a hand to his head. Will caught him and draped Myles's arm around his shoulder. "We can wait longer. Our waterskins didn't burst, so that leaves me with weapons to guard us."

"I'm fine," Myles huffed. "Let's get this over with."

I went to his other side and pushed my aura into him. But I was greeted with nothing but fatigue, and with no wounds, I couldn't do much to take away any aches.

Mercy motioned down the hill. "This way will put us back on course. Might as well gain a little ground while we can."

Sophie and I gathered our things from the pile Will and Mercy had made, before we began our slow process down the hill. By the time we reached the bottom, Myles's head hung towards his chest and he panted. "Will, you are definitely taking first watch."

Will adjusted his grip on Myles as we began our way up the next hill. "My dad says cool-down is like a hangover. You need to sleep it off."

Mercy laughed, glancing over her shoulder. "My dad says your dad stole that analogy from him."

Will waved his free hand dismissively. "Its origins don't matter, only that it's true."

"I don't think I want to ever be hungover," Sophie said. "But from what I've heard... cool-down is kind of like it."

When we reached the top of the hill, Mercy stopped. This hill led to a grassy plain covered in wildflowers. Across the plain, about a mile away, was a village, tall mountains towering on the horizon behind it.

"Are we going into town, Mercy?" Will asked.

"I don't know," Mercy murmured. "I need a minute."

Will nodded and helped lower Myles to the ground to rest

while she discussed with the stars.

I went to sit beside them, but paused. Sophie stood frozen, staring at the distant rooftops, and she flickered wildly.

"Sophie, are you okay?" I asked.

She made a sound similar to a squeak and stepped back, shaking her head. "We need to get out of here. It isn't safe for Mageye."

I stiffened, growing suddenly hyperaware of every aura around us. None seemed to reek of danger, yet I could see waving grasses through Sophie's translucent appearance. "What do you mean?" I asked.

Her quartz eyes shone with fear and grief. "That village is Silverton. The village I was chased out of."

Chapter 13

Myles stood shakily, eyes round with fear as he looked at Silverton. "Soph, how many people know about your power?"

"I don't know." She stepped back, grabbing his hand. "The people of Silverton claim they don't believe in magic, but... I think they do, and they hate it. I don't know what my host family told everyone after I was kicked out."

I took a few steps down the hill, taking in the rooftops. From a distance, the village looked normal enough, and the auras radiating from it didn't spark immense terror... yet this was a town that had attempted to harm Sophie when she was only eight years old.

Myles stumbled, and Will wordlessly caught ahold of him. With Silverton standing between us and the path the stars directed us to take to King Brenton, where were we supposed to go? Myles needed to rest, and the longer he fought against cool-down, the sicker he would feel.

Will helped Myles sit, and Mercy hugged Sophie to her side, her gaze locked on the sun.

"I want to leave," Sophie said. "Maybe... we can go back..." She turned away from Silverton, trembling as she eyed the hill we had just climbed.

A breeze ruffled our hair and clothes, and Myles ran a hand down his face. "It isn't safe for us to be here."

I knelt beside him. "Mercy, is there a shortcut, maybe? Or somewhere we can make a good enough camp that's out of sight of Silverton?"

She shook her head, helping Sophie sit with us. "We can't loop around with Myles in cool-down. There is no good cover and we will be spotted if we skirt Silverton."

"Trees," Myles huffed. He turned and pointed a trembling hand back the way we had come. "That way... we can... go there."

I stood, peering that way. There was nothing but grass and hills. "I can't see them," I said. "I don't think it is a good idea to search for a forest we can't see when you are so far into cool-down."

"We could set up camp here?" Mercy asked doubtfully. "Go back down so the hill blocks Silverton?"

"I don't want to be in the open," Sophie whispered. "Shepherds bring their sheep to these hills. We'll be spotted."

Will glanced at me wide-eyed, and I was sure my expression matched his. With how far into cool-down Myles was, he wouldn't be able to teleport until tomorrow, and from how heavy he was breathing, it was apparent even his ability to walk was waning.

Mercy eyed Silverton, her voice soft. "If they don't know we are Mageye..."

"We could book an inn?" I whispered and Sophie gasped.

"In Silverton?"

"If the stars want us to go through Silverton as the fastest route, and with there being no good campsites nearby, that might be our best option," Mercy said.

"No," Myles huffed, drawing up his knees and putting his head between them. "Not an inn... not in Silverton."

I placed a hand on his back, meeting Will's gaze over Myles's head. Waves crashed in his irises, and the sunlight in them rippled, reflecting his nerves.

"If we are spotted by people from Silverton, they'll have

questions. And I can't use water to fend against them," he said softly, so Sophie wouldn't hear.

I looked down at Myles—who made no reaction to Will's words—then back up at Will. "Can you help him walk all that way?"

He hesitated, turning instead to Mercy, and whispering something to her.

Her expression grew solemn, but she nodded. "There is one," she answered, her gaze flitting to Silverton.

"Take us there," Will directed, taking Myles's arm to pull him to his feet. "Have you ever seen a fawn, Sophie?"

"A fawn?" she echoed, fiddling with her skirts. "No."

He smiled, wrapping Myles's arm around his shoulder. "Their spots work as camouflage; they hide in plain sight." He motioned to Silverton with his free hand. "I think hiding in plain sight is the safest option for us tonight, too. And if you stay invisible the whole time, no one but us four will know you're here."

Tears welled in her eyes. "You want to go into Silverton?"

I pulled her into a hug. "It's safer than making a camp here. Mercy is going to take us to an inn, and we will have beds to sleep in while Myles recovers."

When we pulled apart, she looked to Myles. He slumped into Will, though he seemed to be attempting to straighten himself, still protesting Silverton. The stamina he had when we first discussed our plan to leave had all but faded, and his knees trembled, Will being the only thing keeping him upright.

Her eyes seemed to harden into quartz. "Like with the Mageye earlier," she whispered. "Face my fear. For Myles. For all of us."

"Yes," I agreed. "And we will be with you the whole time, I promise."

She nodded, then wordlessly faded away, small indentations in the grasses the only sign she still stood with us.

When we were all on our feet, Mercy's hand curled around

Sophie's invisible one and Will looked between us. "Is everyone ready?"

"I think so," I said.

He took the lead down the hill, to the flower-filled plain. At the foot of the hill, Mercy released Sophie's hand and led us towards Silverton. A rabbit suddenly darted out of a patch of hemlock, fast disappearing back into the flowers.

"That's like you, Sophie," Will said, pointing after it. "Vanishing into pretty flowers."

A soft giggle came from beside me, though Sophie didn't reveal herself. "Hidden in plain sight."

"Poof," Will said, waving a hand to the air. "Gone. We'll be fine. And Myles, I promise I'll still take the first watch. All you need to worry about is not falling."

Myles cast another fear-filled look at Silverton before mumbling, "I trust you, Will. I trust all of you."

Will shot me a relieved look at Myles's acceptance, and we continued our trek across the field. It took over an hour, and by the time we finally reached the edge of the town, Myles was trembling and putting almost his full weight into Will, but neither made any complaint.

Small shops and wood-walled houses lined the sandstone-cobbled street, welcoming us into Silverton. Though, the friendly appearance did very little ease any nerves.

"The inn is a few streets over," Mercy said, guiding us into the midst of Silverton.

Now that we were in the town, I stuck close to Myles's side. His feet dragged, and his head hung towards his chest.

"You'll be able to sleep soon," I promised.

He shook his head and tried to pull away from Will again. "Not... here..."

"No bad auras," I assured him.

He mumbled something, and I frowned. We needed to get off

the streets before anyone got suspicious.

As we passed through a small market, the vendors watched us warily. Some whispered to each other, so we quickened our pace before we were asked any questions.

"The inn is right around this corner," Mercy said. Her fingers gripped air briefly, before she released Sophie's hand so as not to draw suspicion.

Relief flooded me at the sight of a two-story, thatch-roofed inn. A well-dressed gentleman stepped out, waving to an elderly woman. Silverton didn't appear nearly as dark and scary as I expected.

"Charles's Inn," Will read from the sign out front. "Patrons must be twenty... even Myles is too young."

Myles weakly lifted his head, eyes growing wide as he stared at the sign. "No," he hissed, attempting to pull away from Will, but Will urged him to stop struggling.

Mercy frowned. "This is the only one in town, and we need somewhere to spend the night. Maybe we can ask for an exception?"

"Or maybe someone would be willing to let us stay in their stables?" I suggested.

"Not that," Sophie whispered from somewhere near us.

Will furrowed his brow at the sign, smiling slowly. "I have an idea." He led us past the entrance, and turned into the small alley between the inn and the neighboring building.

He helped Myles lean against the wall and straightened. "Stay here," he directed. "I'll be right back."

Before any of us could protest, he ran out of the alley. Mercy and I exchanged concerned looks. "His ideas are usually out of the box," she whispered, "but nine times out of ten, they're genius."

"I just hope he doesn't draw too much attention," I fretted, watching Myles.

His eyes were slightly unfocused and he hid his face in his

palm, shaking his head.

Sophie kept silent, though a light squeeze to my hand confirmed she was here, and another few minutes passed before Will returned. He was panting and opened his satchel, revealing a bottle of whiskey.

"I'm back," he huffed, kneeling by Myles as he uncorked the bottle.

"What's the whiskey for?" Mercy asked, glancing nervously out the alley. "Did you steal it?"

"Borrowed," Will answered, grabbing Myles's hair with one hand to tug his head back. He pushed the open bottle to Myles's lips, forcing him to drink it.

"Will," I protested. "What are you doing?"

Myles spluttered and weakly pushed against Will, but he wasn't much of a match in his current state.

Will pulled the bottle back and Myles spat out the liquid, gagging. "What was that for?" he croaked.

Instead of answering, Will splashed the whiskey down the front of Myles's shirt.

"What?" Myles protested, tugging the wet shirt away from his skin.

"I'm going to get us a room in the inn," Will said. "Trust me."

Mercy took the bottle from Will and sniffed it. "Ack! Will, what are you doing?"

"I already told you, getting us our ticket in."

"By forcing Myles to drink whiskey?" I asked in disbelief.

"You'll see why," Will answered, tugging Myles to his feet. "Follow my lead, and I'll do the talking."

Myles reeked of whiskey, and I wrinkled my nose as a wave of the stench hit me.

Will looked around. "You still with us, Sophie?"

"Yes," came her soft reply.

Will nodded in satisfaction. "Stay invisible until we get into our room. The rest of us might be able to pass as twenty, but you won't. Mercy and Rose, uh... try and act old."

"Old?" I echoed, frowning.

"Mature," he flashed a smile. "You know, like we're a group of twenty-somethings with our drunk buddy."

Myles took this moment to stumble, and I raised my brow. Drunk buddy, indeed.

Chapter 14

A bell announced our presence in the dark inn, and a stern-looking woman frowned as we approached the bar. Her dress had a stiff-looking, frilly collar, and her cheeks were flushed as if she had indulged in her own alcohol.

Will confidently greeted her. "Good afternoon. We would like to book a private room for the night please. Preferably one with two beds, if you have any."

She shook her head. "I'm sorry, but you must be at least twenty to stay here."

"Are you saying we don't look twenty?" Will asked, looking between me, Mercy, and himself in confusion.

"That's exactly what I'm saying," she replied, sounding cross.

Mercy looked worried, but Will smiled. "Well, thank you for the compliment. Not every day we are mistaken for teenagers again." He readjusted his grip on Myles. "Our buddy here has gotten himself in trouble with the missus. She has a no-drinking rule, and well, as you can see, he has been drinking all afternoon."

"Wha—?" Myles mumbled. "I'm not drunk." But his words slurred together, and our drunk buddy officially looked, smelled, and acted the part. "And I'm not twe—"

Will's hand tightened on Myles's shoulder in what looked like a painful grip.

Myles stopped protesting and Will resumed his relaxed stance.

"Sorry about that. He seems to think that if he says he is sober enough, it will become a reality."

The woman still shook her head. "You four kids have no business here. Drunk or otherwise."

Will furrowed his brow and spoke in a confused voice. "But ma'am, we are twenty." He motioned to me with one hand. "This is my sister, Lily. We've been traveling all day, and when we got in town, Justice here," he continued, pointing at Mercy, "asked us for help with our drunk pal, Abelforth. He's twenty-five and his predicament with the missus has made things awkward. With that said, we wouldn't have stepped foot in here if we were below twenty."

Before the woman could respond or demand we leave, there was a loud crash followed by a *whoosh.*

I jumped; a barrel of rum had fallen from its shelf and burst, dousing half the inn.

"Oh, my," she gasped, hurrying out from behind the bar.

Mercy stepped aside, narrowing her gaze at Will when he expressed his shock.

Myles groaned and took this moment to attempt to pull away. I caught his arm and Will steadied him, scolding, "No, Abelforth." He turned towards the woman with an apologetic look on his face. "Ma'am, I'm so sorry we can't help, but it seems like Abelforth isn't done for the day, and all that rum is tempting him. Would you mind if we grabbed a key from behind the counter and escorted ourselves to our room?"

She hardly glanced up from the wood splinters on the floor. "Room seven has two beds. Leave your payment on the counter."

I hurried behind the counter before she could change her mind. A line of golden keys hung under a short overhang, and I snatched the one labeled seven, tossing what was likely more than enough coins in its place.

Mercy already stood by the stairs in the back of the room, and we followed her. The upstairs was dimly lit and quiet, with room seven on our lefthand side.

I unlocked the door and pushed it open, stepping aside to let Will and Myles pass. Like the rest of the inn, this room was dimly lit. There were two beds, both with brown quilts, a small dresser, and a chair with a footstool in the back of the room.

Will helped Myles sit on the closest bed, and Mercy crossed the room to pull the curtains to let more light into the room.

I hesitated before closing the door. "Are you in, Sophie?"

"Yes," a soft voice said beside me. I shut the door and smiled when I saw her faint outline.

"We'll keep you safe, Sophie. I promise."

She nodded. "Thank you."

Myles sat on the edge of the closest bed, fumbling with the buttons on his shirt. "What are you doing?" I asked, going to him. "You need to rest."

"No," he mumbled. "This shirt reeks. I wanna take it off." He continued fumbling with the button until Will pulled his hands away.

"No," Myles grumbled again.

Will ignored him and helped unbutton his shirt. "Two beds and a chair. This is the best camp we've had since we left the city."

"Not sure I'd call this a camp," Mercy said, sitting on the edge of the far bed.

Will snickered. "Depends on how you define camp, I guess. But no matter what this technically is, we are safe, and as long as we don't cause any problems, that lady shouldn't kick us out."

"Problems like spilling her rum?" Mercy asked.

Will tossed Myles's shirt to the floor with a shrug. "It worked, didn't it?"

"That was you?" Sophie asked, exchanging a look with me. "That cost her time and money."

"I know, but I did what I had to do to get us in."

"And I'm assuming shoving whiskey down my throat was part of what you needed to do," Myles muttered.

Will turned to him. "You're still awake?"

Myles made no reply. Instead, he watched me.

I smiled and pointed to the bed he sat on. "You and Will get this bed, and us girls are going to claim the back half of the room."

"M'kay," he mumbled.

Sophie sat in the middle of our bed, and I joined her and Mercy. "I think I overpaid for the room," I said. "So, even if she is angry about us being young, she will probably be happy with the extra money."

"It will help cover some of the cost for the lost rum, too," Sophie said, glancing at the door when someone spoke in the hall.

The voices faded quickly and Mercy kicked her boots off, sitting cross-legged on the bed.

Will joined us, pointing at Myles. "He's finally asleep."

I looked over and giggled. Will had tucked him in, and hung his satchel over the bedpost.

Mercy leaned over, shoving Will lightly. "Justice?" she asked incredulously. "Where did that come from?"

Will shrugged, smirking. "Would you rather, Vengeance?"

"No, that's worse."

Sophie smiled softly. "I liked Lily, at least."

"Very creative," I said dryly.

Will flourished his hand and ducked his head. "Why, thank you, my dear sister."

Mercy rolled her eyes, though a smile teased her lips. "What's the plan for the rest of the night?" she asked, changing the topic.

"I guess we'll hide out here and wait for Myles to recover from cool-down." Will turned to me. "How are you feeling, Rose? You did a lot of healing back there."

I looked at my hands and sighed. "I'm looking forward to bed," I admitted. "But I'm not in cool-down."

"Well, you're in luck," Will said. "Because there isn't anything else on our agenda for the day besides rest. Myles should be better in the morning, and we'll get out of this town."

Sophie's gaze flit between the window and the shut door. "I have the weakest aura," she admitted. "Does anyone else sense anything... bad?"

I shut my eyes and focused on the auras surrounding the inn. Will's aura mingled with mine. Besides my general unease with our current predicament, nothing suggested we were in danger.

"We're the only Mageye in this inn," Will said. "And I don't sense anything bad anywhere near us, Sophie. We're safe."

"I agree," I said, opening my eyes. "And if you think about it, this inn being for adults only is to our advantage. No one will suspect we are here."

"That's true," Sophie whispered, relaxing her shoulders. "And I trust you all. It's Silverton that I don't trust."

Mercy sighed. "I don't think any of us do. But we just need to get through the rest of the day and tonight."

"Or sleep through it," I said, patting the mattress.

Will laughed and slid off our bed. "I feel bad making you three share this bed. I don't mind taking the chair if one of you want to share with Myles."

Sophie glanced between us. "I actually like the idea of sharing this bed. Can I sleep in the middle?"

Mercy smiled warmly. "Sure, it will be like a sleepover."

"A sleepover in Silverton," Sophie murmured. "I don't think I like that, but it's better than sleeping on the streets."

I stood and went to the chair, nudging the footstool. "Will, can you help me put this in front of the door?"

"Sure."

We each took a side of it and shoved it up against the door. Will flopped onto it and sighed dramatically. "Safe and sound."

Sophie giggled. "Thank you."

Will nodded at her and I turned to go back, but he caught my hand, whispering, "Thanks."

"For what?" I asked, confused.

He shrugged. "For trusting me to take the lead. If you hated the idea of coming into Silverton, I don't think we would have."

"Well, I do hate that we're here," I said, sighing. "But, I think the end result of staying in this inn is the safest option for us. And after that Mageye earlier..."

He grimaced, leaning his head against the door. "Thinking about heights now, it's almost like it's worse again."

An image of Raymond's bloody corpse filled my head and I blinked rapidly. "My fear too," I confessed.

"Yeah," he croaked, staring at Myles unseeingly. "You're right about us staying at an adults-only inn being a good cover."

I glanced at Mercy and Sophie. They lay on our bed, talking softly, and after a second of hesitation, I knelt beside the stool Will sat on. "Can I ask you something?"

He raised his brows and nodded. "Sure."

I sighed a little, pulling Ren's jackknife from my pocket and tracing the *R* with a finger. The illusion Mageye had told us he knew King Duncan matched our powers together, and Will's power had been chosen because water douses fire.

After witnessing our worst fears, the Volcaniacs would now have the ability to recreate them. The mere thought of my bleeding family nearly made me want to abandon the mission and run back to Mageye City. But as long as I was at risk of receiving controlled visions, being far from them was for the best.

Sophie, Myles, and I all had fears that would be difficult to turn into reality. Even Mercy's fear was a bit unique, because it would require her already being kidnapped to recreate. But Will's fear... palaces had tall towers, and with King Brenton's lava, that meant we were heading into a fight of terror only he may be able to defend us against.

"Are you scared?" I asked.

He furrowed his brow. "About what?"

"King Duncan thinks your power might be the key to putting King Brenton's fire out. Does that scare you?" I sighed. "Well, obviously it is scary, but does the fact that it comes down to your power scare you?"

He shifted uneasily. "I don't know if I would say I'm *scared* per se, but nervous, yes. And maybe a bit doubtful about whether or not I will actually be able to defeat him."

"You doubt your powers? Or yourself?"

"Dunno." He stared across the room. "Both, maybe? Do you ever doubt your healing powers?"

I nodded. "Myles once threatened to teleport me off of a cliff if he caught me doubting myself one more time."

He laughed softly. "That sounds like Myles."

"It does," I agreed and he smiled a little, though he now looked nervous. "You're not alone," I said. "None of us are."

He looked over at everyone before offering me his hand. "Shake on it?"

"Shake on what?" I asked, confused.

"That we'll stay a team no matter what."

I took his hand. "Without a doubt."

Chapter 15

"You're walking like you have two left feet," a man laughed in the hallway.

"I have two left shoes," his companion responded, his words slurring together.

"What?" A beat of silence passed, then hushed laughter. "Whose shoe is that? Wait, Oscar, stop..."

Their voices faded down the hall and I climbed out of bed, careful not to bump Sophie. That was the second set of drunk passersby since Will traded shifts with me half an hour ago, and I crept to the door now, quadruple-checking it was locked.

It was, but I gave the stool an extra shove against the door for good measure. This was only my second time sleeping at an inn. The first had been a little over two years ago. A neighbor had asked Raymond to travel a few towns over to pick up a custom table order, and had loaned him his cart. The trip required staying overnight, and Ren, Ryder, and I had begged him to take us. After gaining permission from both our mom and the neighbor, he had agreed.

The inn Raymond chose was smaller than this one and had no bar attached. But we had all woken up in the middle of the night to drunk men outside, arguing over whether the moon was following them.

Ren had called out the window that it wasn't following them, but chasing them, and they had run off, panicked.

We had found that hilarious, but when we calmed down, Raymond reminded us to be careful around alcohol and people who consumed it to the degree they thought the moon was chasing them. It was unpredictable, not unlike magic.

The memory made me smile, but then the image of them collapsing in the woods, covered in blood, came to mind and my smile faded.

I sat on the stool, leaning against the door. The Mageye earlier today had *let* us go, and why would he do that if he hadn't gotten what he wanted?

Knowing our fears and how our powers operated together... What if I was wrong that my fear would be difficult to recreate? We knew he could mask his aura, after all. What if he snuck into Mageye City?

I tucked my feet onto the stool and hugged my knees to my chest. Regardless of whether or not my theory was correct about recreation, there was a certainty that returning home would put my family and all of Mageye City in danger.

Rose.

I looked up at the sound of Myles's voice in my head. He climbed out of bed and picked up his discarded shirt, wrinkling his nose in disgust as he shrugged it on. But he shuffled over, plopping onto the footstool beside me.

"Are you okay?" I whispered. "You're probably still in cool-down; you need to rest."

He smelt heavily of whiskey and I grimaced, though I didn't move away.

"Yeah," he murmured, stretching his legs out. "It can't be much later than midnight, though. Still plenty of time to sleep."

I rested my head against the door. "I don't think I've ever heard you openly admit you want to sleep."

"Several hundred miles," he whispered. "That's... a miracle."

He lifted his hands. "Will was right when he said it should have killed me."

I straightened. "Don't say that. Please... don't..." My heart raced, now picturing his still form after he saved us from the volcano.

He took my hand. "I'm sorry, that wasn't a good choice of words."

I took a shaky breath and gently pulled my hand away. "If you're so tired, you should sleep."

"Probably," he agreed, glancing around our room. "Definitely," he corrected. "But if I wasn't in cool-down, there was something I wanted to talk to you about. And your emotions woke me, so clearly it's a discussion we need tonight, cool-down or otherwise."

"What do you mean?" I sat up straighter, peering at his face in the dark. "Is something wrong?"

"Your fear," he breathed.

I stiffened and pulled back, Mom's expression as she died in the illusion coming to mind. "What... about it?"

He rested his head against the door and sighed deeply, keeping his voice soft. "When I first moved to the palace, there was a maid named Mrs. Susanwool. She was the first person I trusted after my parents died."

Myles had introduced me to several servants in the palace, but none had been named Mrs. Susanwool that I could recall. Nonetheless, hearing about her was a welcome distraction, and I waited for him to continue.

"She passed away," Myles murmured, "when I was eight. I had finally come to terms with the loss of my parents, and King Duncan let me say goodbye to them before officially adopting me... then, three months later, Mrs. Susanwool went to visit family across the city and never came back." He stared ahead of himself, locked on some faraway memory. "I'd teleport to the kitchens and she wouldn't be there, or when someone knocked on my door, it was never her. I started to get scared."

I held my breath as he met my gaze. "That was before I got along with General Cornstone and it left me with two people. General Agar, who had only just joined the Elite Guard and was a favored babysitter, but not a guardian, and King Duncan. My new dad. Whenever either of them left the palace, I was a wreck, convinced it was the last time." He smiled sadly. "And survivor's guilt? If you still feel guilty about not being kidnapped by the trader, since you were the initial target, well, I'm no stranger to that either."

Tears welled in my eyes, and I broke his gaze. But you couldn't hide that type of thing from a mind reader.

"I know you worried about your power reversing its ability to heal others, and you primarily agreed to this mission to protect your family. Have you assigned yourself the duty of being their protector?"

"Kind of," I admitted, fidgeting with the hem of my dress. "My whole life, they have kept me safe. I was the baby, the little sister, the only girl. I have always been the protected, not the protector, but when they were kidnapped..."

"You know that none of them blame you, right?"

I nodded. "But it doesn't change how I feel."

"I know. Trust me, Rose, I *know*. But we have to accept that we can't do everything ourselves. Sometimes we need to trust that they can take care of themselves, even when we aren't at their side."

"Is that what you did?" I asked. "With Mrs. Susanwool?"

He shut his eyes and nodded. "Dad told me that on some level, my fear that any moment could be the last is correct. You never really know what will happen and God doesn't promise tomorrow." He opened his eyes. "But God does promise the rising sun, and He promises to provide. You fear losing your family because you know what it feels like to lose them. But your fear of it is entirely different from it being real. Think about the illusions today and all the terror we felt. That fear was a separate feeling to the *truth*."

"Even if the sun keeps rising and God provides, they're my *family*." I blinked back fresh tears. "I'm scared of being alone. Of losing the only family I have. And right now, they are in Mageye City without me, so what if something happens? What if the illusions today weren't all simply illusions?"

He held up his hand, purple lightning flickering between his fingers. "It's not your responsibility to protect them all the time. It's like I said, there comes a time where they need to protect themselves."

"But what if I want to always interfere? Myles, I'm their sister. I'm my mom's only daughter. I *have* to protect them." Hot tears burned the back of my eyes, and I blinked rapidly against them.

His expression held nothing but understanding. "Ren and Ryder helped you sneak out of the city, didn't they? Even though they didn't exactly like the thought of their little sister risking her life."

I stilled. "They let me go ahead… because they trusted I would come back."

"Exactly. And now it's your turn to gift them with that same trust."

"I still don't want to let them go."

"You're not letting them go," he said. "And remember that being in this inn right now *is* protecting them. I think I can speak for all of us that we'd rather be in our own beds and not preparing to face the Volcaniacs, but we have the city to protect. And we all have a family depending on us, too."

A tear trickled down my cheek and his tone softened. "General Cornstone told me that when I begin to panic, I should lock onto something good. Sometimes that means *happy thoughts,* but that didn't work much for me." He hesitantly reached out and brushed the tear from my cheek. "I usually read people's minds... people I trust. Or I seek out a good aura to calm myself with."

I sniffed. "But that's more if you are having a panic attack. What if I am scared because something bad is happening and I can't do anything to stop it?"

"People will make choices in life that you don't always agree with. And sometimes those choices put them in danger." Myles's gaze met mine. "You can try to protect them, but at the end of the day, you need to let them live with that decision." He waved across the room. "I know I'm a hypocrite, seeing as my whole reason for being upset with this group is because I don't want them here for something I could have stopped, but maybe that means the two of us can learn to trust people with their own decisions together."

I pulled out Ren's jackknife and rolled it in my palm until Myles put his hand over mine. "Fidgeting shows anxiousness, anxiousness shows fear, and fear gives an attacker time to take advantage," he whispered. "Gosh, I hated when my dad said that to me, but there is truth to it. Especially the last part."

My breath caught. "Our fears can't hurt us," I whispered, "but I bet that Mageye from today wants us to believe they do."

He smiled. "He could tell King Brenton to bring an army of elephants to the palace, and I'd still show up." He leaned closer, his voice dropping. "Maybe that's what Will meant by Plan A with added danger."

I laughed a little and tucked the jackknife away. "If I had let my fear for my family's safety paralyze me on our way to The End, we never would have saved them. And if I let that fear take over now, I won't be much of a help to our mission, and then I'd risk losing you four instead."

"Maybe there is even more truth to my dad's old sayings than I thought." He sighed. "I owe him a few apologies when we get back, don't I?"

I smiled softly. "And both of our families have hugs waiting for them as well, don't they?"

"Most definitely."

Chapter 16

Myles pulled the curtains back with a *whoosh*, and I squinted at him. "What are you doing?"

He grimaced. "Sorry, that wasn't meant to wake you."

"Well, it did," I grumbled and he snickered, approaching the bed.

"It is technically time to get up anyway. Will and I have been up for about half an hour."

"Didn't Will take the first shift?" I asked. "And you shouldn't have taken any."

"I didn't." He shrugged. "We got up and told Mercy to get some extra sleep."

The color had returned to his face, and his eyes were no longer glazed, so I smiled and sat up.

He leaned over to nudge Sophie awake and I held my breath, expecting the scent of whiskey. But there seemed to be no remaining smell and his hair was wet. I reached out and touched his hair. "Did you leave the room to bathe? What if someone saw you?"

He shook his head as he pulled back, Sophie now nudging Mercy awake. "I didn't leave the room. Will used one of our waterskins so I could wash the smell of *whiskey* off." He emphasized the end as he walked back around the room and flopped down next to Will.

Will snickered. "Stop complaining. I got us in; no harm done."

"To you," Myles shot back, swatting at him. "And while we are on the topic. How'd you know about Abelforth?"

"What?" Will asked, swinging his legs off the bed to put his boots on.

Myles tucked his arms behind his bed. "You called me Abelforth. How'd you figure out his name? No one is supposed to know it. Heck, even I'm not supposed to know it."

"Huh?" Will looked over his shoulder. "Is your middle name Abelforth or something?" His eyes widened. "Wait, seriously. Is your full name Myles Abelforth Duncan?"

"No, it's not, William Archie Russell!"

Will gasped in offense. "Wait, how do you know *my* name?"

"Myles's middle name is Hilton," I said. "And he said he wasn't supposed to know whoever's name he is talking about, so it can't be his own, right?" I turned to Myles. "Who is it?"

"One of the other generals?" Mercy suggested, clearly fighting laughter.

One of the generals... I sucked in my breath. Myles had told me King Duncan used his last name in his title. Did that mean—

Don't say it! Myles screamed in my head. *Rose, don't you dare. My dad will be furious if he finds out I let you all know his name. Don't say a word.*

I smiled, suddenly giddy with the fact that I was in on such a big secret. *King Abelforth Duncan?*

Rose, he warned, sitting up and glaring daggers at me.

Abelforth? I pressed. *I can't imagine addressing him as that.*

I can imagine myself in a dungeon cell if you address him as King Abelforth, Myles responded, sounding amused, yet concerned.

I sighed dramatically. "Let's change the topic before our names become a full-blown fight. And after this, let's not use our code names again... at least around people we know, because it sounds

128

like someone will be offended."

"Fair enough," Sophie said. "I don't want us fighting."

Will narrowed his gaze at Myles. "As long as I don't hear my full name again." Mercy giggled, and he pointed a finger at her. "Not a word, Miss Justice."

She stuck her tongue out at him. "You're the one who gave us those nicknames to begin with."

"And it got us in." Will threw his hands to the side. "You all seem to forget that. A tragedy. Next time, maybe I won't help."

"Splendid," Myles drawled.

"Myles, you couldn't unbutton your own shirt last night," Will reminded him calmly. "But I digress. What is our plan for today?"

"I want to leave," Sophie said immediately.

Myles nodded. "I want to leave Silverton as well. A group of five traveling teens looks suspicious, regardless of how friendly the town is."

"Well, four," Mercy said as she finished brushing her hair. "Sophie was invisible until we got to our rooms, so I think she should fade away again until we get out of town."

"I can do that," Sophie said.

"All right, but stick close to us," Myles said. "We can't check to make sure you are with us in front of other people."

Sophie nodded. "I know."

"When should we leave?" I asked.

"As soon as possible," Myles answered. "I've been ready to get out of Silverton since before we arrived."

"Do we have all of our things?" Myles asked as we lined up at the door.

Sophie's hands suddenly appeared, raising her satchel, and I giggled, holding mine up as well. She faded away and after a final check around the room, Myles opened the door.

Will nudged him aside, a small smirk on his face. "Don't forget that you're supposed to be hungover."

Myles groaned and put his fingers to his temple. "I don't think it will be hard to fake that, just talking to you is giving me a headache."

Will laughed. "Mercy says I have that same effect on her."

Mercy grinned and walked out into the hallway. "I think you have that effect on everybody."

"Rude," he chastised.

I followed them out of the room. A middle-aged couple stood at the end of the hallway, looking out the murky glass window and across the street. I tensed, expecting them to question our age, but they hardly spared us a glance.

Myles shut the door, but hesitated with the lock. *I can sense Soph's aura. I think she's out of the room.*

A faint tingling told me she was nearby, and almost as if she too could read thoughts, I felt a soft touch on my shoulder.

She's out.

Myles nodded and locked the door, turning to Will. "You led us in. You lead us out."

"You're putting me in charge?" Will asked innocently.

"No, I'm using you as a human shield. If someone attacks us from the front, you'll take the hit."

Will choked. "That escalated way quicker than I expected it to."

"Trust me. You had it coming."

"I did," Will snickered, leading the way down the stairs. The same woman as yesterday stood behind the counter. She huffed when we came in, turning away.

Myles fidgeted nervously, feigning interest in a portrait of a dog.

Will walked up to the counter, giving her an award-winning smile. "Good morning. Thank you for the room last night. It was perfect for us, and *Abelforth* here is feeling a lot better today." He winked. "If you know what I mean."

It was safe to say that Will was having too much fun with his acting, and the supposed-to-be forbidden name-calling.

He passed her the keys and she blindly took them, her expression changing as she looked at Myles.

Myles stiffened, turning from the portrait and ushering Mercy and me out the door. "Come on, *Archie*, the *missus* isn't going to be too pleased with me as it is. The sooner we get back, the better."

Will glanced from Myles to the woman, his brow furrowed. She was still watching Myles and put the key down rather harshly. "Have safe travels," she said, forcing a smile at Will.

Myles practically pushed me outside, calling again for Will—Archie—to hurry.

What's wrong? I asked.

She recognizes me.

Recognizes him? The door shut behind us, but quickly opened again as Will stepped out, looking as baffled as me and Mercy.

"Soph, I am reading your mind. Let me know you are walking with us," Myles said as he broke into a brisk walk.

Will, Mercy, and I followed, and since Myles didn't break his pace, Sophie must have confirmed her presence.

Mercy's worried gaze met mine; the stars in her eyes seemed to be swirling with uncertainty. "What's wrong?" she whispered.

I shrugged, unsure of what to say. She frowned and quickened her pace, taking the lead with the sun as her guide.

We were heading for the mountains and as they rose higher above the rooftops, Myles huffed a sigh of relief. "Straight to the mountains, or are we detouring once we hit the woods?" he asked Mercy.

"We are going to cross the mountains," Mercy explained.

"Good." He glanced over his shoulder, scanning the streets behind us nervously now that we were past the last buildings. "We need to get some distance between us and Silverton."

He reached out and grabbed Sophie's invisible hand before breaking into a run.

Chapter 17

We continued towards the mountains and didn't slow our pace until Silverton was long out of sight.

"Is it safe for me to come out?" Sophie asked from beside Myles.

He scanned the trees carefully. "Yes, we should be safe now."

She reappeared, her hair a mess from running so long. Everyone was out of breath and we passed a waterskin between us, our nerves visible through our continual glances back towards Silverton.

"Myles, what happened? Why'd you freak like that?" Will asked when we had caught our breath.

Myles grimaced. "I was recognized," he confessed.

"By the woman at the counter?" Mercy asked.

"She's the owner," Myles agreed, watching Sophie carefully. "And she... recognized me."

Sophie flickered. "Recognized you from what? I've never been to Charles's Inn."

"I know," he agreed. "But *I* have."

My head whipped back to face him. Myles had told me he met Sophie in the woods, and that after saving her, he never set foot anywhere near Silverton again. And to my knowledge, he had never visited Silverton before meeting her, either.

Myles's gaze shot to me and the lightning flickering in his eyes revealed he carried a secret. "It's not what you all think. Not exactly, at least."

"What do you mean?" Sophie asked. "Is this about what happened to me?"

"Yes," he rasped, faltering in his steps. "I... promised King Duncan I wouldn't tell you."

She flickered again, and Will looked between them uneasily. "Is there a chance anyone from Silverton might follow us?"

Myles stopped walking and shook his head. "Charles's Inn didn't used to have age restrictions."

"You said yesterday you didn't want us to stay at the inn," Mercy prompted. "Did you have something to do with the rules changing?"

He nodded and his expressions seemed to war with each before he sighed. "Soph, about a year after you moved to Mageye City, I returned to Silverton. The plan was for me to scout out your old host family and a few others to confirm that the hunt was entirely finished."

"You went back?" Sophie whispered.

"Yeah," he breathed. "I went back."

Mercy and Will exchanged uneasy looks and I shifted my feet. "What happened?" I asked.

Lightning flickered in his irises again and he looked towards Silverton, his voice strained. "I met your dad."

"What?" Sophie stepped away from him. "My mom and dad are dead, Myles. And my host family disowned me."

"No," he rasped. "Your dad... Soph... Your biological dad, he abandoned you after murdering your mom."

This statement was met with deadly silence, and even the woods around us appeared still. It was as if Myles had sent out a bolt of lightning and shocked the whole group with it, freezing us in a nightmarish twist of past fate.

"What do you mean?" Sophie asked, her voice quivering.

Tears welled in Myles's eyes. "I was eavesdropping at Charles's Inn because the old owner was the head of the town guard. I thought there was a good chance people dining there would know about you, and I could read their minds." He took a steadying breath. "Instead of reading minds, there was a group of men talking about you. And one of those men was your dad, and he was saying some things about you that he should not have been saying. When I realized who he was, I read his mind, and when I found out what he did to you, I lost my temper."

Sophie appeared to be holding her breath, her face frozen in horrified shock.

"I attacked him," Myles confessed, "and everyone who laughed at your expense."

Sophie looked between us, as if waiting for someone to make sense of the situation. The galaxy in Mercy's irises had begun to swirl again, and waves crashed in Will's irises.

"What did he say about me?" Sophie asked shakily.

"That..." Myles stopped himself, looking suddenly nauseous. "I can't repeat it."

"But..." Sophie flickered wildly. "Why would you keep that from me? You attacked my dad over something he said?" Her eyes glossed over with tears and her voice pitched. "He killed my mom? He abandoned me?"

"I'm sorry, Soph," Myles said.

"I think I need some time alone," she whispered and ran into the woods.

"Sophie," Will called, about to follow, but Mercy caught his arm.

"I don't think she'll go far."

Myles stared at the trees she had disappeared into, shoulders slumped with defeat. "When she was younger, all she wanted was a family, *her* family. And... well, King Duncan, General Cornstone, and I were worried that if she found out her father was alive, she would run away and try to find him."

"You did it to protect her," I whispered, holding a hand over my heart. "Myles, if she might have run after him, then I think you did the right thing. But now that she knows... I think she deserves the full story, right?"

"I just wish it wasn't such a bad story," he croaked. "She's my Soph. She's always been... my Soph."

"And I still am," Sophie said, suddenly reappearing next to us. "I want to know what he said, with no filters and no secrets."

Myles stared, heartbreak etched across his face. "Are you sure?"

"Yes," she whispered. Her cheeks were tear-stained, but she straightened her shoulders. "I'm sure."

"Can we explain as we walk, then?" he asked, holding out his hand. "I want to put more distance between us and Silverton."

She accepted his hand and Myles hesitated, turning back to the mountains.

"There were four men at the table," he began. "I don't know who the others were, but one of them confirmed he was..."

"My dad?"

"Yes," Myles agreed, touching Sophie's hair with a trembling hand. "You look like him. Same hair. But the resemblance was only physical. It sounded like he wasn't from Silverton, but was visiting. He was ranting about how you had run away, because... because..." Myles choked up, fresh sparks of old rage flickering in his irises.

"Because of what?" Sophie whispered.

"Because he wanted to finish what he started," Myles whispered.

"What he started?" I echoed, shuddering. "What does that mean?"

"He needed money," Myles said, his voice trembling. "And he couldn't afford to provide for you and your mom, so he tried to sell you both. But no one wanted a mom with such a young child, so he killed her and abandoned you with the plan to... to..." His cheeks flushed. "To come back when you were old enough to be indentured, or worse."

Bile rose in my throat and my legs suddenly felt weak. Mercy too looked faint and Will's face was tinged with green.

Myles took another steadying breath. "He and everyone at the table were ranting and laughing about it, and it was like a fuse snapped. I grabbed your dad and threw him to the floor, punching him over and over before attacking the rest of them. They were all too drunk to put up a fight, and then I went back to your dad." Lightning flickered in his iris. "Everyone was screaming, until a guard hit me over the head with a baton, and I was knocked out."

Sophie had grown deathly pale, though she didn't flicker, as if even her power didn't know how to react. "What happened after that?"

Myles stared at his feet now, his tone softening. "I woke up in a cell, and I tried to explain that your dad confessed to murdering my friend's mom, but they didn't believe me. And when I couldn't tell them your name for fear of the hunt for you being renewed... they locked me away and let the men go free."

Sophie trembled, her knuckles going white where she gripped Myles's hand. "I remember you once disappeared for nearly three months, and everyone was panicked. You said you got lost, but that was when you were kidnapped, wasn't it? It was about a year after you saved me."

"Yes," Myles rasped. "They kept me locked in a small cell for weeks. The head guard was furious I caused such a disturbance in his inn and he made sure I paid for it. The woman from the inn today was his wife; I saw her a few times. She wasn't all bad, but she certainly didn't feel much pity for me."

I looked back the way we had come, eyeing the trees as if Myles's kidnappers could appear at any moment.

"How did you get out?" Will asked. "Did you teleport?"

Myles shook his head. "I didn't use my power when I attacked them, and after I was imprisoned, I was stuck. If I had used my power to escape, I would have exposed the Mageye."

Sophie burst into tears and threw her arms around him. "I'm so sorry." She sobbed. "I'm sorry."

Myles hugged her back so tightly, I worried Sophie might not be able to breathe. "It's not your fault," he told her. "Soph, it's not your fault at all."

"But... but you did it to protect me." She pulled back, sniffing. "Thank you, Myles."

Tears welled in Myles's eyes. "It was worth it to protect you, Soph. It's always been worth it."

Chapter 18

I had never been so happy to stand at the base of a mountain. Well, I never felt particularly strong emotions related to mountains, but the thought that this mountain range would separate us from Silverton was a good one.

"What's your call on direction, Mercy?" Myles asked. "Do we cross over or go around?"

Mercy didn't hesitate. "Over. I don't think staying at the bottom is a good idea. It would put us at a disadvantage during an attack. We want to take the higher ground instead of someone else."

Myles nodded. "Good point. And Will might be able to find some mountain streams, which will give us another advantage."

Will tilted his head back to study the mountain. Trees blocked whatever lay on the ground, whether grass, or rocks, or water, but he nodded. "There is water, but it isn't near the base."

Myles furrowed his brow. "So it's higher up?"

"Yeah." Will grimaced. "We can make it by tonight, though."

"All right." Myles waved at the mountain. "We will find the water and set up camp for the night. Tomorrow, we will cross to the other side, and if I teleport a few times, we should be able to cross the next one."

"The next mountain?" I asked. "How do you know how many there are?"

"Well, have you ever seen one single mountain standing by itself?" Myles asked with a smirk.

I sighed. "You got me there. But I still want to know how many there are."

Sophie turned to Mercy. "Does the sun know?"

"Yes." Mercy shielded her eyes from the bright sunlight. "There are seven mountains total, but we shouldn't need to cross them all. The sun says the quickest route will only require us to cross three."

"That's not bad," Myles said.

"Easy for you to say. You do things like this for a living," Will said. "The rest of us only have a handful of serious endurance training for this kind of thing. Not to mention mountains are *high*."

Myles shrugged. "I thought you said you aren't afraid of anything. And I never said it was going to be *easy*. Only that it wasn't too bad. Particularly compared to what I have done in the past. I once had to cross twelve mountains in less than a week."

"Twelve mountains in a week?" Will gasped.

I crossed my arms over my chest. "You definitely teleported as often as you could."

"Teleported, walked. It doesn't matter, I still crossed twelve mountains in less than a week."

I groaned. "You and Will just want to one-up each other."

Myles grinned. "Maybe Will wants to one-up *me*, but I don't need to one-up him. We both know I'm stronger."

"Excuse me?" Will wagged his finger. "I'm standing right here. And no. We don't know that you're stronger."

Myles casually let sparks fly from his fingertips, a sudden mischievous glint in his eyes. "Are you certain?"

Will's eyes had lit up with an equally mischievous light, and he motioned towards himself with one finger.

Myles made a sudden gagging sound as his waterskin jerked

towards Will from around his neck.

His hands flew up to the strap, and he fumbled with it before he yanked it over his head. He let go, and it flew into Will's hands.

"Your aura might have a farther reach," Will crowed. "But I'm not one to mess with, either."

Myles rubbed his neck, and the corner of his mouth twitched as he fought back a laugh. "All right, I might have underestimated you there."

"*Might* have?" Will asked mischievously. "I've gotten you pinned more than a few times during training."

"Yes, *might*." Myles waved Will off. "You caught me by surprise, that's all."

Will opened his mouth to counter, but I interrupted. "You two can bicker over who is stronger later. Right now, we have a mountain to climb."

I almost burst out laughing at the disgusted faces they both made.

"We are not *bickering*," Myles protested. "Bickering is for toddlers; we are *debating*."

"Yes," Will agreed. "We are having an educated discussion over who is the stronger person. And I'm willing to bet I could take Myles in a power-free fight—I already technically have."

Sophie giggled, and Mercy let out an exasperated groan. "Come on. Us ladies can take the lead while those two have an *educated discussion*."

✕

Lava encased the walls and ceiling of the room I stood in and I spun in a circle, searching for an escape. The lava parted as a door opened and I rushed to it, stumbling back when a broad-shouldered guardsman pushed a young man inside ahead of him. As the door slammed shut behind them, the lava disappeared, replaced by stone walls and a small barred window.

The young man fell to his hands and knees on the dirt floor with a stifled cry of pain, hiding his face as the guard sneered at him. "How dare you cause a scene like that in front of my wife."

When the young man only responded by curling tighter into himself, the guard kicked him. "Look at me when I'm talking to you!"

He lifted his head and I gasped, staring a young Myles in the face. His purple eyes were lit with a mixture of rage and terror, and as the guard continued to yell at him, tears brimmed his eyes.

"I'm not the bad guy," he burst. "I didn't mean to cause a scene."

The guard knelt and held Myles's gaze. "You're right. You're not the bad guy anymore, I am."

Myles's eyes widened and I stepped between them, staring down the guard as my chest heaved. "Leave him alone."

He didn't so much as wince at my words and instead stood, tossing a few final curses at Myles before leaving. The door slammed shut behind him. Myles didn't make a sound, and I whirled back to face him.

"Myles!"

Like the guard, he didn't react and instead crawled to the back corner of the cell, hugging his knees to his chest. "Those men deserved it," he whispered to the cell door. "I could have killed them and I could kill you, too."

Tears welled in my eyes and I went to his side. He appeared to be around fourteen or fifteen, and while the guard didn't appear to be a Volcaniac, this was a nightmare of its own.

Every breath he took seemed to be a drag and a red stain slowly bloomed under his shirt collar.

"Dad," he whispered. "Dad, please... please come..." He held one hand up and purple sparks flickered between his fingers before fading, replaced with an orange glow.

I looked up, but the orange glow seemed to be coming from the air itself, and I turned back to Myles.

He buried his head in his knees, his body shaking with silent sobs. With his sleeves bunched, dark bruises were now revealed and when he moved his leg, I saw he bore wounds hidden beneath his pants as well.

As if his captors didn't want anyone to know they had hurt him.

The ceiling suddenly burst, pouring lava in, and I let out a bloodcurdling scream as it burnt through me, but the young Myles hadn't even looked up.

I woke with a scream and sat trembling as waves of fear washed over me.

Sophie had been keeping guard and rushed to me, along with Myles, who looked spooked.

Mercy and Will shot up, nearly falling over themselves as they looked at the dark woods around us.

"What's wrong?" Sophie asked.

"V-vision," I stuttered as Myles put a hand on my back. He trembled and while his presence and aura were comforting, they appeared to be laced with fear of his own.

"It's over," he soothed, though his voice trembled. "You're awake and safe in our camp. Just... a vision."

I shook my head. "This one was different."

"Different? How was it different?" Mercy asked nervously. "It's been almost a week since the last one, right?"

"I think so," Will agreed softly, glancing between me and Myles.

Myles winced, and his thoughts suddenly filled my head. *I saw something real this time.*

You had one too?

Yes. He stared somewhere in the middle distance. *It was real.*

"Real?" I said aloud, turning to him. "What do you mean, it was real?"

Will sucked in his breath. "Real, as in a prophecy?"

"No," Myles breathed. "It was something from my past. Is that what happened to you too, Rose? A bad memory?" He grimaced. "Full of lava?"

Tears filled my eyes as I met his gaze and saw a terrified younger version staring back at me. "No, Myles. I saw you."

A deadly silence settled over camp, filled by my slowing panicked breaths, and crickets.

"You saw me?" Myles finally asked.

"You were fifteen," I whispered. "When you went back to Silverton, right?"

When he nodded, my heart sank. My vision hadn't only been a nightmare, but a memory. A memory Myles carried deep within himself.

"Was the vision I had real, too?" I asked.

Lightning sparked in his right iris. "If you saw me in Silverton... yes."

Sophie flickered, leaning closer. "The vision was in Silverton?"

Myles stared down the mountain, where Silverton lay hidden. "I wasn't given a trial or a sentencing or anything like that. The inn owner locked me away and punished me."

"Punished you?" Will questioned. The moonlight lit up the concern etched onto his face. "Were you beaten?"

"Yes," Myles breathed. "Tortured is a better word, for weeks. An inspector from the capital finally came and caught him beating me. I was freed that same day in exchange for secrecy and the vow to never set foot in Silverton again. The guard—the husband of the woman we saw today—was arrested and I think sent to the capital, so he wouldn't get pity from the guards he used to work with."

"So, the vision," I whispered, "was real?"

He shuddered, but when he spoke, his voice was steady. "I'd have thought it was only a nightmare, but there was lava. We saw my past in the vision."

"What does that mean?" I asked. "How was King Brenton able to incorporate your past?"

"Fears," Mercy whispered. "Do you think the vision was kind of like an illusion?"

A lump formed in my throat. "But wouldn't they need to know our past to create it? And… and can King Brenton and that Mageye even join together to create a controlled vision?"

"They are both powerful," Myles murmured. "I wouldn't be shocked if there was a way to create visions together."

"But we met that Mageye nowhere near the palace," Sophie whispered.

A grim silence settled over us, and Myles took my hand, the action helping to quell my nerves.

"It seems awfully suspicious that you had a vision that directly reflects the past, the day Myles told us about it," Will said. "Do you think we're being followed?"

I straightened and peered into the woods. My aura swirled with Mercy's, Will's, and Sophie's, but Myles sat still, his voice grim. "I don't think we are being followed. If they were following us undetected, they could very easily capture us."

"That's my point, Myles. We couldn't detect that Mageye when he attacked us, and he let us go for reasons we don't know. How do we know he isn't in this camp right now?" Will said.

"He said he would tell King Brenton to expect us as guests," Mercy said. "I don't think we are being actively followed, not at the moment, anyway. Illusions and visions fall into the same category. If there is a way to send a controlled vision as a team, then the illusion Mageye and King Brenton would make a great team. Maybe that is why he made us face our fears."

"Recreate them," Will murmured, glancing at me.

I swallowed hard. "Memories aren't tangible."

Sophie fidgeted. "King Duncan said the visions won't get worse if we never spend more than one night in the same spot. If that is true, why are the visions mutating?"

"Well," Myles said, "when I started getting the visions, I thought I was reliving the time I had spent in the volcano. So, I have seen real memories before, but they were always directly related to the Volcaniacs. This is the first time it has been something from a different experience."

"Which means that King Brenton is getting stronger," I said quietly.

He stared at his lap. "I can't dispute that. I'm sorry."

His apology seemed to extend past his failure to assure us our concerns were wrong. I squeezed his hand. *From the sounds of it, King Brenton and Marlon and that illusion Mageye weren't the only survivors of the eruption. And maybe some of the Volcaniacs were at the palace already. If you had fallen into the volcano with King Brenton in your arms, we might not know the Volcaniacs are still out there.*

Lightning flickered in his irises and he exhaled slowly. "Maybe you're right," he whispered. "But regardless, whether he is getting stronger or not, we have to stop him and the Volcaniacs for good."

Chapter 19

The atmosphere the next morning was subdued. I packed my satchel quietly, watching as everyone else did the same.

According to Mercy, with no delays, we had nearly two weeks of our journey left. That meant King Brenton had two weeks to grow stronger.

Two weeks to continue tormenting us with controlled visions, or preparing more ambushes. Two weeks to wait for us to come...

I looked up at a soft cooing sound, and smiled at the sight of a Golden Dove. It perched on a branch overhanging the small mountain stream.

Sophie smiled at it too, though her eyes were puffy and rimmed with red. After our discussion last night, I hadn't wanted to sleep again and relieved her of guard duty.

She had cried herself to sleep, despite Myles attempting to comfort her, but now she forced a small smile. "I love Golden Doves. They are so innocent, they make me feel safe."

"I always thought they had an odd shape," Will joked, breaking our peaceful moment. "They look like pears."

"And who said pears are odd?" Mercy teased.

"Pear-shaped pears look normal; pear-shaped birds look weird."

"Are we really discussing the shape of an innocent bird?" Myles asked as he walked past us on his way to refill his waterskin.

Before he could reach the stream, an arc of water rose up and flowed neatly into the uncorked pouch.

Myles jumped back and nearly dropped the waterskin.

Will grinned. "Why walk to the water when the water can come to you?"

"Handy," Myles said, pushing the stopper back in. "Thanks."

"Anytime." Will flourished his hand as he bowed. "Does anyone else need my services?"

"I wouldn't mind them," I said, glad for him lightening the nerves.

Mercy stepped outside of camp, face turned to the sun. When it was time to leave, she confidently led us farther up and around the mountain.

"Can we talk?" Myles asked, putting a hand on my shoulder.

My brow furrowed, but I nodded. "Sure. Is something wrong?"

"No," he said carefully. "But there is something I wanted to talk to you about."

We slowed our pace for some privacy, though it wasn't really necessary when we were no longer talking aloud.

Remember when you first put it together that I can read minds, and I said I felt like I wouldn't want someone else reading mine?

I remember that. He had told me people often found his mindreading frustrating, and that he often tried to hide it because of that.

He ran his hand down his satchel strap, the one he had taken from his house after his parents died. *I don't feel that way with our telepathic connection, but the vision last night...*

Heat rose in my cheeks. *I'm sorry.*

He shook his head, waving to the east and towards King Brenton's palace. *I think King Brenton is the one who needs to apologize. And maybe that illusion Mageye, too... All of the Volcanaics.* His hand dropped back to his side. *King Duncan and General Cornstone know the whole story from Silverton, but that's different from them seeing it. And I assume you have questions, and I think I'd rather you ask them so I can tell you the real story.*

Since joining the Elite Guard, Myles had gone on dozens of missions, and he was no stranger to danger. He had told me that he attempted to befriend a Mageye in a nearby town to Mageye City last year, and instead of accepting the help, he chased Myles off of his property.

Danger was a part of his life, his job, his position as a general. And while Mageye often went by power and experience over age, Myles had been my age now in that memory. Technically, a little younger. As I recalled the tears in his eyes during the memory, tears of my own filled my eyes. How badly I wished I could go back in time for him and push that guard away... Make it so Myles had never been hurt, but I couldn't do that.

Are you okay? I asked instead.

He didn't respond right away, seeming startled by the question. *Sure. That was a long time ago.*

Three years, I responded. *And it seemed pretty bad. You were bleeding, and it looked like every breath hurt.*

He grimaced, touching his chest where the bleeding had stained his shirt. *I was stuck. Like I told Will yesterday, if I escaped, I would be exposing the Mageye. And while my treatment was unjust...*

No, I interrupted.

No?

"You really do blame yourself for everything, don't you?" I whispered, my heart aching for him. "You blame yourself for King Brenton being alive, and back then, you blamed yourself for Sophie's dad being alive."

"There is a reality that if I had dragged King Brenton into the volcano..." He caught himself, his shoulders slumping. "You were right last night, when you said if he wasn't alive, there could still be other Volcaniacs. Still makes me angry, still makes me feel guilty, but..."

"Not your fault."

He shook his head, staring at his feet. "Not sure how I feel about her dad or my treatment. Angry is probably the best word."

"Wronged," I murmured. We passed a section of mountain with missing trees and I gazed across the sea of green below.

A little ahead, Will scurried past the opening, steering Mercy to walk on his right by the now-hidden drop.

Myles watched them too, though his gaze seemed to linger on Sophie, who laughed as Mercy and Will each took one of her hands, swinging them as we walked.

I killed three men in order to protect her, and then, hardly a year later, I found out that the man who wanted her dead the most was still alive, and I couldn't do anything about it, he said. The whole time I was in that cell, I wanted to escape and return to Mageye City to ensure Soph was okay. But I couldn't. Not without exposing the Mageye. When I was sworn into the Elite Guard, I vowed my loyalty to the city even if that meant sacrificing my life.

Lightning sparked between his fingers and he clenched his hands to stifle it, whispering aloud, "It doesn't matter if it is my fault that King Brenton is still alive, or Soph's dad for that matter. My duty is to protect the city." He waved between me, Mercy, Sophie, and Will. "Protect all of you. Believe it or not, but I don't regret a lot of what I've done to keep Mageye City safe. Hurting people, taking lives... I hate it and if I were to quit, it would probably be because of guilt and not my own pain... but I don't regret it."

I took his hand. "I'm sorry that happened to you. You didn't deserve it." My heart skipped a beat as he intertwined his fingers with mine. "I'm glad you got away."

His expression softened and he smiled. "Me too."

I held his gaze, my heart racing. "I couldn't imagine life without you in it. I don't think any of us could, but sometimes..." I hesitated, my cheeks flushing. "I want to be friends forever, no matter what else happens."

A smile twisted his lips. "I think I can promise that."

"Good," I agreed, loosening my grip on his hand. "And you you don't break promises, right? You said that when you promised to get the teleportation crystal in the volcano."

He placed his hand over his heart. "I swear it."

I tentatively placed my hand over his. "Good," I repeated myself and his smile widened.

As we rejoined the others, Sophie pointed at something in the distance. "What's that?"

The mountainside opened into a steep cliff with a waterfall flowing over it. Except, instead of flowing down the mountain, the water appeared to be flowing up.

Will took a few steps closer, eyes round with wonder. "It's magic."

"We assumed," Mercy said. "Seeing as we don't normally see waterfalls going uphill."

He waved her away, studying the waterfall. "Normally, I feel the magic in a source of water long before I see it. Why didn't I sense it earlier?"

"It's magic." Myles shrugged. "Magic is never predictable."

"Always expect the unexpected to be unexpected," I quoted.

"Exactly," Myles agreed.

"Will, can you tell if the waterfall itself is magic, or if it is just the water?" Sophie asked.

He tore his gaze from the cliff. "What do you mean?"

"Would the water still have magic if we took some, or does it only last while in the current?"

"Oh, I see." Will tilted his head, and his aura shifted. "It's both. The waterfall is made of magic water."

Sophie smiled. "Would it be a good idea for you to take some with us, kind of like how Rose has the Golden Dove feathers?"

"That could work, but I want to get closer first," Will said. "I can't be certain from this distance."

Myles looked a little uneasy. "We will have to be careful carrying something magical with us. It will be one more aura for King Brenton and the Volcaniacs to detect."

I fidgeted. "Didn't we decide not to trust auras anymore? At least not without guidance from the stars."

All eyes turned to Mercy and she smiled. "The stars acknowledge the waterfall's existence. It's not an illusion."

"Good," Will mused. "I don't think we need to worry about carrying an extra aura with us, Myles. We aren't masking yet anyway, and even if we were, the presence of magic water shouldn't alarm the Volcaniacs very much."

Myles relented. "Its aura is neutral, though it will likely lean one way or the other depending on who wields it."

"Let's hope my hands make it lean a good way," Will declared, setting off towards the waterfall.

Myles looked between Will and the waterfall, deadpan. "Will?"

"Yeah?" Will glanced back.

"Why walk there when it's in sight and I can teleport?"

Mercy laughed. "Could you teleport us, Myles?"

"Sure," Myles agreed, holding a hand out for me and Sophie. "Thanks for asking."

A purple orb formed around us and we reappeared beside the reverse waterfall.

Will peered eagerly at the water, studying it before splashing in. "Myles was right about it leaning good or bad depending on who uses it."

A light, rejuvenating mist sprinkled us from the water rising over the cliff. The flow continued up the mountain before disappearing into a small cavern.

"What magical properties does it have?" Mercy asked.

Will waved his hand, and water arced high above our heads. "It makes me stronger." He winked at Myles. "And fearless. I'm not even thinking about that cliff right now."

Myles rolled his eyes, but grinned as he took the stopper out of one of our waterskins and poured out its contents, careful not to let it splash into the magical stream.

He held out the empty pouch to Will. "Let's take some. As much as we can afford."

"We have five waterskins between us," Will said. "I think we could use two for the magic water, and the other three will be enough for drinking."

I knelt by the stream and stuck my fingers in. The water was cold and crystal clear. "Water isn't a worry with you around. We will always be able to find it."

"That definitely makes things easier," Sophie agreed, tracing a finger through the water beside me. "And less stressful."

Will finished filling the waterskins and hopped out on the other side of the stream. "All right, I'm ready."

He bounced on his toes, and Mercy smiled. "The magic has really energized you, hasn't it?"

"Yep." Will grinned. "I feel like I could run all the way to King Brenton's palace."

Myles laughed. "I guess we know who's taking the first watch tonight."

Waves crashed in Will's irises, as energetic as his bouncing feet. "Sure. I don't mind."

"Am I the only one worried about what pranks or ideas he's going to come up with, with this much energy?" Sophie whispered to me and Mercy.

Mercy shook his head. "No. I am *very* worried about that."

I laughed. "Me too."

As we began our hike, Will's strides were steady and firm. If only we could have taken the whole stream with us, then we would have no trouble fighting King Brenton.

Chapter 20

It took us another two days to cross the mountains, and with the towering shadows no longer behind us, I felt exposed. Though, that had less to do with the missing mountains on the horizon, and more to do with Mercy's official declaration that, distance-wise, we were at the halfway mark.

With a controlled vision from the night before fresh on my mind, I eyed the trees suspiciously. "I have a question," I announced slowly, turning to Myles.

"Go ahead." He dropped his satchel down as we were taking a break, and I wrung my hands.

"When we broke into The End, King Brenton knew we were inside even when we masked our auras. Now, I know that probably had to do with the map because he lost us when we masked after that, but do you think the controlled visions will alert him once we get within a certain radius?"

"I hope not." Will flopped down by a fallen log. "That would be incredibly inconvenient."

Mercy rolled her eyes. "Not to mention dangerous."

"The danger would be the inconvenient part." Will scrunched his nose. "We have to be able to mask or there isn't a way for us to create any form of ambush."

"Well, from my understanding, controlled visions really only give him access to us when we are sleeping," Myles said carefully.

"Don't sleepwalk into the palace and it should be safe."

Sophie looked between us, the quartz in her irises glittering in the sun. "At what point do we start masking? And... what about our powers?"

"We start masking when we are close enough for our auras to be detected," Mercy mused. "The stars can't tell me that, though."

"But maybe we can," Myles said, tapping his fingers while he thought. "Create an artificial radius?"

"Based off of what?" I asked.

"The map." He sat up straighter. "And our experience from The End. King Brenton had a fifty-mile radius around the volcano, with more protection the closer we got to it. I think it is safe to assume he will have layered protection around his palace as well." He trailed off, lightning flickering in his purple iris.

"All right..." he continued slowly. "The map we found in Gray's hut, and even the staggering of the towers was set mathematically even. Five miles, fifteen, fifty. Divisible by five... We will decide when to mask based off of the presence of auras, but in regards to using our powers, namely my teleporting, let's mimic the map. Since the first Volcaniac we saw was one hundred miles from The End, we can use that as our outer border... and double it."

"Double it?" Will asked. "So, we teleport until the stars say we are two hundred miles away from the palace?"

I frowned. "Two hundred miles would take days for us to travel without teleporting."

"I know." Myles turned east, towards the palace. "The issue is, I don't want to risk suddenly appearing in the midst of danger. At least, with the volcano, we knew in a general sense what it would look like."

"What if we give ourselves that estimate, and we reevaluate once we are within the radius?" Mercy suggested.

"That might be the best option," I agreed reluctantly.

"And will the same rule apply to the rest of our powers?" Sophie asked. "How will we travel two hundred miles without Mercy's guidance from the stars?"

Myles looked between Sophie and Mercy. "Well, you can use powers whilst masked, it just takes more energy. The main trouble is because my power pulses when I teleport, and even shoot lightning. It's really only my mindreading that is never detectable."

I held up my hands and examined my palms. "Last time, when we crossed The End, my sore feet and sunburns healed as we walked without announcing our presence."

"Exactly." Myles nodded. "Certain powers work within their own limits on top of additional control from the Mageye themselves. Rose can't turn off when she heals herself, but she can decide when to heal others. Soph can decide when to turn invisible, or it happens when she feels strong emotions. Mercy's conversations with the stars are constant, but she can ask more direct questions to strengthen the connection."

Will hummed, stretching out his legs. "I have pulled tricks with my power even when masked. It just takes more focus."

"It's like swimming underwater," Myles explained. "Even though we aren't breathing, we can swim, it just has a shorter limit than when we swim at the surface."

Will raised his hand. "Well—"

"Excluding Will's power," Myles said, rolling his eyes. "If we went swimming without you, we would have stricter limits."

I smiled. "So, in that case, the two hundred mile radius is specific to Myles's teleporting. And we will reevaluate once we are able to scope out the area. The rest of us will need to be more cautious with our powers while we are masked, but we can use them as long as we don't unveil ourselves... un*mask*."

"That sounds fair," Mercy agreed.

Will nodded, pulling a branch from behind his back and tossing it aside. "What I got from that is that Myles will be our danger detector once we get closer."

"Isn't he already our danger detector?" Sophie asked with a soft smile.

"Danger detector?" Myles tsked. "What am I to you, some weapon?"

"Well, yeah... that and a source of convenient transport," I said mischievously.

Will snickered. "Precisely."

"Watch your mouths, or I might leave one or two of you behind on our next jump." The corner of Myles's mouth twitched. "Less people is easier."

Sophie began giggling hysterically. "They'll be our lost luggage."

Myles burst out laughing. "Now we're talking."

"Lost? I think in Will's case, it will be blissfully forgotten," Mercy said cheekily.

"Why is it that I'm always the one you all want to yell at or get rid of?" Will protested.

Mercy's eyes sparkled. "Because you're the most annoying."

"I don't annoy you." He turned to Myles for backup. "Do I?"

"I'd prefer not to answer that."

Will put his hand to his chest in mock hurt. "You don't like me? That's offensive. What have I ever done to you?"

"Well, you did shove whiskey down his throat," I reminded him.

Will's face lit up with his signature, mischievous grin. "That was an outstanding performance on my part, don't you think?" He gasped, sitting up straight. "You know what would have made it even better? I should have made the whiskey come out of the bottle and down his throat that way. He wouldn't have spit up nearly as much."

"It sounds like you're trying to kill me." Myles groaned. "What if it went in my lungs?"

Will rolled his eyes dramatically. "I would have called it back out, *duh.*"

"Yeah, Myles. It's not like whiskey in your lungs would cause damage or anything," Sophie sassed.

I giggled; I had never heard her say something so bold before.

Myles buried his face in his hand. "Whiskey burns your throat; I don't want to know what it feels like in your lungs."

"It probably would feel like Will was attempting to murder you," I said.

Myles threw his hands in the air. "*Thank* you. Finally, someone who agrees that I was tortured."

"Wait," Mercy said. "We're picking sides? Then I agree that it was unnecessarily uncomfortable for Myles."

"What?" Will protested. "Are you all on Myles's side? Who got us into the inn, me or him?"

"You did," Myles admitted reluctantly.

"Exactly!"

Myles huffed. "And it worked, but that doesn't mean I enjoyed the experience."

"I enjoyed it," Will whispered, snickering. "Next time, I'll give you a warning."

"Trust me," Myles said, standing. "There won't be a next time."

✕

"What exactly is our plan once we get there?" Mercy asked, turning her gaze from the sun. "King Duncan wants us to finish the Volcaniacs for good. Does that mean we need to track down any Volcaniacs not at the palace? Like the one who created illusions?"

"We need to get rid of King Brenton," Myles said. "Without a leader, the Volcaniacs will be defeated. Once they realize that..." He sighed. "Our job will be nearly done."

"They might seek revenge, though," I countered, kicking a

rock ahead of myself as we walked. "And if we had announced to the illusion Mageye that King Brenton was already dead, he wouldn't have believed us."

"That's true," he confessed. "But some of the weaker members may fall off. Remember, Marlon admitted he wasn't as loyal as we would have expected. And yes, Mercy, I think we will need to track anyone outside of the palace down, unless we get confirmation that everyone is actively there."

Sophie hugged her arms around herself. "What about Mercy's original question? What is our plan when we get there?"

Myles held up a hand, watching lightning flicker between his fingers. "I don't know yet. It's like with my teleporting, we guessed a radius where it will be declared 'unsafe,' but we won't really know that for sure until we are there."

"Yeah," she agreed softly. "I guess so."

"What we need is a magical weapon," Will announced. "The right weapon could answer all of those questions without needing to wait until we get there."

"A magical weapon?" I asked skeptically—watching as the rock I had been kicking bounced under a bush. "How do we find a magical weapon?"

He held up one of his waterskins. "We found the reverse waterfall, didn't we? Magical weapons are out there, you just need to take the time to find them."

"There is a difference between a magical object we can use as a weapon and an actual magical weapon," Myles said cautiously.

"Wouldn't just one more *magical object* be better than the weapons we have now?"

A large fallen tree blocked our path and Myles gave me his hand to help me up. Will lifted Sophie on top and then gave Mercy a hand.

"What kind of magical object are you talking about?" Mercy said as she hopped down on the other side. "I think we got lucky with the reverse waterfall, Will. Yes, it's possible to find magic *weapons*, but I don't know if we can have enough hope in finding one to make it worth it."

"Maybe with the right mindset, a magical object will call us," Will suggested. "Happens with portals all the time."

"How do we know the magical object we sense will be helpful?" Sophie said. "What if we go out of our way to find it, and it ends up being something we can't use? Or a trap, like that fake portal."

"What if we go out of our way to find it, and it ends up being something we *can* use?" Will challenged. "If we go beyond auras and have Mercy confirm it is real with the stars, it won't be a trap."

I patted my pocket over the box I kept the Golden Dove feathers in. King Brenton had plenty of magical weapons up his sleeve; maybe it *was* time to get some of our own.

Myles must have thought the same, because he said, "Keeping a lookout for a potential surprise weapon won't hurt us or slow our pace. What if we stay open to the possibility of going on a detour, and *if* we sense something, we make our final decision then?"

Will nodded. "Fair enough. If it works, great. If it doesn't, we'll think of something else when we get to the palace. For now, we at least have a *potential* start of a plan."

Mercy nodded, but Sophie flickered. "But what if even with the stars, it *is* a trap? Or what if it's in a dangerous location, and someone gets hurt trying to get it? Yes, Rose can heal us, but it would be better if she didn't have to."

"We will be able to tell from its aura if it is a trap," Will encouraged. "And the stars have never tricked Mercy."

Sophie didn't appear at all convinced and Will waved his hand around us. "We don't check out every good aura we sense. If the Volcaniacs wanted to set another ambush, I don't think they would do it that way."

Sophie frowned, but her edges became more solid. "I still

think it is a risky idea."

"Which is why we will decide to pursue it as a team if or when we notice the aura," Will promised. "We won't rush into anything recklessly. If we can't get it safely, we will either find a way to get it, or let it go. But it won't hurt to at least keep a lookout, right?"

Sophie sighed. "I guess you're right. Keeping a lookout won't cause any problems. I'm just worried the Volcaniacs will try to do something. I don't want to face the illusion Mageye again." Her quartz eyes seemed to reflect the sunlight as she continued, "But if he does try to attack us, we will face him together, right?"

"Right," Myles agreed, his expression grim as he addressed me telepathically. *I don't think we need to fear another ambush. They trick us when they want something. With Gray, it was to send us to The End quicker. With the illusion Mageye, it was to learn our fears.*

As logical as that outlook was, it was a risky hope to indulge fully upon. *Wouldn't it be better for them to capture us before we arrive? Otherwise, we will learn how their security works. We are already using what we utilized in The End to prepare for breaking into the palace.*

If we are caught, whether it is before or after we arrive, I don't see them ever giving us an opportunity to escape.

That sent my heart racing. *You mean if we are caught, it's over?*

He shut his eyes and nodded. *We cannot afford to have doubts about the success of our mission, and I truly believe we have the ability to defeat the Volcaniacs.*

But you have more fears than you let on.

Yes.

I had more fears than I let on, too. *Would a magical weapon help relieve those fears?*

Yes, he repeated.

Then we need to find a magical weapon.

Myles glanced at Sophie, then back to me. *Will has thought more about this than he told us. I trust his plan.*

I nodded, and he held his hand out to me. "Let's teleport," he said aloud. "And if anyone senses anything magical, let us know."

Chapter 21

"Good morning," Sophie greeted as I sat up. Her blonde hair glowed in the morning light and she smiled.

I stretched, my body feeling sluggish from lack of sleep. I had tossed and turned all night, but there had been no visions. "Morning. Was your shift peaceful?"

"Yes. I watched the sunrise."

"Hmmm, sunrise?" Mercy mumbled, rolling over and falling back asleep.

We exchanged looks and giggled. "What time are we supposed to wake them up?" I asked, moving to sit next to Sophie.

She hugged her knees to her chest. "I usually wait for Myles, because he doesn't feel as bad about waking us."

"That's because he is only tired when sleep is overdue, not when he wakes up," I said.

"He was like that when he saved me," she said, resting her head on my shoulder.

Sunlight slowly streamed through the trees, and sure enough, when Myles was up, he was on his feet and ready to go almost immediately.

"We'll give them a few more minutes," he said, nodding at Mercy and Will.

Sophie and I exchanged looks and giggled again.

Myles stretched, peering down at us. "What's so funny?"

"You," I answered. "It's weird how quickly you get up in the mornings."

"Maybe the rest of you are slow," he teased.

I don't need to be able to read minds to know you're the weird one, I told him.

He snickered and stepped over Will to grab his satchel from the pile we had left them in. *I have to say, I have never been bullied on a mission as badly as I have on this one.*

Bullied? You haven't been bullied.

I woke up to two of my best friends laughing at me, he scolded. "I see that smirk, Soph," he added aloud.

"What smirk?" Sophie crossed her arms. "I'm not smirking."

"Liar," Myles whispered as he stepped back over. "Now if you two slowpokes will excuse me, I have people to wake up."

Will grumbled when he was awoken, telling Myles to wake him again when it was time to go.

I reached over and nudged Will. "You need to get up quick to prove a point for me and Sophie."

He rolled onto his back, his arms and legs spread out like a star. "Ugh. I'm up."

"Thank you."

Mercy sat up next, pausing to shut her eyes. When she reopened them, the reflection of the night sky was gone, replaced by the galaxy from afar.

After a little more teasing, we started the day with a jump. It was a cool day, and after our agreement that a magical weapon would be beneficial, I sorted through every aura around us for any hints.

Will turned to me, sunlit waves washing softly in his irises. "How far out can you sense auras, Rose?"

"I don't know exactly," I said. "I can usually sense things around the same time as Myles, but he notices them first."

"You can sense out at least a few miles for sure," Myles said.

"But how far exactly? How do you know how far your reach is?" I asked.

"King Duncan and General Cornstone had me practice expanding my aura. One of them would go into Mageye City, and I would have to find them using nothing but my aura. As my aura strengthened, they would have to go continually farther from the palace."

"I didn't know you could strengthen your aura like that." I looked at Myles with wide eyes. "What else did you do for training?"

A sudden mischievous look lit his gaze. "Do you mean training in general, or specifically the training I did with King Duncan and General Cornstone?"

"Why do I have a feeling there is a difference?"

"Because there is," he said innocently, holding a branch out of the way as we walked.

Sophie laughed. "I remember one of the things you did."

"Really?" Myles nudged her, letting the branch swing back into place. "And what, may I ask, is it that you remember?"

She giggled. "Myles isn't allowed in the East Tower of the palace."

"What?" Will said.

"Is that why your room is the only one on the west side?" I asked. "I always thought it was weird that King Duncan and General Cornstone were on the opposite side."

"You exposed me, Soph!"

"You wanted to know what I remember, and that is what I remember!"

Mercy laughed. "What did you do that got you *banned* from the East Tower?"

"I was training," Myles began, "and, well, King Duncan didn't approve of my method."

"What method did you use?" I asked. Being banned from a

part of the palace he was raised in, when he had begun traveling solo as young as twelve seemed... well... like the rumors he was rowdy when he was younger were correct.

"I wanted to practice the timing and precision of my jumps," he explained. "And I decided to practice in the East Tower."

"In the tower or on the tower?" Will asked, switching his satchel to his other shoulder.

"*Off* the tower."

"Off?" Mercy furrowed her brow.

"Yes, off. The East Tower has open windows on every side with nothing but a foot-high ledge to block them. My plan was to jump off and teleport at the very last second, right before I hit the ground. How impressive would that have been?"

"And how dangerous." I stared at him in shock. "You could have died."

He looked suddenly sheepish, but still smirked. "King Duncan stopped me. If he had grabbed me a second later, I would have taken us both off the tower. He was *furious*. Gosh, I've never seen him so mad. He sat me down in his office and yelled for ages. He said if he ever caught me in the East Tower again, he would never let me leave Mageye City. I wasn't allowed to use any of my powers for a month, my room was moved to the opposite side of the palace—so I would be as far from the East Tower as possible—and King Duncan told me I wasn't allowed to go on any missions until I proved that I was responsible enough to be trusted again."

I stared. The only time I had heard King Duncan raise his voice was when he was teasing Myles and told him to get his butt back in his office. "He must have been really furious."

Myles nodded. "I was furious, as well. I didn't speak to him for almost a week after that, General Cornstone, either."

"What made you start speaking to them again?" I asked.

"After I found out my punishment, I ranted to General Cornstone and told him how horrible King Duncan was. Well,

General Cornstone told me I was lucky he wasn't in charge, because if he had a say, my position in the Elite Guard would have been revoked permanently. That, of course, ticked me off, so I stormed out and slammed the door as hard as I could." He smiled a little. "But General Cornstone spoke with King Duncan and managed to convince him that he might have been too harsh."

"Wait, but I thought General Cornstone wanted your position in the Elite Guard taken away?" Will asked. "Why'd he help you?"

"I think he remembered a certain other impulsive thirteen-year-old who got involved in more than a few stupid stunts." Myles smiled, the shadows from the canopy above us making the lightning in his purple iris seem to flash brighter.

An image of a young King Duncan came to mind, racing around the palace while General Cornstone attempted to wrangle him.

King Duncan had been a young king, and similar to how Myles was in line to the throne not through blood but through relationship, King Duncan had no blood relation to the previous ruler, King Fabian. General Cornstone had been twenty-six when the proclamation was made, and from my understanding, he and King Duncan had been inseparable ever since. Though, that was likely because General Cornstone was on babysitting duty for the first few years of King Duncan's reign.

"Do you think you would have been able to pull off the stunt if King Duncan hadn't intervened?" Mercy asked.

Myles ran a hand through his hair. "No, he saved my life. I scared him and that's why he was so angry."

"Imagine getting yelled at by a king?" Will asked, putting a hand to his heart dramatically. "That must be terrifying."

"Not as much as you might think. He raised me, so his yelling at me is more like a dad yelling at his son than anything else. I respect him as my king, but I often look at him outside his status."

"General Cornstone, too?" I asked.

He laughed. "Getting yelled at by General Cornstone is terrifying. I would take a scolding from King Duncan over General Cornstone any day."

"Is it possible," I teased, "that you're *scared* of General Cornstone?"

"Not scared, just cautiously respectful."

"What does 'cautiously respectful' even mean?" Mercy swatted a gnat away from her face. "It sounds like a fancy way to say scared to me."

"I'm not scared of General Cornstone," Sophie said with a smile. "He used to give me piggyback rides and pretend I was a princess."

Myles nodded, his expression softening. "He adores you, Soph. He'd sooner yell at someone for looking at you the wrong way than yell at you."

Sophie smiled, her eyes almost seeming to sparkle. "I love him."

"He's a good man," Myles agreed.

I trailed my hand along the top of some tall wildflowers. "I bet you could jump from the East Tower and time your jump now. That's what you did when the Wolvien Guard almost caught us the first time and in the volcano."

"King Duncan practiced with me," Myles said. "After I was ungrounded. He found a lake with a cliff to jump from and I practiced there."

Will narrowed his gaze. "I'm not sure I like the idea of jumping off a cliff into water... but it's water, so..."

"We should visit that lake when we get back to Mageye City," Mercy said, wrapping an arm around Will's shoulder. "Help you get over your fear since the loft trick with Uncle Ethan didn't work as well as you both thought."

"Or we could find a waterfall," I mused. "Ride down it before graduating to the cliff."

"I'm... tempted," Will admitted. "The waterfall might be a fair start."

Myles slowed his pace as we continued discussing the waterfall idea, and I paused. "Myles?"

His brow was furrowed and I followed his gaze. My heart seemed to skip a beat and a smile teased my lips. A faint aura lay ahead, and it felt helpful.

"What's wrong?" Sophie asked, watching Myles worriedly.

Will was the one who answered, a grin already spreading across his face. "A magical weapon."

Myles nodded, and Mercy turned her gaze to the sun, taking a small breath of relief. "It's real," she said. "Should we try to find it?"

"Yes," Myles and Will agreed simultaneously.

"It feels helpful," Myles added, quoting my previous thought. "I think we should check it out."

Sophie fidgeted. "I don't sense anything."

"I don't either," Mercy said. "But the stars do, and they have never led me astray."

I took a small step towards the aura. "I agree with Will and Myles. I think we should pursue it."

"Are you sure it isn't dangerous?" Sophie fretted.

"Positive," I assured her.

She sighed, but nodded. "I trust you all. Let's try to find it."

Mercy wasn't as hesitant. "I think we should take any help we can get."

"All right!" Will pumped his fist into the air. "It's settled. Let's get ourselves a magical weapon and not die in the process!"

"How about we don't die, period?" I said with a raised eyebrow.

"That's what I said. Don't die."

"You said don't die in the process of getting the magical weapon. You didn't say anything about whether or not we can die *after* we get the weapon. And I say we don't die at all."

Mercy laughed. "It sounds like what Will meant to say was, 'let's get ourselves a magical weapon and not die at all!'"

"Much better!" I agreed.

✕

"Does anyone have any idea what the aura could be coming from?" I asked once Sophie and Mercy had also picked up on the magical presence.

"Not really," Myles said. "I imagine it is some sort of plant or stone. Something tangible that we can pick up."

"Would plucking a flower destroy its magic?" I asked.

"That would depend on the flower. We'll have to see when we find it."

As the aura strengthened, the assurance it was something good strengthened with it. And then something tugged my waist, as if an invisible rope was gently reeling me in. "It's calling us," I said with a smile.

"Yes." Will looked pleased. "It wants us to find it."

Soon though, I noticed a second aura, but unlike the first, this one was uneasily familiar.

Myles glanced at me. *Are you okay?*

There is another aura.

He turned back in the direction of the aura calling us and paused. "Wait a second," he said.

"What's up?" Will asked.

"Rose noticed another aura." His brow furrowed. "I know that aura," he murmured. "But from where?"

I nodded. "I recognize it, too."

"What do you mean?" Will looked between us, his head cocked to the side as he searched for the aura. "That baddish one? It feels pretty weak to me; it's probably only a territorial squirrel or something."

"A territorial squirrel doesn't have a bad aura, Will," Mercy said dryly.

"And how would you know? Have you ever come in contact with a territorial squirrel?" He gave a fake shudder. "I have. It wasn't pleasant."

Myles stared at him, and I could sense he was reading Will's mind. Finally, he said, "I did not need to know that. And the aura we feel right now is only vaguely familiar. I don't think it is anything to worry about, at least not yet."

Sophie stepped back and the trees became visible behind her. "Is it bad that you and Rose both recognize it?" she asked.

"I don't know," Myles said. "But we shouldn't let an uncomfortable feeling stop us from getting the help a magical object is offering."

A non-territorial squirrel skittered up a nearby tree, flicking its tail as it watched us pass.

Both auras continued to strengthen, but the good one outweighed the bad, and I let my stance relax.

Will smiled. "There's a lake."

I squinted ahead and flashes of blue lit between the trees. Sand surrounded the water and something stood on the beach. Something red and orange.

It looked like some sort of tarp or canvas. Maybe someone had a camp by the lake?

The others hadn't noticed, and I hesitated before catching up to them. Will was theorizing what the magical weapon would be, but I kept my gaze locked on the glimpses of red and orange until a break in the trees allowed the cart into full view.

I stopped walking and opened my mouth to give a warning, but no sound came out.

No wonder I had recognized the bad aura; it belonged to the man who had almost torn my life apart. A man I had assumed was gone from my life forever now that his job was done.

My voice hardly sounded like my own when I finally got the warning out. "The trader."

Chapter 22

The flamelike pattern on the canvas was unmistakable. The trader was here. Within shouting distance. Maybe even within sight.

Myles stepped past me, hand on the dagger at his waist, and I snapped out of my frozen state enough to grab him. My fingers dug into his wrist, but he hardly flinched.

"Myles," I said.

He stepped back. "We're going to get rid of him," he vowed.

"He's dangerous," I whispered, glancing at Mercy, Will, and Sophie. "And maybe he will have information we can use."

"Who owns the cart?" Will asked. Waves crashed in his irises and he had his finger on the top of his waterskin, ready to pop it off and defend us with its contents.

"The trader…" Sophie said softly. "Rose?" Her voice pitched. "Didn't a trader with a flame-covered cart kidnap your family?"

I nodded, and Mercy gasped.

"He's the one who kidnapped your mom and brothers? That means he's—"

"A Volcaniac." Myles's jaw ticked.

"Which means we need to get rid of him," Will echoed Myles somberly. "But why is he here? Why has he stopped so close to the magical object we are searching for?"

"He's not a Mageye, is he?" Sophie asked. Despite the severity of the situation, she was fully visible, as if her power was saving itself for when it was truly needed.

"No. But his eyes are open, which means he might be able to sense the item we are looking for—and us. It depends on how sensitive he is to magic," Myles said.

"He must be pretty sensitive, since he used so much magic to kidnap my family," I said, still gripping Myles's arm. "Raymond told me he used magic ash to make them fall asleep until he was far enough away from Sunset Hollow to not get caught."

"Magic ashes?" Will asked. "That sounds like something King Brenton would use."

"It does..." Mercy's breath caught. "What if the magical object is *in* his cart? What if he has access to our magical weapon already?"

Purple lightning flashed in Myles's right iris. "Then we'll make him give it up."

I released my tight grip on him and took Ren's jackknife instead, my gaze returning to the cart. A breeze ruffled the tight canvas over the roof, making the flames seem alive. A heavy presence filled my chest and it took me a moment to recognize it. Loathing. Not even King Brenton and his controlled visions filled me with this kind of loathing. Instead, it almost reminded me of the level of fear the illusion Mageye had triggered. A feeling that went down into my very veins, a feeling that went beyond emotions and instead tangibly existed.

I had never been a hateful person, but I carried nothing but loathing for the trader who kidnapped my family. "Whether or not he has our magical weapon, we are confronting him," I stated.

Myles lifted a hand towards the cart, but caught himself before blasting it with lightning. "We need to find him first. He might not be inside."

My knuckles were white around the jackknife in my hand, but I didn't loosen my grip as we approached through the trees.

Will's breath hitched. His eyes had glued to the lake, excited waves crashing in them like a temperamental sea. "It's in the lake," he breathed.

"The trader?" Sophie asked doubtfully.

Will blinked a couple times, refocusing on us. "The magical object. It's not in the trader's cart. It's in the lake."

"In the lake, or it *is* the lake?" Mercy clarified.

"In."

Myles took a step back. "Can you tell what it is?"

"Yes," Will murmured, awe filling his gaze as he continued examining the lake. "It's a crystal, but I don't know what it does or what it looks like."

"That's good. I don't want him touching it," Myles said. "We need to find him before we figure out how to handle this."

His voice filled my head. *He isn't going to hurt your family again.*

Tears filled my gaze, and I wiped my eyes before they fell. *He isn't going to hurt* anyone *ever again. Not after this.*

Myles stared straight forward, but nodded. *Never again.*

Tall reeds stretched along the side of the lake, and we used them as cover to get closer.

Myles suddenly froze, motioning for us to stop. "There he is," he declared, his voice tight.

The trader stood by the far edge of the lake at the base of a sheer cliff. He paced, staring at a specific spot on the water. From where we stood, there wasn't anything special about the spot.

"That's where the crystal is," Will whispered. "The spot he's looking at. But there is no way he will be able to get it without the help of magic. The lake is deep, and the crystal is at the bottom."

"Shh," Myles shushed, a concentrated expression on his face. No one spoke while Myles strained to read the trader's mind. "He sells magical items," he said slowly. "And creatures."

"Who can you sell magic to in Alveraada?" Will asked. "The Volcaniacs, obviously, but if he is one of them, would they really be his clients?"

Mercy crossed her arms. "It sounds more like a black market

to me."

"That's exactly what it is," Myles said, watching as the trader approached the water.

"Does he have any magical creatures in his cart now?" Sophie asked, tears welling in her eyes.

"Yes," Myles said stiffly. "I can sense their auras. But don't worry, Soph, we'll free them."

"Surely he has weapons," Mercy said. "Doesn't that make this risky?"

"It does, but it's no riskier than defeating the Volcaniacs at their palace," Myles said. "Right now, all I know is that he can sense the crystal and is trying to get it because he knows it will be worth a lot of money in the magical world."

"You mean he's not getting it for King Brenton?" I asked, my grip loosening on the jackknife. "But he's a Volcaniac."

"I don't know." He hesitated, adding darkly, "But I wouldn't hesitate to bet that he would love to bring *us* to King Brenton, regardless of anything else."

"We won't give him that chance," I said, tracing my thumb across the *R* on the jackknife. "We need to find out what he knows about King Brenton's current plan, then dispose of him."

"And we still need to get the crystal," Mercy pointed out.

The reeds we hid in rustled as Myles moved to get a better angle of the trader. "We need to deal with the trader first. If he catches us trying to get the crystal, it will only make things worse."

The trader and the crystal. He waded ankle-deep now, before turning and moving farther along the lake.

The sun shone as mid-afternoon, and my heart began to sink. "I don't think we have time for both. By the time we deal with the trader, it will be dark, and we can't afford to stay in one place too long."

Will's expression fell and Mercy looked to the sun for another answer, but there didn't seem to be one. It was one or the other.

"Or both at once," Myles said as if reading my mind—which he had probably done.

My eyes widened. "How would we do that?"

Lightning flickered in his right iris. "Will, is it possible for you to keep someone else from getting wet, or can you only keep yourself dry?"

"It's like your teleporting. I can do multiple people, it just takes slightly more energy. Why?"

"I think you and Rose should get the crystal, while Mercy, Soph, and I interrogate the trader and hijack his cart."

"What?" Sophie said, growing translucent. "Split up?"

"Yes. Rose and I can communicate telepathically. And the three of us can ensure the trader doesn't try to stop them."

"That sounds pretty dangerous," Mercy said. "What if something goes wrong with one group? How will the other group help?"

"King Duncan said part of the reason our powers work so well together is we can stay in contact with each other even if we split up. I think it's time we do that," Myles urged.

I shook my head. "I want to talk to the trader." My voice shook. "I can't not confront him, not after what he did. He didn't just wrong me, he kidnapped my family, he burned our home, he tried to destroy our *lives*. And for what? Because King Brenton asked him, or because he wanted a reward? Because he is an awful excuse for a human being? I... I want to..." My voice caught and I took a small step back despite myself, speaking in barely above a whisper, "I want to see his face when he realizes he has lost."

Myles straightened his stance, his gaze locked on my face. *I don't want him hurting you. He has caused enough harm already.*

He kidnapped my family, I argued, waving my hands for emphasis while Mercy, Will, and Sophie watched, no longer able to hear the conversation. *I want revenge. Or justice. Whatever you want to call it.*

He doesn't deserve the satisfaction of laying his eyes on you after what he did. Myles stepped closer. *I need to be in the group that confronts him because my mindreading and lightning gives me the best-suited power for an interrogation. At the end of the day, he is a normal human who can see into our world, and I can take him from it.*

My thumb again traced the R and I studied the trader. He was walking back to his cart, probably to get some sort of magical tool to retrieve the crystal with. Oblivious that standing across the lake was his biggest mistake.

Me.

And Myles.

But more than my family was at stake this time. All of Mageye City depended on us. I sighed, reluctantly slipping the jackknife into my pocket.

Myles took my hand. "We are too close to the crystal to pass it up, and with the trader in front of us, we can't let him slip away."

"All right," I agreed. "You win. Will and I will get the crystal, and you three will end the trader."

Relief flitted across his expression and he released my hand, leaving me with strangely empty air in my grip. "What does everyone else think?"

"I don't mind it," Will said. "But we need a rendezvous point."

"How about we meet back where we first saw the trader at sunset?" Mercy suggested.

Myles shielded his eyes to judge the angle of the sun and nodded. "That should give us plenty of time to finish our jobs."

Sophie took a deep breath and tied her hair back from her face. "This is what we are here to do, isn't it? Stop the Volcaniacs for good."

She was right. This was our first chance to ambush a Volcaniac and not vice versa.

We had to take it.

Chapter 23

When Myles, Mercy, and Sophie disappeared with an electric snap, I stared at the spot they had stood. *God, please watch over them.*

Will turned away first. "We need to get in the lake without the trader seeing us."

The trader was currently rummaging through his cart, but he could turn at any moment, which made running straight into the lake from the reeds too risky.

It seemed no matter how close the reeds or trees went around the lake, there was empty sand that would allow us to be spotted.

The reeds rustled as we pushed closer to the lake for a better look. About a quarter of the way around the beach, large boulders rose from the water and scattered about on the sand. Many of them were large enough to provide cover.

"Is there a limit to how far and long you can keep us both underwater?" I asked.

Will's eyes narrowed as he studied the boulders. "Water gives me energy, remember?"

"Yes. But too much of whatever fuels your power can be a bad thing," I said, reflecting on how Myles had attempted to overload King Brenton when he caused the volcano to erupt.

"That would be true in a stormy sea. In a calm lake, it won't overpower me."

"Then can we sneak in using those boulders as cover?"

Waves crashed in his irises. "This will be fun."

With our backs to the trader as we wove through the reeds, I grew stiff. The man who kidnapped my family was within *shouting distance*.

"Myles told me he is hoping to interrogate Volcaniacs with his mindreading," Will said quietly. "You know, to make sure we aren't missing anything. So, I really think it's for the best we split up like this."

I sighed. "I'm angry at the trader for what he did."

"Of course you are. And the two of us are going to steal the crystal he wants from right under his ugly nose."

My lip twitched. "I hadn't thought of that." The reeds now blocked our view of the trader and I relaxed my shoulders. "Thanks, Will."

He nodded, now studying the still surface of the lake. "Want to tell Myles we're about to go in?"

"Yes." I shut my eyes, shifting the conversation to telepathic. *We are about to go in the water.*

The comforting pressure of Myles's aura presented itself. *Good luck.*

Will waited, and when I turned back, he offered a hand. "We need to hold hands so I can keep you dry."

"Like how Myles prefers to hold hands when we teleport?"

He nodded. "I don't need to hold Mercy's hand anymore, but I think that's because we spend so much time together."

I accepted his outstretched hand and we ducked behind the boulders, hurrying to the edge of the water. When the water washed against my ankles, I could feel it, yet my boots and skirts remained dry. It reminded me of my first impression of portal walls. Water that wasn't wet. Using the boulders as cover, we waded out until the water reached our shoulders.

"Ready?" Will asked.

"Is it like swimming?" I asked.

He nodded. "You're going to think this is fun, I promise."

We ducked under the surface and Will created a bubble with us suspended inside. The sides rippled with the movement of the water, but nothing broke through.

I reached out to touch it with my free hand, but froze, turning to Will. "Will it pop if I touch it?"

He touched it, his fingers sliding through. "Nope, I'll keep it intact. Try not to touch it without giving me a heads up, though, or it might break."

Similar to a portal, my hand went out the side without any resistance. I wiggled my fingers curiously. They were wet, as if I were reaching into a bucket of water instead of a submerged bubble in a lake.

My hand dried as I pulled it back in, droplets jumping from my skin and molding back with the bubble wall. "I can see why you think this is fun."

"Water powers," he agreed. "I see no downsides."

I laughed, watching a fish suddenly startle and dart away. "Which way is the crystal?"

"Straight ahead," he answered confidently, making a motion like swimming that drifted him forward.

I copied, keeping a tight hold on his hand and watching the bubble move in awe. Though we remained suspended within the bubble, it morphed as we traveled, giving us the appearance of swimming.

"How are you doing this?" I asked.

He shrugged, looking out at the water. "How do you heal yourself?" he countered.

I hesitated; he had a good point. "But you're controlling it, aren't you? Or are you controlling the water?"

"I'm holding the water back and using this bubble so we can breathe."

I stiffened, almost releasing Will's hand. Wouldn't we need to replenish the air in the bubble? After all, he controlled water, not *air*.

"What's wrong?" he asked, tightening his grip on my hand.

"Is the bubble going to run out of oxygen?"

"No. There is oxygen in water, and it is filtering into our bubble."

I sighed in relief. "Phew."

"Don't breathe like that, though. Taking deep breaths uses it up faster than I can replenish it."

"What?" My heart raced, and I struggled to steady my breathing in a balance between panicked gasping and holding my breath. That was, until I noticed Will was fighting laughter. "Will!"

He lost the fight against his laughter and snickered. "I'm sorry, it was too tempting."

"I can see why Mercy shoves you sometimes," I scolded, glaring at him.

He held up his free hand. "You're right, that was mean. I swear, you aren't going to drown on my watch, though. I would never be able to recover my pride if that happened. And Myles would probably kill me."

"Funny how both of those disadvantages don't involve the fact that I would be dead."

"Whoa, there! You and Mercy made us agree not to die on this mission, remember?"

"This is the part where my brothers would die out of spite. Lucky for you, I'm not in the mood to die today."

"I want to meet your brothers," he decided as we swam deeper into the lake.

I eyed him. "You and Ren would get along a little *too* well." He practically beamed, and I sighed, squeezing his hand. "I'll introduce you, as long as you keep your promise not to let me drown."

He cheered and vowed to the deal. As we continued swimming downwards, I could see why Will had said the lake was too deep to access without magic. A ship could sink in the lake, and you would never know.

Sunlight shone in streaks through the water above, but the rays slowly weakened.

Myles's aura loosely surrounded me like an extension to the bubble, and I ensured I offered him the same assurance that everything was going well in the lake.

A dark shape loomed ahead and we swam straight for it—the cliff we had seen by the lake. It was sheer even under the water, and the pull from the crystal came from the bottom. My fingers itched to grab it as its pull intensified.

Will dropped us at speeds much faster than we could swim, yet everything in the bubble remained calm and free-floating. A soft glow lit up from below, as if a candle was shining through the water with all its might.

"Do you see that?" I asked.

"I think it's the crystal."

As if it understood his words, the magical pull strengthened to the point where it almost felt like we were being physically pulled through the water.

"Yep," Will said. "Definitely the crystal."

We see it, I told Myles.

Good. He has more magical items in the cart than I am comfortable leaving him access to when we confront him. He is searching for the crystal again, and I teleported us inside.

I squeezed Will's hand with my nerves. *Is there anything useful?*

Not to our mission. He had magical butterflies, though, and Soph is freeing them.

My grip relaxed on Will. *Be careful.*

We will.

"They're in the cart," I told Will. "Ransacking it before confronting him."

"That means he might notice the crystal move when we grab it," Will said smugly.

"Distract him further," I agreed with a smile.

The soft glow continued to brighten and we swam to the bottom of the lake. Will directed me on how to get my feet under myself to stand, and we now walked along the sandy bottom.

Nestled at the base of the cliff was a small crystal, roughly the size of a walnut. A blue-white glow shone from the glasslike white crystal, lighting up the lake softly.

"Do you think we can grab it barehanded?" Will asked.

"I don't see why not. It is calling us."

He knelt, keeping a tight grip on my hand as he picked up the crystal. He admired it before handing it to me. "Your pockets are deep enough that it will stay safe."

It was unexpectedly heavy and cold, even though it had just been in Will's warm hand.

"What do you think it does?" I asked as I slipped it into my apron, patting it with satisfaction, and casting a glare towards the beach where the trader likely stood.

Will's face lit up. "Ice."

"Ice? You think it can freeze things?" The weight of the crystal pressed against my thigh, the coolness of it leaking through the fabric.

"Myles will probably know more than we do, but that's my best guess. It is cold and looks like frosty ice."

A slow smile teased my lips. "Ice magic would explain why it was calling us."

His brow furrowed. "It would? I figured it was because we wanted a magical weapon."

"It is. But it's probably also because of what ice does to fire."

"Ice stops fire," Will breathed.

I felt suddenly giddy, proud of our accomplishment. "We did it, then. We found a weapon that stands a fighting chance against King Brenton."

Will grinned. "Now, all we need to do is get back."

Chapter 24

The sunlight streaming through the water strengthened as we rose from the depths of the lake and swam back to the boulders.

"Can you ask Myles if the trader is nearby?" Will asked. "And for a general update."

"Good call."

Myles's aura shifted as I spoke. *Is it safe for us to leave the water? If you look along the lake, there is a cluster of boulders we are using as cover.*

He won't see you, Myles answered. *He is in the woods now and we are following him. The more space between him and his cart, the better.*

Thank you.

"Myles said they are following the trader into the woods," I explained.

Will nodded. "Let's head to our rendezvous point, then."

When our heads broke the surface, the bubble burst and droplets rained around us. The water shed off of me and we crept out of the lake.

Despite Myles's assurance the trader wasn't nearby, we ducked behind the boulders before darting back into the reeds.

Will had kept his hair wet and pushed it out of his eyes now, chest heaving. "That was the longest underwater trip I've gone on in a bit."

"Do you need a minute to rest?" I asked, eyeing the sun for an estimate on time. "It looks like we have another hour before we need to be back at our meeting spot. You can take your time."

"I'll rest when we get back to our spot." He uncorked a waterskin and took a few sips, smiling. "I'm not near cool-down."

I led the way back through the reeds, the cold weight of the crystal against my thigh putting a bounce in my step.

Will and I are heading to our meetup spot now, I told Myles.

He didn't reply and I was cautious to not distract him with my aura. Myles, Mercy, and Sophie must be confronting the trader at this very moment.

We were quiet once we left the reeds and crept back through the woods.

"Besides his cart, I don't sense anything bad nearby," Will murmured. "They must have followed him fairly deep into the woods."

"Maybe the trader found another magical object," I suggested.

A fallen tree worked as a bench and I smoothed my skirts once we were settled.

We're back, I said to Myles. He again didn't answer, and I hesitated. Even if he was fighting, he should be able to talk to me. Myles had a remarkable ability of maintaining multiple conversations simultaneously. *Myles?*

No reply came and I turned to Will. "Myles isn't responding."

"Can you still feel his aura?"

Myles's aura felt as it had since we parted ways in the reeds, and I nodded.

Will stretched his legs out. "Then I'm sure he's distracted or too busy fighting to respond. This is Myles we're talking about. I'm sure he's fine."

I eyed the sun as it neared the start of sunset, sighing a little. "You're right. And we agreed to meet at sunset, so they should be here within the hour, anyway."

"And we'll be able to ask Myles about the crystal. My bet is still that it is related to ice."

I pulled the cold crystal from my pocket and rolled it between my fingers. It cast a light, barely perceptible glow, that grew as the forest around us was cast in shadow from the sun's descent.

Will held his hand out for the crystal. "It looks like a teleportation crystal."

I nodded in agreement; teleportation crystals were a powerful magical object. I had used one once before, when my family, Myles, and I were escaping the volcano. Well, my family used it—I had been unconscious during its actual use.

Will tossed the crystal into the air and caught it. I yelped. "What are you doing?"

He casually tossed it again. "Nothing."

"What do you mean *nothing*? You said it yourself; it looks like a teleportation crystal, which means it might activate by being thrown."

I held my hand out, and he reluctantly handed the crystal back, picking up a regular stone to play with instead.

As we waited, the sky slowly bloomed with pink and orange. Myles was still not answering my attempts to communicate and I fidgeted. *Myles?*

Will tossed the stone he had been playing with aside. "They will be here soon," he said firmly as his gaze darted around the forest.

A sudden feeling of intense fear struck me and I nearly doubled over, my hand to my stomach.

"Rose?" Will asked, grabbing my arm.

"Myles..." I whispered. The anxiety wormed its way through my gut, fueled by the connection provided by our auras, and I jumped to my feet, desperately hoping to pinpoint his direction. "Something's wrong. I can feel it in Myles's aura."

No matter the distance between us, my connection to Myles made it seem he was by my side, but right now, nothing but his aura suggested his heart was still beating. Everyone else, Mercy, Sophie, and the trader, were entirely missing.

Will stood beside me, his voice sounding tight. "Something happened."

"I can't sense any of them."

"Me either." Will exhaled loudly. "We need to find them."

"We can't," I whispered.

"What do you mean?" Dark waves crashed in Will's irises, and I couldn't tell if they had darkened with fear or if it was the oncoming twilight that made them appear that way.

"We don't know what the situation is, and if we get involved, we could put them in even more danger. What if they have a plan, and we barge in and ruin it?"

"We can't *not* help," he argued.

"We don't even know where they are." My voice shook. "I don't like leaving them hanging, but our involvement might cause more harm than good."

"Our involvement could also save their lives."

"But what if they come here for help and we're gone? What then?" I turned in a slow circle, searching desperately for any sign of them.

Will stilled. "Can you tell if he needs help, even if he isn't using words?"

Myles, what's wrong? Will and I can help—what do you need?

There was no answer, and I began playing with the ties on my apron out of frustration. "I can't reach him!"

"Is he upset?" Will peered towards the lake, his aura searching like mine was.

"What do you mean?"

He turned back, his expression suddenly serious. "Do you think anyone has died?"

At that, I stiffened, then slowly shook my head. "No. Not yet. There is no grief in his emotions."

"Good." He ran his fingers through his hair. "That means they have time and we can..." His shoulders slumped and he shook his head. "I don't know what we can do. I feel helpless."

"Me too."

He looked again towards the lake, where we had separated, but I now stared towards the trader's cart. It was too dark to see, but judging from the auras inside, empty. "Do you think we should explore the cart?" I asked. "What if there is something inside? Some clue about what happened or where they could be? They followed the trader into the woods, maybe he had a reason that is left behind in the cart."

"I don't want to leave this spot," Will fretted. "It's like you said, what if they come back and we aren't here?"

"The cart is in shouting distance," I said slowly. "And I can let Myles know. But Will, I can't sense any of their auras. If we were right about both of us having near the same reach as Myles, they're over five miles away, at least."

Will stared. "Is there a chance Myles had a teleportation crystal on him?"

I shook my head. "He used it on his last mission. King Duncan wanted Myles to take another, but they are so rare now that Myles refused."

"What about the trader?" Will's voice had become unnaturally calm and matter-of-fact.

I froze. "Maybe. But... but normal humans can't find them, right? Only be given them?" Before he could answer, fresh fear pumped into me. "He used one to take my family to The End, so it is possible he has others."

"That's not good," Will murmured. "Maybe we *should* explore his cart. We can try to find clues and if that doesn't work, we will wait here. We can't follow them with no trail. It's not like the training Myles said he did in the city, we can't safely wander until we sense them out here."

I took a shaky breath, pulling Ren's jackknife out. "Let's try."

We crept back through the woods and crouched in the bushes at the edge of the trees. A sliver of moon sparkled on the lake and the trader's cart silhouetted against it. His horses walked along the beach. Evidently, Myles, Mercy, and Sophie had unhitched them when they broke into the cart.

Will scanned every inch of the scene before speaking. "We need to stick together, but let me lead. If I get hurt, you can heal me, and I will use the lake as a defense."

"The cart's empty, right?" I asked.

"I hope so." His expression was carefully masked, and prickles went down my spine at the realization he feared the worst.

We darted from the cover of the trees, flattening our backs against the cart. My chest heaved and I reached for Will's hand through the dark, squeezing tightly.

"It's just an empty cart," I whispered, though it was partially to comfort myself.

He squeezed back. "Just an empty cart."

When our breathing steadied, we inched around the side and stood at the open back. The canvas was torn aside, revealing a mess empty of people and bearing no evidence of a fight, but deliberate destruction.

Will climbed up first, crouching to offer me a hand. Vials had been uncorked and the contents spilled, the same with boxes, and every drawer in the cupboards had been removed and tossed aside. Not one piece was broken, only overturned.

"This has our group written all over it," Will whispered as he reached inside a small cage that had been left unlocked. He pulled his finger out to reveal a butterfly sitting on his fingertip. "And I don't see any evidence of a teleportation crystal being used here."

"When we realized the trader used a teleportation crystal last time, only Myles could see evidence of it. What if neither of us are strong enough to see it this time?"

Will stared down at the floor, shaking his head. "I think God would show us."

"You're right," I agreed, watching as the butterfly flew off of his finger and twirled into the night. "And we are both more in tune with magic than I was then."

"Let's see what else we can find," Will suggested with a sigh.

Our movements were stiff and quiet, alert for any sounds from outside. I sifted through some spilled stuff, wrinkling my nose at a bone, covered in marks from a small canine.

"There is nothing here," I eventually admitted. "Now what?"

Will sighed, looking out the open back of the cart. "We wait."

I paced in the small clearing while Will stood with his arms folded, staring in the direction of the lake. We had returned to our meeting site over an hour ago, and neither of us had spoken since.

"At what point do we start looking?" I finally asked.

Will sighed and uncrossed his arms. "Where would we even start looking? I know some Mageye can see flashes of auras like a trail, but I've never really been able to. I think one of us would have seen the colors of a teleportation crystal had they used one, but that's about it."

He was right; we were glued to this spot, at least, until we sensed them coming. If they came.

"What do you think happened? They obviously didn't get in a fight in the cart, but why are they so far away?"

"As long as you can still feel your connection with Myles, there's a chance."

"Maybe they're lost?" I said doubtfully.

"Not with Mercy." His voice cracked, and he clenched his fists. "Not with Myles."

I resumed my pacing, but Will caught my arm. "Don't wear yourself out. They might need you when they get back."

My hand shot into my apron pocket, clutching the small box Ryder had given me with three Golden Dove feathers.

Will released my arm. "This is my fault. If I hadn't had the stupid idea of looking for a magical weapon." His voice rose with his anger. "This never would have happened if it weren't for me. And what was it for? Some *stupid* rock that's barely the size of a walnut? What use is that against the strongest Mageye there is?"

He whirled around and threw a punch at the nearest tree. His breath hitched with pain, and he held his fist tenderly with his other hand. "Gosh, I'm an *idiot*," he groaned.

I rushed to him and tried to pull his fist away from his injured hand, but he pulled back. "No, Rose. Save yourself for the others."

I wordlessly shook my head and took his injured hand, cupping it with both of mine.

"It's not your fault, Will," I told him. "We all agreed it was a good idea, and I still think that. The trader is outside of this."

He fell silent, watching me heal his hand. From the aching in my own hand, I could tell he had broken a couple fingers.

"I'm scared for them, too," I whispered.

He let out a slow breath. "I'm sorry, Rose. I shouldn't have lost control like that."

I looked up and met his eyes through the dark. "Remember at Charles's Inn when we agreed we would be a team no matter what?"

"Yes."

"We're a *team*, Will, and teams make decisions together. This isn't your fault. Looking for a magical weapon was a good idea, just like faking Myles being drunk was a good idea. Just like asking you to join our mission was a good idea on King Duncan's part."

Will remained silent, his gaze boring into me, and I didn't need light to tell waves were crashing in his irises. "Thank you," he finally rasped.

As the last of his fingers mended themselves, I released his hand, flexing my own as the pain faded.

Will's face suddenly lit with purple light and electric crackling filled the woods.

Myles stumbled through the bushes, blood trickling from a wound on his head and soaking his shirt. He cradled Mercy in his arms and practically fell to his knees, careful not to jolt her.

"Help."

Chapter 25

"Mercy!" Will shouted as we ran to them.

Myles gently lowered Mercy to the ground, and I knelt beside her, surveying her injuries.

It was too dark to see, and Myles wordlessly lifted a hand to allow lightning to crackle between his fingertips, illuminating the area enough to see her wounds.

Sophie stumbled after Myles, covered in bruises, but Mercy's skin was badly blistered.

"He burned her," Myles rasped.

She was unconscious, and I put my fingers to her wrist. Her pulse was barely detectable. I shuddered, taking her hand and squeezing tightly while I scanned her body for the worst injuries. She looked ghastly in the purple light provided by Myles's lightning. Even without connecting to her through my power, the thought this was too much came to mind.

Will stroked Mercy's hair with shaking hands. "Rose?"

I shook my head and pulled the box with Golden Dove feathers out, fumbling with the lid and grabbing the first feather tightly. Many of her wounds rivaled each other as the worst, so I took her hand and pressed the feather between our palms, praying it wasn't too late.

Pain blossomed over every inch of me, each beat of my heart pulsing with the weight of agony the trader had wielded upon

Mercy. Tears welled in my eyes and I blinked rapidly, squeezing her hand with all my might.

"Rose?" Will said again, his voice desperate. "Why isn't she healing? Why isn't she—?"

Sophie tried to pull him away. "Will, you need to be calm. You're distracting Rose."

He pushed her aside and shook Mercy desperately. "You can't die, Mercy. You can't..."

"Will," my voice cracked. "I need you to stop jolting her. I can't heal her if you don't move."

"But—" He sobbed and pulled back, practically collapsing into Sophie as she hugged him.

The worst pain blossoming through me was over my chest. Fresh tears pricked my eyes as I reached for Mercy's chest, pressing my palm over the burns. My breaths were shaky and her skin was hot to the touch, so hot that my palm now ached with burns despite her palms being unscathed.

Sweat rolled down my back and I whimpered, releasing her hand and panting as the feather dissolved into ash. With it gone, I put that hand over a gash on her head, which bled heavily.

The pain was blinding and I screwed my eyes tightly shut, pushing every ounce of myself into her. When my arms trembled and gave out, Myles caught me with his free hand, holding me up.

Will hovered beside me, but made no move to touch Mercy again, and Sophie continued soothing him.

"You can do it," Myles whispered, breaking through the sounds of our cries. "You can save her."

The blood pooling beneath her faded and the pounding in my skull from her gash faded with it, replaced by a pounding from cool-down. But her pulse was still thready, and I took her hand again.

Her chest rose slowly, fell, and then hit a stronger rhythm. I pulled back, swaying and catching onto Myles's shoulder.

"Is she...?" Will asked.

"She's alive," I whispered. My chest and arms still burned with her pain, and Myles lowered his hand, keeping a grip on me as he moved to Mercy's other side, pulling me close before I collapsed.

Are you okay?

Yes... She's alive. She's alive... My head swam, and nausea swept over me even as the agonizing pain from the burns began to fade. "What else?" I asked.

Will moved back to Mercy's side, his hands trembling as he stroked her hair.

Sophie crawled closer. "Rose, you need to lay down. That was..." She choked up. "That was a lot."

I weakly shook my head. "You and Myles are hurt. Let me help."

I turned in Myles's arms and reached for him, but grasped empty air. I blinked and refocused, realizing I had been reaching for nothing.

"Rose," he said, worry leaking into his voice.

"Let me heal you. Then I'll rest."

"No." He lifted me carefully and carried me to the fallen log Will and I had been sitting on when we first began to worry.

I tried to start healing him, but couldn't focus enough on any one wound while I was in his arms.

He gently placed me down. "Soph and I aren't seriously hurt. We'll be okay until you're out of cool-down."

I tried to argue, but my eyes were already falling shut, and I finally gave in to sleep.

Chapter 26

Myles's arms wrapped around me, holding me close. The sun had risen, and I blinked a few times before lifting my head.

"Rose." Myles sat up straighter and looked over me worriedly.

Blood had dried above his eyebrow, and I pulled my arm from his hug, putting a finger against his wound instead. He winced and gently took my wrist to stop me. "Don't heal me if you aren't ready."

I hesitated, looking across the clearing to Mercy. Will had moved her under the base of a tree, letting her head rest in his lap as she slept. Sophie slept beside them, her dress stained with blood.

"I'm okay," I whispered.

He pulled me closer and buried his face in my hair. "I'm sorry."

"For what?" I lifted my head. "What happened?"

The trader. His expression soured and his mind suddenly went silent, blocking me from the events that had led to the night before. "I'll explain once everyone is up," he finished.

I gripped his hand tightly and rose on my knees, peering through the trees to the lake. Branches swayed over the picturesque scene, devoid of any hint of flames. "His cart's gone."

"I know," Myles croaked.

The whole word suddenly seemed to shift and Myles steadied

me before I fell. "He's... alive?" My mouth felt full of cotton and I sat heavily. The trader had been so close and now he was gone again, safe while we picked up the ashes of pain. Exactly like I had been forced to do in Sunset Hollow.

"I don't think he is aware your family escaped," Myles whispered. "Or even the full details of the eruption in The End." He brushed hair from my eyes with a trembling hand. "I'm sorry."

I blinked rapidly against my tears and put my hand to his eyebrow again, healing the gash before he could complain. Neither of us spoke as I healed the rest of his wounds, and I paused when I finished, watching his chest slowly rise and fall with every breath.

Myles was alive. So was my family. So was Mercy, and Will, and Sophie. No one died last night.

That was all that mattered.

Will looked up when Myles and I approached. Dark bags shadowed his eyes and the usually active waves appeared dull in his irises. Evidence he hadn't slept last night. "She hasn't woken yet," he rasped, looking back at Mercy. "But she's breathing."

I knelt beside her, gently taking her hand and feeling for injuries. She looked peaceful in her sleep and I released her hand. "The injuries took a lot out of her, but she will be okay."

Relief washed over Will's face. "Thank you... thank you for healing her."

I smiled. "That's what I'm here for."

He nodded, and his gaze locked back onto Mercy's face. His posture had relaxed some and he smiled a little. "Never lived a day without you," he whispered. "Don't want to start now."

Myles reached behind Sophie, taking a waterskin and passing it to Will. "Drink that; you look exhausted."

Will stared at the waterskin blankly, but straightened and accepted it. "Thanks."

While he drank, Sophie stirred and lifted her head. I went to her, glancing over her bruised skin in concern. "Where are you hurt? I am going to heal you now."

She yawned, sitting up a little straighter. "Are you sure? You won't hit cool-down, will you?"

I shook my head. "I feel better, and I don't want to see you covered in wounds regardless."

"All right." She overturned her palms and I gasped. They were covered in blisters and I took them gently, wincing at the burning in my own hands as her wounds healed.

"What are the burns from?" I asked.

"The trader," she whispered, tears welling in her eyes. "He had more magical weapons than I've ever seen someone wield at once."

"I couldn't block Mercy," Myles whispered, staring at her face unseeingly.

Sophie took his hand. "You can't take every hit. And if it had been you and not her, I don't think we would have escaped." She looked down at Mercy. "I'm not happy she was hurt... but at least we are all alive."

Myles grimaced. "I still can't believe how strong he was."

"Why wouldn't you have been able to escape?" Will asked.

"I was in cool-down," Myles admitted. "We spooked him and he used some form of teleportation magic that made the whole world a blurry rainbow and dragged us through the woods. I tried teleporting us out of it and got so dizzy, I was helpless when the dragging stopped."

"Teleportation magic?" I whispered. "Like a teleportation crystal?"

He ran a hand down his face, shaking his head. "Not as powerful, but it caught us off guard."

"We tried our best," Sophie whispered. "But he fought mean."

A chill went down my spine. Fought mean. That was a good way to describe it. The trader's cruelty knew no bounds, and when you carry morals in a fight where your opponent does not, it certainly complicates things.

"I tried to teleport us out of there, but the orb was too weak from cool-down. We had to fight our way out and then I still couldn't teleport right away."

"You were so far into cool-down, you couldn't teleport at all?" I asked.

"Not safely." He rubbed his temples. "Not with Mercy as injured as she was. I couldn't risk it going wrong and dropping her in the middle of the jump. I couldn't risk making it worse."

Will's fists clenched, and his face contorted with rage. "You mean he is still out there?"

"Yes," Myles whispered. "But he isn't working for King Brenton anymore. I tried reading his mind as we fought and he seemed pretty occupied with wolves."

"Like the Wolvien Guard?" I fretted.

He shook his head. "Wolf *pups*, or something... I don't know, but he doesn't have a reason to return to King Brenton."

Sophie gripped her skirts in her fists. "What if our attack gives him a reason?"

"I don't think he will. He doesn't know who I am, and he doesn't know that I helped Rose free her family. All he thinks is that we are three crazy Mageye who attacked him. And he saw us as an opportunity to make money. If he captured us, he could have sold us." Myles's face suddenly darkened, and a sickening feeling filled my stomach.

"Sold you to who, exactly?" I asked.

"Well, we suspected there was a black market, and now we know for sure." Myles turned his gaze towards the spot where the cart had stood. "People kidnap and sell Mageye for their powers. Or they turn them over to hunters to be... killed."

"*What?*" Will snapped. "What do you mean?"

"I don't really know," Myles confessed. "But I'm willing to bet whatever it is, it is run by the Volcaniacs. We stop the Volcaniacs, we stop the trader, we stop the black market. All in one strike."

"The black what?" Mercy mumbled.

Will nearly shoved her off his lap in his surprise. "Mercy! Oh, gosh, Mercy. You're awake!"

She blinked, looking at us in confusion. "How'd we get here?" Stars flickered in her irises, reflecting her sudden rush of fear. "Where's the trader?"

"Not here," Will soothed, pulling her up to hug. "Myles got you out, and Rose... Rose healed you."

Mercy's gaze turned to Myles and me. "The last thing I remember was the... fire."

Lightning sparked in Myles's purple iris. "The trader threw something at you and your skin caught on fire. Sophie got the flames out, but you were already unconscious."

Sophie fidgeted, eyeing her palms. "It didn't burn your clothes, so I smothered the flames."

"And he's gone now?" Mercy whispered.

Myles swallowed hard. "I teleported as soon as I could and he... he got away, but that also means he gave up chasing us."

"Oh..." Her eyes flickered and Will helped her sit up on her own. "I don't know what to say. But... thank you... for helping me. All of you."

"We're a team," Sophie said. "More than a team."

Will helped Mercy drink some water, and I reached for Myles's hand. *He's gone, at least.*

I'm just sorry it's not for good when he is causing so much harm to the world.

"We're all alive," I whispered. "Here and in Mageye City."

"That's right," he agreed, a sudden look of overwhelming relief lightening his expression. "We made it back to each other."

"Good," Will whispered. "I wouldn't accept anything less."

That got a soft laugh from Mercy, and Sophie wiped her eyes, smiling a little. "Did you both find the crystal? Maybe something went fully right yesterday."

"Fully right," Will agreed. "We found it. Stole it from right under that idiot's nose."

I pulled the crystal from my pocket, and Myles sucked in his breath, taking it with trembling fingers. "An ice-diamond."

"An ice-diamond?" Will asked. "Rose and I weren't sure what it did, but it's cold and looks like ice."

"Exactly." Myles passed the ice-diamond to Sophie. "It can temporarily freeze people. It could allow for an escape."

"Freeze people?" Sophie handed the diamond to Mercy, who admired it with wide galaxy eyes. "Does it turn them to ice?"

"Kind of. It is the equivalent of freezing in a snowstorm without the presence of the storm. The size of the crystal determines how powerful it is and how long the freeze lasts."

Will's shoulders slumped. "This one is only the size of a walnut; we'll be lucky if we get a millisecond out of it."

Myles shook his head. "No, I would consider one the size of a pea above average. This one is *huge*."

"How long do you think the freeze will last?" I asked.

Myles took the ice-diamond from Mercy and weighed it in his hands. "I'd say about five minutes. Enough time to escape, *and*," he looked between us, "more importantly, this one is large enough that it should be able to freeze multiple people, if needed."

"How does it work?" Sophie asked. "Do you throw it like a teleportation crystal?"

"Exactly like a teleportation crystal. They come from the same magical family. All you need to do is throw it at the feet of whoever you want to freeze and then run."

Mercy rested her head on Will's shoulder. "Why is it called an ice-diamond and not an ice-crystal, if it is in the same family as a teleportation crystal?"

"Because diamonds form under pressure, and ice-diamonds are very compact." Myles held the crystal to the light, and rather than shining through, it seemed to refract off. "No matter how much pressure you put them under, they won't warp or crack. But when you throw it, it shatters."

"Can it be used more than once?" Will asked.

Myles lowered his hand. "No, it's one and done. The shattered pieces will melt. Besides, retrieving it would cut into your escape."

"Fair point," Will admitted.

I took the ice-diamond back. "Now what?"

"We finish what we started," Myles said. "Right?"

Mercy was the first to answer, holding her hand to her chest where the worst burns had been. "King Brenton would be happy if he found out we got scared away by someone who isn't even a Volcaniac anymore."

Will raised a brow. "I want to ensure nothing like last night happens again. To anyone."

"No more magical black market," Sophie whispered.

I looked towards the lake. "Technically, with the controlled visions, my hand was forced into the decision to come. But I want Mageye City to be safe, so I think I would have made it anyway."

Myles shut his eyes. "I let King Brenton escape unscathed once, now the trader. That's not going to happen again."

A heavy silence settled over us, and I drew my knees to my chest. The trader might be gone, but maybe there were worse people to worry about. After all, King Brenton had been the one to order my family's kidnapping, the one to hold them, and the one to attempt to pawn them off.

I reached for Myles's hand and he straightened his back, a cool confidence settling over his expression. "If we can keep up the pace we have been carrying, I think we can get there in a week."

"Or less," Mercy breathed, her gaze locked on the sky. "There's a shortcut."

Chapter 27

Stars shifted across Mercy's irises, and I held my breath as I waited for her to clarify what she meant by a shortcut. The color had returned to her cheeks, and she smiled softly. "There's a mountain portal."

Myles tugged his hand from mine in his excitement, leaning towards Mercy instead. "A mountain portal? Are you sure?"

Sophie sat up straighter and some of Will's exhaustion seemed to fade as he also leaned closer to Mercy.

I looked between them, confused. "What's a mountain portal?"

"Legendary magic," Will said, smirking.

"Mountain portals are specialized portals that take you *through* the base of a mountain," Myles explained.

"You come out on the other side of a different mountain," Will finished. "I've never used one."

"I've only used two," Myles said. "They are hard to find because they tend to keep themselves a secret."

"It's like the magical world is gifting us with a shortcut," Sophie said, smiling. "God's hand."

"Sounds like both God and magic are on our side," Myles agreed.

"Well, of course," Will said. "What's not to love about us?"

"Hopefully not much," I said. "At least until our mission is over, we need all the support we can get."

"Every ounce of it," Myles said, leaning back on his palms. "I don't sense it yet, Mercy, so you will have to guide us. Are you up for that?"

"Yes." Mercy watched the sun again. "The sun can guide us."

"I like when the stars guide us," Will said, resting against the trunk of the tree again.

I studied him closely. Despite his excitement over the mountain portal and overwhelming relief that Mercy was safe, his eyes held a twinge of dullness from his exhaustion. "When are we planning on leaving?" I asked.

Myles's brow furrowed. "Well, if that mountain portal is waiting for us, we should probably leave soon."

Sophie agreed, but I hesitated, looking from Myles to Will. Myles tilted his head, glancing at Will and pausing. "Will, do you need some time to rest?"

Will frowned. "Why me, specifically? I'm ready to go when the rest of you are."

"You didn't sleep last night, and I'm assuming the swim you took with Rose took a lot out of you as well," Myles said.

Mercy gasped. "You didn't sleep?"

Will avoided her gaze. "Not when you were so sick. I thought I was going to lose you."

Mercy sucked in her breath and threw herself into his arms. They squeezed each other so hard I began to fear that I might need to heal broken ribs.

When they separated, a tear slipped down Will's cheek. "I've never been scared like that."

Mercy sniffed, hugging him again. "I'm safe. Rose healed me. She saved me."

"I know she did." He pulled back from Mercy and spread his arms to me. He smelt like fresh water and crisp mountain streams. "Thank you," he whispered into my ear. "And thank you for before that, too. Thank you for believing in me.”

“We’re a team,” I whispered back. “No matter what.”

Waves crashed in his irises, and flashes of sunlight seemed to bounce off of them as his emotions tumulted between fear and relief. He took a deep breath. “Sleep or no sleep, we have a mountain portal to find.”

Sophie stood slowly. “Are you sure?”

“Positive.”

“How about we take a walk to the lake first?” Myles suggested. “We can refill our waterskins and give Will a chance to charge up.”

“Charge up?” Will asked with a small smile.

Myles shrugged. “I thought you’d appreciate the term.” He waved towards the lake. “And we’ll put you to use with fishing, if you’re up to it. Before we got, well, dragged off, we stole some of the trader’s food. Tonight, we will feast.”

My lip twitched a little, but it quickly settled into a frown as I looked in the direction Myles had waved. “Extra food is good, but what about the trader himself? His cart is gone, but what if he is still in sight?”

Myles followed my look towards the lake. He didn’t speak, so I sent my aura out, my shoulders slumping at the vaguely familiar aura. Will was right last night when he said there wouldn’t be a doubt if a teleportation crystal had been used.

“He used a teleportation crystal, didn’t he?”

“Let’s hope it was his last one,” Myles said grimly. “But at least now, we don’t need to worry about bumping into him.”

We took our time at the lake for Will’s sake, and once we left with stomachs stuffed with fish for breakfast, Mercy took the lead.

“Does a mountain portal work like a regular portal?” I asked.

“Kind of,” Sophie said. “They don’t glow, though. In order to use it, you need to find its entrance. A cave will lead into the heart of the mountain, and halfway through, you will be transported to the next mountain. When you come out the other side, you will have traveled thousands of miles."

I stared. "Really? Does the teleportation feel like anything?"

She shook her head. "No. Well..." She turned to Myles. "I don't remember noticing it?"

Myles nodded in confirmation. "It happens in the dark, so you won't notice it unless there is a temperature or terrain change accompanying it."

"Sophie, have you used a mountain portal?" Mercy asked.

"Myles and I took one after the men chasing me died. We wanted to get away and leave the bad memories behind."

Myles tapped his fingers against his thigh. "That was the first time I found one on my own. The only other time I used one was with King Duncan when I was ten."

"Why did you use one with King Duncan?" Mercy asked.

"He found one and wanted me to experience it while I had the opportunity."

Will lifted his head. He had been unusually quiet since we left the lake, seeming too tired to participate much in our conversations. "King Duncan used to go on missions like this?"

"More than you might expect," Myles said. "He has always been an *adventurous* king."

"I guess that's what happens when you unexpectedly become king at thirteen. The rules change," I mused.

"Exactly." Myles smiled. "But I think he made some good changes. If I ever become king, that's how I want to rule."

Mercy paused. "I forgot... You're in line for the throne, aren't you? After General Cornstone?"

Myles nodded. "Yes. I'm second in line."

"I knew you were in line, but I don't always think about it. You never mention it."

He sighed. "It's complicated. I don't really *want* to be king. I wouldn't refuse it, but I'm not actively seeking it."

"What do you mean?" I asked.

"It's complicated," he repeated, watching a robin scurry across a tree branch. "And it is likely that it will eventually happen... If I outlive King Duncan and General Cornstone."

My steps faltered. "To become king would mean they're gone?"

Lightning flickered in his purple iris. "Unless they step down from the throne, but that would make them unfit and," he shook his head, "I'm not counting the days for it, but I will take the crown when it is time."

Sophie nodded, a contemplative look on her face. "That won't happen for a long time, though. Even General Cornstone isn't that old."

"That's true," Myles agreed. "And who knows, maybe by then I will be keener towards it. But for now, I'm happy as a general."

"General *Duncan*," Will snickered. "If I were you, I'd use my fancy title all the time."

I smirked. "Everyone else on the Elite Guard goes by their titles, but he is just Myles."

"That's not true," Myles protested.

"Yes, it is," I argued. "Who calls you General Duncan?"

"The other members of the Elite Guard, for starters. You know... on formal occasions."

I raised an eyebrow, giggling. "*Do* they? Or are you trying to get some of your dignity back?"

"I had Marlon call me General Duncan, didn't I?"

"That's because you were annoyed with him."

Will snickered and Myles bit back a smirk of his own. "Well, I've had my title long enough that he should have recognized me... though, since my dad was letting him heal, he might not have mentioned me before we went to interrogate him."

"That's true," I relented. "But I still haven't heard your title used often."

"I don't flaunt it, but I could at any time. So be careful with that teasing, miss."

Sophie giggled. "We're sorry, General Duncan."

"General Abelforth," Will whispered and I laughed, both of us earning scoldings from Myles.

"How long have you been a general?" Mercy asked when we stopped laughing. "Since you were ten?"

Myles wagged his finger at me a final time before answering. "I started working when I was ten, but I wasn't a full member of the Elite Guard until I was twelve. I got my title after my first completed solo mission."

That piqued my interest. "Is that how things will go with Raymond? He will become a full member once he completes his first solo mission?"

"Yes and no," Myles said slowly. "Oftentimes, it has to do with your first mission, but it truly comes down to self-sacrifice. We swear to protect Mageye City no matter the cost, and when that is proven, we earn our title. Raymond might not be a Mageye, but he has the experience that qualifies him to join the Elite Guard. Anyone who can put up a fight on a broken leg deserves a spot on the guard in my book."

"That's true," I said, pride bubbling in my chest. Raymond certainly had the admirable traits required for the guard. "Raymond has wanted to be a guards-member for a long time. Before we moved to Mageye City, he had been planning on personally training with General Jacobs in Sunset Hollow this fall."

"He told me that."

I smiled; Myles and Raymond had hit it off right away. They had very similar morals and life goals. Not only that, but they were practically the same age, and since Myles spent so much time with me, he was bound to see my brothers often.

He was close with the twins as well, but they already had each other as built-in best friends. Things had always been a little different for Raymond. Ever since our dad had died of an unknown illness when Raymond was seven, he had carried the title of the "head of the house." As goofy as he could be, he was always the first to snap back into business mode, a trait he shared with Myles.

Chapter 28

Mercy had announced earlier in the day that she was hopeful we would be able to sense the mountain portal's aura by sunset, but as the sun began its descent, the wish wasn't fulfilled. However, she was confident we would reach it tomorrow regardless, and the sun and stars hadn't failed us yet.

Will had hardly spoken a word all afternoon and lagged behind now, dragging his feet. His shoulders were slumped, but he made no complaint.

I think we need to stop for Will soon, I told Myles.

He looked over his shoulder and his expression softened. *He's dead on his feet.*

Is there a safe spot nearby?

Myles didn't answer, though his aura shifted and he nodded to himself. "I think we should set up camp now," he announced. "I know it's early, but last night took a lot out of us, and we will be taking the mountain portal tomorrow. We shouldn't over-exert ourselves."

He generalized his announcement, not directing it at Will, and I smiled. While Will was adamant about complaining over waking up, he never seemed to like being the one to hold us up during the day.

"I like that idea," Sophie said. When she noticed Will, she looked like she was about to say something, but caught herself, casually saying instead, "I could use extra sleep if we are stopping early."

"That works for me," Mercy agreed. "Where should we set up camp?"

"There is a safe spot nearby. We can make a camp in the center of it."

"I want that," Will mumbled.

Mercy stepped over to him. "Are you all right? Do you need help walking?"

Will shook his head but made no reply. His hair covered his eyes as his head drooped towards his chest. "Sleep," he finally said.

"Yes, you can sleep through the whole night," she assured him. "We don't want you getting sick."

Unfortunately, the safe spot Myles had found didn't provide much cover. Ferns hid the forest floor, and we settled amongst them, using them as a cushion—a very leafy cushion.

Myles leaned against a small boulder. "I'll take first watch. Who wants second?"

"I can take second," I said, sitting beside him. "Wake me up when you start getting tired."

I mean it, I added, remembering the times on our first mission when he tried to push his exhaustion aside so I could sleep.

He looked at me guiltily. *Fine... but I am going to wait a full minute after I need to switch to wake you.*

A full minute is a very serious crime, I scolded, shaking my head in disappointment.

He grinned. *I am a dangerous man.*

I grinned back and settled closer to him while I split some of the food we carried. Mercy braided Sophie's hair, and I could see a flattened-out layer of ferns beside them where Will must have already passed out. We took turns sipping from a jar of soup from the trader's cart since it wouldn't take very long to spoil, though we were careful to save a fair amount for Will.

"I'll take the third watch," Mercy said when we finished dinner, looking up from Sophie's braid.

Sophie pulled away, turning back towards her. "No, I will. I know you feel better now, but you were very close to... to dying last night. I think you should sleep the whole night through."

Mercy opened her mouth, but before she could argue, I leaned forward. "I agree. You deserve a full night's rest."

Myles nodded as well, his hands now folded behind his head. "We don't want you overworking yourself, Mercy. You have been in constant communication with the sun all day and will be doing the same tomorrow."

Mercy sighed, turning back to Sophie's half-finished braid. "All right, but if any of you need an extra person to keep watch, wake me. I don't mind."

"If we need you, we'll wake you," I promised.

"And Will can enjoy the full night," Myles said.

"I call waking him up in the morning." Mercy giggled. "He will either be very chipper or pretend he went into a coma overnight."

The ferns surrounding the flattened ferns shuddered, but Will didn't appear. "He earned the rest," I said.

"No!" I screamed as lava rose from the pool in the center of King Brenton's amphitheater, arcing over my brothers' heads.

Time seemed to freeze for one paralyzing second, and then the lava crashed down, and they were gone. The sound of their screams echoed in my ears... over and over and over...

"Rose!" a worried voice called. Someone shook me, and I opened my eyes with a gasp. "Rose!" Myles said again, his eyes practically glowing in the dark. *You're okay,* he soothed telepathically. *Calm down. If it was a controlled vision, you're awake now.*

I shakily pulled myself upright, tears burning at my eyes. "Not real," I whimpered.

"Not real," Myles agreed. "You're shaking." He hugged me to his side. "Take some deep breaths."

I sank into his hug without a second thought, glancing around our camp to ensure no remnants of the nightmare remained in the shadows. Three holes seemed to have formed amidst the ferns where Will, Mercy, and Sophie slept.

Myles waited patiently, and I tentatively leaned further into him, listening to the sound of his soft breaths. *My brothers and I were back in the volcano's amphitheater,* I began. *And when King Brenton caused the wave of lava to arc over them, you weren't there to block it.*

He drew in his breath. *So, you relived a twisted memory?*

Yes.

Are you okay? I know that's your greatest fear.

Tears rolled down my cheeks, and he opened his arms to me. I buried my face in his chest, sniffing. *I'm scared.*

I know.

Those two words that I heard from him so often brought me comfort, and I lifted my head, resting it on his shoulder instead.

Thank you.

For what?

For always knowing what to say.

He stroked my hair gently. *I'm a mind reader, that's what I do. Now, are you sure you're feeling better?*

Yes.

He hummed softly, whispering, "I don't know why I asked that when I knew the answer from your thoughts and emotions." I giggled and he snickered. "Oh right, that's why I asked. Got you to laugh."

"You manipulated my feelings?" I teased, wiping my eyes with my hands.

"Maybe. I don't feel very bad, though."

"Mean," I whispered.

He snickered again, shimmying to lay down and pulling me with him. *Are you okay to take over on guard?* he asked. *I feel bad asking right now, but I was about to wake you anyway. I might have been able to stop the vision...*

It's okay. I took his hand and squeezed it. *It's been a few days since we had one, so if you start getting restless, I'll wake you.*

X

Myles slept soundly beside me, his head leaning against my shoulder. I held very still, not wanting to disturb him. King Duncan had once told me that Myles's hugs used to be coveted in the palace. Apparently, when he was little, he was clingiest to the people he trusted the most, and it took King Duncan over a year for Myles to start unveiling that side of himself.

With Myles and I, it had taken less than two weeks for me to hug him for the first time, after Gray attacked us. It was nice to have a friend that wouldn't flinch away from my touch, and having him next to me after one of the controlled visions that connected us seemed to push some of the fear aside.

An owl hooted, and I looked towards it, narrowing my eyes to peer through the trees. The upper branches were too thick to see it, and the woods were otherwise quiet.

Myles mumbled something before turning away, his head no longer on my shoulder. I took the opportunity to stretch my legs, taking a careful walk around the fern patch.

The owl hooted again, and I jumped as it suddenly flew past me, stifling my yelp before accidentally waking the others. I scurried back to Myles and sat beside him again.

Once I relaxed, I took a moment to thank God for the warm weather. If it was winter, I would be freezing right now. Ironic, seeing as we were on our way to fight a fire king.

And there was a week, tops, before we fought him. That was

how long Myles and Mercy thought the rest of our journey would take thanks to the mountain portal. And then we would be in King Brenton's palace. Fighting him once more.

Except this time, we would defeat him. There simply wasn't another option. Not when Mageye City depended on us.

Myles shifted beside me, snapping me out of my thoughts. He was growing restless and I nudged him. "Myles."

His eyes snapped open, and he jerked upright, relaxing when he saw that I was the one who had awoken him.

"Are you okay?" I asked.

"Yeah." He laid back down shakily. "Vision. I saw what you saw. Back in the amphitheater."

"That's what I thought," I whispered, taking his hand.

He squeezed it gently. "Thanks for waking me," he mumbled as he drifted back into sleep.

I stayed by his side, his hand clasped in mine until I was too tired to stay up any longer. I reluctantly let go of his hand and woke Sophie, returning to Myles's side when she was up.

Chapter 29

Will leaned over me. The color had returned to his face, and waves crashed in his blue irises. "Myles said to get you up," he explained.

I rubbed the sleep from my eyes, mumbling, "You look a lot more alive."

"I *feel* a lot more alive." He leaned back, waving at Myles and Mercy. "They're talking about today's plans."

I sat up. "We're going to use the mountain portal today."

He nodded. "Sophie told me."

Will had ferns stuck in his hair, and I teased them out for him. He laughed and plucked a few strands from my braid. "The ferns made a soft cushion," he declared.

"They did," I agreed. The flattened holes where we had slept had partially risen, giving a crumpled appearance.

Anymore nightmares? Myles suddenly asked. I looked up as he stepped away from Mercy, who had turned her attention to the sun.

No. Did you have any?

He shook his head, sharing his thoughts with me while he took a drink of water. *Since we don't know how close to King Brenton's palace we will be when we leave the mountain, we want to set up camp early again tonight so Mercy can talk to the stars.*

I tilted my head, studying his relaxed demeanor. No one seemed to have any doubts about the mountain portal, and while

225

the idea sounded good, it relied heavily on, well, convenience. What would happen if there were no mountains near where we wanted to travel? After all, mountain portals supposedly took you from one mountain to another.

There will be something for us to exit from, Myles answered without me directly asking. *If the mountain portal is having the stars direct us to it, there must be mountains between us and the palace.*

As long as it lets us out somewhere closer, I'll be happy.

Me too. He put the stopper back in the waterskin and addressed us all. "Is everyone awake enough to pack up?"

"Ready as I'll ever be," Will said, picking up his magic waterskins.

Myles sighed wistfully. "You know, I think I'm already missing tired Will. Yesterday was peaceful."

"Eerily peaceful," Mercy said. "It might have been relaxing for you, Myles. But for me, it was worrisome."

"The lack of mischief was nice, but I'm with Mercy. It worried me," Sophie agreed.

"Well, I'm alive and feeling good now." Will offered me a hand up. "No promises about mischief, though. Sounds like I have some to make up for."

✗

A harsh gust of wind nearly swept Sophie off her feet, and I laughed as I caught her. "Are you okay?"

"Yes," she huffed breathlessly. "My dad once said I'm as light as a kite; maybe he was right."

Another harsh gust blew and this time we both stumbled. Myles took each of our arms, also laughing. "Let's see if I can take us somewhere with better cover."

Will caught my free hand, tugging Mercy over. "Flying seems like something I'd prefer to avoid," he announced.

"It's exhilarating," Myles said as a purple orb crackled around us. "In the right environment."

The orb snapped and we reappeared in a forest with trees so thick, it looked like we would have to travel single file through them.

Mercy patted the nearest trunk, eyeing the sky through the leaves. "Less windy, at least. And we're getting close."

Myles stepped between the first trees and we followed, listening to Mercy's instructions. A faint magical presence mingled with the air and I glanced around the dark trees. There didn't seem to be a direction the presence was coming from, giving it the appearance of being laced over the trees.

"I feel magic," Will announced from behind me. "Good magic," he added when Sophie frowned.

"I think that's the mountain portal," Myles said. "They don't pull you in like a regular portal. They let you know they are there and trust you to find them yourself."

"Then how's it letting the stars guide Mercy?" Will asked.

"Well, I don't really know how to explain Mercy's power. But my assumption is that the mountain portal gave the stars permission to guide her. Right, Mercy?" Myles turned to her.

She motioned to the sky. "If the portal didn't want the stars guiding me, the stars would keep its secret."

"So, you're saying the stars keep secrets from us?" Sophie asked.

"Well, not necessarily because they want to. But if something, particularly a *magical* something, doesn't want the stars to tell me about it, they won't. Our powers have limits—if the stars told me everything, I would get overstimulated and hit cool-down."

"So, that's how you hit cool-down," Sophie said. "It takes energy to talk to the stars."

"Yes," Mercy agreed, pausing to squeeze between a particularly tight gap between trees. I followed her, and Will grumbled as he squeezed after us. "In general, the stars are a constant presence, but when I ask them directly for something, that is what takes more energy. General directions to King Brenton's palace versus direct directions to this mountain portal."

"What about you, Sophie?" Will asked. "Are you unable to turn invisible when you hit cool-down?"

Sophie brushed a stray strand of blonde hair from her eyes. "I become fully visible, even if I'm scared. My emotions often activate my power." She laughed. "As I'm sure you've all noticed! When I am scared or nervous, I can't always control it. Unless I consciously choose to become visible. But when I am in cool-down, I am powerless."

"Can you see yourself when you are invisible?" I asked.

Will laughed. "What?"

"Well, Sophie, what changes when you turn invisible? Can you see through yourself?"

She wasn't having as much of a struggle to squeeze between the trees and hardly paused as she side-stepped through two of them. "Yes. I turn invisible to myself, too."

"So, you can't see yourself at all?"

"Nope." She held her hand out, and it disappeared. "It isn't an illusion. I turn fully invisible to everyone around me, as well as myself."

"I think you have one of the most unique powers I've seen," I said.

"Thank you." Her hand reappeared, and she waved it through the air, allowing it to turn translucent. "I don't think I would be able to control it if I was able to see myself even when fully invisible."

"I don't know if I believe that," Myles said over his shoulder. "You've always had a strong hold of your power."

Her expression fell a little, whispering, "Until I was caught."

"If you hadn't been caught, we never would have met," he countered.

At that, Sophie smiled again. "That's true."

"If you think about it, none of us would be here right now if we hadn't gone through the trials we each have had," Mercy said. "If we hadn't all learned how to control our powers and the magic, we never would have met."

"Well, the two of us would have met," Will piped in.

"Fair point; you've *always* known me." Her smile grew mischievous. "I, on the other hand, was blessed with a month of peace."

"And then I came along and, bam! Your life was suddenly a lot more exciting."

She shut her eyes as if reminiscing. "I think I miss the quiet."

He flicked her arm and she swatted him away, both snickering. They continued teasing each other and my gaze drifted to Myles.

Had my family not been kidnapped, all of the bad I had gone through since discovering my power wouldn't have happened. But the good wouldn't have happened, either. Meeting Myles, moving to Mageye City, making friends with Mercy, Will, and Sophie—though by now they were much more than friends.

Myles took my hand, snapping me out of my thoughts. *Family,* he said contentedly. *General Cornstone once told me blood doesn't make his family and it doesn't make mine either. Or, it doesn't have to. Sometimes, actions mean more than blood.*

I swung our intertwined hands. *I followed my family when they were taken because they are my family, not because we share blood.*

I don't share blood with you all, but I would stop at nothing to keep everyone here safe.

I squeezed his hand and he squeezed back, lightning sparking in his irises. Myles's presence was like a pillar of comfort, and we continued weaving through the trees in a contented silence.

"There's no way anyone but Sophie can fit through this," Will announced, waving his hand.

The trees now formed a wall of tangled limbs and towering

trunks. Sophie stepped up to the largest gap and attempted to wiggle through, but didn't get farther than her shoulders. "I can't fit through, either."

"Time for another jump," Myles decided. "No amount of sucking in my stomach will get me through that."

Mercy took his free hand. "I don't know how to describe this other than I know where to go, but not how to put it into words. Can you read my mind?"

He nodded and shut his eyes. A purple orb lit up around us and snapped, freeing us from the constricting forest.

While the forest hadn't seemed particularly dark, the sky above brightened, and I squinted as my eyes adjusted. Mercy smiled, turning her face to the sun. "I feel the magical presence now."

"Me too," Sophie agreed.

"I more than feel it," Will announced. "I see a mountain." He pointed above the trees and the tip of a mountain shown above them.

"Which mountain is the mountain portal on?" I asked. "Can the stars tell you, Mercy?"

She nodded. "It's the one we can see right now."

"That narrows our search, then," I declared.

Myles smirked and I glanced between him and the mountaintop. *What?*

You asked which mountain in the plural, he explained. *Remember last time when I told you mountains always come in groups? You agree.*

I stuck my tongue out at him. *I will neither confirm nor deny that.*

He raised an eyebrow. *Your thoughts suggest a confirmation.*

Sophie nudged me. "Whatever you're arguing about, I'm on your side," she whispered.

Myles fake-gasped. "I heard that, Soph."

"Heard what?" Mercy asked, glancing over her shoulder.

"Soph has betrayed me," Myles said mournfully.

"Understandable," Will immediately said.

"What?" Myles stared at him. "I thought we had a pact to have each other's back?"

"Oh, right," Will swiftly corrected. "Not understandable," he told Sophie.

I laughed. "Since when do you have this pact?"

"That is top secret information, Rose," Will informed me seriously. "To reveal that would be to betray each other's trust."

When Will helped me get the smell of whiskey off at the inn, Myles said while staring straight ahead. *Before you three got up.*

I fought to hide my laugh, but Will noticed. "I am incredibly disappointed in you, Myles. *Incredibly.*"

Myles waved his hand dismissively. "Think of it as us being even now."

"Even from what?"

"From when you agreed with Rose and Soph two seconds ago."

"I corrected myself, didn't I?" Will argued, waving his hands to generalize the statement. "Mine was a mistake, yours was a direct betrayal."

"If you are even now, does that mean you have forgiven Will for forcing you to drink whiskey?" Mercy asked innocently.

"Oh, no! That is an entirely different situation." Myles deadpanned.

Sophie laughed. "I thought you said bickering was for toddlers."

"It is!" Both gasped at the same time.

"If you're sure," she said through giggles.

I smiled and motioned her and Mercy away. "We should make a pact, too," I whispered. "Seeing as they have one."

Mercy crossed her arms. "My thoughts exactly. And our pact will be better since we don't bicker."

Sophie's eyes seemed to sparkle. "I agree. This will be fun and beneficial. We will all be on the same page."

"All right," I said with a smile. "We agree to have each other's backs if and when it is needed."

"No matter what and no matter when the need arises," Mercy added.

"Big or small," Sophie finished. "We have each other."

Our meeting was interrupted by Myles. "I don't think I like you three whispering like that," he called, walking backwards to face us. "Besides," he raised his hands as if to display the land behind him, "we have reached the mountain. Now we need to find the entrance to the portal."

Chapter 30

The pull of the mountain portal beckoned us forward, and yet, it gave no direction.

"Where on the mountain is it?" I asked. Now that we were at its base, the mountain rose too high for us to see its top.

Myles hummed. "They're normally on or near the base. We have to walk straight through the mountain, and we can't do that from the top."

Sophie scanned the mountainside, a thoughtful expression on her face. "How did you find it last time, Myles?"

"I played hot and cold with the aura. The strengthening and weakening of the pull as we turned towards or away from it guided me."

Will rubbed his hands together. "All righty then, everyone. We're about to play the most intense game of hot and cold in our careers."

Mercy laughed. "I'm going to crush you, Will. I always have."

Will held his hands out in a calming gesture. "This isn't a competition, Mercy," he said with a mature tone. "We all have the same goal in mind here."

Mercy shoved him. "Shut up, Will."

He playfully shoved her back, and I crossed my arms. "I'm experienced with hot and cold myself. I've played quite a few rounds of it in my day."

"Ahh, yes," Myles said, eyes sparking. "Back in the olden days when you were a young'un."

"Hey!"

He laughed and stepped closer. "Ready to play?"

Sophie laughed. "I want to make sure we are all on the same page; this can't be a real competition since we need to stick together."

"Darn," Will said. "I hadn't thought of that. I guess we'll have to make it a competition another time. For now," he pointed to our left, "it's thatta way."

Myles agreed, and we set off, Will in the lead. We spent the next hour traipsing along the lower base of the mountain, the magical presence never tugging us but continually growing stronger.

"It is close," Mercy called back to us. "Myles, what do you think?"

Myles didn't answer right away, studying the mountainside closely. He pointed at a large hawthorn bush. "It's behind that."

How he located it, I wasn't sure, but when we stepped around the bush, a small hole in the ground led into a dark cavern.

"Oh," Mercy whispered, stepping back. "I thought it would be more open. Not so... tiny... and dark."

Will rubbed the nape of his neck. "I thought the same thing. But we are going through together. You won't be alone for a second."

"The stars won't be with us," she whispered.

"They're not going anywhere," Will soothed. "It's like closing your eyes. You can't see them, but they're there. Or what about a thunderstorm? That completely blocks the stars, but you know they're still there, on the other side of the clouds."

"That's different. There is nothing... nothing *physical* separating me from them. But the cave... We're walking through a mountain—there will be an entire mountain between us." She turned to the rising slope of the mountain and shuddered. "I won't even be able to hear the whispers."

Sophie hugged her. "Remember how terrified I was in Silverton, but we made it through safely? We're going to help you get through the mountain, just like you all helped me."

Mercy shook her head, and stars flickered in her irises. "Myles... is there another way? Please?" Her bottom lip quivered.

He placed a hand on her shoulder. "I know you're scared, Mercy, but we'll be okay. Think of it this way. The stars guided us here, didn't they? They wouldn't do that if they didn't want you to use the portal."

"You're right," she whispered. "They wouldn't guide me somewhere that would sever the bond... I don't think."

"Your magic is a part of you," I said. "Your power wouldn't guide you somewhere that would take it away."

She took a shaky breath. "I can do this." She stepped back up to the hole and stared into it. "I can do this. We have to do this."

"Yes." Will pulled her back again. "I'll hold your hand the whole way. I'm not going anywhere."

Her knuckles turned white with how tightly she gripped him. "Thanks, Will."

Myles squatted by the edge of the hole. "I can light it up so we can see. Would that make it better, Mercy?"

"Yes," she whispered.

"All right." He looked us all over before turning to me. "I'm going to climb in first to see what it's like down there. Then I'll call you down, Rose. Then Soph." He glanced at Will and Mercy. "I think Will should go next and then Mercy, so that when she comes down, we are all there to meet her. Does that work for everyone?"

Everyone nodded, including Mercy. "I can do this," she said firmly. "Everything is going to be okay."

"Exactly," Will and Myles said simultaneously. They grinned

at each other before Myles looked back into the crevice.

"When we come out the other side, I don't want to teleport right away. We might be within the radius we created where we are on foot only."

A heavy silence cloaked us and I turned to the east. Less than a week suddenly seemed like a much smaller timeframe.

"That's what we're here for, isn't it?" Sophie said, surprising me by breaking the silence first. "Stopping King Brenton? We have almost made it."

"Almost," Myles repeated, swinging his legs into the crevice. "I'll start calling you down once I'm sure it's safe."

We crowded the hole, and he huffed as he landed below. A flickering purple light lit up the cave, crackling softly, and he looked up at me.

"The drop was bigger than I anticipated," he called, his voice echoing through the chamber. "But it's all clear down here. Do you want me to catch you?"

I eyed the dark walls the purple light bounced off of. "Yes, please."

"All right. I don't want to shock you, so I'm going to let out the light. Jump straight down, and I'll catch you."

I sat and swung my legs into the hole. The crackling stopped as the lightning flickered out and I leaned over. "Are you ready?"

"Yes, I'm standing below you."

My stomach jolted as I dropped, gasping as Myles caught me. He gently placed me on the ground in the dark and held his arm above his head to again light up the cavern. The lightning lit up his face in an eerie purple glow. "You good?" he asked.

I nodded. "Thanks for catching me."

He simply smiled before looking up at Sophie's nervous face.

"Can you catch me, too?" she asked.

"Of course." He motioned towards the stone wall on the far side of the tunnel. "Stand back, Rose. I don't want to bump you."

When Myles saw I was safely out of the way, he lowered his arm and stopped the lightning. Now, the only light in the otherwise dark tunnel was from the crevice above us.

"Whenever you're ready, Soph," Myles called. "I'll catch you."

"I'm ready." She swung her legs over and dropped in. Myles caught her easily, gently placing her down as he had done to me.

"Thanks." Sophie huffed. She took a look around the tunnel. We were at a dead-end portion, and it led straight into the heart of the mountain. "I forgot how... unmagical... mountain portals are. It looks like a normal cave."

Myles nodded. "That's why they're so hard to find." He again let purple lightning crackle in his hand. "We're ready whenever you are, Will."

Neither he nor Mercy were in sight above us. Will peeked into the cave, his hair covering one eye. "Give us a minute," he called. "Mercy isn't quite ready."

Myles stepped back. "Tell her she can take her time."

"Thanks," Will said before disappearing again.

Myles joined me and Sophie by the wall of the cave. "I wish I could teleport us to the center to make it quicker for her, but that would interfere with the portal's magic. It might break it."

"Break it?" I repeated, eyeing the dark tunnel extending before us.

Myles nodded. "The mountain portal is supposed to take us; we aren't supposed to add to it. If I teleported, it could overwhelm the portal and get us stuck."

"I remember you saying that last time," Sophie agreed.

Myles smiled, the purple lightning lighting up his and Sophie's faces in flashes. "That's because King Duncan yelled at me my first time. I wanted to double our teleportation by jumping through... That earned me an earful of a lecture."

Sophie and I shared a look as we giggled. "It's still hard for me to picture you getting yelled at as often as you imply," I said.

"You didn't know him when he was my age," Sophie teased. "Getting scolded was a part of his daily routine."

"Not *daily*," Myles protested. "Maybe every other day."

"Every day," Sophie whispered to me, raising her brows. "Sometimes every hour."

Will interrupted before Myles could reply. "I'm coming down. You don't need to catch me, but keep the space lit, so I don't collapse."

Myles raised his arm to light up more of the tunnel. "Works for me."

Will landed in a crouch, rising slowly and looking farther into the heart of the mountain. "I didn't realize it was so dark. I thought it would be semi-lit."

"I did too," I said.

Mercy peered into the cavern. "You'll catch me, Will. Right?"

"Right," he confirmed, moving below her. "Remember that time you were scared to jump off that tree branch you were stuck on, and you jumped down into my arms? This is like that."

The memory cracked a small smile from Mercy. "I was stuck because the branch we had climbed up from cracked beneath you, and you fell out of the tree."

Myles snorted. "Minor detail you forgot there, Will."

"That's not the point," Will interjected. "The point is that Mercy was scared to jump, but I promised her I would catch her, and I *did*. Also," he added, "the branch cracking wasn't my fault. How was I supposed to know it would break? We both used it to get up. I thought it would support me on the way down, too."

"That's true," Mercy said. "Although, it was really funny to watch you fall."

"What?" Will questioned. "Well, if that's the case, maybe I won't catch you this time."

"Don't worry, Mercy," Myles assured her. "If he doesn't catch you, I will."

"Thank you." Mercy took a deep breath and let it out slowly. "I'm ready."

She stuck her legs into the cave and jumped into Will's arms. Her eyes were tightly shut and she clung to him. "I'm in a cave," she whispered frantically.

"I know," he soothed. "But caves have entrances and exits, right? We'll be out of this one before you know it."

She cracked her eyes open and let Will set her feet on the floor. "Thanks for catching me. Now," she cast a final look to the sun before turning to the heart of the mountain, "we have a mountain portal to use and a king to stop."

Chapter 31

Lightning arced between Myles's outstretched fingers, creating a glow bright enough for us to see by.

It was quiet inside the mountain, the only sound being our echoing footsteps and Will's whispers to Mercy.

"How will we know when we teleported?" I asked, my voice echoing loudly.

Mercy jumped.

"Sorry," I whispered.

"It's okay. Can we all keep talking, actually? I think that will make this easier."

"Of course," Myles said, glancing over his shoulder. "To answer your question, Rose, since we won't feel the teleportation, the only way for us to tell will be if this mountain and the next have different interiors."

"Or the temperature could change," Sophie added. "That is another telltale sign."

"The other side will have an opening, right?" Will asked. "Because, you know, I said entrance and exit, but sometimes that means the same thing, so..."

"What?" Mercy yelped. "No, there has to be an exit on the other side! There *has* to be."

Will stumbled over his words as he tried to correct himself. "Stupid thing to say, I'm sorry. It's a portal to take us somewhere else, so obviously it will have an exit. I don't know why I even asked about it being different."

Mercy trembled, clutching his arm tightly. "Are you sure?"

"There will *definitely* be an opening," Myles assured her. "It might be big and let us walk straight out, or it could be like the entrance and we will need to puzzle our way out. But whatever the exit looks like, it will exist."

"When Myles and I took a mountain portal together, the exit brought us to an abandoned fort and it was the safest we had felt for days," Sophie encouraged. "We will make it out of this one safely, too."

"We'll make it out," Mercy repeated. "We're going to make it out."

"You know something Myles told me once?" I asked her.

She took a shaky breath. "What did he tell you?"

Myles laughed nervously. "Should I be concerned?"

I shook my head. "No. It's a good thing." I met Mercy's gaze. "When we were trying to save my family, I was really scared that we might not be able to. And Myles told me that he knew they were going to be okay because he wasn't willing to take no for an answer."

"I'll just say no thanks and take the outcome I want," Myles finished, nodding his head.

"Exactly. And we can use that same logic now. We *are* going to make it out because none of us are willing to let it be any other way."

Mercy finally began to relax. "We'll make a way if we have to."

"Now we're talking," Will said with a smile. "We've got this. All we need to do is keep walking until we reach the end of the tunnel. Then we will get out, and we won't let it be any other way."

Sophie smiled. "I like that outlook."

"I do too," I said, meeting Myles's eyes through the dark. "Myles was right about it when the situation was much more dire.

So, of course it will work out the same here."

X

There was no way to keep track of time inside the mountain, and everything looked the same. Dark and rocky.

"Is it me, or is it weird there are no bats in here?" Will asked.

"I don't think so," Myles replied. "Only powerful Mageye can find mountain portals. So, nothing else can get in."

"You mean the entrances are invisible to non-magical beings?" I asked.

He nodded. "I don't know what they see. But it wouldn't be an entrance."

"Is it to protect the magic?" Sophie asked.

"Yes. As well as normal people and animals."

"Does that mean mountain portals can be dangerous?" Mercy asked, her voice pitching.

"We're Mageye," Myles soothed. "We'll be okay." He stopped walking, staring at the ground. "It's dirt," he said.

"What?" I looked at my feet. Sure enough, the floor of the tunnel was no longer made of stone, but dirt. When I looked at the walls and even back the way we had come, the entire interior of the tunnel had changed.

"We're halfway," Mercy breathed in relief.

"Yes," Myles said. "That means..." He trailed off, brow furrowed.

"What's wrong?" Sophie asked, her power giving her the appearance of fading into the shadows.

"Is it safe for me to keep lighting up the tunnel?" he pondered. "We have no idea how close we are to King Brenton's palace. In fact, should we consider masking our auras until we are able to confirm how close we are?"

Will frowned. "I hadn't thought of that... as for masking our auras, it won't hurt, minus causing a bit of a strain. But getting rid of our light? That's asking for someone to trip. Then Rose would unnecessarily need to use her powers."

"I also don't want to walk in the pitch dark," Sophie said. "There is no other light down here."

Mercy's breath started to quicken. "Please don't stop, Myles." She huddled closer to Will. "It's like the walls are closing in."

"They're not closing in," he soothed.

"Um... actually," I said cautiously. "The walls *are* closing in."

"What?" Myles's head whipped to the walls beside us.

The entire mountain began to rumble, and I stumbled into the walls as the ground shifted. Loose dirt rained down from above, and I looked frantically down either end of the tunnel, hoping for an exit, but there were only shaking floors and shrinking walls.

"Run!" Myles shouted, yanking Sophie back to her feet from where she had tripped and shoving her ahead. "Now!"

Mercy screamed, and her legs seemed to give out from under her. Will grabbed her arm, tugging her upright and practically dragging her down the tunnel after Sophie.

Myles took my arm and pulled me after him. "Faster!" he shouted. Purple lightning sparked off of him, lighting up the tunnel just enough for us to see the walls closing in.

"What's happening?" Will shouted. He doubled over to protect Mercy from the stones falling from the roof of the tunnel.

I put my arm over my head as the small stones rained down, yelping as they pelted me.

"I think the portal's shutting down," Myles shouted back.

The walls were now so tight they forced us to run single file, rough dirt and stone pressing against us. Myles shoved me ahead of him, and I twisted sideways as the walls were too thin for me to run straight through.

"We're not going to make it, Myles!" I screamed.

"I know!" He reached his arm over my head, and the tunnel

lit up with purple lightning.

My chest squeezed and the pressure fast constricted my ability to breathe, but then there was an electric snap and air flooded my lungs.

Bright light burned my eyes and a loud groan escaped me as my back slammed into the ground. Green, blue, and stone mixed together across my vision and dazzling stars accompanied a crack as my head slammed into a large rock. Branches whipped my skin, and then I was in freefall, my hair and skirts whipping around me.

I swung my arms wildly, screaming as Myles fell after me. He disappeared into the bushes and rocky ground scraped my skin as I skidded down a mountainside.

My fingers seemed to refuse my commands to grab something to stop the fall, and instead, I went flying forward as Sophie slammed into me, identifiable by a flash of blonde hair.

We flew apart and a loud crack sent fire erupting through my ribcage. I screamed, weakly hugging my ribs with one arm.

A few leaves twirled across my spinning vision from above and I rolled onto my stomach to vomit, sobs making the aches worse.

Branches continued cracking and then a bloodcurdling scream tore through the air, quickly followed by Mercy screaming Will's name. "Will!"

I gritted my teeth and a high-pitched whine escaped me as I lifted my head. Mercy stared over a ledge, screaming, "Oh no, oh no, oh no. *Will.*"

Will's screams went on and on, completely agonized and I staggered upright, bracing myself against the tree and staring at Mercy. My knees threatened to buckle, but Mercy was too close to the edge. Too panicked. Too at risk of falling after Will.

"Mercy!" I shouted, but it was more of a croak and she didn't react.

The spinning resumed as I took my first step and I screwed my eyes tightly shut, blindly reaching for the tree I had fallen against.

The soothing touch of my power gave me the strength to open my eyes and I stumbled forward again, Mercy still not reacting to my shouts.

"Myles?" I called instead. "Help!"

Sophie sat curled into herself, blood staining her blonde hair crimson. Her quartz gaze met mine, tears rolling down her cheeks. "Find Myles," I told her. "We need his help."

She slowly uncurled from herself and I turned back to Mercy, my pace quickening. She stood as if frozen, shrieking and listening to Will's screams.

I reached out and touched her arm. "Mercy?"

She jumped so high she nearly fell, and I tugged her back as she screamed, "He's going to die! Rose, he's going to die! It's bad... it's really bad... Will.... He's... he's..."

Will's screams had faded to faint whimpers and violent, choking sobs. I braced myself and leaned over the edge, bile rising in my throat as I took in a towering drop coated in red.

Will had landed on a bed of stone, and blood gushed from a gash on his leg, a jagged piece of white bone sticking out.

He twitched as his screaming renewed, his head rolling back, wordless screeches making my stomach flip with nausea.

My vision went fuzzy and I rubbed my eyes, wheezing as I stared at him. *What do I do?*

The cliff was dizzyingly jagged, with a straight fall down. If I jumped, I would end up with broken bones, and attempting to climb down was too risky.

The cliff stretched to both my right and left before blending into a steep slope, curving around and keeping Will cupped in a crescent.

Mercy collapsed, ducking her head between her knees and gripping the grass in her fists. I touched my throat with trembling fingers, my shout to Will coming out as a whisper. "I'm coming... Just hang on... hang on until I can get to you."

His only response was continued screaming.

Chapter 32

The slope leading around the crescent-shaped cliff was steep, but I ran to it anyway, leaving Mercy alone. Will's screams had stopped again and I tripped, grabbing the branch of a sad-looking tree for balance and practically hurling myself down the slope.

Branches smacked my face and my ankle rolled as I stepped on a tree root. Pain reverberated up my leg and I staggered sideways, gripping a thick trunk for balance. The spinning had started again and I dug my palms into my eyes in frustration. "God, please," I begged, cracking my eyes open.

The world stilled and I gasped, running forward and continuing my ungraceful descent of the slope.

Each step sent more pain up my ankle, and each breath felt like a drag. But, when I finally reached level ground, I broke into a run back to the cliff.

A few birds startled and flew out of my way, but I ran straight past them, trees snagging my hair and dress until I stepped onto the stone bed.

Will lay ahead of me, blood covering the stone around him and even the bottom of the cliff.

My hurried steps clicked across the rocks and I froze halfway to him. I had watched Myles die and he had looked less injured than this.

Both of Will's legs appeared gravelly damaged, the tibia

sticking out of his right calf making me gag as I crept closer, whispering his name. His left arm was twisted underneath him and a buzzing filled my ears.

Every fiber of my being seemed to tremble, but my voice came out shockingly calm as I threw myself beside him. "I'm here, Will," I announced my presence. "I'm going to help you."

Tears rolled through the dirt and blood on his cheeks, and he made no sign of recognizing me.

I blinked rapidly as I fumbled with my apron pocket to pull out the box of Golden Dove feathers, looking back at Will.

"These will save you," I croaked, pulling out the first feather. I grasped it firmly in my hand but hesitated to touch any part of him. "God," I whispered. "Please save him. Please help me..."

There was no reply, but a resolve entered my heart as I turned my attention to the jagged bone sticking from his leg. I placed my hand over it, the feather cupped in my palm, and Will's back arched. The sound that came from him shot terror through my resolve and planted itself into my heart. I had never heard a human scream like that before.

"I'm sorry!" I pleaded, putting my second hand over the break even as he wordlessly begged me to stop. It would heal faster if I touched the worst of it directly. But that also meant more agony for Will.

"Rose!" someone shouted from above me.

I lifted my gaze, nearly bursting into tears at the sight of Myles. Mercy and Sophie's panicked voices floated down from somewhere behind him, but Myles stood still, staring at us in horror.

"Oh no." His jaw went slack and despite his horror, no lightning flickered around him. As if he had forgotten he had a power.

Before he could say anything else, I screamed. The pain blossoming in my leg was indescribable, as if my very bones betrayed my body.

Lightning crackled and Myles suddenly knelt at my side. His breaths were shallow, and a trail of blood made its way down the back of his neck, soaking his collar.

Will jerked beneath me, and Myles put his hands on his shoulders, then froze. "I don't want to make it worse," he whispered.

I made no reply other than a shuddering sob. Every breath I took seemed to intensify the waves of pain and I bit my lip until blood began pooling in my mouth.

I rose onto my knees, my right leg nearly buckling beneath me as I braced myself. The bone beneath my hand was slick but firm, and I pushed down on it.

Will's strangled shriek cut itself short and his eyes rolled back into his skull, going terrifyingly still. But then the bone shifted and the pain that reverberated from my leg in the matching spot sent so many stars across my vision, the world went white. Myles put a hand on my shoulder, and I sucked air through my teeth, blinking until I could see again.

"Is it in place?" I whimpered, unable to see through my tears.

"Looks like it," Myles croaked, his voice shaky. "Are you using a feather?"

I nodded in reply, sweat dripping from my brow as Will's calf slowly closed over the bone. With the bone hidden where it belonged, Will looked no better and I pulled back, taking him in, in horror.

It was too much. His face was covered in bruises and scrapes, and blood gushed from wounds I couldn't see. I had never seen someone so pale, and his breaths had become flighty and altogether too shallow. The only sobs now belonged to me and Myles by Will's side, and Mercy and Sophie above us. It was fast sounding too quiet without Will's screams.

Myles held me upright and I reached for Will's other leg with a trembling hand, ignoring how every part of my body screamed for me to stop.

The blood surrounding his leg slowly crawled back inside, and I started breathing through my mouth to try and quell the nausea.

Another wave hit me and I swayed, pulling my hand back. "I can't," I whispered, fear gripping me.

Myles grabbed my hand, pushing it back over Will's chest. "He needs you," he whispered.

I dug my fingers into Will's chest, sharp sobs escaping me. My own wounds were still healing and there was no way for me to put that on hold. Every inch of my body was burning, aching, stinging, stabbing, and painful. And Will's wounds were *too much*.

The other feather, Myles said. *You need to use the final feather.*

I sobbed, screwing my eyes tightly shut. "Myles... it's still too much."

He sucked in his breath. "Water." He jumped to his feet, his voice steadier. "We need water."

"The magic water," I practically screamed. "Find his magic water."

Myles disappeared with an electric crackle, and I grabbed my final feather.

Chapter 33

When Myles reappeared beside me with the magic water, I slumped into him. The second feather crumpled to ash as the last of the blood on Will's legs faded, leaving his torso and upper limbs caked in crimson.

Myles supported me. "Are you okay? You're in cool-down, aren't you?"

"I need to heal his arm," I whispered, weakly reaching for the water. The world spun, but my grasp was firm as he passed it to me. "Are *you* okay?" I asked. "Sophie was bleeding, and I didn't notice any bad injuries on Mercy."

"Don't worry about the rest of us. We're banged up but not in danger. Heal Will."

I struggled with the stopper and paused with it uncorked, unsure of how to use it. Myles gently rolled Will and pulled his arm out from underneath him.

Blood spurt from a gash, splattering Myles's face and filling me with fresh dread. Myles put his hand over the worst of the wound, squeezing tightly as the blood continued to squirt between his fingers.

I went rigid, staring at the blood gushing from between Myles's fingers in horror. No wonder Will had gone so pale. Before I could second guess myself, I splashed the contents of the waterskin over Will.

Dust and blood washed off of his skin, and I wet his face and hair, taking a deep breath as I set the last of the water aside and gripped Will again.

Myles kept his hand over the gushing wound, using his shoulder to wipe the blood from his face.

Stars again flickered across my vision, but no longer from pain alone. My power seemed to be draining from me and I slumped over.

Myles caught me with one hand, holding me up as I tightened my grip on Will and pushed harder and harder. Myles's aura mixed with mine, and I gasped as energy surged through me again, taking the edge off of my pain. I pushed it all into Will and his blood began mixing with the water, before reversing back into him.

Color slowly returned to his face and with its return, the pain I felt began to fade. Myles gasped as the blood seeping from between his fingers began to roll the other way, and he pulled back shakily. The blood on his hands disappeared and Will's open wound invited the life-sustaining liquid back into his veins.

The reversing continued and Will's eyes shot open. He lifted his head, his eyes meeting mine as his chest heaved. Waves crashed in his irises, and the wet strands of hair hanging over his face seemed to bring life back into him.

My hand slipped from him, but he continued healing on his own. The bruises on his right arm, and the blood on his face, all faded as if they had never been there. Blood from the rocks and our clothes and Myles's face disappeared, and Will reached for me, taking the hand I had healed him with. "Rose?" His voice shook, but not with pain.

I had healed him. Will was going to live.

Chapter 34

Everything ached and I opened my eyes slowly, drawing in a careful breath. My ribs throbbed and I lay still, staring at the stars above my head. Sore muscles had fast become foreign since discovering my power, yet the fogginess that seemed to be pulling me back to sleep suggested I was still in cool-down.

A cliff towered above me and I lifted my head, wincing when my muscles protested. I lay on the bed of stone I had passed out on after healing Will, and everyone had gone quiet. No more screaming or crying or panic.

Myles slept beside me, one hand resting on my stomach, and the stars provided enough light for me to see the dark trail of dried blood down the back of his neck. I cautiously placed my hand over his, my breaths shallow. Having him by my side, especially after the ordeal we had just survived, seemed... *right*.

Sophie and Mercy slept a few feet from us and I furrowed my brow, sitting up slowly. Was no one on guard?

Will gasped when he saw I was up, having been huddled at the base of the cliff. "Rose," he whispered. "Are you okay?"

"Are you on watch duty?" I mumbled, gently moving Myles's hand off of me. The fog in my head wasn't clearing, and I leaned my forehead in my palm.

"Yeah," he answered, moving closer.

Someone touched my shoulder gently, and I looked down to

see Myles. "Are you okay?" he asked.

I blinked a few times, realizing I never answered Will when he asked. "Yeah... tired... and sore."

"Sore?" Will's eyes widened. "It still hurts?"

"I think it's cool-down," I mumbled.

Despite my assurance, he studied me in concern, and I, him. He looked perfectly fine. In fact, he looked better than fine. He looked as healthy as he had the day we met.

"The magic water went inside of him when you healed him," Myles said. "I think that's why his wounds finished healing themselves."

Will nodded. "It's like it—" His voice caught, but he pushed on. "It's like it never happened."

"Good," I whispered, shuddering as I looked up at the cliff he had fallen from.

Will touched my hand. "Thank you, Rose. I don't remember much... but the pain. So much pain..."

I accepted his hand. "It was... bad. I don't know if I would have been able to heal you without the feathers and water. But I'm just happy you're okay."

"Feathers?" Will jerked his hand back and turned to Myles. "You said she used the water. You said nothing about the feathers." He turned back to me. "You wasted them on me?"

"Wasted? Will, I needed them. You would have died!"

"I know, but..." He trailed off. "I don't want to die," he finally whispered. "But two is too much, it's more than I'm worth."

"Will," Myles said firmly. "You're worth more than two feathers to us."

I nodded in confirmation. "We're a team, Will," I said. "We help each other. No matter what."

"But now our feathers are gone because of me," he whispered.

I leaned over Myles to rest my hand on Will's chest, over his heart. "I'd rather have a beating heart than feathers."

"Yeah," he admitted slowly, placing his hand over mine. "Me too."

"Me three." Myles put his hand over both of ours.

Will smiled a little, looking up when Mercy and Sophie joined our small huddle.

"Rose," Mercy said, tears welling in her eyes. "I'm sorry I... I made it worse. I made everything worse. I'm sorry."

Sophie put a hand on her shoulder. "You didn't make anything worse. You were scared."

"No." She shook her head. "I couldn't stop screaming, and—"

"Sophie's right," I interrupted. "We all panicked. Nothing was your fault."

Myles began gently rubbing my back. Almost as if he were stimulating healing, some of the soreness in my muscles began to fade. "If anyone needs to apologize, it's me," he rasped.

"What?" Will frowned. "Why you?"

"I panicked when the portal was closing, and pulled us up as high as I could. I didn't mean to drop us on the top of the mountain. If I had teleported right when it started, we would all be fine. And we wouldn't have been forced to use magic we were saving for emergencies."

"But why did it shut down?" Sophie asked. "That *was* an emergency. And it's no one's fault that Rose had to use the feathers and some of the water. It was the only way to save Will."

"It happened right after we made it through the halfway mark," Myles said. "It must have been weaker than we realized."

"But it shut down with us *inside* of it," I said. "The portal could have killed us. Myles, without you there, we would have been crushed."

"I know."

A heavy silence fell over us, and Myles continued rubbing my back. "The portal was willing to take us. I think the problem was that the portal wasn't strong enough for all five of us to go through."

"We overloaded it?" Sophie asked.

"I think so. I mean, I don't really know that for certain, but it makes sense."

Mercy hugged her knees to her chest. "But we're out... and I'm never going in another one again."

Will looked at the cliff he had fallen from and shuddered. "Me either."

Just the thought of the shaking walls and crushing ceiling made me want to flee. I gave my own shudder and leaned against Myles's shoulder with a yawn. "What time is it?"

"Past midnight," Will said. "It's been quiet the last couple of hours."

Myles leaned over to see my face. "You're still in cool-down, aren't you?"

"I'm not as sore anymore, but my body's still tired."

"All right." He sighed. "You should get more sleep, then. In the morning, we'll figure out what to do next, as well as how close we are to King Brenton's palace."

I turned to Mercy. "Can the stars tell you now?"

She stared at her lap. "I'm having trouble talking to them. I think I forced myself into a kind of mental cool-down."

I reached over and took her hand. "Take your time, don't force it."

She sniffed, but nodded. "Thanks, Rose."

Despite the aching tiredness being gone from my body in the morning, Myles wanted me to pace myself with healing him, Mercy, and Sophie. So, I healed them one at a time with a break before helping the next.

Myles insisted on being last, and when he finally relented, I cupped the side of his face in my hand. His headache was worse than I anticipated and I grimaced. *You shouldn't have made me wait so long to heal you.*

You're healing me now, aren't you? Our gazes met and he smiled. *I feel loads better already, if that makes you feel better.*

Limited consolation. I moved my hand from his face and took his hand instead, flipping his palm to examine it. It looked as if he had attempted to grab hold of a branch when we fell, as his skin was raw and scraped.

He sat quietly as I healed him and when I finished, he didn't move his hand right away. "Thank you."

"You're welcome." I waited as the rest of his pain faded from my body, before turning away. "That is everyone, right? No one is hiding anything else?"

Will looked up from sharpening his dagger. "No secrets."

"Good."

Sophie had been picking berries from a bush nearby and brought them back to split with us. Mercy declined them, instead sitting on a boulder nearby, her faced turned to the sun. "My connection is back," she said simply.

"Take your time, Mercy," Myles assured her, adding a thanks to Sophie when she gave him some of the berries.

Her fingers were stained with their juices and I wet a kerchief for her to wash up with. "Thanks for finding Myles yesterday," I told her.

She took the kerchief. "I'm sorry it took me as long as I did. When I found him, he was unconscious."

I turned to Myles. "You got knocked out?"

He rubbed the back of his head where the worst pain from his headache had been. "After that first drop. I fell after you and blacked out. The next thing I knew, Soph was shaking me and saying you and Will needed help."

Will winced. "Can we not talk about... that?"

"Sorry," Sophie said.

He shook his head. "It's fine." He stared farther down the mountain, and some of the color left his face. "Myles, what are the odds of me convincing you to teleport us down to the bottom?"

"It depends on how close we are to King Brenton's palace," Myles replied. "I'm sorry."

"Yeah..." Will stood slowly. "I'll ask Mercy."

When he left, I turned to Myles. *What was that about?*

Heights.

My heart sank. Will had already been battling with the height of some of the mountains we crossed, and after yesterday...

His fall made it worse. He told me earlier, because he knew his emotions would make it easy for me to accidentally read his mind.

Did he suggest any way we can help him? Like he said his dad tried to do?

Myles sighed. *You mean help him get rid of the fear? No. Fears have to be conquered by the one they're feared by. We can support him, but he has to be the one to conquer it.*

Like when we met the illusion Mageye for the first time.

He is well-versed in fears, Myles answered, a faraway look in his eyes. *Too well-versed.*

Chapter 35

"All right," Mercy said as she and Will rejoined us. "The mountain portal took us farther than we expected." She pointed to the horizon. Another ridge of mountains loomed in the distance, their tops touching the clouds in the sky. "The palace is on the other side of those mountains."

Sophie flickered. "How close to the mountains?"

"We'll be able to see the palace once we cross them. Or we'll at least be able to see the start of King Brenton's land. Myles and Rose said The End was surrounded by charred land, so I think we can assume his palace will be the same way," Mercy explained. "He will have it protected, somehow."

"I agree," Myles said. "We will need to cross that land, too. Hopefully, there is more cover this time around."

I examined the tops of the distant mountains. "And a shorter distance. Five of us out in the open for days..."

"Not good," Will said. He was the only one who hadn't so much as looked at the mountains, though he seemed calm and poised.

"I wonder..." Sophie trailed off, her blonde hair swaying as she tilted her head. "I wonder if there's a way for me to enhance my powers and turn you all invisible?"

"Have you ever tried to turn anyone else invisible?" Mercy asked.

"I have, and it never works. But my clothes turn invisible when I do, same with items I'm carrying if they are in my hand before I turn invisible. So, there has to be some way to take it a step further, right?"

"Did you hold hands with people when you tried before?" I asked.

She nodded. "It has never extended to other living beings. I've tried animals, too. I used to have a pet bunny and my mom and dad said it looked like it had a magic power of its own."

"Cocoa Amber Hughes," Myles said, laughing softly.

"Let me guess," Will said. "It was brown with amber eyes?"

"With floppy ears," Sophie awed. "Even if I put her under my dress, she was visible."

"Hmm." I examined my hands. "I would have said holding hands seems like a good baseline. But that would be risky even if it worked, because we would trip over each other and break the chain."

"That's true," Sophie mused. "But what if there was something for me to draw upon? Like a magic rope... as an invisibility conductor?"

"I don't think I know of any ropes that work like that," Mercy said. "But that concept sounds like a lead."

Myles gasped, straightening as if struck by lightning. "Maya Moths!"

"Maya what?" I asked.

"Maya Moths," he repeated. "They can turn invisible, which means we might be able to use them to enhance Soph's power. The fur on their wings is what turns them invisible. It coats them like a fine dust, so if we rub their wings, it might enhance Soph's power and help her turn us invisible. Of course, we would still have the issue of walking together without tripping, but we can figure that out when it comes to it."

Sophie's eyes widened, the sunlight reflecting off the glittering quartz in her irises. "How do we find Maya Moths?"

"We can find them tonight." Myles examined the cliff towering above us. "They live in mountains—hiding in caverns during the day and coming out in the evening."

Will swept hair from his eyes. "Does that mean we should stay put for today? Or try to find a cavern they will be coming out of?" He eyed the cliff, grimacing. "Actually, can we move away from this spot?"

"Yes," Myles agreed. "We can start heading down the mountain and look for a cavern. It will make our hunt for moths easier tonight."

Sophie turned to look down the mountain. "But how will I use the moth dust?"

"You might be able to use it like I use Golden Dove feathers," I suggested. "I hold them in my hand so my aura can harness their power."

"So, if I cover my palm with the moth dust and hold someone's hand, I might be able to turn them invisible?"

"I think so," I said with a smile.

"All right." Sophie turned back to Myles. "It won't hurt to give it a try."

None of us needed much coaxing to leave the cliff Will had fallen from, and we began our trek down the mountain.

The crescent shape formed by the surrounding rocks and trees led us out into a bare and rocky mountainside, which was unfortunate for Will as it did little to block the height of the mountain.

He kept his eyes on the ground, and Mercy put a hand on his shoulder to encourage him.

Our pace was slow, examining the rocky outcrops for caverns, and being careful not to slide down any steep slopes.

"There's a cave," Sophie announced. The cave she pointed at was small, but when we gathered around it, Myles declared it to look like the perfect cave for Maya Moths.

"I have one question about this plan," Will said, keeping his back to the height of the mountain. "How exactly do we find something invisible?"

"They're not *always* invisible. They can just turn invisible," Myles replied.

"Well, then how do we *catch* something that can turn invisible? Won't they disappear when we try to grab them?"

"Oh." Myles hesitated. "You have a point."

"Wait, we're catching them?" Sophie asked. "Against their will?"

"Well... kind of," Myles said. "We will release them, but we need to catch them to get their dust."

"No." Sophie stepped back from the cave. "I thought we were going to try and touch them, not grab and capture them. I don't want to do this if we are going to scare them."

"We aren't going to hurt them," Myles promised. "It will be quick. Find the moth, grab it, brush dust off, release."

Sophie crossed her arms. "They use their invisibility as a defense. It's not right for us to catch them and use them."

"I think it's kind of like how I get feathers from Golden Doves," I suggested.

"No, because they *give* you the feather, you don't rob them."

"It's not *robbing*," Myles assured her.

She looked between us all and shook her head. "I'm not doing it if there is a chance we're going to hurt them."

"What?" Myles stared. "Soph, we aren't going to hurt them. We need to capture them, brush their wings, and let them go. That's it, I promise."

"*Myles*," Sophie said, and he paused.

His expression slackened. "It's not like that, Soph."

"It is to me," she said firmly.

"But." Myles tapped his fingers to his thigh, studying the

cavern. "We need help and these moths can provide it. It isn't like what happened to you, I promise."

Mercy's expression softened. "Oh... yeah, Sophie, we aren't doing this to hurt the moths."

Sophie flickered, but stood tall. "I'm sorry, but if we can't find a way to be gifted their dust willingly, I don't want to do it."

Myles hesitated and Will, Mercy, and I exchanged awkward looks. Sophie waited for Myles to answer and he finally sighed. "You're right, Soph, I'm sorry. If we can't find a way to get the dust without scaring or hunting them, we won't do it. But would you be willing to try if we can find a way to get the dust without any of that? Maybe you can turn invisible and pet one?"

She relaxed and nodded. "I think so. Thanks, Myles."

His expression softened. "You're too good for the world, Soph."

She giggled suddenly. "The only times I've gotten into mischief have been with your influence."

"And you enjoyed it," he teased. "Maybe you do have a mean streak."

"Mean streak?" she whined.

Mercy and I glanced at each other and smiled. "Sophie's not mean."

We said it simultaneously and Sophie stepped between us. "Thanks."

"We made a pact for a reason," Mercy whispered. "Now, should we wait here for nightfall?"

Sophie giggled, crossing her arms and tilting her chin. "Yes, we can wait right here."

✕

Will was careful to never look directly down the mountain, but as the sun set and the height hid itself under darkness, he relaxed.

"How much longer until the moths come out?" Mercy asked,

watching as the first stars appeared in the sky. "Should we begin preparing?"

Myles shoved the last bite of his dinner in his mouth. "Moths are attracted to light, so if we light a small fire, we may be able to get them close enough that we can touch them."

"Is it safe to light a fire at night?" I asked doubtfully. We had lit one earlier to cook meat from a turkey Myles hunted, but that was entirely different to creating a beacon through the dark. "What if there are Volcaniacs around, and they see it?"

"I don't sense any bad auras," Myles said. "And they won't necessarily assume a light is us. We are still far enough away that it would be reasonable to assume we are passersby. I think we're safe."

When we all agreed, he lit a small fire near the entrance to the cave, and I pulled the box I had kept the Golden Dove feathers in from my apron pocket.

"We can use this to store the dust."

"Good idea," Sophie said, gently taking it from me. "Once we test it, I will keep it in my apron for when we are ready."

"We also need to find a way to all turn invisible at once," I added.

"That will be our next step after we collect the dust," Myles said.

A slight movement behind him caught my eye and I peered at the cave. A small brown moth flew from it and into the night sky. Its wings looked fuzzy, even fuzzier than a normal moth's wings, and as I watched, it disappeared. "I saw one!"

"Saw what?" Myles asked, turning behind himself.

"One of the moths." I pointed to where I had last seen it. "It flew out of the cave and disappeared."

He grinned. "We're in the right place."

"What did it look like?" Will asked. "You know, before it turned invisible?"

"It was small and brown. And it looked soft."

"Looked soft?" Mercy repeated.

"Yeah. It had fuzz on its wings."

"The dust!" Sophie said, a smile on her face. "I want to touch one. Maybe they will come to me since I can turn invisible, too. Like how Golden Doves come to Rose. And that way, they won't be scared or feel used."

Myles nodded. "It looks like you're about to get a chance." He pointed at a small moth hovering by our fire. As we watched, it faded, and suddenly reappeared on the other side of the fire, but now it looked bigger. Maybe there were two.

Sophie took a careful step closer to the fire. "Could you give me some space?" she asked. "So they can approach me."

"Of course," Myles said.

He, Mercy, Will, and I crept away cautiously, watching her disappear.

"Do they live in colonies?" I asked once we were a safe distance away. "Or are we lucky?"

"They are very shy creatures," Myles said. "They stick together for safety. My old tutor, Mr. Langley, believes they can see each other even when they are invisible."

"Why?" Mercy asked. "Did he have a reason for believing that, or was it a theory?"

"He pointed out that it would be hard to stay in touch with an invisible group. If they cannot see each other when they are invisible, then how do they always stay together?"

"That's a fair point," Mercy conceded. "Do you believe it?"

"It makes sense, and it wouldn't shock me if it were true. But part of my brain could never wrap my mind around the concept of being able to see something invisible."

"Let's hope Sophie understands it," Will said. "If that theory is true, maybe we won't need to hold onto each other for the dust to work."

"That would be the best outcome," Myles mused. "Visibly invisible... no clue how that works, but if it does, it does."

"That is a very ironic thing for someone who can read minds to say," I pointed out.

"That's different." He shrugged. "I don't see thoughts, I hear them."

"How is that any different?" I argued. "You connect using an invisible conductor. And how about when you teleport? You create lightning out of thin air and disappear into it!"

"It's definitely different. Thoughts are not a physical object you can touch. And lightning is made of energy, so I increase that energy to create lightning."

"What about the invisible lightning you created in The End?"

"We could see it," he pointed out. "Like heatwaves."

I pouted, and he made a face back, but I could see amused lightning sparking in his right iris.

"You're not going to beat me on this one," he said.

"I can try."

"How?" he snickered. "You can't tell me how my own power works."

I crossed my arms. "We'll see."

"I think all of our powers are invisible to some degree," Mercy said.

Will put a hand to his temples. "This conversation is going to give me a headache."

Giggles swept over us, but we stopped when Sophie suddenly appeared.

Her gaze was focused on an empty branch I assumed carried a Maya Moth.

"What's your plan, Soph?" Myles asked.

"I'm waiting," she replied without moving her gaze.

"Waiting for what?" Will whispered to me.

I shrugged. "Probably for it to feel right."

"This sounds like the raising eyebrow thing all over again," Mercy said with a slight laugh.

Will flashed her a grin and raised an eyebrow. "It does, doesn't it?"

"Pretty sure we're all going to have a headache by the end of the night." Myles laughed. "Let's give Soph more space. She is going to get us our invisible key into the palace. I can feel it."

Chapter 36

"I touched one," Sophie announced as she suddenly appeared beside us. She held the box out, and when Myles lit the area with purple lightning, it made the dust inside the box sparkle. "Only one so far, but it worked. I waited for it to come to me, and it let me take some of its fur—some of the dust."

She grinned, turning to Myles excitedly. "And I could see it! Even when we were both invisible. I could see us both when it touched me, but we disappeared as soon as it flew off. It was like we connected."

"That's great," Myles said. "No, actually, that's *perfect*. That shows that the dust should work." He looked back into the box. "We're going to need a lot more, though..."

"I know. I think they can tell we need it for good. It will take time, but I can do it."

"You're the best-suited for the job, Soph." Myles smiled at her. "I bet they will start coming to you now that you've done it once."

"I hope so," she agreed, shutting the box carefully.

"Is there anything we can do to help?" I asked.

She shook her head. "I don't think so. You can sleep if you want. I will stay up until I collect enough dust to fill the box, so I can keep watch."

"Are you sure?" Will asked, brow furrowed. "You'll be exhausted tomorrow."

"I'm the only one who can collect the dust," Sophie replied. "And since the moths are nocturnal, I need to do it now."

"We can stay here so Sophie can rest tomorrow morning," Mercy suggested. "Then tomorrow afternoon, we can work on learning how to use the dust, and we will start traveling again the day after."

Myles nodded. "We shouldn't move any closer to King Brenton's palace until we have our plan for turning invisible. If this doesn't work, we will need to figure out something else."

"That works," I agreed. "But Sophie, if you need us for anything, wake us."

"I will." She disappeared, her footsteps the only sign that she had returned to the small fire by the cave.

"I'm going to stay up," Myles told us. "In case she needs anything."

"All right." I sat beside him, stretching my legs out.

"This area is safe," he declared contentedly.

I nodded in agreement. After our initial crash-landing on the mountain, the auras had settled. The mountain was peaceful, and I was thankful we still had another full day here.

"Rose?"

I shielded my eyes from the sun, yawning. Sophie leaned over me, smiling as she held up the box I had given her.

"I did it," she whispered. "The Maya Moths helped me like the Golden Doves help you!"

I sat up. "Really?"

She carefully opened the box, revealing that it was filled nearly to the brim with a fine, translucent powder, glittering in the morning sun.

"Wow," I awed. "Sophie, that is great!"

Myles stirred. "What?" he mumbled, only half-awake.

"Sophie collected the dust," I told him.

His eyes snapped open, and he sat up. "Where?"

Sophie laughed and passed the box of dust to him. His eyes widened. "This is perfect."

"Yes." Sophie sat across from us. "It took all night, but I did it."

"You must be exhausted," I said.

She nodded, giving me a tired smile. Her eyelids drooped and she sighed softly. "Can I sleep now, and we can figure out how to use it this afternoon?"

"Of course, Soph," Myles mumbled. He looked tired too, but he stood to shake off the last of it.

Will and Mercy were gone, and Myles frowned, relaxing after a moment. "I think they went to watch the sunrise," he told me as Sophie laid back.

I nodded, standing beside him and stretching. "No visions," I observed.

"Yeah." His gaze locked on the distant mountains that hid King Brenton's land from view. "Soon, they'll be gone for good."

"I hope so." I took his hand, and he started, turning from the mountains and smiling at me.

"I know so," he replied with a grin.

Voices distracted us, and we turned to see Mercy and Will climbing over the rocky mountainside.

"Morning!" Mercy greeted, waving a fistful of what looked to be leaves. "Did she do it?"

"Yes." Myles showed them the dust.

Will stared at the dust. "How many moths did she touch to get that much?"

"No idea." Myles laughed. "But it was enough. We're letting Soph rest before we play around with the dust."

The leaves Mercy had brought with her turned out to be from an evergreen tree, and we boiled water in one of the jars we had taken from the trader's cart to make tea. When we finished, Will gleefully announced he was going to take a bonus nap, and ended up sleeping until past noon. When he got up, we agreed to give Sophie a few more hours and didn't wake her until mid-afternoon.

Myles gently nudged her awake. "Hey, Soph. Are you ready to try the dust?" he asked.

Sophie yawned, blinking sleepily, but mumbled, "Just give me a minute."

Myles stood, careful not to bump her. "Take your time." His eyes landed on me. *I'm going to let her do what feels right. Her power should guide her through trial and error for this.*

You have a lot of experience helping people unlock new layers of their powers. I turned to Sophie, who was slowly rising to her feet. *I think it's going to work. The moths let her collect the dust, and that's a good thing, right?*

It should be.

"Where is the dust?" Sophie asked.

Mercy handed her the box. "Do you know how you're going to use it?"

Sophie cracked open the lid and studied the sparkling dust. "I think it's going to come down to touch. Kind of like how Rose needs to touch the wound she is healing, or how Myles needs us to hold onto him to teleport. Well, to teleport a farther distance."

"That makes sense," Will agreed. "And you can use the dust as a conductor."

"That's my hope," Sophie replied. She pinched some of the dust between two fingers, rubbing them together to coat them in a fine layer of dust.

"What's your plan, Soph?" Myles asked.

"I think if I hold hands with someone, I might be able to turn them invisible with me. I don't know how much dust to use, and I don't want to waste a lot while practicing. So, I'll start small and use more if needed."

"You're the boss." Myles held out a hand and Sophie giggled as she took it.

She stilled and shut her eyes, taking a deep breath before vanishing with Myles. I sucked in my breath; it worked!

"I'll try more dust," Sophie said. "I want to give this way a few chances before considering something else."

"What?" Will asked. "It worked."

"What?" Myles echoed. He and Sophie reappeared, and Myles was already giving Will a skeptical look. "Did you say it worked?"

"It did," Mercy said. "You both disappeared."

"No, we didn't," Sophie said, looking at her dusted fingers in confusion. "Nothing changed. I could see Myles the whole time, and I could even see myself! I was expecting to, at the very least, disappear myself, but even that didn't work."

Myles nodded in agreement. "What are you talking about?" he asked Mercy and Will.

"Wait," I interjected. "No. You both turned invisible. All three of us saw it."

"Huh?" Myles turned back to Sophie. "Try again," he told her.

She took his hand, and they disappeared.

"Can you see us?" came Myles's voice.

"No," I said.

They reappeared, and Will tilted his head. "Could you see each other that time? We couldn't see you."

"We could see each other," Sophie said. "I don't get it... is it only partially working?"

"Wait a second," I said. Everyone turned to me, and a smile grew on my face. "Myles, remember what you told us about Mr. Langley's theory? How he thought that Maya Moths could see each other whilst invisible? And Sophie, didn't you say you could see yourself and the moths even when invisible when they were in direct contact with you?"

When everyone nodded, I continued, growing excited. "I

think Mr. Langley's theory is correct! The dust turns the moths invisible, but only to those not using it. The reason Sophie and Myles could still see each other even though the rest of us couldn't, isn't because the dust wasn't working properly. It's because they were connected by the magic dust!"

Sophie's face lit up. "That means we will be able to see each other even when we are invisible, which gives us an advantage. We won't need to worry about tripping, because we will be able to see each other the whole time."

Myles grinned. "We have three-fourths of our problems solved. We collected the dust, figured out how to use it, *and* we have the bonus that we can still see each other. Now all that's left is figuring out how to use it all at once. We can't all hold onto Soph directly, so will it work through us like a chain if we all have dust on our hands?"

"What if..." Will began, eyeing the box of dust in Sophie's hand. "Sophie... Do you think you could control *just* the dust?"

"What do you mean?" she asked.

"Hypothetically speaking, if we were to coat our hands in the dust, could you then control the dust to turn us invisible without touching? Kind of like how Myles can create individual orbs if needed."

"I don't know. You might need to be covered in it from head to toe, and I don't have nearly enough for that."

"All right." Will furrowed his brow. "Can you try it? I might have an idea, but it depends on if this works."

"Sure." Sophie took out another pinch of dust and sprinkled it on Myles's outstretched hands. He rubbed his palms together, and the sunlight sparkled off the dust.

"Let us know if he disappears," Sophie said, tucking the box away. She turned to Myles and disappeared, but Myles remained solid... Well, his body did.

"Your hands," I said. They had disappeared. He held his arms up to his face, eyes wide.

"I can see it. Well, I can see that they disappeared."

His hands suddenly reappeared, as did Sophie. "You looked normal to me, but you said your hands disappeared? That means you're right, Will. I can control the dust itself, but only the parts of your body that have dust on it."

"That's better than nothing," Mercy said. "Maybe we could put it on in patches all over us?"

"We'd look like a moth-eaten coat," I pointed out.

Myles snorted. "I'm sure that's the last thing King Brenton would expect."

Will grinned. "Yeah, but what if we could surprise him by showing up *completely* invisible?"

"That would be preferable," Sophie agreed. "But I don't have enough dust. And it would take a couple of days to collect enough—days we don't have."

"And what if the dust gets brushed off or it rains?" I asked. "Since we would be able to see each other perfectly, we wouldn't be able to monitor whether it fades."

Will shook his head. "That's not what I'm suggesting. I think there might be a way for you to turn us all invisible from the inside out."

"What do you mean?" Myles asked. He paused, raising his brows as he assumedly read Will's mind. "Are you suggesting we *eat* the dust?"

"No. Drink it. If we mix the dust with water, I can control it from the inside and distill it into our bloodstreams. Speed up the extraction of nutrients, or in this case, moth dust. Then, Sophie can control the dust and turn us invisible."

Myles grinned. "You might be a genius."

Will grinned in return. "Took you long enough to notice."

"Couldn't that be dangerous?" Mercy asked hesitantly. "How do we know we can eat it?"

"If we get sick, Rose can heal us," Will pointed out. "We can combine our powers to make it work."

I nodded slowly. "And healing a reaction to any potential toxin wouldn't remove the dust, which means my healing won't stop the dust from working."

"Until it leaves our system," Myles said. "It doesn't take that long for water to digest. Granted, Will is going to distill the dust into our bloodstreams, so we will have more time, but not forever."

"It takes about twelvish hours for our bodies to fully digest something on a full stomach. But to be on the safe side, let's give ourselves ten hours. That is, if Sophie can hold it that long, which I think she can," Will mused. "We are relying on the logic that the dust will give her a boost, and that would include increasing the length she can maintain invisibility. If we drink it on a full stomach, we can get the maximum time. And then, depending on how far the area is that we need to cross, we can either make it in one go, or, after ten hours, drink more of it. We should have enough for us all to take two doses."

"How do you know how much we need to take?" I asked.

Will paused, theorizing slowly. "Well, let's say we wanted to poison someone—"

"I'm going to stop you right there," Myles said. "And redirect this conversation. Think of it like using a pinch of salt in your broth. A little goes a long way; the same thing goes for magic. Take the ice-diamond; it is small but incredibly powerful. We have enough dust for us all to take a few pinches."

"That makes sense," I said.

Mercy felt her arm with her fingers. "How do we know that Sophie won't just turn our insides invisible? After all, when she tried to turn Myles invisible, only his hands did. What if it only turns our organs invisible, making us look hollow?"

"I don't think that will happen, since our bloodstream delivers nutrients to all the cells in our bodies. The magic would be everywhere," Will said.

"And we will do a test run on someone to ensure they are fully invisible," Myles said. "That will also help us estimate how long we have and how much dust we need."

"We can test on me," I volunteered. "That way, if there are any medical repercussions, I will heal."

"All right," Myles said, taking the box of moth dust from Sophie. "Let's test."

Chapter 37

Myles directed me to sit, in case there were any negative side effects to consuming the dust before my power took over. Once I was settled, he rifled through his satchel and pulled out a small glass vial. "Will, can you fill this with water?"

"Sure." Will uncorked a waterskin, and a small arc of water shot up and neatly filled the vial.

"Thanks," Myles said, turning to Sophie. "Soph, put the amount of dust in that you think you will need."

She took the vial and pinched some of the dust in her fingers. "Can you mix it, Will?"

Will's eyes flashed and the water in the vial began to swirl like a whirlpool, and it soon took on a shimmery, almost silver color as the dust mixed in.

"Reminds me of the stars," Mercy observed, smiling.

"It's pretty," Sophie agreed, sitting across from me. "Are you ready to drink it?"

I nodded and took the vial, turning to Will. "Will I be able to feel you distilling it?"

"To be honest, I haven't done anything like this before, so I don't know how it feels. But all I'm doing is speeding up what your body already does. If it hurts, tell me to stop."

"Easy enough." I took a deep breath before tilting my head back and drinking the vial. It was crisp, crisper than any water I had ever had. When the vial was empty, I set it aside. "I'm ready."

Will nodded, squinting at my stomach. "I'm going to get it into your bloodstream now."

I nodded, and a sudden chill went through my body, starting in my stomach and quickly spreading across my chest and into my arms, as well as down my legs. "I can feel it."

The chill immediately stopped, and Will stared. "Does it hurt?"

"No, it feels like you're tickling me from the inside. But it doesn't hurt."

He smiled. "It's a new trick, then."

Mercy groaned. "Will is going to start randomly controlling our organs now."

"I hadn't thought of that," Will said as the tingling resumed. "Thanks for the idea, Mercy."

"No! Don't do it," she argued.

He beamed. "No promises." The tingling slowed again and he grew serious. "All right, that should do it. And its effects should last until it leaves your system."

I examined my hands and arms, but they looked normal, and the tingling had faded completely. "I wonder if my blood would sparkle?"

Myles laughed. "I guess that depends on if the dust dissolves like salt."

I wrinkled my nose. "That's a weird thought... Are you ready to test it, Sophie?"

She went to take my hand, but paused. "Actually, I'm going to try without touching you. Since that is our goal."

"Good idea," Myles said, watching closely. Will and Mercy did the same, and Sophie closed her eyes.

When she opened them, they seemed to be glowing, as if a candle had lit behind them. "Did it work?" she asked.

I turned towards Myles. He, Mercy, and Will all had identical grins on their faces.

"Sure did!" Will cheered. "I can't see either of you."

"Really?" Sophie gasped.

"Yep," Will grinned at her, and I realized she must have made us visible again.

"Do you feel a strain when you do it, Soph?" Myles asked.

"A very slight one, but it is manageable." A small smile appeared on her face. "Even for a day-long journey with five people."

Myles nodded in satisfaction. "It looks like we have a way to sneak in. Now we need to know how long the effects truly last. I think we should test every fifteen minutes or so, to get the timing as exact as possible."

"When we officially do it, we should have a little more time," Mercy said. "Because we will be on a full stomach, and none of us have eaten in a couple of hours right now."

"That's true." I put a hand to my stomach. "I'm not hungry, but I'm not full either. That might cut the time a little short."

"That's all right," Myles replied. "We will have a rough estimate. And we have some berries leftover from yesterday. How about you eat some now?"

✕

Nine hours. That was how long the full effects of the Maya Moth dust lasted. After that, Sophie could only get me translucent, and eventually nothing at all.

And that wasn't on a full stomach. Had I had a full stomach, we likely could have gotten even more time.

"This is good," Myles said. Darkness had long since settled, and he had relieved Will of his post, keeping watch. "When we all use it, we won't be able to tell when the effects fade, but if we drink more after about nine hours, we will be able to get eighteen hours total."

"We should have a little more than that if we drink it on a full stomach," Sophie reminded him. "Plus, the effects don't stop all at once; it fades slowly, so that will buy us extra time."

"That's true," I agreed. "We might be able to squeeze a full day out of it if we play our cards right."

Myles nodded. "That would be ideal."

Soon after, Sophie fell asleep, and I lay next to Myles. "Tell Mercy to wake me if she gets too tired during her shift," I told him.

He wrapped one arm around me, pulling me closer. "You've been up all night testing the effects with Soph," he argued. "I'll tell her to wake me instead."

Flush rose in my cheeks and I stared ahead of myself, fighting a nonsensical smile. "Deal," I whispered, inching closer.

"Good," he murmured. "Now, sleep."

"Mmm," I replied as I drifted to sleep in his arms.

When I opened my eyes, my friends were gone and the sky was dark. Not with night, but with a deadly storm.

Flashes of orange filled the sky as the top of the mountain exploded, lava spurting high into the air.

I screamed and scrambled to my feet to run down the mountain, shouting my friends' names.

They didn't answer.

"Myles!" I shouted again, stumbling over a loose stone and twisting my ankle. I fell to the ground, scraping my hands and knees as the lava raced towards me.

Streams of it flooded around either side of me, closing up and blocking my way of escape.

"Help!" I screamed, looking around wildly and calling again for Myles. My ankle ached, and my palms and knees burned, heat from the lava making it hard to breathe. "Myles!" I cried.

This time, there was a reply. A man walked through the lava towards me, his one eye the color of a burning ember.

King Brenton.

His mouth twisted into a wicked grin. "It looks like I didn't need to send Tara and Mark, after all." He waved his hand to the mountaintop, where lava continued to arc into the sky. "I see you."

Chapter 38

My eyes snapped open, and I fought wildly against the person holding me down. "Let go of me!" I whisper-screeched as I struggled, scared to scream and make the dream reality.

The person let go, and I scrambled away, my heart racing.

"Rose!" Myles called. "Rose, it's me. It's only me."

I stilled, tears blurring my vision as he rushed over, pulling me back into his arms. I buried my face in his chest and sobbed. "I'm sorry," I whispered.

"Shh, it's okay. You're okay. You didn't hurt me."

I only hugged him tighter, gripping his collar in my hands.

"What happened?" he asked gently. "Was it a vision?"

I nodded, still refusing to lift my head from his chest, even as my heartrate returned to normal. I didn't want to leave his arms.

"He spoke," I finally said.

Myles stiffened. "Who did?"

I didn't have the strength to say it aloud, so I switched to thoughts. *King Brenton. The mountain turned into a volcano, and I was all alone. The lava surrounded me, and I called for you, but you weren't there. Then King Brenton came, and he said something about people named Tara and Mark, and that he could see me.*

See you? That means... Oh no. Myles's thoughts came to an abrupt halt as he shut me off from then.

I pulled back. "It means what?"

"Three nights," he whispered. "We've been here for *three nights.*"

"For the dust," I said, confused. "Why does that..." I stopped, a sudden chill going through me. King Duncan had told us that if we stayed in the same spot for too long, King Brenton might be able to see our location.

I pulled out of Myles's arms. "Does that mean... Do you think he meant it? Do you think he was actually able to see me?"

"I don't know," Myles said, purple lightning flickering in his right iris. "I don't..." He looked to the top of the mountain and jumped to his feet. "We need to move. Now."

I didn't argue. Instead, I began gathering our things while Myles woke everyone else.

"Pull in your auras," Myles directed once everyone was awake, or at least half-awake.

"Huh?" Mercy asked. "Pull in our auras, why?" Her voice pitched. "Are we being attacked?"

Will was already on his feet, gripping a waterskin tightly in his hand.

"Rose had a vision," Myles explained. "We... We shouldn't have, ugh!" He groaned in frustration. "How could I have been so stupid? It was the *one* warning King Duncan gave us."

"What was the one warning King Duncan gave us?" Sophie asked, peering into the darkness nervously.

"Not to stay in the same spot for more than one night. King Brenton saw Rose in the vision—the vision was of *this* mountain. We need to get out of here; he might be coming."

Any lingering tiredness vanished in a flash, and we began a hurried descent. Sliding in the dark, it took us nearly an hour to reach the base of the mountain.

"How far should we go?" Will asked. "We don't even know for sure if the Volcaniacs are coming, much less from which direction."

Mercy took the lead, watching the stars instead of the ground at her feet. "There is a good hideout nearby. We can stay there until morning, and if no one has shown up by then, we should be safe, since I'm sure King Brenton will assume we are going to move."

"That's true," Myles agreed. "And our auras are hidden, so if someone shows up, we will be able to ambush them and not the other way around."

"And maybe it was only him trying to scare us," I said. "After all, this was the first vision either of us has had in a while. Wouldn't he need to create a vision multiple days in a row if he wants to see us?"

Myles hesitated. "But if the vision was of that mountain..."

"You're right," I agreed, reaching for Ren's jackknife and rubbing my thumb on the handle. "He also referenced people I've never heard of."

"Who?" Sophie asked nervously.

"Tara and Mark."

Will frowned. "Volcaniacs?"

"The hideout is up ahead," Mercy announced.

A huge rock formation loomed above us, and cracks between the piled boulders provided cover while still allowing us to see out.

We crawled in and found a hollow center with the rocks piled over our heads. We sat in a circle, our feet touching in the middle. Gaps allowed the stars to shine in from overhead, and a safe aura seemed to rest on us like a weighted blanket.

"We should be safe here," Mercy said, peering out of one of the cracks to see the stars.

Myles nodded, taking my hand and rubbing circles with his thumb. "He said he saw us, not that he was coming. But if he recognizes the mountain and knows how close it is to his palace..."

Sophie hugged her knees to her chest. "It's not like we're only a day away, right? And... and they probably don't know exactly how Mercy's power works."

"That's true," I agreed softly. "Mercy never used her power around the illusion Mageye, because the stars never hinted about the fake portal he created."

"He knew our powers worked together, but that is pretty obvious," Mercy added.

Myles's thumb stilled and his shoulders relaxed. "That gives us an advantage back... and he gave Rose names. Tara and Mark, we can use that."

"How?" Will asked.

"Uh... I don't know yet," he confessed. "But when Rose and I were in the volcano, some of the Volcaniacs thought we were members. Now we have names to pretend we got orders from, right?"

I shut my eyes, resting my head against the rocks. "Silver lining kind of stuff."

"Exactly," Myles agreed. "We won't ever forget Dad's instructions again. I'm sorry I let that happen."

"We all forgot," Mercy said. "We got distracted with getting hurt and the Maya Moths."

"Another silver lining." Will grimaced. "The mountain portal led us to the moths... but I don't think I'd do it again if we could go back."

"Definitely not," Mercy agreed, grimacing. "Never again."

"Should we get up early?" Sophie suggested softly. "I know we are getting too close to teleport safely, but we could at least have a head start to the day."

Myles nodded. "I think we should head in a less obvious direction starting tomorrow. With Mercy's power acting as a secret weapon, we can come in from another side."

Will stretched his legs out, careful not to kick anybody. "What if instead of cutting through the mountains, we go around them? It would take more time, but he would expect us to go the quicker route."

"That would make us easier to ambush," Mercy pointed out. "Having height is an advantage."

Will shook his head. "It comes with disadvantages too—we could fall."

"Well, we could get crushed by an avalanche at the bottom of the mountain," Mercy said, but as she continued, her tone softened. "We won't let you fall again, Will. And we aren't going to climb straight up to the top and back down; that would waste time and energy." She made a curving motion with her hand. "We can loop around it."

"I agree that getting stuck in between mountains isn't a good idea. But Will does have a good point," I said. "If the palace is on the other side of the mountains, the obvious route is straight through."

"Well," Myles said with a frown. "Since we are assuming King Brenton doesn't know about Mercy's power, he doesn't know that we have his exact location pinpointed."

"But he knows that we were on a mountain, and that we are heading to his palace, so the only way to go is straight through." Sophie fidgeted with the hem of her dress.

Mercy nodded in agreement. "Besides, even if we didn't know his palace will be in sight on the other side, we know what direction to travel in. East."

"At the end of the day, whether we continue cutting straight through or take the long way around, our end goal stays the same," I said. "King Brenton knows we're coming, and that won't change no matter what route we take."

Everyone stared at me, but no one could come up with a counterargument.

"You're right," Myles finally said. "We don't have the element of surprise with us. Which means that all we can do is avoid any lurking Volcaniacs."

Chapter 39

"Will, can you dry my feet?" I asked after trudging through a puddle. Since our scare with the controlled vision, we had been careful to lean into the advantage gifted to us by Mercy's power. Myles had never had the vision—our first time not sharing one since we left the city, nor had any come since.

All of which we took to be signs in our favor, and we had stopped masking our auras once we had determined the Volcaniacs weren't coming for us. We were now traipsing in what Myles declared was a parabolic route up and over the last mountain shielding us from King Brenton's palace. As if that wasn't enough to make us anxious, the day was cold, damp, and foggy. But Will had kept us dry, bending the drizzling rain around us.

Water rushed from my boots, leaving my feet dry but cold. "There you go," Will said.

"Thank you." I peered through the mist. "We should be getting to the back of the mountain soon, right?"

Mercy pointed at the sky. "I think so, but the fog is messing up my communication with the stars."

"Hopefully, the fog will clear," Sophie said. "Once we reach the other side, we might be able to see the palace. We don't want it to suddenly take away our cover when we start walking towards it."

"That's a good point," Will said. "We need the sun to come out, and the fog will dissipate. It's too cold for the water droplets to evaporate."

"Can you make the fog move?" I asked. "Since it's so moist?"

He narrowed his gaze at the fog, but the movement of the droplets was the equivalent to blowing on smoke. It did nothing but provide a swirling effect. "I guess fog isn't quite my area of expertise. Only the rain."

"Better than nothing," I said, inching around a puddle that suddenly jumped out of the way. "Thanks."

"We might need to wait out the fog once we reach the back of the mountain," Myles decided. "That way we can scout the area before we try sneaking to it. Give us a chance to plan an ambush, so to speak."

"I can't sense any bad auras," I added. "So we still have a ways to go."

"True," Will said. "And I kind of like not being able to see it. Once we do, everything is going to feel a lot more real."

"Much more real," I agreed, my steps slowing until I stood frozen, staring at the dissipating fog that revealed we had made it to the back of the mountain.

Barely visible in the distance was the outlined shape of a dark palace, surrounded by miles of dreadfully familiar charred black land.

"Is that..." Will started to ask, then stopped. "It is."

The mountain range we had crossed was much larger than I had realized, spreading out on either side of us in a large crescent shape, caging in the palace. Similar to how we had been caged at the bottom of the cliff Will had fallen from. I shuddered; it was safe to say we would all be happy to cross back over these mountains and leave both them and the palace behind for good, once the Volcaniacs were defeated.

It looked as if the blackened land merged into flat grasslands, and separating us from the grasslands were miles of thick forest.

We stared in silence, waiting for the rest of the fog to dissipate to get a better look.

"Well, we will have cover until we get to the grasses and charred parts," Myles finally said.

Weak sun rays struggled to pierce the clouds and Mercy stepped into one of the rays, turning her face to the sky. "There are about fifty miles between us and the start of his land, and then another twenty-five separating the grasslands from the palace. The grasslands themselves are only about five miles."

"Eighty total," Will murmured.

"Not as protected as last time," I observed.

Sophie nodded, adding, "Volcanos are bigger than palaces."

Myles turned away from the palace. "He's still regaining his power. It has only been a few months, and I'm sure he's still rebuilding his army."

"But he's been getting stronger," Will pointed out. "We can't underestimate him."

"I agree," Myles said, his expression solemn. "Expect the unexpected to be unexpected."

Another silence settled over us as we again observed the distant palace. From afar, it looked like a portrait made from charcoal, but it wasn't nearly as pretty as the art Ryder made with his charcoal.

"What's the plan?" Sophie asked. "We can use the woods as cover, and once we get to the grasslands, we will need to use the Maya Moth dust. But when do we start masking our auras?"

"We should mask our auras once we turn invisible. That way, we will be undetectable," Myles said.

Will shifted his feet. "We already haven't teleported in a few days, but now," he waved his hand over the forests and grasslands, "we're fully on foot, aren't we? Even portals will be unlikely at this point, since they don't usually linger in bad areas."

"Well, the Wolvien Guard used them, and the mountain lion Myles and I saw," I said.

"Anyone, good or bad, can use them," Myles explained. "But what Will said is right, they don't often linger where they can get tainted."

"Oh." I eyed the palace again.

"Well, if we are going to mask our auras and be invisible, we'll have our element of surprise back," Mercy said.

"Exactly. And I intend on keeping it," Myles agreed, his expression growing determined. "We have a palace to break into and a king to kill."

It took us three days to cross the forest separating the mountains from the grasslands. No longer was our mission able to be mistaken for friends on a camping trip; it was now a mission to defeat the Volcaniacs through and through.

Will had suggested that Myles should climb a tree and attempt to scout out the grasslands before we left our camp this morning, but the idea had been set aside when Mercy told us she suspected we would be leaving the woods behind today, anyway.

Now, as a faint sense of danger made my aura tingle, I paused. It came from ahead of us. "Is that aura something coming towards us, or is that the grasslands themselves?" I asked nervously.

Myles frowned. "The grasslands themselves. It has the presence of danger, but not immediate danger."

"Can either of you sense it?" Will asked Mercy and Sophie.

Both nodded. "It's faint, though," Sophie said.

"It's faint for everyone," Myles said. "Bad auras can't hurt us, they are meant to deter us."

"Well, it's not going to work," I said. "We're coming, whether King Brenton likes it or not."

Lightning flickered in Myles's purple iris. "That's right." He took a few steps closer to the auras and paused. "I know we decided to wait to mask until we are invisible, but maybe we should do it now."

I shut my eyes, imagining swirling green smoke being folded up inside of me. When I opened my eyes, Myles nodded as the comforting blanket of his aura faded. Will, Mercy, and Sophie followed suit, though Mercy didn't move her gaze from the sun as she did so.

"We are almost at the start of the grasslands. Once we leave this forest, there won't be any cover," she said.

"Which means we will need to start using the Maya Moth dust," Will said.

"We need to plan how we will use it." Sophie pulled the box of Maya Moth dust out and opened it, studying the glittering contents. "I think I want to see the grasslands first."

A slow feeling of anxiety seeped into my veins and I took a careful breath. "Let's take a look, then."

The faint auras lingering in the forest grew slowly stronger, until glimpses of swaying grasses appeared through the trees. We crept as close as we could without losing cover and studied the fields in silence.

Were it not for the blackness framing the grasses from behind, the field would look relatively normal. The grasses appeared to reach about knee high and they danced in the light breeze.

I braced my hand against a nearby tree and stood on my tiptoes, straining my eyes to get a glimpse of the palace. According to the stars, about thirty miles separated us from it.

Myles put a hand on my shoulder. "It's not as tall as the volcano, so we likely won't be able to see it until we are much closer."

"How much closer?" Will asked.

"Depends on how tall the palace is and how flat the charred land is," Mercy murmured.

Sophie hadn't said a word, and instead stood to the side, clutching the box of Maya Moth dust in her hands. Her irises seemed to glitter as light hit them and she studied the grasslands in painstaking detail. A memory to be seared into her vision until the Volcaniacs were defeated for good.

"Myles, can I have the vial?" she finally asked.

He nodded and pulled it from his pocket, passing it to her and then putting a hand on her shoulders. "Is it okay if we move back into the forest for better cover?"

She only nodded, already eyeing the vial and stumbling blindly after us. When we were a safe distance away, she lowered the vial from her face. "I'm going to say one vial gives us nine hours to play it safe, and I have enough dust for all of you to take two vials, with a little leftover."

"That's good," Will said. "And I should be able to distill it into us even out there. My aura won't flash out very much."

"Good," Sophie murmured, now eyeing Myles. "I think Myles will need to take more than the rest of you, since he's so much taller."

"I hadn't thought about that." Myles looked down at himself. "I probably should have tested it, too. Height and weight will make a difference."

"Well, it ultimately comes down to when the dust leaves your system," Sophie continued. "And nine hours is what worked for Rose without taking a full meal, so nine hours is less than we should actually have. If you each take it twice, we will have roughly eighteen hours within our safe estimate. The question is, can we cover thirty miles in eighteen hours?"

"I don't think we have a choice," Mercy said. "It's certainly doable after all the walking we have done. But holding in our auras will add strain, not to mention, we don't know what the charred terrain is like."

Will turned back to the grasslands, now hidden behind the

trees. "We can do it. But what about when we get to the palace? I find it hard to believe we will be able to complete every part of our mission in under eighteen hours. We will likely turn visible again at some point inside the palace."

Sophie flickered, but took a deep breath and steadied herself. "The main reason we want to remain invisible is so we can sneak in. Once inside, we can find cover or a hiding place, and our presence will eventually be known, regardless."

"And how will we get back out?" I asked.

"Well," Myles said, "our mission is not only to eliminate King Brenton, but to destroy *all* surviving Volcaniacs. Ideally, we will be able to walk out when we finish."

"And then we'll hunt down the rest of them. Find any stragglers and finish them, too," Will said softly.

"We may need to keep King Brenton alive for a little bit," Myles admitted reluctantly. "So I can read his mind and find out where everyone else is."

"How would we do that?" I asked. "Unless he hits cool-down, even if we tie him up, he could still use his powers."

"We could use the ice-diamond," Mercy suggested. "Myles can ask him where everyone else is, read his mind, and finish him before he unfreezes."

I pulled the ice-diamond from my pocket, letting the cold crystal roll in my palm. Its chilly presence had been a constant against my leg that I had fast become used to.

Sophie gently took it from me, eyeing it nervously. "But what if we need it as a weapon? That's what we got it for. Unless we finish everyone else off first, we should at least keep it in mind as an escape."

Myles nodded. "I agree with both of you. We should keep it as a form of escape, and if we don't need it, we will use it so I can get a chance to read King Brenton's mind. If we have to use the ice-diamond before we face King Brenton, we will figure something else out."

"If I surround him with water, he won't be able to save himself," Will suggested.

"You want to drown a fire king?" Mercy asked.

"Or douse him."

"Extinguish his flame," Myles pondered, lightning flickering in his right iris.

I accepted the ice-diamond back and dropped it into my pocket. "A lot of what we'll end up doing will come down to what the interior of the palace is like. If he is in a room like the amphitheater in the volcano, there would be more lava than water."

Will looked down, his voice suddenly soft. "I know."

Myles paced, tapping his fingers against his thigh. "What we need to focus on now is reaching the palace without getting caught. Rose is right about needing to see what we are up against first."

Will lifted his head and squared his shoulders. "In that case, we will need to time our arrival. We have eighteen hours to get in, so how do we want to use that time?"

"We need to get every second out of the dust that we can, so we shouldn't take it until we are ready to leave," Mercy said. "And we should all take it at roughly the same time so we are all on the same timeline for the second dose."

I glanced at each of the bags we carried. With Will's ability to fish in every stream or lake we passed, and Myles's ability to shoot lightning and hunt, on top of any foraging we did, food hadn't been a big concern. However, we often ate lean and the Maya Moth dust required us to take it on a full stomach to get the maximum time.

"I don't think we have enough food to be completely full," I observed. "So, we might need to find more food first, and we will eat as close to when we leave as possible."

"That's a good point." Myles stopped pacing. "I also think we should rest before we leave. Once we step out of this forest, rest won't be an option."

"Not something to rush." Will eyed the trees blocking the grasslands again.

Myles nodded slowly, his gaze flicking over each of us before he straightened. "All right, it is what, roughly two in the afternoon? What if we spend a few hours hunting and collecting food, and then rest until about midnight? At midnight, we will get up and eat until we are full, then take the dust and start crossing the grasslands. If all goes well, we will arrive at the palace around noon tomorrow. Since we are invisible, we can use the daylight to our advantage."

Will was the first to agree with the proposal. "I think that is as solid of a plan as we will get."

I nodded in agreement. "If we can break in during the day when we can see, I vote we take that opportunity."

"I agree," Mercy said. "My connection to the stars will be cut off in the palace, anyway. I can see them through windows but not have a full conversation with a roof over my head. So I won't be able to give directions once inside during the day or night."

"If it isn't going to make a difference for your power, then breaking in during the day is the way to go," Will said. "And it also comes with the bonus that King Brenton will probably expect us to break in at night. He doesn't know we have a way to turn us all invisible."

"We really do have advantages, then," Sophie said, smiling softly. "They don't have the upper hand like they seem to think."

Myles smiled. "Now, we just need to play our cards right."

Chapter 40

We spent the next couple of hours gathering food for our *midnight feast*, as Will had cheerfully named it. He had gone fishing in a nearby stream, and though the fish were small, he had caught plenty of them.

Myles and I had spent the time gathering hazelnuts from a nearby grove, and Mercy and Sophie had collected more berries than we would probably be able to eat.

When Will returned from fishing, he held a two-foot-long, sturdy-looking branch in his hand.

"What's that for?" Myles asked.

Will held it up. "A makeshift baton. I have room in my bag, and it isn't too heavy, so I thought, why not?"

"And what are you going to use a makeshift baton for?" Mercy asked doubtfully.

He demonstrated swinging it. "I'm going to send King Brenton flying off the edge of Alveraada!"

"Have you ever used one of those in a fight?" Myles asked, holding out his hand and giving it his own test swing.

"Not against a living thing. But I've hit enough rocks with these to know it's worth having as a backup."

Myles handed the baton back to Will. "I would agree with that. A well-aimed blow to the head will take someone out. Trust me. I've been the victim of one."

"Should Will test it on you?" I asked sweetly.

Myles's eyes widened. "What? No! He can test it on the first Volcaniac that crosses our paths."

"At that point, it won't be a test," Will said somewhat solemnly.

My shoulders slumped and I looked towards the grasslands. With all of the hours we had spent training, practicing fighting tactics, surprise "attacks" from each other, and general endurance, it was easy to feel prepared. But, what was a month of practice going to do against decades of strength? Only time would tell, and prayer, as God must surely be on our side.

Sophie's gaze lingered on the baton. "At least we'll be together."

"Till the end," Myles said, sitting across from Will. He patted the spot beside himself, and some of my anxiety faded as I sat beside him. "In a little while, we will gather some sticks for a fire. I'm not really in the mood for raw fish."

Mercy wrinkled her nose. "Me either."

"Gross," I said. "I'd almost be willing to take the Maya Moth dust on an empty stomach over raw fish."

"Good thing we're going to cook it, then," Myles teased. "You know what, why wait? We should have the fire doused by the time it's dark. We're too close to risk the flame being spotted through the trees."

I glanced towards the grasslands nervously and stood to help gather sticks.

We were cautious with the fire, and after it was extinguished, we ate a light dinner of berries, keeping the rest stored for later.

"Rose." Myles leaned against a fallen log. "I don't know if it's safe for us to sleep so close to the palace. King Brenton is a day's journey away, and we can't risk having a vision when we're this close."

A lump formed in my throat, which I swallowed back. Neither

of us had had a controlled vision since the one I had on the mountain, but if King Brenton truly knew we were getting close, he must certainly be preparing to attempt another vision soon.

"Well," I said slowly, "I guess a sleepless night tonight will make sleep tomorrow even better. No more Volcaniacs, no more controlled visions."

"We can keep watch together," Myles said. "Hold each other accountable."

Will frowned. "That doesn't seem fair, especially since I'm sure we will need both of your powers tomorrow."

"Rose's power can probably help with any side effects of exhaustion," Mercy said, turning to me. "Right?"

"Well, I can't do much for nausea," I said. "But for sore feet and headaches, I can help."

"I've stayed up for two days straight before," Myles said, nudging me. "And Rose's brother did that right before we left. If he can do it for his trial, we can do it for this trial."

I smiled a little, though my heart ached. "We'll make Raymond proud."

Will hesitated. "Is there a way to avoid a vision by only letting you sleep for brief intervals?"

"At that point, it wouldn't even be worth it," I said, sitting up straighter. "We don't really have a choice, and even if we did, I don't want to risk it."

"All right, if you are sure."

"We'll be fine," Myles assured. "We've done this type of thing before."

"And hopefully, this is the final time," Mercy said. "For all of us."

"Yes, after King Brenton is defeated, the rest of the Volcaniacs will be nothing," Sophie added. "Even if we have to search for them."

"If we have to search for them, we will end up facing them one at a time," I said.

"Piece of cake," Will declared, laying down with his arms folded behind his head.

"We should have a cake to celebrate when we finish this," Mercy said, giggling. "The sweetest thing we've had since we left are berries."

"Well, technically we had those stuffed rolls Will's mom packed," Sophie pointed out.

Myles chuckled, stretching his legs out. "I could go for a cake. One with extra frosting."

"Buttercream," I hummed. "Now I'm too hungry to sleep even if I wanted to."

"Me too," Myles agreed, smiling.

The woods were eerily quiet, no chirping crickets or rustling leaves accompanying night creatures. I rested my head on Myles's shoulder, my eyelids drooping with exhaustion.

"Rose." Myles moved his shoulder away, and my eyes snapped open.

"Sorry," I mumbled, blinking the sleep away.

"It's okay." He took my hand and helped me to my feet alongside him. "Here," he said, "sometimes standing helps."

I buried my face in his chest. "It does," I murmured.

He chuckled, wrapping his arms around me. "Can you keep a secret?"

Of course.

Want to know how the professionals stay awake without getting tired?

I lifted my head. "The professionals? You mean the Elite Guard?"

"Mmhmm." A spark of purple lightning flickered in his right iris. "We fake it."

"What do you mean?"

"It's what General Cornstone taught me. Pretend you aren't tired until you have everyone fooled, even yourself."

"Is that what you do?"

He tilted his head. "I try."

I pulled back. "Want to know what I do to stay awake?"

"What?" he looked curious, and I smiled.

"This!" I jumped up and down, careful not to step on Sophie, who slept near us.

Myles laughed. "That's one way to do it."

"Your way is probably more professional," I confessed.

"I said it's how the professionals do it, didn't I?" He sat again, this time laying down and tucking his arms behind his head. "It will be easier to stay awake if we talk."

I lay beside him, also tucking my arms behind my head. "The forest is so quiet... it kind of reminds me of Gray."

He wrinkled his nose. "Me too. At least we don't need to face him tomorrow."

"Yeah..." Judging from the moon, we only had another couple of hours until midnight. Somehow, that didn't seem like very much time, and yet too much.

"You know, the whole controlled visions and everything have to do with our auras merging when you saved me," Myles said. "And King Brenton targeting us has to do with us breaking into The End. Saving your family, me not killing him..."

I nudged him. "Not your fault."

He lifted his head a little and smiled softly. "That's not what I was trying to get at."

"Oh." I settled down again. "What was your point, then?"

He turned his gaze back to the canopy above us. "If there was one person I'd want this connection with, it's you. You're my friend in a way no one else has been my friend."

I knocked my feet together. "What do you mean?"

"You're my closest friend," he answered. "You know, I've

gotten nightmares before, outside of these controlled visions. And one of the things my dad and General Cornstone taught me was to seek out someone good. Often, instead of searching for a safe aura, I enter the mind of someone I trust." He turned his head to face me again, smiling softly. "I do it most often to King Duncan and General Cornstone, but now I do it to you, too."

My heart seemed to skip a beat. "You're my closest friend, too."

"Good," he whispered. "I think one day I'll marry you."

"What?" I half-sat up in my shock. "Marry me?"

"Well, my whole family is made of people who stepped up when my parents died. My dad, my godfather... and Soph is like a little sister. Now, you came along and things are all complicated. You see, you already have enough brothers, and you don't need a fourth. But I don't want to just be friends, so I figure I'll marry you."

I sat up the rest of the way, staring down at him as my cheeks flushed. Was he saying marry me solely as some kind of formal arrangement, or was he saying marry me because he wanted to be more than friends as we were now?

"I... wouldn't mind another brother," I said softly. "But I don't think I want you as a brother."

He reached out and took my hand. "Plan on it, then."

I had a feeling that plan involved a ring, and I bit my lip to keep from smiling too wide. My best friend and future husband... Sure, we were too young to stage a wedding this instant, but in a few years... Given our telepathic connection, there was simply no way I could ever be as close to another man as I was with Myles. So, why not marry him?

"Plans made," I whispered.

He rolled onto his side and propped up on one elbow. "Sometime I want to stay up with you all night. We can start by watching the sunset and end with the sunrise."

"I'd like that," I agreed. "No pressure from the Volcaniacs, just us."

"Just us," he breathed, sounding awestruck. "Yes. King Duncan and I like to sleepover on the speech balcony. That's where I'll take you."

"I've never been on the speech balcony."

"There's a lot of the palace you haven't seen," he teased. "I'll have to show you."

"Like what?"

"Like the East Tower," he whispered dramatically.

I giggled, feeling suddenly daring. "I have an idea," I whispered back.

"What is it?"

"What if we sneak into the East Tower for our sleepover? And spend the whole night up there."

Myles's face lit with a mischievous smile. "You are a very bad influence."

"I'm not the one who is banned from a part of my own house."

He laughed but quickly stifled it before he awoke the others. "All right, you win. It's a date."

My heart fluttered. "Yes," I breathed. "A date."

Chapter 41

We spent the rest of the wait talking. And even though every second that passed brought us closer to our attack on King Brenton's palace, Myles's presence helped me to forget.

At midnight, we reluctantly woke everyone. The moon was no more than a slit in the sky, which meant we had to stumble through the dark to find them.

Once we did, we slowly found our way to the edge of the woods. A light breeze swept through the grasslands, creating an eerie wave of rustling grass. *God, be with us.*

Sophie stumbled into me. "Sorry, Rose." She shrank back from the dancing grass. "I don't like this."

"I don't either. It looks a lot creepier at night," I agreed.

"It's okay," Mercy said. "The stars say we're safe. It only looks creepy."

"Easy for you to say," Will said. "You're the one with night powers."

"Night powers?" Mercy questioned, eyes narrowing.

Will shrugged. "Sorry, but you know what I mean."

"Let's take a few steps back," Myles said. "We'll eat, and then drink the Maya Moth dust."

A cluster of thorns near the edge of the woods served as a barrier between us and the grasslands.

We had pre-split our food to save time, and Mercy passed

everything out now. There seemed to be an almost electric current between us, though no one spoke. I ended up passing my leftovers to Myles, and Sophie offered hers to Will. Despite not consuming the dust herself, our packs would be lighter without any food, and she could use all the energy she could get.

When we finished, we returned to the edge of the grasslands.

"Nothing scary yet," Will said, forcing a determined smile. "Just drinking dust we gathered from a bunch of moths."

"Refreshing, right?" Myles also forced a smile, and pulled a small vial from his pocket. "Are you ready, Soph?"

"I think so." She pulled the box of Maya Moth dust out and took the small vial Myles offered her.

Will unscrewed a waterskin and filled the vial with an arc of water.

"Thanks." Sophie sprinkled in the dust, and it began to swirl in a steady whirlpool. "Who's first?"

"I should probably go first," Will said. "I haven't distilled something into myself before, so the rest of you will have to make sure it works. Sophie and I won't be able to tell."

"Good point," Myles said.

"All right." Will took the vial from Sophie and downed it in one gulp. When he finished, he turned to me in awe. "Rose, you didn't tell me it was the best water you've ever tasted." He eyed the empty vial. "And to think I was being sarcastic about drinking moth dust. This is my new favorite drink."

"It was oddly refreshing," I agreed. "And it doesn't have a bad taste, either."

Will passed the empty vial to Mercy and looked down at his body, holding his arms half-out to his sides. He wrinkled his nose. "It does kind of tickle, doesn't it?" We watched quietly, and he lowered his arms when he finished. "I'm ready."

Sophie handed the dust to Myles. "It'll disappear with me if I hold it." She faded, and a moment later, Will disappeared, too.

"It worked," Mercy declared.

"Really?" Will's voice came from the spot he had vanished from. "That's good. Now let's get the rest of you set quickly. So we will have the same amount of time."

Mercy went next, and I took the vial after her. This time, I could tell when I had disappeared because Sophie, Mercy, and Will were suddenly visible again.

"Welcome to the invisa-party," Will said with a grin.

Myles raised an eyebrow. "I might not be able to see you, but I can still hear you." He tilted his head back and took the vial like a shot.

Nothing changed, but he looked towards us, which meant the Maya Moth dust had turned him invisible alongside us. "Is everyone ready?"

We fell silent, turning towards the grasslands behind the thorns. When we walked back around them, another breeze rustled the grasses. This one made the grasslands appear almost alive, beckoning us onward.

Have sweet dreams tonight, King Brenton, because they will be your last.

✗

Once we were out in the open grasslands, it was easier to see. Mercy led the way, using the stars to guide us along the safest path. Everything looked identical to me, and the auras felt the same in every direction, yet she carefully guided us around invisible points of danger and through shortcuts no one else could see.

A breeze continued to rustle through the grasslands, and Myles shook his head. "The breeze is coming from behind us, which means it is blowing our auras *towards* the palace. I don't like that."

"But we have our auras masked," Will pointed out. "And they don't know we are coming tonight, so they probably aren't actively looking."

313

"They might not know that tonight is the night, but they know that we *are* coming," Myles countered.

I frowned. Myles was right. "They likely have guards stationed day and night. Whether we continue right now or wait another week won't change that," I said. "And there isn't anything we can do about the wind."

"Unless we had a Mageye with us that could control the wind," Mercy said. "Then again, using their power like that might not be a good idea when we're this close to the palace. It would be noticeable even when masked."

"Whatever the case," Myles said. "We need to be ready at any moment... just like them."

"Well," Will said, "the point of our ambush is that we don't want them to be ready."

"Shouldn't we be able to sense the auras from the charred land by now?" Sophie interrupted. "We are already halfway across the grasslands and everything is the same as it was before we came out here."

"It is getting stronger," Myles said. "It's very slow, though. The wind is pushing it back."

"That means we are less than five miles from it," I said.

Mercy nodded. "The grasslands are about five miles. You and Will should be able to sense the charred land soon."

As she spoke, a gripping fear swept through me, the feeling that something dangerous lay ahead. I turned my gaze to the shadowy land before us. "I can feel it."

"Same here," Will said. "You two girls get ready, don't let your hold on your auras slip."

"We won't," Mercy said.

"We *can't*," Sophie whispered.

The shadows before us slowly darkened and eventually blended into scorched miles of land. Unlike the relatively even border between the charred land and forest at The End, these were clawing arcs of blackness reaching into the grasslands. As if the evil auras were dragging themselves forward, expanding King Brenton's domain.

I carefully avoided one of the slashes, staying on the grass for as long as possible.

It was too dark to make out any distinct shapes in the land before us. There were no signs of any guard towers this time, and if there were, we likely wouldn't see them until we were much closer, anyway.

"We have about seven hours of our first dose of dust left," Myles said. "Which means we don't need to worry about taking more for a bit."

"That's good," Mercy said distractedly, studying the land. "Do you think anything will happen when we step onto it?"

"No," Myles said. "But let me go first, just in case." He stepped across and cringed. "The aura is much stronger on this side of the magical barrier," he warned. "Don't cross until you're ready. It would be better to wait an extra minute than step across and lose your hold on your aura."

Each barrier Myles and I had crossed in The End had had the same effect. Layers of increased fear and heat, until we made it to the volcano. I took a deep breath, squared my shoulders, and stepped out of the grasslands. As Myles had said, the auras heightened, and I almost involuntarily doubled over from their sudden weight.

Are you okay? Myles asked, taking hold of one of my hands.

Yeah, I just need a second to adjust.

Will and Mercy stepped across together. Both grimaced under the heightened aura but forced themselves to relax, as did I.

Sophie followed last, flinching under the aura. She closed her eyes and took a deep breath. "It's just the aura. We aren't in immediate danger," she murmured.

Myles put a gentle hand on her shoulder. "You're exactly right.

It's the false fear from the aura, not real fear. We're okay, we're together, and we're going to stick together."

"That's right. We're a team," I assured.

"We're a team," Sophie echoed, offering a tight-lipped smile.

"Relax, Sophie, the best that you can. It makes it easier to keep a grip on your aura that way," Will said. "Otherwise, you'll start to feel the strain."

"I know," she said softly. "I've done this before with Myles."

I nodded, turning to look at the dark mass of trees, that were now hardly small blips in the distance. Same dangerous auras, same charred land, and same Volcaniacs waiting... but this time we weren't saving anyone, but ending lives. I shuddered. "If we're all adjusted, we should keep going."

Mercy took a deep breath and stepped further onto the charred land. "Follow me."

"Can we rest for a few minutes?" I asked as the first streaks of dawn kissed the horizon.

Surprisingly, I wasn't feeling the effects of the sleepless night, but rather, my feet were sore from the rocky, burnt land, and I wanted to heal them.

"Only a couple of minutes," Myles said. "We are winding down on our first dose of the dust, and I want to stretch it as far as possible."

I nodded and sat on the burnt land to tug my boots off. I was met with instantaneous relief and the soreness quickly faded as I wiggled my toes. "That feels so much better." I looked up. "Are anyone else's feet sore? I can take this chance to heal them."

"I don't think you want to touch everyone's feet, Rose," Will said with a laugh.

I wrinkled my nose. "I can touch any part of your skin; it doesn't need to be your feet."

"Really?"

I nodded, and his face lit up. "In that case, yes, please." He flopped down beside me with his legs stretched out. "I thought it was a weird request, so I didn't ask."

"That's what I'm here for, to heal you all if you get hurt."

"Yeah, you're here to heal wounds, not our sore feet."

I grabbed his ankles, and as I felt my powers flowing into him, he leaned back on his forearms, his head tilted back and his hair spreading on the ground around him. "That feels so *goood*," he groaned.

The pain in my feet increased and then faded as I released him, and my body took over the healing.

Will hopped back to his feet. "You all should have her do that. The best foot massage I've gotten in my life."

Sophie laughed and sat beside me. "You don't mind?"

I shook my head and grabbed her skin, repeating the process for Mercy and Myles.

When I finished, I stood. "Are we ready to continue?"

"I think so," Mercy said, her gaze locked on the disappearing stars.

Once the sun rose high enough for us to truly see the surrounding landscape, we stopped to take it in. It looked eerily similar to The End, but instead of a volcano looming in the distance, there was now a distant outline of a crumbling black palace.

"Why are there no barriers?" I asked. "I know King Brenton is weaker than last time, but he should still have something, right?"

Myles tapped his fingers against his thigh. "Last time, the barriers started about fifteen miles out from the volcano."

"And we are nearing that point now." I waved my hand ahead of us. "They should at least be in sight. And last time, we could feel the magical heat. Right now, it isn't unnaturally hot."

"Maybe he's weaker than we realize," Will said. "The

317

controlled visions are likely taking a lot out of him. That could also be why he doesn't send them every night."

"Are you saying that you think he is focusing more on taunting Myles and Rose than protecting himself?" Mercy asked.

"Potentially. I mean, he knows we're coming, and that illusion Mageye let us go. Maybe he let us go because he got what he wanted with knowledge of our fears, or maybe he let us go because he couldn't kidnap us by himself." He paused, adding, "Either way, it seems pretty clear that King Brenton is waiting."

"Waiting for what?" I asked.

"Us," he answered grimly.

Myles frowned. "We know he wants us dead... but maybe he doesn't have the strength to stop us on the outside. He is waiting for us to come to his domain."

Sophie paled, and I got the feeling that if we weren't using the moth dust, we wouldn't be able to see her. "Like an ambush?" she asked.

"I hope not," Mercy said.

"He can't set up an ambush if he doesn't know when we are coming," Myles assured us. "He might be prepared for a counter-strike, but not a surprise attack."

"Fair enough," Will said. "And like I said, he might be weaker than we think. Maybe he just *wants* us to think he's strong."

"That would explain why the illusion Mageye let us go," I conceded.

"Whatever the case, we can't turn back now," Myles said. "We have as solid of a plan as we are going to get and a window of opportunity we might not get again. We can't waste it."

"We *won't* waste it. We are here to finish what we started in The End," I declared.

Myles nodded, his determined gaze meeting mine. *And fix my mistake. I know I am the only one who truly blames myself for King Brenton surviving the eruption, but that doesn't change the fact that I feel* a responsibility to fix this.

Fixing this is exactly what King Duncan has asked us to do, I replied. And tonight, we will sleep without fear of controlled visions, make a plan for finding any stragglers, then go home and sneak up to the East Tower for a sleepover.

His fierce expression softened and lightning flickered in his purple iris. *I can get behind that plan.*

Consider it a date, my telepathic voice sang. But first, we need to handle the Volcaniacs.

Handle the Volcaniacs, he echoed, turning his gaze back to the horizon. Together, and with no not being an acceptable answer. We can do this.

Chapter 42

"Something's not right," I said, looking ahead of us. We had taken the second dose of dust a couple of hours ago and, by the looks of it, would be able to break inside the palace before the effects wore off. We had seen no barriers of any kind, but now, with the dark outline of King Brenton's palace slowly gaining more focus, something looked off.

"What do you mean?" Myles asked, lightning flickering in his right iris.

"Why is the land around the palace glowing?" I squinted my eyes; it wasn't just glowing. It looked as if the ground gave out near the palace, and an orangey-red light shone from below, like rays of sun coming from beneath the surface of the earth.

The palace itself was entirely black and had what appeared to be a bridge leading up to it, though it was hard to make out clearly from this distance. A light pressure nudged my aura as Myles read my mind, before voicing my thoughts. "It looks like a moat."

"A what now?" Will asked.

"A moat with a bridge," Myles said. "A moat is like a canyon that goes around a palace to protect it. It's normally filled with water, but judging from the glow, I think this moat is filled with..."

"Lava," I finished, and Myles nodded grimly.

Will stared, eyes wide in horror. "A canyon as in a *canyon-canyon*, or a canyon as in an exaggeration of speech?"

"They mean a canyon-canyon, Will," Mercy said, putting a hand on his shoulder. "I think that's why it looks like the ground plateaus. It is a sharp cliff."

Will gulped. "Well, we're still far away. Can't exactly pinpoint those exact details yet."

"There is definitely lava below the ground that we can't see," Myles said, shielding his eyes from the sun. "We know that for sure because of the glow, and unfortunately, a moat is the most logical guess."

"Is there a way around it?" Will asked. "Even the Volcaniacs would think a canyon full of lava is sketchy."

"The point of a moat is that you can't go around it," Myles explained. "You are forced to cross the bridge, and normally that means getting caught before you cross. But right now—thanks to Soph—we will be invisible, so we can cross unseen."

"Moats normally have a rope bridge. If so, the bridge will sway, and they will notice," Sophie pointed out.

"They could blame it on the wind," I said. "And if it isn't a super wide moat, and we cross it quickly, we might get away with it, even if it sways."

"Maybe it isn't a rope bridge," Will suggested dully. "Maybe it's a wide, flat, sturdy one... one you can't see over?"

Myles shot Will a sympathetic look. "Maybe," he said. "We'll figure everything out when we get there, Will, okay? Don't stress about it."

"That is easier said than done," Will said meekly.

Mercy grabbed his hand. "Let's think about something else."

"Like how pretty the sky looks," Sophie suggested.

We looked up. The sky looked pretty sky-ish to me, but I voiced my agreement anyway.

"That cloud looks weird," Myles said abruptly.

"Which one?" Mercy asked.

Myles pointed at a very misshapen cloud.

Will gave a half-smile. "I agree."

I grabbed Myles's hand and squeezed. He glanced at me and offered a grim smile.

We continued discussing random topics, not only to distract Will, but to distract us all. An evil aura seeped from the palace, and every glance I dared spare towards the moat showed the fiery glow getting brighter.

✕

"Is this a bad time to say I really need to pee?" Will asked as we neared the bridge. His gaze was firmly fixed on anywhere but the very obvious cliff ahead of us.

"Yes," Myles said. "Don't even think about that."

"But I've been holding it since we took the second dose," Will complained. "I thought I'd share my agony with you all."

"Now I need to pee," Mercy said. "Thanks a lot, Will."

Will flashed a mischievous grin. "No problem."

"Let's change the topic," Sophie interrupted. "We need the dust to stay in your systems as long as possible, so let's not tempt anyone."

"I'm not tempting anyo—"

"Stop," Myles hissed.

At first, I thought he was snapping at Will, but then I followed his gaze and froze.

"What are those?" Sophie whispered, inching closer to Myles.

A cackling screech tore through the air, causing us all to flinch as a huge, mutant-looking bird circled above us. It screeched again and turned to fly back to the bridge and the dozens of other birds that circled above it.

"I don't know," Myles said darkly. "But they're magic, whatever they are."

"It looks like they're guarding the bridge," I said worriedly.

Will took a half-step back, bumping into Myles. "Sorry," he

said distractedly, staring at the inevitable trial before us.

The bridge was not made of rope, as we had thought, but of a dark stone. It was barely three feet across, with nothing but a chain-like railing separating its occupants from the deadly fall.

Mercy offered Will the last of our non-magic water. "Here, drink this. It will help calm your nerves."

He took it with trembling hands and tipped his head back. "Thanks," he croaked when he finished.

"We don't know what the birds can do, but they can't see us. So, if we are quiet, we should be able to sneak past," Myles said.

Another one swooped away from the moat, circling a little to our right before looping back. Guards. But bird guards certainly seemed better than the Wolvien Guard. Or even the mountain lion Myles and I had fought in the volcano, for that matter.

When we arrived at the bridge, Will swayed and Sophie caught his hand to steady him. The sheer cliff stretched on either side of us, eventually curving out of sight behind the palace. Lava bubbled at its bottom, the heat of which seemed to be stopped by a hazy orange shield. The drop was inestimably high. Even without the lava, it would be deadly.

Huge pillars held the bottom of the bridge in place, and even as I watched, a few stones crumbled from the side. It had the same ruin-like look of the palace that rose behind it.

Easily the size of King Duncan's palace, this one held no beauty—only power. Blacker than the land around it, it too was crumbling, and yet, nothing but strength seeped from it. The darkness of it seemed to suck out the light of the day, filling the air with a chill that threatened sparks.

"All right," Myles said softly, stepping purposefully in front of Will to block his view. "We need to cross, and then we will figure out how to break in. It looks like the bridge leads right to an entrance of some sort." He pointed at the arch that stood only a few yards from the bridge. It appeared to lead inside, with many similar dark pillars and arches surrounding it.

"What about the birds?" Mercy whispered. "Do we ignore them?"

"We have to, at least until we learn what they do."

"Have you ever seen any birds like them before, Myles?" I asked as one of them swooped low enough for me to get a good look.

It was about the size of a coyote and had impure white feathers speckled by black. The tips of its wings resembled burning embers, and as it slowly flapped its wings, an ashy tip burnt off, as if already alit.

"No. But they look like a cross between a crow and a seagull," Myles replied darkly.

"A cross?" Mercy echoed worriedly. "You don't think King Brenton created them, do you?"

I reached into my pocket and squeezed Ren's jackknife. "Like the Wolvien Guard?"

"Look at their eyes," Myles said.

I looked, and my blood chilled. Their beady eyes were alit with flames. Another bird screeched, and Will flinched, grabbing my arm for support. Waves crashed in his irises, resembling a stormy sea.

"I don't like them," he rasped.

"I don't either," Sophie whispered.

Will still held onto me and I caught myself before voicing my fears out loud, asking Myles instead. *You don't think the Wolvien Guard will be here, do you?*

Myles's gaze flitted to me and I nearly sobbed in relief when he shook his head. *I can't promise the answer is no, but I am fairly confident. Even the six hunting us were there and if any survived, King Brenton probably would have sent them after us.*

The birds are smaller, at least, I said.

Myles nodded and turned his attention back to the birds.

"They're only guarding the bridge, I don't see any farther down the moat."

My brief relief dissipated. "If King Brenton created them as guards..."

I know, Myles's voice filled my mind. *Who knows what they can do? But you're right... they're smaller than the wolves, and unless they can somehow burn us with their feathers, all they can really do is peck us.*

"We need to cross now," he said aloud. "The longer we are at a standstill, the more likely it is for someone to find us."

Will shook his head frantically, taking a staggering step back. "Please, no," he whimpered. "I can't do it, Myles. It's too high. I can't do it."

"We have to, Will." Myles gently pried Will's fingers from my arm. "If I could teleport us across, I would, but that's not possible. I know you probably can't imagine a worse way to access the palace, but I will walk with you the whole time if you want. I can even hold onto you. No matter what happens with everything else today, you *aren't* going to fall."

"But—"

"Will," Mercy said. "As backward as this is, the fact that this is King Brenton's bridge should be an encouragement. It's not only the only way for us to cross, but the only way for the Volcaniacs to cross. Which means this bridge has to be sturdy."

Will nodded slowly, and some of the crashing waves in his irises seemed to calm. "Just don't look down, right?"

"Exactly," Myles urged. "Don't look down and don't think about it. Half the fear you are feeling is from the palace. It isn't *real* fear."

"It feels real," Will mumbled.

"That's King Brenton's goal," I said. "He wants to deter us."

"Fine," Will said with only a slight quake in his voice. "Myles, can you follow me, so I don't fall?"

Myles nodded. "Of course."

"Thanks." Will's gaze flicked to the birds. "I was going to look up instead of down; now I don't know what's worse."

"You can watch me. I'll go first," Mercy said, taking the first step onto the bridge and glancing back to ensure we were following. "Are you ready?"

"Not really," Will grumbled as he stepped after her.

Myles stayed close to him, and I urged Sophie ahead of me. With everyone on, I released my grip on Ren's jackknife and put my first foot onto the bridge.

For my family. For Mageye City. For all of Alveraada.

I eyed the birds as we walked, and none of us spoke for fear of being overheard. Besides taking turns flying part of the way onto the charred land, they stayed relatively close to the bridge. They were silhouetted against a bright sky, but far in the distance were the beginnings of an accumulation of dark clouds.

I don't see any Volcaniacs, Myles said telepathically. *Which means they must all be inside... but I don't sense their auras.*

It is probably like the volcano. Peeling back layers of the Volcaniac onion.

He paused, glancing at me in confusion. *That's a new term.*

Under normal circumstances, I would have started snickering, but the screeching of birds made my amusement dissipate before it could rise.

Our progress was slow but steady. Will trembled, but held back his panic enough to keep pushing forward.

"Halfway there," Myles encouraged under his breath, but he was cut off by a sickening screech.

Something slammed into me from behind, and I crashed to the ground. I rolled onto my back, attempting to scramble away, but I had nowhere to flee from the mutant bird flying at me.

Myles yanked me away from it and shot the bird with a bolt of purple lightning, sending it spiraling over the bridge as the rest of the birds swarmed above us, their brackish shrieks making my ears ring.

"How can they see us?" I gasped.

"I don't know—keep us invisible, Soph," Myles shouted as he swung his fist at the nearest bird. "I shouldn't have used my lightning," he panted. "It was reflex."

"I'm trying!" Sophie shouted, though I couldn't see her. She was the only one still invisible.

Will's eyes had grown so round I could see their whites. "We need to get off the bridge," he rasped. "We can't fight here."

Mercy swung her dagger at the oncoming birds, and as more swooped down, I grabbed Ren's jackknife and did the same.

A bird grabbed my arm, talons piercing my skin as it pulled up, and my stomach dropped as my feet left the bridge. I swung frantically with the knife in my right hand, and the bird let go with a screech. I rolled to a stop, digging my fingers into the crumbling stone to anchor myself.

"Rose!" Myles pulled me up, arms shaking.

"They can lift us," I said, my voice pitched.

One of the birds flew into Will's face, talons outstretched. He yelped, stumbling into the chain railing of the bridge. He grabbed the bird and threw it away from himself, his face bleeding as he barely managed to catch his balance, clinging to the chain for dear life.

Sophie suddenly reappeared, shaking her head. "With you all moving, I'm having trouble calling on the dust. It isn't working."

"That doesn't make sense." Myles grunted as a bird flew into his chest. "We should have still had hours with the dust, and how come they only just now saw us and not when we first walked on..." He froze. "The halfway point. Everyone off the bridge *now!* We need to find cover before the birds attract the Volcaniacs."

Mercy grabbed Will's hand and dragged him after her, running towards the palace.

Sophie ran behind, flickering wildly. "Something's stopping

me from hiding you," she fretted.

A bird swooped down and grabbed her arm, yanking her off her feet. Sophie screamed, kicking wildly as her feet caught on the chain railing. With a harsh tug, the bird pulled her from it.

"Sophie!" Myles screamed as he dove for her, grabbing her ankle and attempting to pull her back.

But the bird was too strong, and he was lifted into the sky with them.

"No!" I screamed, jumping toward Myles, but he was out of reach. I could do nothing but cling to the chain and stare helplessly as the bird flew away from the bridge, Myles and Sophie hanging from it.

Someone grabbed my arm and pulled me away from the edge as the bird released Sophie's arm, sending her and Myles plummeting into the lava below.

Chapter 43

My bloodcurdling scream was certain to attract the Volcaniacs, but I couldn't stop it. Will caught me before I threw myself after them. The waves crashing in his irises were full of horror as he pushed me to the ground behind him.

"Both of you, get down," he shouted. His arms shook, but he no longer sounded afraid. He sounded angry.

I reached towards Mercy helplessly, but couldn't get my hand to grab her, my heart still frozen in shock. They hadn't even had time to scream.

Mercy threw herself down beside me, and Will stood above, shielding us from the continued onslaught of the birds.

He grabbed his wooden baton and swung it at the nearest bird. It screeched, spiraling out of sight.

I doubled over, hugging my stomach as I fought the urge to scream again. There was nothing I could do. There was nothing anyone could do.

Unless Myles teleported in time, they were gone. *Myles.*

Mercy put her hand on my shoulder, stars raining in her irises as her eyes filled with tears.

Will took a step back. "We're going to need to make a break for it," he huffed. "Mercy, help Rose. We need to get off of this bridge and find somewhere to hide."

Mercy took my arm and half-pulled me to my feet, so we

crouched, waiting for Will's signal before we bolted out of his protection.

A bird came swooping at Mercy from behind, but Will saw it and smacked it away with the baton.

He took another step back, and Mercy and I tensed, ready to run—when electric crackling filled the air.

I shrieked as Myles and Sophie appeared. Myles pushed Sophie down behind Will, with Mercy and me, and took a position on our other side. His back was to us as he raised his arms above his head and sent out a wave of lightning, striking the rest of the birds.

Before we could react, he whipped around and grabbed Will's arm. A purple orb formed around the five of us, and we disappeared with an electric snap, reappearing under the cover of a rocky overhang at the base of the palace.

Mercy and I stumbled apart, and I threw myself into Myles's arms, sobbing into his chest. "I thought you were going to die!"

He hugged back, enveloping me in his arms and squeezing so hard it hurt. When he let go, I embraced Sophie.

Tears stained her cheeks, and she moved to Myles next. "Thank you for saving me," she cried.

"I'm sorry," he whispered, holding her close. "I'm sorry."

Mercy sank to the ground, her back pressed against the charred rocks behind us. Her chest heaved and she stared over the moat, shaking her head.

Will clutched the baton to himself, eyes so wide I could see their whites. He had talon marks on his face from the birds, and his blood looked ghastly against his deathly-pale skin.

When Myles and Sophie pulled apart, he looked us all over, mouthing numbers. "Five," he croaked out loud, sagging against the wall with relief. "Five."

"Good number," Will said hoarsely, still gripping his baton as if his life depended on it.

I wobbled to him on weak knees, and touched my fingers to his face. The crimson blood seeped back into his cuts, and the pain from both my and his healing wounds faded.

"Thanks," he rasped as I stepped back.

He loosened his grip on the baton and blinked a few times as he looked at Myles.

"Don't ever tell me you can't face heights," Myles said, stepping forward and embracing Will. "You kept Rose and Mercy safe."

"Still don't like heights," Will rasped, hiding his face. When they stepped apart, he added, "But that wasn't as bad as it could have been... Right?"

"We all survived," Mercy said softly. I knelt and healed her wounds.

When I went to Myles and Sophie, I was surprised to see their wounds had all faded during our hugs.

Myles met my gaze and I embraced him again. *I thought I had lost you.*

I know. I thought so, too. He gave me one final squeeze before stepping back. *We need to stay strong right now, and we can take out our fear on King Brenton.*

He turned to everyone. "I don't know why no one came out when the birds attacked. We either got lucky, or they are waiting inside."

Mercy stood slowly, putting her palm against the wall of the palace. "What kind of stone is this? I don't recognize it, and it looks... well, it *feels* like magic."

I put my hand against the palace, surprised to find it warm and almost alive. When I pulled my hand back, it was covered in black dust, like charcoal.

Myles frowned. "I know what that is. It's otologicoal... It creates a double-sided, soundproof barrier. What happens inside is heard only inside, and what happens outside is heard only outside."

"That explains why no one came out when we were on the bridge," I whispered, looking down at my hands. "But what happened to our invisibility?"

Myles shook his head. "The birds reacted when we were exactly halfway across the bridge. I can't say this for sure—since we could see ourselves the entire time—but I think there is some sort of magical barrier that took away our magical defenses when we crossed it. We are no longer invisible."

Sophie wiped away the last of her tears. "But how would a barrier like that be created?"

A heavy silence fell over us, and Will cleared his throat. "What are the chances that the illusion Mageye is here?"

"High," Myles said darkly, scanning the palace looming above us.

"Well," Mercy said nervously, "we will have to take him down eventually, right? We can kill two birds with one stone..."

"Please don't mention birds right now," Sophie squeaked.

"Sorry." Mercy put a comforting hand on Sophie's shoulder. "That wasn't the best choice of words."

I bit my lip, again putting my palm against the wall of the palace. "We will take them out one at a time. God-willing, they will be in separate rooms. If not, we might need to wait it out."

Myles nodded in agreement. "Take them out and hide the bodies. We can't risk our presence being discovered."

"Who do we go for first?" Will asked.

"We're going to cut the snake off at the head," Myles replied as a determined bolt of lightning flashed in his right iris. "Aim for the king."

Chapter 44

"We need to find a way to sneak in," Myles said. "The palace is in ruins, so we might be able to find a broken window."

"More like a hole," Will muttered as he tilted his head back to look at the charred palace.

"As long as you all aren't seen," Sophie fretted.

Mercy pursed her lips. "You're right."

I stepped up beside Myles. "The otologicoal means they won't hear us at all until we are in, right?"

Myles nodded. "But it also means we won't be able to hear *them* until we are in."

"We have Sophie," Will said. "She can look in whatever entrance we find and ensure it's empty."

Sophie squeezed the fabric of her dress in two tight fists. "I can do that."

Myles mouthed a prayer as he turned to lead us around the base of the palace, away from the birds and the distant clouds I had noticed.

We stepped carefully over scattered chunks of charred obsidian, wary of any tripping hazards. Birds squawked behind us and I cast a look back towards the bridge. "More birds," I breathed. "What if they warn the Volcaniacs the others are gone?"

"Our auras are still masked," Will whispered. "So, they all kind of died... without a trace."

"There isn't anything we can do about it," Myles said, eyeing the sky. "The sooner we are inside, the better. With all of the birds gone, they will either assume we fell off the bridge with them or are still outside."

Mercy stepped around Myles and Sophie to take the lead. "I think there is a good spot for us to enter through ahead."

"Good," Will said, eyeing the moat and gently steering me around his side, closer to the palace.

"Thanks, Will," I whispered.

He only nodded, smiling grimly despite his fear. The palace wall was cracked in many spots, but nothing provided a crevice large enough to enter through. Mercy stopped us by an outdoor balcony and I breathed a sigh of relief at the sight of glassless windows.

The balcony was more like an outside terrace made of obsidian. The width appeared to be that of an average hallway and it had one entrance leading into the palace.

It was silent, but that could still be the otologicoal at work. "Soph," Myles breathed. "Climb onto me and look inside. If you see anyone, think it and I will know."

"Okay," Sophie whispered as she disappeared. Myles knelt on one knee and reached up to brace his hand against something invisible to steady Sophie as she climbed on his leg.

There was a moment of silence, then Sophie became translucent enough that we could see her. "It's empty," she whispered.

Myles lifted her off his knee. "The otologicoal will block everything from outside the palace as soon as we are in."

Will rubbed his hands together. "And the auras will probably increase too, right?"

Myles nodded and turned to the balcony. He braced his hands on the edge to slide through one of the open windows. "Brace yourself and know you are feeling the presence of evil, not immediate danger."

He winced when he made it to the other side and said something, though we couldn't hear him.

The otologicoal, he said. *You can't hear me, can you?*

No, I said.

He nodded and stepped back.

Mercy whispered goodbye to the sun before following Myles inside.

Will helped Sophie climb in before turning to me with a forced a smile. "I hate that this is an upgrade from the moat."

I cast a look at the moat and wrinkled my nose. "Myles will be able to teleport us back across it soon."

That got a real smile, and he offered a hand. "Want a lift?"

"Yes, please."

He helped me in and as soon as I crossed through the barrier, the auras intensified. In contrast to the heightened auras, I could hear Myles, Mercy, and Sophie again.

"Is everyone ready?" Myles asked once Will was safely inside. Lightning sparked between his fingertips, until he curled his hand into a fist.

"Yes," I replied, and he crept down to the shadowed entrance to the palace.

"Will," Myles breathed as we plastered ourselves against the walls on either side of the doorway. "I'll take the lead, and you bring up the rear. If someone attacks from the front or back, we can hopefully take them out silently."

Will nodded. "I can do that."

"All right." Myles scanned everyone's faces. "We have to aim to kill. I know you might not want to, but we don't have a choice. We can't risk any survivors rising again." He sighed. "If it is you or them, choose yourself and remember that also means you are choosing Mageye City. It doesn't make you a monster."

I could sense resignation in Myles's aura. He hated killing as much as the rest of us, but since joining the Elite Guard six years ago, he had fought against many people who aimed to kill him and forced him to offer the same.

"For Mageye City," I whispered, adding to myself, *And my family.*

"For Mageye City," Myles agreed. He cautiously straightened from the wall, leading us into the palace.

Sophie flickered as we walked down the first corridor, settling into a translucent state.

The corridor ended with only one hall, leading deeper into the palace. Myles stopped before turning the corner, and I half-expected an ambush, but instead, he turned back. Purple lightning sparked in his right iris. "Victory to me means that everyone gets out. And we are here to be victorious."

I slipped my hand into my pocket and clutched Ren's jackknife. "I agree."

"We all do," Mercy added.

Myles hesitated for another moment before stepping into the next hall.

"Can anyone sense King Brenton?" Will asked. "If we're cutting the snake off at the head, we need to find the head."

"I can," Myles said solemnly. "That's where we're headed."

He led us through several dark hallways, and soon, a fiery-orange glow began to illuminate them, coming from the direction we headed in.

"Where is that glow coming from?" Sophie asked.

"Lava," Myles and I said simultaneously. We shared a concerned look. The last time we had faced King Brenton, he wielded the lava as a weapon. If we were walking toward both him and the lava now, it meant we were walking into an evenly-matched fight.

We still have surprise on our side, Myles assured me.

I met his gaze. *Yes. But will that be enough?*

✗

The orangey-red glow of the corridors continued strengthening the farther into the palace we went. It was almost like a maze, and despite the otologicoal no longer preventing us from hearing the Volcaniacs, it was quiet.

"Maybe there are less of them than we thought," Will breathed.

"I hope so," Sophie whispered.

I eyed the dark walls. Despite the strength seeping from every inch of the palace, the suggestion it was relatively abandoned was an assurance.

"Who are you?" a deep voice called.

I jumped and stumbled into Mercy in my surprise. A man stood in the entrance to a doorway we had passed. His eyes were a deep forest green, and it looked as if the shadows of leaves shifted in them.

Vines trailed out of the room around him, but Myles had already reacted. He teleported behind the man, putting one hand over his mouth and holding his dagger at his neck.

"Not a sound," he ordered. The vines continued growing from behind them, but Mercy pulled a dagger from her waist and quickly cut them. I helped her gather the cut pieces and followed Myles into the room the man had come from.

Will ushered Sophie in and stood guard at the open doorway, the half-empty magic waterskin in hand.

Myles stood in the middle of the room and lightning sparked in his right iris. "I'm going to ask you some questions, and if you try to lie or make any noise, I will shock you."

The man struggled, but Myles's grip on him only tightened, the very tip of his dagger drawing blood. "No, I'm not letting you go to answer. I'm reading your mind instead. I know you plan on shouting a warning the minute I release you."

The man let out a muffled yell, and lightning sparked off of Myles's fingertips, shocking him. He stilled, his chest heaving, and a vine began curling around Myles's foot.

"How many people are in this palace?" Myles demanded, kicking the vine from his ankle.

The Mageye struggled for a moment longer before slowly relaxing into Myles's grip.

Myles glanced at us. "Fifty-four. Including him."

"How many are Mageye?" Mercy asked, taking a step closer to the man.

"Thirty," Myles said immediately, raising his brows. "Including the illusion Mageye... Mark."

"Like the controlled vision," I breathed. "King Brenton referenced a Tara and a Mark."

Will shifted his stance. "Who's Tara, then?"

Myles looked down at the man with a scowl. "Their queen."

"Queen?" Mercy echoed.

"And is she here, too?" Sophie asked softly. "You said fifty-four in the palace, but are there more Volcaniacs elsewhere?"

The Mageye let out another muffled yell, grimacing as Myles shocked him again. He huffed and glared at us, while a look of relief crossed Myles's face. "They're all here."

Fifty-four Volcaniacs in this palace and then we were done, with no need to hunt anyone else down. Stragglers like the trader or other members of the magical black market would have no one to trade with, without the Volcaniacs to facilitate things.

Myles returned his gaze to the man in his grip. "Where is King Brenton?"

Instead of mentally answering, the man attempted to elbow Myles in the ribs. Electricity crackled, louder this time, and the man slumped to the ground, unmoving.

Myles held his hand to where the man had attempted to elbow him. "He was using vines elsewhere in the palace, trying to get attention."

Sophie stared at the dead man in horror. "Can we leave this room?" she whispered.

"Yes." Myles stepped over the body with a grimace. "King Brenton is in his throne room."

"He has a throne room?" Will asked. "Who made him king, anyway? Where is he getting his title and power?"

"Himself," Myles replied. "He crowned himself, and his queen, apparently."

"And we are going to dethrone them," Mercy said.

"Exactly," Myles agreed, stepping back into the hallway.

I followed. "Which way is the throne room?"

Will pointed down the hallway the way we had been going—the illumining orange glow seeming brighter down there. "That way?"

"Yes," Myles said. "We're almost there."

"And what's our plan when we get there?" Sophie asked softly.

Myles sighed. "Kill him."

Chapter 45

"Sophie, can you look in that room?" Myles asked. "Don't go inside, just look in from the doorway."

The room he referred to was dark, the first area of the palace that had no fiery glow, as if something inside was absorbing the light.

Sophie nodded quickly and disappeared. We waited in tense silence until she reappeared. "Nothing is in there. I don't know why it's dark."

"Could it be a sign of weakness?" I asked. "Maybe his hold isn't throughout the entire palace?"

"I doubt it. Something in there feels magical," Will said.

"An outlet of power?" Mercy suggested grimly. "Aren't they usually dark to preserve the energy?"

"What is an outlet of power?" I asked.

"Think of it as a way to store excess power. You force your aura into it, and over time, as you regain your full strength, the outlet of power also strengthens," Myles explained. "Something to draw upon."

I took a step closer, peering into the blackness. The aura seeping from the outlet of power was dangerously familiar. "I think this is where he creates the controlled visions."

Myles's expression slackened, but he nodded. "He is using it to fuel them," he breathed.

"When we kill King Brenton, will this room shut down, too?" Sophie asked nervously.

"Yes, his hold will break, and everything will return to the way it was before he took over," Myles assured her.

"Just like the land in The End refilled with life when you broke his hold last time," I added.

Myles nodded. "Exactly."

I bit my lip. "What if it happens the other way around?"

"What do you mean?" Mercy asked.

"What if we break the outlet of power?"

Will raised his brows. "Is that even possible?"

I turned to Myles, expecting him to have the answer. Instead, he stepped up to the dark doorway. "I don't know."

"So, what do we do?" Will asked. "Can we use our auras to... taint it?"

Myles glanced back and set his jaw. "We're about to find out. Let's go in."

I pulled out Ren's jackknife and clutched it tightly. "I'm ready."

Myles was the first to step into the room, his footsteps echoing eerily throughout it.

Mercy let out a soft squeak. "Can I stay here and be a lookout?"

"Yes," Myles agreed. "That will let me light it up without worry of someone noticing. Let us know if you see anyone."

Will and I followed him in. Sophie took a couple of steps, but lingered by the doorway.

The aura inside the room was thick—almost as if a layer of evil coated us. Myles lifted his hand above his head and lit up the dark room with purple sparks.

I caught a glimpse of a podium in the center of the room, but then, the palace rumbled.

Will stumbled into me. "Sorry," he huffed.

"What was that?" I asked.

Myles let his sparks go out. "I don't think we're supposed to blend auras inside of here," he whispered, stepping away from the podium. "Tainting or otherwise."

"What does that mean?" Will asked.

Myles shook his head, though the room was too dark to see his expression. "King Brenton first, and then the outlet of power."

We left without another word. Mercy and Sophie met us in the hallway.

"Why did the palace rumble?" Mercy asked.

Myles grew solemn. "I think it was the outlet of power. It reacted to me using my power... though I don't sense anyone near us, so we should be okay, at least for now."

"Should we leave the outlet of power, then?" Sophie asked.

Myles nodded. "We need to destroy it before we leave... but once King Brenton is gone, that should be easy."

"If everything will revert back to how it was once he is gone, the outlet of power should take care of itself," Will said, casting the dark doorway a final glance. "Or dissipate with time."

"That would be even better," I agreed grimly.

✕

"Get out!" a distant voice shouted. I froze. That was a voice I recognized. The corridor we stood in glowed brightly, as if torches or lava lit the halls—though nothing but dark stone was in sight.

Purple lightning crackled from Myles's fingertips, but he quickly suppressed it as we paused in the hall.

"King Brenton," I whispered.

Myles nodded grimly, stepping around Will and Mercy and taking the lead. "We're almost there."

King Brenton didn't shout anything else; evidently, whoever he had been yelling at hadn't needed to be told twice.

An open arch led down two wide stairs, and the end of the tunnel was illuminated with a strong orange glow.

We crept down the hall, plastering ourselves against the walls on either side and using the shadows as cover.

The orange glow of the palace came from the lava that flooded this square room. Obsidian stepping stones led to the throne from four different entrances, and the four walls were all lined with seats.

It looked as if King Brenton had more than a new palace, but he had a new amphitheater as well.

King Brenton himself paced in front of his throne, orange streaks etching slowly through his obsidian crown. "Odol should have taken care of his brat before taking mine."

Odol? Who was that? Besides King Brenton, the throne room was empty, and he continued to pace, muttering to himself. Whatever bad news he had received seemed to have left him distracted, and Myles lifted his arm towards King Brenton, though he didn't attack him... yet.

"He's alone," he breathed. "But surrounded by lava."

Mercy shifted her feet. "He is better armed than we are as long as he is in this room."

"Not if we catch him by surprise," Will said. He uncorked one of the magic waterskins, and took a swig from it. "Myles, could you drop him right now?"

"We wouldn't be able to interrogate him," Myles said. "We know from that other Mageye that everyone is here... but that is it. His thoughts implied that there are three Mageye here believed to be stronger than us. King Brenton, Mark, and... Queen Tara. I want to know more about who we are facing."

"There are fifty-three Volcaniacs left," Sophie whispered. "Fifty-two, not counting King Brenton."

"We can face them blind, like they are facing us," I breathed as I stepped forward. "Myles, this is our chance—we can strike him down while he is oblivious."

"You're right." Myles squared his jaw and raised his arm once more, but Mercy grabbed his wrist, stopping him.

"Someone's coming," she hissed.

At her words, another aura swept over us, dangerously familiar, but in a way I couldn't place.

King Brenton must have felt it too, as he turned, a smug grin on his face. "Just who I need to see," he said as a mountain lion emerged from another entrance.

Sophie faded until she was translucent and Myles stiffened as a mountain lion elegantly leapt across the stepping stones and gracefully approached King Brenton. An X-shaped brand was etched into its left shoulder. A lump formed in my throat. This was the same mountain lion that had ambushed me and Myles twice before. Once, when we first met, and again in the volcano before we saved my family. It had the ability to scratch its prey from afar, no physical contact necessary.

"Hello, Tara, dear," King Brenton hummed as the mountain lion rubbed its head along his thigh.

Myles and I shared a horrified look as the mountain lion purred loudly, rubbing its entire body against him like an overly friendly kitten.

Will's nose wrinkled in disgust. "His queen is a cat?"

"Shh," Myles hissed, and Will fell silent as the scene continued unfolding before us.

Tara bumped her head against King Brenton's palm, and he stroked her, to which she responded by deepening her rumbling purr.

Then she began to transform. Fur turned into a head of hair, her tail shrank, and her legs turned into arms. A woman now knelt at King Brenton's feet.

A slit in her lacy black dress went up her thigh, and her shoulders were covered with nothing more than a thin lace. Her long brunette hair reflected the orange glow of the lava and made her appear to be a light of her own. As King Brenton continued petting her head, the edges of her lace lit with a never-ending flame.

As she rose to her feet, she appeared to climb him, one hand over the other, until she stood at his side, hanging off his arm lovingly. Even in her human form, she continued to purr, and when she reached up to straighten his obsidian crown, words flew from my mouth, "Ms. Kaser!"

I quickly slapped my hand over my mouth, but it was too late. My neighbor's yellow eyes pierced through the shadows of our corridor, and her mouth split into a menacing grin, revealing sharp fangs.

King Brenton snapped his head in our direction, and lava shot straight into the air around him and his throne, but then it froze, as if he too was in shock.

He stepped away from Tara Kaser. "I want General Duncan," he said, a hungry flame catching in his iris.

"Not happening," Myles spat as he shot a bolt of lightning at him.

King Brenton simply waved his arm and lava rose in front of the bolt.

"We need to run," Mercy squeaked.

"Yeah," I agreed, backpedaling as the lava arced towards us.

Will was the only one to step forward. He motioned up with his hands to create a wall of water that caught the lava—if only for a moment. He turned back. "More than run, I think we need to teleport."

Chapter 46

Purple lightning formed around us, and as the lava burst through Will's barrier, we disappeared.

We stumbled out of the orb in an empty room.

"How is Ms. Kaser here?" I demanded. "She's a Volcaniac?" I shuddered at the thought. She had been in my house. She had made us a pie, and I had *eaten* it!

A reflection of my shock displayed itself on Myles's face. "We were laughing with her about having a good night's rest, and now..." He stopped. "She was a spy, which means the Volcaniacs might know our plan."

"I'd like to be let in on that plan," Will said. "What do we do now? If we can't fight them together, how do we fight them?"

"The ice-diamond." I pulled it out, clutching it in my hand. "We can use that to freeze and then... well, kill them."

"No." Myles turned to me. "We need to take Tara alive and figure out how long she has been spying on Mageye City."

"Take that thing alive?" Will questioned in disbelief. "It is one thing to try and demand answers from King Brenton, another to take Tara as a prisoner and bring her back to the city with us."

"We have to," Myles said. "She spied on the city."

"And told King Brenton about you," Mercy interrupted.

Myles stilled, his lips parted, then he shook his head. "He didn't know who I was in the volcano, but he knows my title now.

That's why I want to take Tara with us. We need to know what other information she fed to the Volcaniacs."

"But if we destroy all of the Volcaniacs, everyone she gave information to would be gone," I said.

"The secrets will die with them," Sophie whispered, flickering.

"Maybe you're right," Myles conceded. "So, we need to defeat King Brenton, Mark, and Tara."

"How do we do that?" I asked.

An ear-splitting shriek echoed through the palace and we all jumped. Myles's gaze hardened. "They're looking for us."

"And they'll find us soon enough," Will said as he strode to the door. "We are sitting ducks in this room."

As he spoke, several men ran past the door—but thankfully didn't see us.

"Pick them off as we go," Myles ordered. "We have to."

Sophie stepped past Will and disappeared to check the hall before her hand appeared again, waving us out. Myles rested his hand on her shoulder briefly as he stepped past.

Mercy fiddled with her dagger, and Will looked both ways, waves turning his irises into a stormy sea.

"Where in the palace is everyone else?" I asked.

"All around you," a new voice said.

The voice seemed to come from the walls themselves, and I turned in a circle, scanning for any clue as to where Mark stood.

Myles raised his arms and purple orbs formed around each of us, but he didn't snap them. "Come out, you coward," he spat.

His order was met with a howl and I shrieked as a pack of wolves ran around the nearest corner, fangs bared.

Our protective orbs flickered out as we took off running without a second thought, but with a flash of fiery-red light, the wolves vanished.

Mark laughed from somewhere behind us, and I spared a glance over my shoulder fearfully.

"We need to get away from Mark," Will panted. "We can't tell what is and isn't real with him around."

"I know—" Myles huffed, but was interrupted by Sophie.

"Myles!"

The orangey-red corridors around us had begun to shift, the entryways flashing before settling in a new order.

Myles backpedaled, but it was too late. He ran into the open corridor in front of us and came to a crashing halt with a sickening crunch. "Not this one," he groaned as his right hand flew to his face, where blood gushed from his broken nose.

"How do we get out?" Sophie asked. "Feeling for the right corridor will only take more time!"

Mercy pressed her hands to the open corridor, sliding them along the invisible wall for an entrance, and Will stepped forward, swinging his second waterskin off his shoulder. He dumped the contents onto the ground and the water sprang to life. It washed against the walls in small waves before swirling down through what appeared to be a solid barrier. Will took off at a sprint through the illusion. "Follow me!"

I grabbed Myles's hand as we ran, sending my power through him to heal his broken nose.

His grip on my hand tightened. "Thanks, Rose."

Neither of us let go as we ran through more illusion-filled corridors. The last time we had run through lava-lit corridors together, I had almost lost Myles. And if I had thought I couldn't survive without him then, I *knew* I couldn't survive without him now, throbbing nose and all.

Mark's laughter had faded but the illusion continued, sending us running through wall after wall.

Sophie's long hair streamed behind her as she ran, and Mercy's aura swirled around us, searching for any clue the stars might offer through the illusion.

"Almost." Will wheezed as the water swept through another

solid wall. We ran after it and burst onto an open balcony.

I backpedaled, tugging Myles back with me before we ran into the railing separating us from a fall to the courtyard below.

"Oh no," Mercy huffed, staring at the sky above the square courtyard. Mutant birds circled overhead, smudges of darkness against the gray clouds gathering above, slowly blotting out the sun.

In the center of the courtyard, a fountain gushed lava into the air, lighting our faces in eerie orange flashes.

Myles grabbed Mercy's hand and pulled her away from the edge as several Volcaniacs ran into the courtyard.

One pointed at us. "There!"

Myles raised his arm to shock them and two fell, but the third dodged the strike. "I want to get down, so we aren't on the same floor as Mark," he announced.

Will screwed his eyes tightly shut and leapt off the balcony, using the water to catch himself. Mercy leapt after him without a second thought, and he caught her too.

Myles grabbed my wrist and Sophie's hand, teleporting us below.

The remaining guard was armed with a staff, but when he realized we were all coming for him, he backed away.

His aura seemed to pulse and my stomach filled with dread—the others in the palace would likely notice us all using our powers.

As if on cue, the lava in the fountain rose high into the air, and King Brenton walked out from another entrance.

Myles shocked the guard and raised his arms towards King Brenton. "What do you want with Mageye City?" he demanded, taking a step back as King Brenton stepped forward.

Sophie faded away, and I gripped Ren's jackknife tightly. More Volcaniacs came out from around the courtyard, and the birds shrieked as Tara paced on the balcony we had leapt from. Her tail was lashing side-to-side.

Will and Mercy stepped closer to us, glancing between the Volcaniacs in vain.

"Power," King Brenton answered, exactly like Marlon had told us in the dungeons all those weeks ago. "I *crave* it."

Myles gulped. "You are a strong Mageye, but there is such a thing as too much power."

Mercy raised her weapon, her gaze locked on a woman behind us who was armed with a staff and slowly approaching.

I locked eyes with another Volcaniac and gripped Ren's jackknife tighter.

"Not for me," King Brenton announced. He stuck his hand into the lava fountain and lifted out a fistful as if he were cupping water.

Myles shot a bolt of lightning at him, and at the same time, Will sent a wave towards the fountain itself.

Parts of the fountain sizzled, and Will quickly called the water back, his main weapon dwindling.

Suddenly, everything went black, then the courtyard flashed. Another man approached from behind, an exact replica of King Brenton.

The woman Mercy had been keeping an eye on too, changed, as did the man I had locked gazes with.

"Mark," I gasped.

Several Volcaniacs ran forward, but with no way to tell who the real King Brenton was, we could only pray we didn't get burned.

Will grabbed his baton and cracked it against a Volcaniac's skull, and I slashed my dagger across someone's wrist.

Sophie flashed in and out of sight, and Myles raised his arms, sending out a wave of lightning, but still they came.

Tara leapt from the balcony—the only one still in her true form—and stalked towards me.

"The ice-diamond!" Mercy shouted.

Myles caught my eye and nodded, so I plunged my hand into my pocket and clutched the ice-diamond in my fist.

I hurled it at the ground and all of the Volcaniacs froze—covered in frost—except for King Brenton.

A purple orb formed around us and we disappeared with an electric snap.

Chapter 47

Myles panted as we reappeared, but didn't break stride. "King Brenton is the only one not frozen, we need to take our chance."

He had taken us above the courtyard, and we ran back onto a balcony, near where King Brenton had stood.

Everyone in the courtyard was still frozen, including Mark, which meant that for a moment, his illusions were gone. My gaze skipped over the Volcaniacs nervously, suddenly unsure which one was Mark. We had seen him after he taunted us with our fears, but now he seemed to blend in with everyone else.

King Brenton strode to Tara, and when he touched her, she unfroze.

She quickly changed forms, and knelt before him. "Rose did that!" she spat. "She froze me."

"With an ice-diamond." King Brenton nodded. He said something else to her and Will raised his arms.

The last of his water rose in a wave and gushed towards them, the perfect chance to douse King Brenton's fire.

At the last second, King Brenton turned, and with a single flick of his hand, lava arced from the fountain, and the water sizzled as the two waves collided.

Will's jaw dropped. "What? That's not fair. You can't do that!"

Mercy grabbed his arm, pulling him from the edge of the balcony. "Let's not taunt the enemy, Will!"

"But—" Will sputtered. "He took away my ability to *fight*."

"He's trying to kill us, Will. That's the whole point," Myles said as he grabbed Will's other arm and forced him to run back into the palace. "New plan," Myles huffed. "We're playing cat and mouse; wear them out and pick them off."

"Won't that wear us out first?" I asked.

Myles glanced at me, lightning sparking in his irises. "What else can we do?"

"The outlet of power!" Mercy panted. "What if we go there and try to destroy it? They already know we're here, so it won't matter if it causes another earthquake. If anything, it will unsteady them."

"How do we break it?" Sophie asked.

"I don't know," Myles said. "But we might as well give it a try."

"Do you think it will work?" I asked.

"If it doesn't, we will be trapped inside," Will said.

Myles shook his head. "It is hard to get trapped when you are with someone who can teleport."

We passed a window and Mercy skidded to a halt. There was no glass separating us from the outside, though the otologicoal meant we heard nothing from the other side.

She leaned out the window and turned her gaze to the sun. "It's above us," she panted as she ducked back inside. "There are stairs on our right."

"How'd that happen?" Will asked.

"How did what happen?" I asked.

"We are below it? It was on the first floor and we went up a floor to get above that courtyard, not down."

"That doesn't make sense," Sophie said, eyeing the ceiling.

I paused, feeling suddenly uneasy at that realization. The outlet of power and throne room had been on the first floor, and Mark's illusions must have been on the second, since Myles teleported us before King Brenton doused us with lava.

Myles looked down the hall the way we had come. "I don't know."

Sophie grew faint at his words, but her eyes glinted like sharp pieces of stone. "It will be okay," she whispered.

Myles shook his head, but forced a smile. "Lead the way, Mercy."

She ran ahead, glancing through each archway and corridor until she found the stairs. "The stairwell is empty."

"Good." Myles squeezed around her and led the way up the stairs, his shoulders tense.

The stairs were made of a rough, blackened stone, and I could feel heat rising from them through my boots.

"Why are the stairs hot?" I asked.

Myles bent, brushing the steps with his fingertips. He quickly yanked his hand back, hissing in pain.

"Are you okay?" Sophie asked.

"Yeah..." Myles trailed off, looking down the stairwell and his eyes widened in horror. "Off the stairs, *now!*"

He pushed Will ahead of him and grabbed Mercy's hand to pull her up. I glanced over my shoulder and yelped. The steps were sinking through the floor, lava rising in their places.

"We're going to get trapped in the middle!" Will shouted.

I grabbed Sophie's hand and ran a step after Myles. The top stairs, too, had begun to sink, lava welling in their places.

"Jump it," Myles called, pulling Sophie from me and pushing her ahead.

Will didn't hesitate. He leapt across and ran out to give the rest of us space.

Mercy jumped after him, and Sophie followed. She stumbled out of the way as Myles and I reached the edge of the stairs. Myles grabbed my hand, and we jumped across together.

We slumped against the opposite wall, panting as we caught our breath. "No more stairs," I huffed, trembling.

Myles nodded in agreement, his cheeks flushed. "We need to get away from here."

I looked down the hall. "Which way now, Mercy?"

"Right," Mercy replied. She took the lead, continually glancing out the windows.

"Gotcha!" A man jumped out of a room, grabbing Mercy and pinning her arms behind her back.

Mercy yelped, kicking at him in vain, but he held her away from himself to prevent it.

"No!" Will wrenched the man off of Mercy, using a move he and Myles had practiced often on our way here. The man's arm twisted behind his back, and he attempted to kick Will's legs out from under him. Before he could attempt a second kick, he was struck with purple lightning and collapsed.

Will dropped the man and hurried to Mercy, his voice trembling. "Are you okay?" He took her arms and examined the marks left from the man's tight grip.

"Yes." Her voice shook, and shooting stars flashed in her irises, but she was otherwise unharmed. "Thanks."

"I'll take the lead from here," Myles huffed, briefly touching Sophie's hand. "I don't sense any other auras on this floor."

"They must still be near the courtyard," I whispered. "Didn't you say you hoped the ice diamond would give us several minutes?"

He nodded. "Unless King Brenton unfreezes anyone else, yes."

As we continued down the hall, the fiery-orange glow dissipated, growing dimmer until we stood in near pitch blackness.

"Is the outlet of power expanding?" I breathed.

Myles stopped walking, the purple lightning arcing between his fingers lighting the corridor in faint flashes. "No," he breathed back.

"Then what..." Will started to ask, but stopped as something growled from within the darkness.

Sophie whimpered and a heavy force slammed into me, knocking me to the ground. I screamed, finding myself pinned under Tara's large paws. She grabbed my arm in her mouth and her teeth sank into my skin. A swift jerk of her head made my shoulder pop and I shrieked.

"Rose!" Myles shouted. He blasted Tara with lightning, and she released my arm, howling as she scrambled back into the darkness.

Myles shot a bolt of lightning after her, but the streak of purple simply soared until it was devoured by darkness. Mercy skidded to her knees beside me.

"Are you okay?"

I rolled onto my stomach and vomited, overcome with a blinding pain. "Your power will fix it soon," she whispered, tenderly bracing my dislocated arm as she helped ease me up.

Myles backed toward us, arms spread and lightning crackling between his fingers. "I don't think this blackness is the outlet of power. I think we are the only ones who can't see."

"An illusion," Will said grimly. He spat on the floor, and though it was only a little water, it sprang to life.

"Look out!" Sophie shouted as two women ran from either side of the dark corridor. The staffs they carried lit with flames, and Mercy tugged me back as swirling mud rushed past us alongside one of the women.

My shoulder shifted and popped, and I sat up a little in Mercy's arms. "I'm healing." I panted.

Sophie jumped out of the way, but turned back, swiping her dagger through the air. The woman shouted and turned, but before she could raise her staff, a purple orb appeared around Sophie and she reappeared on my other side.

Mercy reached over my head and tugged Sophie down, the three of us now all crouching at the floor. "Help me guard Rose," she said. "Myles and Will have better powers for this fight. We

359

can't see until they are too close."

Sophie flickered, crouching and resting a hand on my shoulder as it continued to heal. "Will said he thinks the darkness is an illusion."

"I think so too," I whispered, watching in fear as the women fought with Will and Myles.

Will tugged his baton from his satchel and his spit jumped into the air, reflecting the light of the torch of the woman bearing down on him. He swung the baton and the wad of spit flew into the woman's eye.

She screamed and clutched at the wound, giving Will the chance to knock her off her feet.

Myles threw his dagger at the woman attempting to corner him, striking her heart. She slumped to the floor, her mud drying into dust.

Then he turned to the woman Will was fighting and shocked her.

"Thanks," Will huffed, looking both ways. "They are attacking from both sides."

"Which means we need to pick a way to fight for," Mercy said, helping me to my feet.

Sophie rose on my other side, swiping blood from my arm even as it began reversing into the punctures left from Tara's teeth.

Shadows swirled around us and I shouted as another Volcaniac ran out of the darkness. "Myles, watch out!"

He whirled around just in time, and bent backwards, standing quickly and plunging his dagger between the man's ribs. A hand grasped my arm and I screamed as my healing shoulder was jostled.

"Your queen awaits you," the Volcaniac dragging me growled, but Sophie screamed and kicked him between his legs, sending him doubling over in pain.

Purple lightning struck him and he dropped to the ground, Mercy tugging Sophie away as he fell.

I clutched at the arm the Volcaniac had grabbed, slowly rolling my shoulder as the pain eased. There was only one queen who could want my presence, and the punctures from her teeth were only just leaving my skin.

The shriek of a mountain lion echoed down the dark hall, and I released my hold on my arm, stepping past Myles. "Let me fight."

Chapter 48

"Rose!" Myles protested as I ran past him towards a coming Volcaniac. Gripping my jackknife as I had practiced, I slashed through the air, blood splattering from the man's arm. He shouted and pulled back, raising his other fist. I kept swinging as he attempted to corral me against the wall. "What are you doing?"

"I can heal. I'll be fine," I shouted, stumbling back when the man raised a sparkling dagger.

Purple lightning lit up the black tunnel and my attacker collapsed. Myles grabbed a fallen staff and threw it to me.

"At least use this," he huffed. "I don't want them getting too close with so many illusions around."

I caught the staff, but faltered as the shadows shifted again. An orange glow followed King Brenton as he approached from behind Myles, the black walls slowly merging into lava.

"I will make a deal with you, *General Duncan*," he announced, stopping a safe distance away. Lava continued coursing down the walls and Mercy stepped closer to the center of the corridor, tugging Will with her to avoid the heat.

Myles raised his arm to shock King Brenton, but narrowed his eyes. "What is it?" he spat.

"I will let all of your friends leave... if you join my army. Gray is gone and I am in need of a new advisor."

My heart jumped to my throat, but Myles didn't hesitate to

answer. "I will never help you." He stepped back from King Brenton. "I am here to kill you."

King Brenton smiled slyly. "It was never a question of if, but when. If you will not vow your loyalty to my Volcaniacs by your own free will, then I will force you." The embers in his iris lit with flame as the rest of the walls and ceiling encased us into a tunnel of lava. "I will use force on *all* of you."

The walls of lava began to inch forward and I trembled, tugging Sophie away from them. Mercy clutched her dagger so tightly her knuckles went white. "Stop it!" she cried. "Myles, get us out! It's too small and we'll get burned."

A purple orb formed around the five of us, but then it flickered out, and Myles groaned, putting a hand to his temple.

King Brenton stepped forward. "You've never been forced into cool-down before, have you?"

"And today won't be the first time," Will snapped. He took Myles's arm and his aura shifted, seeming to merge with Myles's.

"Thanks," Myles huffed, slowly pulling his hand from his temple. He turned back towards King Brenton, but he had disappeared, and in his place was a wall of lava. Unlike the walls and ceiling, this barrier jumped to life, surging towards us.

Exactly like the first controlled vision Myles and I had shared in Mageye City. All this time, Myles had been right. The nightmares were more than visions. They were prophecies.

Will grabbed Mercy's hand and practically dragged her after him. Myles caught my hand, grabbing Sophie with his other arm. He held her close and I nearly lost my balance until he jerked me upright. "Keep running," he huffed.

The tunnel appeared endless and the wall behind us continued surging forward, always just on our heels. When Myles was certain I was running on my own, he released my hand to get a better grip on Sophie.

Purple flashes filled the bright orange tunnel as Myles created a forcefield down the length of it, protecting us from the lava.

"I see the end," Mercy shrieked as she broke out of the tunnel and skidded to a halt at the edge of the wrap-around courtyard balcony.

I backpedaled, my heart racing as I realized I wouldn't be able to stop myself in time. Will grabbed my arm, and tugged me back, sending us both crashing to the ground.

I landed on top of him and he wheezed, but held me tightly. "Are you okay?"

"Yes," I panted, struggling to disentangle myself from him. "Thank you."

Myles still clutched Sophie, and Mercy's eyes widened when the lava caught itself at the end of the tunnel, before flickering out and confirming it was yet another illusion.

Will helped me to my feet, and Myles put Sophie down, shaking his head. "We're in a madhouse. How do we keep ending up in this same courtyard, even when we move to different floors?"

I peered down the dark corridor, once again alit with only an eerie orange glow. "They are too strong," I said. "Last time, our mission was to get in and out."

"What are you saying?" Will asked.

Myles voiced my thoughts for me. "They have an advantage in the palace. We can't defeat them while we are in their domain."

"*Everywhere* is their domain," Mercy said, wiping tears and ash from her cheeks. "If we leave the palace, they have the moat. If we leave the moat, they have the charred land. If we leave the charred land, they have the grasslands."

Sophie stepped away from Myles and shook her head. "We need to get away from the lava."

"How?" Will asked.

Myles paused and turned his gaze to the sky. "We might be in luck," he breathed.

The dark clouds from earlier had hidden the sun completely

in preparation for a storm. "Lightning," I whispered.

"What now?" Will asked. He too looked at the clouds, then back at Myles, understanding dawning on his expression. "We need to get you out in the open."

"We *are* out in the open," Mercy pointed out.

Myles shook his head. "We need to put distance between ourselves and the illusions."

A brackish screech tore through the air, and I looked up. A bird was now silhouetted against the storm clouds. Followed by more of its flock.

One of them circled lower, before diving. Myles raised an arm to shock it, but stumbled as the ground beneath our feet rumbled. The fallen stones of the ruin-like palace bounced as the palace shook, putting us all off balance.

I shielded my face with my arms and gasped as electricity crackled, looking up in time to see Myles had recovered and shocked the bird before it attacked. But more were coming.

"Around the balcony," Mercy called. "That takes us to a different part of the palace than we keep getting trapped in."

As we ran around the balcony, loose stones flew through the air, affixing themselves to the walls of the palace. Almost as if they were returning to their rightful place, their *real* place. The lava in the courtyard fountain seemed to swirl with red and orange, growing brighter as the clouds darkened the sky.

"What's going on now?" Will shouted, shielding his head from flying debris.

Loose stones in the balcony began to solidify and I backpedaled too late, my foot landing firmly on stone. Somehow, that was worse... because if the true walls of the palace were rebuilding themselves, then that had to mean...

"The palace," Myles said grimly. "It was an illusion. *Everything* here is an illusion."

"So now that the palace looks stronger..." I started, glancing at

Myles.

We are seeing their true strength. The palace looked rundown to trick us into thinking he was weak, but he's not. He's stronger than he was the last time we fought him. We fell into his trap.

What else is an illusion? I asked, watching as the last small chunks of the palace slid into place.

Everything except for the sky above our heads.

Chapter 49

Once we were back inside the palace, Myles created a forcefield over the entrance to stop the birds from following. The illumining orange glow greeted us, but this time it bore no semblance of illusions or the presence of Volcaniacs.

We ducked into the first empty room we found, and Will slammed the door behind us. He pressed his back against it and held the knob tight, so it couldn't twist from the outside. "What's your plan, Myles? Should we teleport out right now?"

Myles shook his head, his chest heaving. "I will need to create as much lightning as possible once we are out there."

"Out where?" I asked.

"The charred land." Myles squared his shoulders. "I am going to create a forcefield around us and with luck, it will attract more lightning. When we are struck, I will blast it outwards and destroy anyone who follows us."

"So, the goal is to lure them out?" Mercy asked. A trickle of blood ran down from the corner of her mouth, and I went to her and rested my fingers on her cheek.

"Yes," Myles agreed. "God-willing, enough Volcaniacs will follow that this incapacitates them." He glanced at the ceiling and restructured walls. "Maybe even destroy part of the palace."

Sophie clenched her dress in two tight fists. "But the otologicoal..."

"You're right." Myles licked his lips. "They won't be able to hear us... but they will see us. And anyone who doesn't follow won't know what happened, hopefully, until it is too late."

"If we let them chase us out, that will be too risky," I said. I ran my tongue over the spot where most of Mercy's pain had been in her lip. "The moat is filled with lava. Crossing the bridge will be a death sentence."

"Only if they witness us crossing the bridge," Myles said.

"If we are luring them out, then they will know we are crossing the bridge." Will straightened and pressed his ear to the door, listening for any Volcaniacs. "They could knock us off," he added in a hushed voice.

"They won't be able to hear us," Myles said. "The minute we step outside the palace, we can start running. They are looking for us inside, not out." He spoke faster as the idea solidified in his mind. "We will cross the bridge and when we are halfway across, whatever barrier that stopped the Maya Moth dust from working will lose its effect. If Soph can reactive it, we can put some distance between us and the palace, and then I will create the forcefield, and we will unmask our auras. They will notice our auras and follow us out."

Sophie dropped her hands from her skirts. "How long has it been since the second dose of Maya Moth dust? We've been sweating and crying and... What if it is out of your systems?"

"Then it's out of our systems." Myles broke off when the palace rumbled, though this rumble seemed to come from above and not below.

"What was that?" I fretted.

Myles smiled. "The storm, it's coming. I can feel it." He looked between us. "Regardless of whether the Maya Moth dust works, if we can get a head start, I can create a forcefield to protect us as we run. And I will strengthen the forcefield when we are ready for the lightning to attract them if they haven't spotted us."

Mercy stared practically through the ceiling as the palace rumbled again. "I think we need to do it."

"Sounds like our best bet," Will agreed, straightening from the door. "Which way is out?"

Mercy went to the door by Will, and opened it cautiously. A window across the hall revealed a thin streak of light, fast growing dimmer as more storm clouds rolled in. "There is a short staircase down the hall," she whispered.

Will winced. "We can't trust the stairs."

"She said it's short, so we can jump it," Myles said. "Or I can teleport. That shouldn't take much energy from my forcefield outside."

"Won't teleporting flash your aura?" I fretted.

"We'll decide when we get there. For now... I don't sense anyone in the hallway."

Sophie stepped up to the door. "Let me look," she whispered.

She disappeared and Will inched aside to let her out. I held my breath until her silhouette appeared again. "It's empty."

Myles stepped around Mercy and Will, and glanced down the empty hall. It now glowed with a stronger orange light as the light from outside faded.

Mercy had said the staircase was to our left, but as the palace rumbled again, no one moved. Finally, I stepped closer to Myles. "Ready?"

He touched my braid with trembling fingers. "Yes," he breathed.

Auras pulsed somewhere deep within the palace, but we managed to find the staircase without any Volcaniacs finding us first. The staircase was only five steps down, so instead of teleporting, we jumped them.

I stumbled and Myles caught me. Our gazes met and I whispered, "I'm scared."

"Me too," he whispered back.

Will hopped down beside us and Myles broke our embrace. "We are *almost* out."

The eerie-orange glow slowly replaced itself with a gray light from outside. Similar to the entrance we had used into the palace, this corridor ended with an arch. This time, though, it wasn't made of roughly charred stone, but of smooth bricks and ashy obsidian.

Sophie crept to the exit first, fading away to ensure it was empty. "It's safe," she said softly.

Myles thanked her and stepped out. As I passed through the arch, thunder boomed and everyone jumped. Wind whipped our hair, and I pushed my skirt down with one hand.

The otologicoal had been blocking the sound of the storm, and now, it would block our voices, too. The black sky was tinged with the orange reflection of the lava in the moat. A few birds circled above, but as they got buffeted by the wind, they swooped away.

Mercy pointed around us. "It's a straight shot." She raised her voice above the wind. "But farther than I would have hoped. Should we go back in and try to find something better?"

Will peered back into the corridor we had exited from. "I don't want to go back in there."

I swallowed hard and stepped away from the arch. "I don't either."

Myles frowned, judging the distance between us and the bridge. From where we stood, it looked as if I could cup it in the palm of my hand.

Sophie flickered. "Do we run or walk?"

"Run," Myles decided, his shoulders slumping. "I doubt the Volcaniacs will expect us to be outside. That might turn our lack of cover into cover."

Thunder cracked again and Mercy glanced at the sky. When she looked back, the stars in her irises glowed brightly. "I'm ready."

"We all are," Will said.

"Then let's run," Myles said. "As fast as you can, and Soph, the second we are halfway across the bridge, try to call upon the Maya Moth dust."

She braced herself to run, and nodded. "I'm trying already."

Thunder cracked and someone shouted. I turned, stumbling away from a woman who had exited the tunnel after us, flaming staff raised. The wind snuffed the flame and a stick suddenly flew past me, knocking the woman out. Will grabbed my hand and pulled me after him. "I told you that the baton would help!"

Wind buffeted us and I squinted my eyes, locking my gaze on the distant bridge. We had to make it. We *had* to.

Myles likely could have run a lot faster, but he matched his pace to ours, hands half-raised to create a forcefield or shoot lightning if need be.

"Don't fall behind, Mercy!" Will shouted. He grabbed her arm and pulled her after himself until her strides matched his.

A stitch in my side made me wince and I panted, relieved when my body took over the healing, though my throat still burned from running. The bridge now looked as if it would take two hands to hold it, maybe three.

Regardless, it was too far.

Don't think that, Myles ordered. *Focus on running. Every step is a step closer...*

Four hands to hold it.

Five, he answered, evidently having been reading my mind this whole time.

"Can't... run... much... longer," Mercy huffed.

"It's the distance between our houses now," Will encouraged.

Sophie suddenly yelped, falling to her hands and knees. "My ankle."

I skidded to a halt to turn and heal her, but Myles pushed me towards the bridge. "Keep running, I'll grab her."

I hesitated but he had already scooped her into his arms and broke into a sprint again.

Lightning flashed and hope lit in my chest. The lightning was still too far away for Myles to use, but we were running towards it.

Myles reached the bridge first and didn't break his stride as he ran to get Sophie across.

"Remember, they can't hear us!" he shouted, his voice nearly getting lost in the wind. "Hurry across and Soph will activate the moth dust."

I glanced over my shoulder, gasping for breath. Will was right at my heels, and Mercy was only a few steps behind.

Will and I bounded onto the bridge simultaneously. It shuddered beneath us, and I flailed my arms wildly in an attempt to catch my balance.

He grabbed me and pulled me away from the edge. "I got you," he panted.

The bridge shook again, and he looked behind me, horror striking his expression. "Mercy!"

I whirled back, and time seemed to slow as Mercy was dragged off of the bridge, caught in King Brenton's grip. She screamed as he lifted her into the air, her legs kicking wildly and hair whipping across her face in the strengthening wind.

"Mercy!" I stepped toward her and found my foot plunging into open air. Time snapped back into motion as stone fell from the bridge and Will caught me again, dragging me away from the gap forming between us and Mercy.

Mark appeared out of an illusion of thin air, his laughter being washed out by the strengthening wind. A faint shout echoed from behind us and I turned. Myles had put Sophie down at the halfway mark and braced himself to teleport, but the lightning quickly flickered out.

I can't teleport her out of his grip. He began running back as more stone crumbled from the bridge, forcing Will and I farther from

Mercy. Tears streamed down her face, and Will let go of my arm.

"Catch her," he said, just loud enough for me to hear.

"What..." I stopped, screaming as he leapt the gap. "No!"

Clearly not expecting him to jump, both King Brenton and Mark stepped back in surprise, giving Will the chance to grab Mercy and pull her free.

She clung to him but he shook his head and ripped her hands from his neck, throwing her back to the bridge. *Catch her.* I ran forward as she landed on her stomach, clawing at the crumbling edge, that threatened to drop her into the lava far below.

A deafening crack of thunder boomed, shaking the very air around us. I grabbed her hand with both of mine and heaved, pulling her up and dragging her away from the crumbling edge.

"Jump, Will!" Sophie screamed from the center of the bridge, waving her arms wildly.

With Mercy on her feet, I turned, holding my arms out. "Jump," I shouted. "I'll catch you."

Neither King Brenton nor Mark seemed to have recovered from their shock and Will stepped forward, but faltered at the edge of the growing gap.

Myles reached us, grabbing Mercy and pushing her towards Sophie. Another orb formed around him, but again faltered as King Brenton dragged Will from the edge.

The crumbling bridge suddenly dropped, and Myles and I jumped, nearly falling as we scrambled backwards.

Myles pushed me behind him as he had with Mercy, holding his hand towards Will, who was now held in a similar position to Mercy, helpless but to writhe in the air.

King Brenton adjusted his grip on Will, holding him in front of himself like a human shield. Myles dropped his hand. There was no way to stop King Brenton or Mark without risking a deadly shot at Will.

Will's chest heaved and he slowed his struggle, a wild look of panic in his eyes. "Go!" he screamed.

"No!" Mercy screeched. "Will!"

"Go!" Will shouted again. "Myles, continue with the plan. Save yourselves."

A gut-wrenching sob tore through me as more of the bridge crumbled away, forcing us even farther from him. Myles tried again to teleport him, but the entire bridge jolted, and he stumbled, losing his focus.

I shrieked as the bridge shuddered and the tip slowly sank towards the lava, promising a fiery death unless we ran from Will.

Mercy sobbed, and I took her hand, tugging her with me from the crumbling edge.

"I can try to avoid him." Myles's voice shook. "Or blast the palace instead. That will distract them and if King Brenton releases Will..."

"You have to try," I said firmly.

Sophie shrieked as she began sliding down the ramp towards us, her skirts whipping in the wind. Myles caught her and she steadied herself on the iron rails.

This time, instead of raising his arms towards Will, Myles raised his arms to the sky. A purple orb encased us, lit up by lightning from the coming storm.

Mark stepped forward as King Brenton dropped Will to the ground. A bloodcurdling scream erupted from Will's throat and he writhed, helpless as a second, smaller orb of lightning formed around him, shielding him from the Volcaniacs. But they didn't look deterred.

A bolt of lightning struck down and connected with the forcefield around us. The static sound tore through my eardrums, and our hair rose on end.

But as it touched the orb, everything turned white. I reached out to touch it and didn't get shocked.

It was an illusion.

"Myles, no!" I screamed, but it was too late. He had already snapped the orb.

Chapter 50

We reappeared with an electric crackle and fell out of the orb. My head rang with the silence around us; the thunder and wind suddenly gone.

Myles stumbled to his feet and looked around, whispering our names as he counted heads.

He never said Will's name.

The world spun and I staggered to my feet, looking around in confusion. "Will?" I called out into the surrounding... trees?

More silence, and Myles's knees gave out. "I don't feel his aura. But... but I snapped his orb with ours, so..." He leaned forward, palms on the ground. "I left him. I *left* him."

Sophie stood beside me, tears streaming down her cheeks as she faded. "What happened to the palace?"

Mercy stared at Myles numbly, stumbling around in confusion. "Will?" Her voice rose to a frantic screech. "Will!"

He didn't reply. I turned in a slow circle, whispering his name. As if he would suddenly respond, laughing as he came out from the trees. As if it were only a prank, but there was nothing funny about where we now stood.

Moments ago, we had been face-to-face with King Brenton, and then Mark had created an illusion that Myles had somehow snapped. And now we were here... in a forest with grass the color of emeralds.

Myles sobbed, and I sank to my knees, tracing the grass with a trembling finger. Mercy took another look around us, then she too, fell into the grass.

The trees that surrounded us weren't green and brown, rather, the leaves were a bluish color and the trunks purple.

I blinked a few times as the spinning finally stopped. Had Mark created another illusion?

Sophie slowly reappeared and a breeze swept past, rustling our hair as well as the leaves of the trees. Everything about our surroundings, including Will's missing place, seemed very real.

"Where are we?" I whispered. "Where did Mark send us?"

Bonus Content

I wrote in my note at the beginning of the book that *Illusion of Fear* has gone through the most changes between drafts. But the biggest change of all happened even before I pantsed my way through that first draft. And that change has a name, *Tara Kaser*.

Will, Mercy, and Sophie introduced themselves to me on the same day, but they weren't alone. They brought another character with them, a character by the name of Margaret.

Margaret was going to be an elderly Mageye with the ability to turn into any animal, though she always favored cats. She had seven cats at her house and could often be found in the form of an elegant, long-furred, silver cat. And most importantly, she was going to be a main character in *Illusion of Fear*.

Instead of a group of five, there was going to be a group of six, but Margaret fast started making things, well, awkward. I couldn't find a way for Myles to take the lead when a sixty-year-old woman was in the group. There was simply no way he would boss her around, but she also wasn't fit to lead since she had never gone on a mission like this before.

Ultimately, I cut Margaret, but I also couldn't bear to let her go. So, I started thinking of a new role for her, and her more cat-like qualities... You can probably guess the rest.

That is Tara Kaser's backstory, but what about the other characters who were left behind in the city? Here is your chance to learn more about two of the closest duos in all of *The Mageye Trilogy*. Ren and Ryder, and Mercy and Will.

RYDER

A light breeze blew through the window, causing the curtain to flutter. I looked up from my drawing and at the moon.

Crickets chirped steadily outside and I sighed, glancing across the room at Ren, who was sound asleep. The room we shared was lit by an oil lamp, which I used to draw by. I had begun work on a portrait of a young Mageye I had seen a few days ago. He had stood on the bottom rail of a fence and held both arms up to the sky as his dad called a group of sparrows to fly around his head.

Ren appeared to be in a deep sleep, and I returned to my drawing. Before we had been kidnapped by the trader, staying up late to draw by candlelight while Ren slept had been a way for me to relax. Now, it was impossible for me to go to sleep until late every night, instead keeping watch, waiting for the cries.

His night terrors had started in the volcano, but there, he would wake up in a cold sweat, silent tears rolling down his cheeks. They hadn't seemed to extend past that initial panicked awakening. But soon after we moved to Mageye City, Ren had climbed into my bed and sobbed in my arms, telling me how bad the nightmares truly were. Since that night, his nightmares were no longer silent, and his cries showed how truly un-fine he was, no matter how much he insisted it in front of Mom and Raymond.

Usually, if he could make it past midnight, he could sleep relatively peacefully the rest of the night. Often, I waited until nearly one to leave my desk and return to my bed, and it was nearing midnight now. I rolled my wrist to ease the cramp, studying the paper. Something was missing...

Ren whimpered and I looked up. He cried again and I pushed my chair back, nearly tripping over it as he sobbed. "Nooo, please stop... Please... It burns..."

I ran to him and pulled him upright, hugging him tightly. "Ren, shh. It's me, it's Ryder. You're safe."

Sobs racked his body and he jerked away, but I caught him before he fell out of bed. "You're safe," I soothed. "It's only me. It's no one bad."

He grabbed my arm when he finally broke through the terror and recognized me. "Ryder..."

"I'm here," I promised. "I'm not going anywhere." I held my arms out, and he collapsed into me.

"I was back there." He sobbed. "I was back, and it hurt..."

"I know, Ren. I'm sorry. I'm so sorry." My voice shook, and I couldn't keep my own pain from it.

There had been a Mageye in the volcano who could produce fear, and the trader who kidnapped us had used that Mageye to torture Ren as revenge for telling him off for being rude to Rose. The Mageye had made Ren face his worst fears. Alone. His screams had echoed through the volcano, still ringing in my ears if I listened hard enough.

"When's it going to end, Ryder?" Ren whispered as his sobs slowed. "When am I going to be normal again?"

"I don't know," I confessed miserably. "I'm sorry, Ren, but I don't know."

"Every night," he whispered. "I hate sleeping."

I rubbed his back like our dad used to do when we were little, before he passed away. "You don't need to be scared of sleeping as long as I'm here," I promised. "I'm not going anywhere."

He pulled away slowly, wiping his eyes with trembling hands. "Do you even sleep?" he croaked.

"Sure I do," I said, covering my hand with my sleeve and

wiping his face patiently. "I draw."

He looked at my desk, where my art pad still lay open.

"What were you drawing?" he asked, clenching the blanket in both fists.

I stood and retrieved my art pad from the desk, offering the book to him.

He unclenched the blanket and carefully took the book. His finger traced over the drawing, but he was careful not to touch it directly and risk smudging.

We had gotten into countless fights over him getting too close to my artwork, and now he was as cautious around my sketchbooks as I was.

"He's a Mageye," he whispered.

I sat back on the edge of the bed. "A young one."

He only nodded, slowly pulling his hand back. "Ryder?"

"Yeah?"

"Do you think Mom and Raymond... Do you think they can help me, too? Like you do?"

Finally. I had been desperately waiting for him to ask me that, feeling helpless as my efforts to help him appeared to only offer support and not healing. "I know they will, Ren," I whispered. "All you need to do is ask."

His eyes filled with fresh tears. "Rose, too? I know she will, when she gets back?"

I nodded. "They will all help you. You're not broken, and this isn't forever." My voice caught. "I'll be with you every step of the way, Ren, I promise. I'm not... I'm not ever going anywhere, and they aren't either, so don't worry about any of that. We will help you."

A tear slipped from his cheek and landed on the drawing, causing a small splatter. He sucked in his breath, but before he could apologize, I cut him off.

"Don't worry about it."

"But—"

"It's all right," I soothed. He handed the book back to me, and I stood, but he grabbed my wrist, holding me back.

"Please don't leave."

"I'm putting this away. I'll come right back."

He shook his head, still holding my wrist. "Please don't leave," he repeated. "I need you."

At that, I sat on the edge of the bed, gently tossing the book onto the floor, letting it lie open and out of the way.

"What do you need?" I asked.

He took a shaky breath. "You," he croaked. "I need you... and... and Mom too, and Raymond, and Rose, just not... not yet."

"That's okay," I whispered. "They'll help you when you're ready, and until then, you've got me."

He laid down slowly, his breathing finally returning to normal. "Thank you, Ryder," he whispered.

"I'll stay here until you go back to sleep," I promised.

He reached for my hand and squeezed it tightly, but his grip slowly loosened as he lapsed back into sleep. I waited a while longer, watching his chest rise and fall, until I was certain he was in a deep sleep.

I gently pulled my hand from his and stood, grabbing my art book and placing it back on my desk.

My bed was on the opposite side of the room to his and I frowned. Too far. I looked back at Ren, and returned to his bedside, climbing under his covers.

He rolled over as if somehow aware I lay beside him, and hugged his arm around me. I pulled him close, breathing deeply as I buried my face in his hair.

Soon, I would convince him to get more help. So instead of being unable to do anything but comfort, we could help Ren overcome his nightmares for good.

WILL

(Seven Years Ago)

"You look like an old man." Mercy giggled, knocking the large branch I used as a cane with one of her own.

I snickered, lifting the cane as if it were a sword. "To trick my enemies!"

Her galaxy irises seemed to flicker with lights and she lifted her branch, waving it at me.

I blocked it, the wood clacking together as we swung and parried with each other. A few cows stopped their chewing on grass to watch, and I jumped over one of the calves, Mercy leaping right after me.

"You two better not be playing leap frog with the calves again," Dad called, and I stumbled to a halt, my chest heaving as I turned to face him. He stood on the other side of the pasture fence, wagging a finger at us. "Get out of my field if you're going to be rowdy."

"Sorry, Uncle Ethan," Mercy called, driving her stick into the ground.

I waved my branch in the air. "We're making it so they are nice and not scaredy cats."

Dad turned to go, calling over his shoulder, "Well, since you are both eager to help with the cows today, you can help shovel out the barn."

Mercy and I exchanged looks. "That's the smelliest job," she observed.

I raised my brows, tugging her branch from the ground and passing it to her. "We don't need to do it if he can't catch us."

I took off running before she could reply, dodging cows and leaping over an occasional sleeping calf until I made it to the far end of the pasture. Mercy wasn't far behind and she put both hands to the fence, leaning her chest against it and laughing.

"Now what?" she asked.

I shrugged, tossing my branch over the fence and watching it land in the bushes, leaves shivering as it passed. "We stay out of the way so we don't get stuck with any smelly jobs."

The fence had a lower rung that offered the perfect height to swing my leg over the top from, and I climbed up, hopping down the other side.

Leaves rustled as Mercy's branch landed somewhere in the woods beside mine and she followed me over the fence. "Let's go to our swing," she decided, turning right and leading the way back around the fence to where our parents' fields connected.

"The water is happy today," I said, tilting my head as we walked. A large river went through our land and its very existence felt like life in my ears in a similar way to auras.

"So is the sun," Mercy agreed, kicking a pinecone. It bounced against a tree and rolled to a stop beside a still form.

A small sparrow lay on the ground, its wings folded over itself and body still.

"Oh no," Mercy said. "I think it's dead."

I peered at it. "Its wings kind of work like a blanket."

"That's sad."

I shrugged, looking towards the cows in the field behind us. Mercy and I had seen plenty of death on the farm, but for every life lost, we saw more being born every spring. "It is in bird Heaven now."

Mercy knelt, gently cupping the bird in her hands and stroking its head with her thumb. "Don't you need to be buried to go to

Heaven?"

I blinked, turning back. "No... that's not how my mom made it sound."

"Maybe..." She placed it down and began scraping at the dirt with her hands. "Even if it is in bird Heaven already, it will get eaten by wild animals out here."

"Are you going to bury it?" I asked, watching her dig.

"Yes, and we can put a rock over it so nothing can dig it up."

My eyes widened and I turned in a slow circle, scanning for any good rocks. When I found one, I hefted it up, lugging it back to the hole Mercy had dug.

Already, it looked deep enough and she carefully picked some flowers, laying them in the bottom of the hole like a cushion.

"There," she whispered as she lay the bird atop the flowers. "Now you can fly straight to bird Heaven."

I plucked a large leaf from a tree and put it over the bird as if it were a blanket, and we pushed the dirt back over it together.

"Now the rock," she said and I hefted up the rock again and dropped it over the burial site.

"There," I declared. "Safe forever."

"And that can be my good deed for the day," Mercy said, wiping her hands on her pants.

"I found the rock," I said. "So that counts as mine."

"And we helped the calves become less jumpy," she added.

"*And* we moved those branches out of the field," I declared, continuing on our way to our swing.

Mercy hummed, skipping after me until we found the river. We took a moment to wash our hands and I trailed my fingers through the water, each lapping wave against my palm like a breath of fresh air rushing into my lungs.

"Where do you think you want to be buried?" Mercy asked.

I flicked water at her. "What do you mean?"

She lifted her shirt to wipe her face. "Like the bird. Would you want to be buried in the woods?”

“Oh.” I sat on the ground, sticking my booted feet into the water. “I think I would want to be buried near the water. Then I could listen to the sound of it until I go to Heaven.”

Mercy plopped down beside me, sticking her boots into the water next to mine. “That definitely isn’t how Heaven works.”

“How do you know?” I challenged. “Have you ever died?”

“Why would you be able to hear if you were dead?”

I wrinkled my nose. “You thought the bird couldn’t go to Heaven until it was buried.”

“I’ll ask Mom during Bible study tonight,” Mercy decided, laying back in the grass. “But if you could choose where you were buried and couldn’t hear, where would it be?”

“Still the water,” I decided, laying back and stretching my arms above my head. “What about you?”

She shut her eyes, basking in the warm summer sun. “Under the stars,” she said simply.

“Me with the water and you with the stars.” I snickered. “I wonder if Mageye with dirt powers want to be buried extra deep?”

She laughed, opening her eyes and turning her head to face me. “I promise to bury you by the water if you die first, if you promise to bury me under the stars if I die first.”

“Deal.” I offered my hand. “But if you die, could you do it after your chores? I don’t want to do double.”

“Why would I die *after* my chores when I could die before and get out of them?”

“Like we did today?” I lowered my voice. “What if you die halfway through chores? Then I won’t be forced to do them ever, because everyone would feel bad.”

“Or we can die together and get our answers about bird Heaven,” she suggested, grasping my hand.

We shook on it. “We die together, or not at all,” I declared. “And if it is together, then we can die before chores.”

"Double deal!" Mercy agreed. "Now... let's get to the swing before we are caught on your half of the yard. Uncle Ethan can't scold us for skipping chores if we are on joint property."

PLAYLIST

Looking to add songs to your playlist that remind you of the Mageye, and more specifically, *Illusion of Fear?* Look no further! (As always, songs are in no particular order to keep you on your toes. Because, yes, some of them remind me of how *Illusion of Fear* connects to *Beldestine.*)

"Counting Stars" by One Republic— Mercy and Will are as inseparable as Ren and Ryder. Exploring them and their bond has been my favorite part of developing their characters, and this song was practically written for them.

"Run Devil Run" by David Crowder— If *Illusion of Fear* was a movie, then I think "Run Devil Run" would be playing while the main cast runs from Mark when he changes the corridors in the palace. Though the song is about making the devil run and not running from the devil, something about it has always fit this scene in my head.

"King of Me" by The Rend Collective— There is no plot relevance to this song being on *Illusion of Fear's* playlist. But, when I was first drafting the Maya Moth scene, it began playing and now every time I hear it, I am transported back to that mountain.

"Sharks" by Imagine Dragons— I have loved Imagine Dragons for a long time, and many of their songs are on my writing playlist(s). But this song was added to my Mageye playlist even before I finished hearing it for the first time. Why? Well, in honor of Mark (the illusion Mageye), of course.

"Bleeding Out" by Imagine Dragons– "Bleeding Out" isn't technically a song that inspired any scene that occurs in *Illusion of Fear*, but it does fit the bond between two of the characters very well. Myles and Sophie (or should I say, his Soph?) and the past they shared together.

"Crushing Snakes" by Crowder– No background or secrets needed to explain why "Crushing Snakes" is on this playlist. All you need to do is listen, and you will know exactly why I have it here for *Illusion of Fear*.

ACKNOWLEDGEMENTS

To the guard rail on Misty Lane where this story was born… The dedication of this book was never meant as just a joke, but it is a story shared between me and God. Why He chose that short twenty-foot guard rail as the spot for Will, Mercy, and Sophie to introduce themselves, I will never know. But up until my family moved, I always saw them standing at that guard rail.

Mom: For always believing in me, encouraging me, and reminding me that everything will work out in the end—I just need to trust His plan. Thank you.

McKenna: Thank you for cheering me on through every step of the process. And thank you for responding patiently to my concerned texts about whether Myles's favorite part of his room was his office or bathroom. (It was always meant to be the office, but the wording got concerning.)

Lea & Aaralynn: With the hundreds of comments you left throughout the beta reading process, there was never a single one I felt might have been "off." Rather, there were many times where your comments were near-exact reflections of each other, even though you were on separate documents. Thank you for the assurance that your feedback is honest, and an even bigger thank you for helping this book become so much better.

Michaela: Thank you for all of your help and support with *Illusion of Fear*. Receiving my manuscript back just days before Christmas felt like opening a present early!

YOU (my reader): Thank you for picking up this book. For you to be reading this note, you must have read *The Mageye* too. And that thought is one that always brings a smile to my face.

To the best dogs that have ever existed: Pac, Belle, and Fiona.

To Fritz: Rest in peace, sweet angel. Try not to smack too many dogs, even if they deserve it. (But if you do, make sure to go for your triple-whack combo.)

COMING SOON

The Mageye:
Beldestine
April, 2026

Paris Kaufman is a college student with a love for creative fiction. With her writing, she hopes to spark the same passion for reading she acquired as a young teen. When not writing, you can find Paris cooking, painting, or tending to her many animal friends.

Instagram: @parisandherbooks

YouTube: @parisandherbooks

Email: parisandherbooks@gmail.com

Website:
https://parisandherbooks.wixsite.com/parisandherbooks